WRITTEN IN BLOOD

A MIDSOMER MURDERS MYSTERY

CAROLINE GRAHAM

HEADLINE

First published in paperback in 1994 by
HEADLINE PUBLISHING GROUP

First published in this paperback edition in 2016 by
HEADLINE PUBLISHING GROUP

1

Cataloguing in Publication Data is available from the British Library

ISBN 978 1 4722 4368 3

Typeset in 11/13.5 pt Sabon

Printed and bound in Great Britain by Clays Ltd, St Ives Plc

Headline's policy is to use papers that are natural, renewable and
recyclable products and made from wood grown in sustainable forests.
The logging and manufacturing processes are expected to conform to the
environmental regulations of the country of origin.

HEADLINE PUBLISHING GROUP
An Hachette UK Company
Carmelite House
50 Victoria Embankment
London EC4Y 0DZ

www.headline.co.uk
www.hachette.co.uk

Caroline Graham was born in Warwickshire and educated at Nuneaton High School for Girls, and later the Open University. She was awarded an MA in Theatre Studies at Birmingham University, and has written several plays for both radio and theatre. Her highly acclaimed series of novels featuring Detective Chief Inspector Barnaby inspired the hit ITV drama *Midsomer Murders*.

By Caroline Graham and available from Headline

The Midsomer Murders Mysteries

The Killings at Badger's Drift
Death of a Hollow Man
Death in Disguise
Written in Blood
Faithful unto Death
A Place of Safety
A Ghost in the Machine

Standalone novels

Murder at Madingley Grange
The Envy of the Stranger

For Frank and Linda Belgrove
Life Savers

Without some sort of anxiousness
writing loses its charm.

Nicholson Baker, *U and I*

Foreword
by John Nettles

Twenty years ago, a producer came to see me where I was working up in Stratford-upon-Avon. He was clutching a bunch of books by Caroline Graham about the adventures and exploits of a Detective Chief Inspector Tom Barnaby who worked for Causton CID. 'We want to make a television series out of these novels,' he says, 'and we would like you to play the part of the DCI. What do you say?' At the time, I thought that after playing a policeman in Jersey, I was not about to play another one in Causton. But the producer, Brian True-May, had come a very long way to see me, so I politely agreed to read the books and get back to him with a decision.

Reading the books that summer in Stratford was my first introduction to the world of Caroline Graham and Detective Chief Inspector Barnaby. And what a happy experience it was! The books are wonderful. I found Tom Barnaby quite fascinating; he's an ordinary, decent man who continually finds himself in extraordinary and often indecent circumstances, yet he still makes time to tend his garden and endure his wife Joyce's appalling cooking with an almost god-like equanimity. And, of course, he loves his daughter Cully (the only girl with that name in the known universe) to distraction, like most dads love their daughters. He has no obvious faults or tics, injuries or addictions, depressive illnesses, failing relationships. He doesn't even own an antique car, the usual badge of a television detective. Tom Barnaby is a four-square, well-mannered Englishman and I love him for that. After reading Caroline Graham's books, there was no question. I knew that I had to play him . . .

There began *Midsomer Murders*, one of the most successful British cop shows of all time, shown in every country and every territory known to man. Around the world, Tom Barnaby is celebrated as the top English cop.

The television shows are great, but, good as they are for the viewer, they are not as good as the original books can be for the reader, because when you read the book you can make up your own pictures of the characters, and they are the perfect creations for *you*. But there is something else that makes the Barnaby novels better than their television counterpart: the variety and depth of the characterisation, to say nothing of the complex and satisfying plotting.

On television, because of the need to tell a story quickly, the novels have to be simplified; the characters are less rounded, and many fascinating details left out. In the books, Barnaby is a much more interesting character than we managed to convey in the television series. His style of non-confrontational, even conversational, interrogation that is so quietly absorbing in the books does not work on the box, which demands a noisier, more muscular approach from a copper. Likewise with Troy, the character you see on the screen is quite different from how he appears in the books. In the novels, Troy is an amazing creation, as far removed from Tom Barnaby's character as the North Pole is from the equator. The character was softened and made more attractive to a TV audience. It is true there were hints of his original red-top attitude, but they weren't ingrained or obvious enough to be character defining. In fact he became a lovable character in the television show and it must be said that, despite the simplification involved, Troy remains one of the best-loved characters in Midsomer.

In Caroline's novels, unlike the television series, the size of the social canvas is vast, with a huge variety of characters from all social classes: the lords and ladies; the poor; the young; the old; the disadvantaged; the indulged; the psychotic; the deranged; the loved and the unloved. The lives of all these characters are intimately and entertainingly delineated and explored, the murder mysteries are character led, in a way that the television versions are, very often, not – the television plots concentrate almost exclusively on the exotic methods of murder rather than the character of those who commit them. They have succeeded on this level beyond all expectation, but there is always a price to pay for turning books into a television series. Very often, the human interest is lost in the pursuit of ever more lurid and sometimes ludicrous plot lines; and while the results of this chase can be as entertaining as they are popular, something essential to good whodunnit storytelling is undoubtedly lost.

But despair not! In Caroline's books you will find that humanity restored, the drama therefore more real and the satisfaction absolute. Enjoy!

John Nettles
July 2016

Contents

The Invitation

Afterwards, talking to the police, no one could quite agree as to who had put forward Max Jennings' name. One or two people thought it was Amy Lyddiard, who was sure it was her friend Sue Clapton. Sue disagreed, suggesting Rex St John, who said it certainly couldn't have been him because he had never heard of the man let alone read his books. Laura Hutton admitted she might have been responsible, having recently come across an article in *Harpers* describing the author's recent move to a village barely twenty miles away. Brian Clapton said whoever it was had inflicted on him the most boring evening he had ever spent in his entire life. But what Amy and Sue both agreed on was that poor Gerald's reaction to the suggestion had been most dramatic.

No sooner were the words 'Max Jennings' uttered than, according to Amy who wrote block-buster fiction, he had apparently jumped, blanched, trembled, been taken aghast, stared wildly round or winced as if from some mysterious blow. And then he had dropped his coffee cup. There was immediately much fuss over the stained trousers and what with that and scraping the sugary residue off the carpet it was some ten minutes before the group reassembled. Sue made some fresh coffee using the special chocolate-truffle variety that Gerald had left ready and which Brian said he couldn't tell from cocoa.

When she took the tray in Gerald was standing in front of the gas fire holding damp trousers away from his scalded knees and saying, 'Terribly sorry about all this. A sudden twinge . . .' He laid his hand briefly against his white shirt front.

'You must go and see the quack,' said Rex.

Laura thought, it's his heart, and felt nauseous and quickly cold. But he's not fat. Or even overweight. The right age though. And you didn't have to be fat. There were all sorts of other factors. Oh God. *Oh God.*

'I think Rex is right—'

'It's just indigestion. Some jugged hare—'

'Even so—'

'Do you think we could get on?' Brian made a great show of looking at his watch. He didn't like Gerald for a variety of reasons and thought more than enough time had been spent fussing over him. 'I've got marking to do before I go to bed. We're not all members of the leisured class.'

They returned to their discussion, which was on the difficulties of finding a guest speaker. Just before the accident Amy had suggested a woman who lived in nearby Martyr d'Evercy and wrote about the humorous antics of her Pekinese dogs, of which she had a very large number.

'I know who you mean,' said Sue. 'She produces the books herself and takes them round to all the local shops.'

'Vanity publishing is strictly *verboten*,' said Brian. 'We want real writers or none at all.'

'It's only four times a year,' said Honoria Lyddiard, picking up the last pimento-and-cream-cheese vol-au-vent. There were two flaky frills resembling the wings of infant angels sticking out. She placed it on her large tongue like a pill and swallowed it whole. And that makes eight, observed Amy quietly to herself.

'I would have thought,' continued Honoria, 'that between us we could manage that.'

Between us was stretching it. Although quick to deride most of the names mentioned, Honoria rarely suggested anyone herself. The people who did come she nearly always deemed unworthy and was often extremely rude about them, not always waiting till after their departure.

'We could ask Frederick Forsyth,' said Rex, who was writing a thriller about a hit man, code name Hyena, and his attempt to assassinate Saddam Hussein.

'No point,' said Brian. 'These people always pretend they don't have time.'

This was demonstrably true. Among the people who had not had time to address the Midsomer Worthy Writers Circle over the past few years were Jeffrey Archer, Jilly Cooper, Maeve Binchy and Sue Townsend although she had sent a very nice letter and a signed paperback.

Only once had they had any sort of success. A poet, garlanded with prizes and praise and visiting the Blackbird bookshop in Causton for a signing session, had agreed to come and talk to them on the same evening. It had been a disaster. He had only stayed an hour, which was spent drinking, reading out his reviews and telling them all about the break-up with his boyfriend. Then he burst into tears and had to be driven all the way back to London by Laura, the men in the party having declined the honour.

And so the group perforce had had to be content with

far lesser luminaries – a journalist from the *Causton Echo*, an assistant producer (tea boy really) from the town's commercial radio station and a local man who published from time to time in *Practical Woodworking* and consequently thought himself too grand to attend on a regular basis.

'What about that idea you had at breakfast, dear?' Sue Clapton smiled timidly across at her husband. She was as neat and smooth as he was untidy, with long stringy hair the colour of milk chocolate tucked behind her ears and large round glasses with multi-coloured frames. She wore a long wrapover skirt the colour of clover printed with tiny daisies and her feet, in unlovely leather clogs, were placed just so. 'The one—'

'Yes, yes.' Brian flushed with annoyance. He had planned to introduce his suggestion coolly; absently, almost throw it away when the usual bickering had reached its nadir. 'I do have a contact who might – repeat might – just come and talk to us.'

'What does he write?'

'He doesn't.' Brian gave Gerald an amused smile. 'He's a devisor.' He chuckled and his ironic glance spread to include them all. Plainly no one knew what a devisor was. Typical. 'Mike Leigh?'

'Now that would be a coup,' said Laura, crossing elegant silk-clad honey-coloured legs. The friction produced a whispery hiss that had an effect on all but the man it was meant for.

Sue wished she had legs like that. Brian wished Sue had legs like that. Honoria thought the movement extremely vulgar. Rex boldly fantasised a wisp of lace and a suspender. And Amy smiled at Laura in simple friendliness – paying for it later over the Horlicks.

'I didn't say it *was* Mike Leigh.' The colour on Brian's cheeks deepened. 'I was merely making a comparison. Last week the school had a visit from Nuts N Bolts – theatre in education? – who gave this really brilliant account of a day in the life of a comprehensive—'

'Bit coals to Newcastle, what?' said Rex.

'Oh dear, oh dear.' Brian shook his head and laughed. 'You just don't get it, do you? Bouncing their own experience back to these kids but in a new dynamic form gives their lives a thrilling authenticity.'

'Pardon?'

'They recognize the grammar of the narrative as being identical with their own.'

'I see.'

'Anyway,' continued Brian, 'I caught up with Zeb, the guy who runs it, while they were loading the van and asked if he'd come and give a talk. We'd have to pay—'

'Absolutely not,' said Honoria. 'We never pay.'

'Just expenses. Petrol and—'

'Honoria's right.' Rex struggled to inject a note of regret into his voice. 'Once we start doing that sort of thing . . .' He tailed off, wondering, as he had often done, if such parsimony wasn't perhaps counterproductive. Maybe if they'd offered John le Carré his expenses? Honoria was speaking again. Loudly.

'Of course if you'd like to fund a visit from this person yourself?'

Honoria regarded Brian coldly. He really was an absolute mess of a man. Straggly hair, straggly beard, straggly clothes and, in her opinion, an extremely straggly political viewpoint.

Sue watched apprehensively as her husband retreated into a sulk, then started to play with her hair. Beginning at the scalp she lifted a narrow strand and ran her nails down it, pulling the hair taut before letting it go and starting on the next piece. She did this for the rest of the evening. It was only half an hour but all present felt by then that they had, at the very least, entered the next millennium.

And so, eventually, through many digressions and much argument, the conversation described a full circle and Max Jennings' name came up again.

'I really feel we might have a chance with him,' said Amy, 'living nearby. Also he's not a hundred-percent famous.'

'What on earth's that supposed to mean?' said Honoria.

'I think,' said Sue, 'Amy means just quite well known.'

'I've never heard of him,' said Brian, drumming his fingers on the arm of his chair. Whilst having no time for the rich and famous he also had no time for the not really all that rich and only very slightly famous. Truth to tell, if you were not at the very bottom of society's dung heap and being ground further into the primeval sludge by every passing jackboot, Brian would almost certainly be giving you the complete kiss off.

'I heard an interview with him on the radio,' said Amy. 'He sounded really nice.' Too late she remembered it should have been 'wireless' and waited for Honoria to click her tongue. 'I'm sure it's worth a try.'

'I can't stand these poncy nom de plumes. No doubt for Max we are meant to read Maximilian. Probably born Bert Bloggs.'

'I read his first novel, *Far Away Hills*. He was brought up in absolute poverty in the Outer Hebrides. His father was a terribly cruel man and drove his mother to her death. She killed herself when he was still quite young.'

'Really.' Brian sounded more cheerful. 'We could give it

a try, I suppose. Not as if we have anyone else in mind.'

'There's Alan Bennett.'

Brian sniffed. He was rather off Alan Bennett. At the beginning Brian had been very much under the writer's influence. He had hung around outside the village shop and the Old Dun Cow with a tape recorder, talking to the villagers, hoping to unravel the rich and poignant complexities of their inner lives as he understood was the great man's way. It had been a dead loss. All they talked about was *Neighbours* and football and what was in the *Sun*. Eventually a drunk had called him a nosy piss pot and knocked him down.

Laura said, 'I thought we were keeping him for an emergency.'

'Let's take a vote shall we?' said Rex. 'Asking Jennings?' He put his hand up as did the others, Honoria last of all. 'Gerald?'

Gerald had turned his still damp trousers back to the fire. He looked over his shoulder at the six raised hands then back to the artificial blue and yellow flames. However he voted it could hardly affect the outcome. Yet he could not let this terrible suggestion pass without some form of protest.

He said, 'I think it'll be a waste of time,' and marvelled at the neutrality of his voice. At the even tone. The regular and unhurried spacing between the words. The words themselves so mild in contrast to the torment raging in his breast.

'Sorry, Gerald. You're outnumbered.' Brian was already pulling on his knitted hat.

'Even so,' (he couldn't just give up) 'I don't think there's a lot of point—'

'If you won't write I will,' said Brian. 'Care of his

publisher, I suppose. In fact I might ring them up—'

'No, no. I'm secretary. I'll do it.' At least that way matters would stay in his own hands. 'No problem.' Gerald stood up, wishing only to be rid of them. He saw Laura covertly watching him and managed to stretch his lips in the semblance of a smile.

He did not sleep that night. He sat at his desk for the first hour quite motionless, drowned in recollection. His head felt as if it were being squeezed in a vice. To see the man again. Max. *Max*. Who had stolen his most priceless possession. To have to speak words of welcome and no doubt be forced to listen to hours of self-aggrandisement in return. Gerald knew he would not be able to bear it.

At three o'clock he started writing. He wrote and wrote and wrote again. By six he was exhausted and the waste basket was overflowing, but he had the letter. One side of one sheet of paper. He was as sure as he could be that the balance was right. It was out of the question that he should beg Max not to come. Even at the time – even at the very moment of that terrible betrayal – Gerald had not begged. Victorious Max might have been but that was one satisfaction he would forever seek in vain.

Now Gerald, gripping his pen hard in his right hand and holding the paper down firmly with his left, started to address the envelope. Necessarily he began with the name. M.a.x. J.e.n.n.i.n.g.s. The pen slipped and twirled in his sweating fingers. It was as if the very letters had the power of conjuration. He could hear the man breathing, smell the fragrance of his cigar smoke, look into the brilliant blue eyes in that bony, sunburnt face. Feel the old spell being cast.

He read the letter again. Surely no one comprehending the emotional turmoil from which such an invitation must inevitably have sprung would accept.

Gerald affixed a first-class stamp, put on his muffler and overcoat and left the house. As he set off for the post box the milkman's float materialised out of the dark.

'You're up early, Mr Hadleigh.' The man nodded at the white square in Gerald's hand. 'Making sure you get your pools off.'

'That's right.'

Gerald strode off, his spirits curiously lightened by this mundane encounter. The real world rushed in, familiar and banal. It was the night now that seemed unreal. A hot-house of unhealthy imaginings.

He quickened his pace, filling his lungs with fresh winter air. By the time he was starting back towards the cottage the bitter reflections that had so tormented him just a short while before now began to seem no more than over-heated fantasies. He was projecting his own wretched memories on to someone else. For all he knew Max had practically forgotten about him. And in any case, even if he hadn't, Gerald could not somehow see him driving nearly thirty miles just to talk to a bunch of amateur scribblers. He was successful now. Each new epic in the *Sunday Times* Top Ten without fail. No, the more Gerald thought about it, the more insubstantial and unfounded his previous fears now seemed.

There were streaks of rose pink, lemon and silver on the horizon as he let himself back into the house and put on the coffee pot. And by the time the sun's scarlet rim had appeared he had persuaded himself that writing such a careful and painstaking letter had been a waste of time and effort. Because there was no chance in the world that Max would come.

* * *

Almost a month to the day after the group meeting Laura stood by her kitchen door, knowing what she was about to do even as she entertained the delusion that she might yet change her mind. In her hand she held an empty sealed envelope. Laura did not own a dog and had more sense than to walk around an English village in the dark for no apparent reason.

On her last excursion (just under a week ago) she had met the Reverend Clewes coming out of the vicarage with Henry, his basset hound. They had all walked along together and Laura had been compelled to post her envelope before being accompanied all the way back home and seen safely inside. She had not dared to venture out again and had gone to bed fretting miserably with deprivation. But tonight Henry had gone trotting by with his master, and trotting back, a good half hour ago.

Laura buttoned her dark reefer jacket up to the neck. She wore jeans, strong leather gloves, black boots and a sombre head scarf concealing distinctive coils of hair that glittered like copper wire. She stepped out into the still, silent night, locked the door, turned the key very gently and stood for a moment listening.

There was no sound from either of the houses flanking her own. No cats being put out or let in. No chink of milk bottles or rattle of dustbin lids. Or friends being seen off the premises. She set off, hushed on rubber soles, turning left without even having to think.

She walked quickly, keeping close to tall hedges – the Englishman's modest horticultural version of the medieval stockade. Suddenly a crumpled-silver-paper moon occupied the sky and Laura stepped into a negative. Pumice-stone houses, black trees painted with pale light. Previously lost in the anticipation of journey's end, she was shocked into self-consciousness. Exposed, like a solitary actor on a brilliantly lit stage.

It was still several yards to the post office, which was, in fact, nothing grander than the properly fortified sitting room of Wiworry, Mr and Mrs 'Midge' Sandell's bungalow. The pillar box was by the gate and as Laura drew level with it the moon became obscured by clouds again. She put the envelope into her pocket and walked on. This was the tricky bit, for if she ran into an acquaintance now she could hardly say she was on her way to post a letter. But luck was with her and she saw no one.

Plover's Rest was the last house to face the Green proper. From then on the divided road joined up again and the property on either side consequently became less valuable. There was a gap of around thirty yards before these houses began and this area had been left wild. It was filled with a tangle of hawthorns; sloes and wild crab apples and was a godsend to Laura for, like most of the houses on the Green, Plover's Rest had a halogen lamp which any direct approach set off immediately.

She made her way through the tangle, holding vicious briars away from her face, staring into the blackness unafraid, desire outweighing apprehension a hundredfold. Then, heart pounding, she crept out of the tiny copse, made a left turn and squeezed through a second gap, this time in a waist-high wattle fence. She was now in Gerald Hadleigh's back garden.

Laura stood for a moment, keenly aware of her surroundings – a massive beech tree, empty ornamental urns, the barely visible outline of patio slabs sparkling with frost. Over her head the sky was crammed with stars. Avoiding the gravel, she tiptoed softly forward, preceded by puffs of her own breath immediately visible on the icy air.

There was a light on in the kitchen but, as Laura approached, it was plain that the room was empty. Boldly she stared in. There were some dirty dishes in the sink. A half bottle of claret and a glass on a tray. Changing her position slightly she could see the long shelf of boxed spices and narrow glass jars with dried shavings of fungi and ginger and some brackish curly stuff the colour of dried blood.

Gerald had mentioned once that he liked to cook Japanese food. Laura had at once said she adored it too and asked if he would give her a lesson. He had smiled and said he wouldn't dare but next time he cooked teriyaki she was welcome to try some. She had waited, in a daze of happiness, for that invitation, which had never materialised.

Eventually, driven by longing, by a vision of the two of them sitting at a candlelit table drinking glasses of warm sake she reminded him of his promise. He assured her he had not forgotten and how would next Thursday at seven be?

Laura had danced away to steam her skin and brush her glorious hair and massage scented lotion over immaculate, slender legs. On Thursday at six forty-five she had put on her Jasper Conran maize jacket and ivory silk shirt and narrow damson crêpe skirt and hung glowing cornelians in her ears. She looked lovely. Everyone said so – the Clewses, Rex, the couple from Windy Hollow who were in computers. A first invitation, she discovered later, for all of them.

Anyone else would have learned from that. Laura, crying herself to sleep, awoke to the conviction that Gerald was simply nervous. Socially not at all gauche where romance was concerned, Laura told herself, he was simply out of practice. He wanted to entertain her in his home but, the first time, needed other people present. That had been nearly a year ago. The invitation had never been repeated.

Wretchedly unhappy, needing to protect herself, Laura struggled to create in her mind an alternative situation, charting the progress of an imaginary affair to Gerald's disadvantage. He was a rotten lover, a boring conversationalist, faddy and finicky and set in his ways. Completely self-absorbed. After no time at all, light-hearted and free as a bird, she left him. With a huge expenditure of imaginative energy Laura could hold on to this comforting fiction, sometimes for days. But then, of course, she would see him again.

Sound and light! Bathed in panic she dodged from the window and pressed herself flat against the cottage, feeling the flints jab into her back. But it was only Brian, Gerald's nearest neighbour, putting his permanently red-nosed Volkswagen away. The headlamp's beams were gradually eaten up. The garage doors banged shut. She heard him walk down the side of the house and go in. A bolt was shot. No doubt Sue would, even now, be making bedtime drinks. Laura felt a fleeting pang of envy. Not, God knew, that she, or surely anyone in their right senses, would want to be married to Brian. But there was undoubtedly a brand of cosiness obtainable à deux that was simply not on the menu when you lived alone.

Oh, what am I doing here? Laura pounded her gloved fist on the wall, scraping the leather. I am a grown-up thirty-six-year-old woman. I am attractive and have even been called beautiful. I am not neurotic. I have friends and I have known love. I run a successful business and have a pretty house full of beautiful things. Children smile at me.

13

Cats and dogs give me the time of day. Men ask me out. So why am I creeping around like a criminal at eleven o'clock on a freezing February night on the off-chance of catching a glimpse of a man who couldn't give a damn whether I'm alive or dead?

Falling in love. She had never understood before how literally, physically true the phrase was. One minute she had been choosing oranges in the village shop, the next she had stepped back and trodden on a man's foot. A tall man with greying curly hair and rather cool hazel eyes. What happened next (the falling) was quite extraordinary. Laura had seen a film once – Hitchcock perhaps – where someone in their dreams tumbled down and down into a black and white spiralling vortex. And that's just what it had been like. She closed her eyes, feeling again the force of it, tugging on her heartstrings like a falcon's jesses.

Sure that he would be married, Laura had become weak with relief on hearing that he was a widower. Such a tragedy. His wife died several years ago. Leukaemia. They hadn't been married long. He's never got over it. And she, confident of her femininity, her lovability, thought: I will show him how to get over it. I will make him happy again. And when I do he will forget all about her.

New to Midsomer Worthy, she attended the harvest supper in the hope of seeing him. He was not present, but she did discover that the village boasted a writers' circle of which he was a member.

Though having no talent or interest in the subject she joined immediately, under the pretence that she was transcribing a mass of letters, papers and receipts she had bought in an auction job lot. And so, once every four weeks at the very least, she was sure of seeing him. Not just to smile and wave at across the Green but truly to be with for two and sometimes nearer three hours. She thought of these periods as quality time. Time spent doing what mattered to you most in all the world. She had come across the phrase in a magazine article about parents with only limited access to their children.

Telling him was out of the question. She was not even remotely tempted. Everything would inevitably change, perhaps – no, almost certainly – for the worst. Things were easy now between them. Or at least Gerald thought they were, which is what mattered. But how might he handle a passionate declaration of undying love that he was either unable or unwilling to return? It would place him in an intolerable position. He would be embarrassed when they met. View her perhaps with distaste. Or worse, with pity. He might even drop out of the group to avoid an awkward evening. Goodbye, quality time. Hello, end of the world.

God, it was cold. Her feet, even with thick socks inside the boots, were frozen. Laura moved on to the grass at the side of the house where she could, inaudibly, stamp up and down. I must be mad, she said to herself. I'll be seeing him in twenty-four hours.

She had a sudden sharp perception of how she would appear to an observer. A peeping Thomasina. A voyeuse. And vowed to give up. Tomorrow.

A vehicle was approaching. The sound became louder, filling her ears. It was not Gerald's Celica. This car had a much heavier, louder note. And when the door opened and closed it was with a louder thunk. Laura ran into the trees on the far side of the cottage. Then, dry-mouthed with apprehension, moved swiftly forwards to where she could see what was happening.

A taxi stood in the drive. A woman, her back to Laura, was paying off the driver. She wore a smart black suit and a little hat with a veil. The driver called out something of which Laura could make out only 'safely in . . .'. The woman rapped on the cottage door. As the cab drove away, the door opened and she stepped inside.

Laura let out the breath she had not even realised she was holding in a low moan. She clapped her hands over her mouth and waited, rigid with alarm, in case someone had heard. But it seemed no one had.

As she stood absorbing the shock other feelings were released. Misery, jealousy, a great bursting sadness and rage at her own gullible complacency. Because Gerald had shown no interest in her she had been vain enough to assume he had no interest in any woman. How completely she – indeed all of them – had been taken in by the pose of grieving widower.

Knowing she would be sorry, yet driven to turn the knife, Laura moved away from the shelter of the trees. As she did so a branch pulled at her scarf. The velvet curtains in the sitting room were not quite drawn. She stood in the flower border, past caring by now whether she was seen or not, and applied her eye to the chink.

She could see part of the bookshelves, the section of the sideboard supporting the wedding picture with Grace, appropriately enough, cut off. Half a vase of pink viburnum. The woman came into view. She was carrying a glass of red wine, presumably the claret. She had taken off her hat and thick fair hair tumbled in waves over her shoulders. She was beautifully made up but, thought Laura, older than I am. Much too old for him.

The woman lifted her glass, smiled and spoke. Then drank deep. Gerald's wine. The intimacy of this very ordinary little ritual nearly drove Laura mad. She could no longer see for tears. Certainly she never saw or heard old

Mr Lilley from Laburnum Villas walking by with his collie dog.

Amy could remember quite clearly the moment she became aware that servitude had entered her life. She had been living at her sister-in-law's for several months and had tried to make herself useful from the start, being only too keenly aware of her inability to contribute financially to the household.

The moment in question had occurred on a sunny afternoon in May. Honoria had been sitting at her desk surrounded, as usual, by genealogical charts, old letters and other documents relating to the Lyddiards' family tree and books on heraldry. The doorbell had just rung and Amy had put the pillowcase she had been mending aside, looked across at Honoria's broad back, half got up, hesitated. Honoria did not even turn round. Just jerked an irritated finger in the direction of the sound.

Until that moment Amy had dignified her increasingly lengthy range of daily tasks under the term 'being useful', which she certainly was. Within a month of her arrival Amy had taken over the shopping (village store daily, Causton once a week), garden maintenance, collecting wood for the boiler, washing and ironing and helping Honoria with her research. But there were certain things that she might not do. Duties that were below the salt. Although only a relation by marriage she was still a Lyddiard, which meant no kneeling. Mrs Bundy came in once a week for that sort of thing, which was called 'the rough'.

On the rare occasions when visitors were present Amy was not even allowed to clear away the tea things. 'As if,' she had grumbled during one of her secret conversations with Sue, 'they are going to think we've got a black and white maid hiding in the kitchen.'

Sue had nodded sympathetically, remarking that she'd never known anyone so snobbish.

Amy disagreed. To call Honoria a snob was like calling Alexander the Great a bit on the bossy side. The worshipful veneration she entertained for her position and that of her ancestors on the map of English history beggared belief. Amy thought she was a bit mad. Since her brother's death Honoria had spent all her time fiercely tracing this blood line, fortifying every discovery with as much primary material as she – and now Amy – could discover.

Many cardboard boxes filled with rubber-banded index cards attested to a most assiduous ferreting out of information. A vast square of white card, weighted at each corner, was permanently unfurled on a large table where it was gradually being imprinted with the family tree. When this was complete Honoria planned to have the details transferred to the finest vellum, professionally calligraphed and illumined with gold leaf, whereupon it would be framed and hung in the main hall.

Amy had long tired of it all. She had wondered more than once how Honoria came by her obsession, for it certainly did not run in the family. Ralph (or Rafe as his sister still insisted on calling him) had been the least class conscious of men. He would talk to anyone and everyone in an easygoing and friendly manner. Unlike his sister he just liked people.

Honoria despised people. Especially the lower orders. 'Unwholesome barbarians breeding like bacteria in their squalid little hutches' was one of her less extreme descriptions. How her aristocratic spirit looked down on them! Barely civilised rabble.

Ralph had always laughed at this nonsense and could not understand why Amy didn't do the same, but she found Honoria's insistence on a 'natural aristocracy of the blood' far from funny. To Amy it seemed dehumanising, smacking of eugenics, born leaders and chilling attempts at social engineering.

'Are you listening to me?'

'Yes, Honoria.'

Amy sighed as she lied but was glad of the interruption. Every recollection of her husband could so easily tip her into a spiral of unhappy nostalgia. She tore open a plastic carrier and placed it over a tray of brown-bread cartwheels containing Primula cheese and asparagus tips. Honoria was still going on about the asparagus, even though the tin had been reduced to half price because it was badly dented. Amy had defended her purchase, saying everyone would be taking something special out of respect for the celebrity speaker.

'Anyone would think he was a reincarnation of William Shakespeare,' Honoria had grumbled, adding, 'if there are any left make sure you bring them back.'

Amy finished arranging her second tray. Triangular sandwiches with the crusts cut off filled with cucumber and home-made mayonnaise. She would much rather have used shop-bought. Not only did it taste nicer but the consistency was much more satisfactory. This stuff either ran out in little puddles or seeped through the bread so it looked like mustard-coloured blotting paper. But Hellmann's was deemed too costly.

'People seem to be going mad,' persisted Honoria. 'Laura spoke of buying something from that ridiculously expensive pastry shop and Susan is baking a cake, no doubt full of the disgusting hamster food they all seem to thrive on.'

'An iced carrot cake actually.'

'He's coming from the far side of High Wycombe.' Honoria, already wearing an old Barbour, now rammed a tweed pork-pie hat over her short, straight, iron-grey hair. 'Not the North Pole.'

'Where are you going?' asked Amy, meaning, as she always did, how long will you be?

'Just to Laura's.'

If Max Jennings was coming from the North Pole, thought Amy, shivering in spite of two jumpers, a cardigan, tights, leg warmers and ankle boots, he would certainly feel at home in Gresham House.

She went into the library, where Honoria, having finished work for the day, was letting the fire go out. Amy crouched over the smouldering grey-white remains and rubbed her frozen fingers. She wondered whether to go down to the cellar and kick the boiler. This was a voracious wood-burning contraption connected to iron skirting pipes which it was supposed to feed with hot water. There were two or three dials to be twiddled as an alternative to physical violence, but neither method was wholly satisfactory. The pipes never had more than the chill taken off. The water was never more than lukewarm.

Amy decided against it. By the time she had got down there and attacked the thing she could be in her room and writing. Never a day without a line had been Olivia Manning's dictum and Amy tried her best to live by it.

Her novel, *Rompers*, was safely locked away in a shagreen hat box on top of the wardrobe. She had described it to the group, not untruthfully, as a family saga, but just what type of families they were and what sort of thing they got up to remained a secret between herself and Sue. Although the sexual shenanigans were pretty decorous compared to some bestsellers and although she had, so far, been unable to bring herself to use the 'f' word, which seemed to look so dreadful written down, there was still enough hot stuff sizzling in the rich and glamorous stew to give Honoria serious pause for thought. A process which might well lead to the conclusion that the loose-moraled person producing such unsavoury rubbish was not worthy to reside beneath the Lyddiard roof. And then, thought Amy, where would I go? A woman of forty, completely unskilled and without a penny to her name.

This was not Ralph's fault even though, in the eyes of the world, he had not been a success. A sailor when Amy met him, she often thought it was a mistake that he left the service. But he was worried about abandoning her for long periods and she, of course, had missed him dreadfully. He had no special gifts and talents and, while not un-intelligent, never really discovered what he was cut out for. With a legacy from his parents – Honoria got the house and a small annuity – he opened a second-hand bookshop. This failed, as did other idealistic ventures – growing olives in the Evvia, picture framing in Devizes. Finally, having almost exhausted the money, they bought a tiny cottage in Andalusia with an acre of stony soil and struggled towards some sort of self-sufficiency. It was during this period that Ralph became aware of the first signs of the cancer that was to cost him his life.

Stop it! Stop it! Amy shouted the words, forcefully vanquishing her beloved husband, the tiny ill-equipped Spanish hospital, Honoria's enraged descent and the dreadful flight home. If she was going to write herself out of her present miserable existence she would not do it by endlessly picking over the past.

She took down the hat box, removed the manuscript

and re-read the last three pages to get in the mood. She was not entirely dissatisfied. The prose seemed to her quite robust and she had been careful to keep out even the slightest hint of irony. But how would it come across, Amy now asked herself, under the hard commercial eye of a tough fiction editor?

At least this time round (for *Rompers* was her third attempt) she had got the social class and settings right. At first, when Sue pointed out that the quickest way to make pots of money was to write within a genre which she called 'cuddling and buying things', Amy had quite misunderstood. Her heroine, Daphne, a dental receptionist, had been shyly approached by a divinity student while selecting a cauliflower in Tesco's. Now, stylishly renamed, she was wheeling and dealing in Hong Kong.

Amy chewed on her Biro. When she was just thinking above writing it seemed so easy. All sorts of jolly phrases leapt to mind. Pacy, beautifully shaped, packing a punch. But when the time came to deface the dreaded blank page they never seemed to belong in what she was working on.

Likewise individual scenes. Great fun to write; difficult to fit in to the grand overall scheme. Amy had wondered about missing this step out entirely. Why should not readers buy all the bits – perhaps in a prettily decorated box – and assemble them to their own designs in their own homes? After all, people did it with furniture. It could be a new trend. And publishers were supposed to be always on the lookout for originality.

Amy looked at her watch and gasped. Half an hour since Honoria had left. All that time wasted in sad recollection instead of working towards a better future. She seized her pen.

'Damn, damn and damn again!' cried Araminta saltily as she picked up Burgoyne's latest fax with trembling lips.

Honoria cycled alongside the Green in solitary and deluded splendour, pursing her mouth savagely as she spotted a single Coca-Cola tin lying meekly on its side beneath the village notice board.

Powerfully present on the parish council, Honoria had so far fought successfully against the placing of a litter bin on, or even anywhere near, the beautifully maintained verdant oval. But if this sort of loathsome despoliation was to be the result she may well have to think again.

Without doubt the article in question had been thrown down by someone from the municipal dwellings. Although these hideous breeze-block buildings were placed, quite rightly in Honoria's opinion, on the very edge of the village proper, the social pariahs housed within seemed to think they could go wherever they liked, shouting, playing music, revving their disgusting motor bicycles. In the summer they even swarmed all over the Green to watch the cricket, bringing pushchairs and picnics and hideous tartan rugs. If Honoria had her way the dozen or so council houses would be contained behind high wire fences and patrolled by armed guards.

She turned into the driveway of Laura's cottage and dismounted by crossing one stout leg in front of the other and jumping down. She leaned her bicycle, a large old upright with a semi-circle of yellow oilskin laced over the back wheels and a fraying wicker basket, against the garage and tapped on the front door.

Honoria was there by invitation. At her own request Laura had been looking out for a stone figure to grace the Gresham garden's clematis walk. She had rung the previous evening to say that a catalogue had arrived for a coming sale in Worcester containing pictures of some charming statuary. Perhaps Honoria would like to come and look at them? She suggested tea time the following afternoon, which was early closing at her shop.

Honoria rapped again, but no one came. She lifted the latch, which was very old, a highly polished brass heart with a lion's paw handle, and the door opened. All was quiet but for the tock-tocking of Laura's tall ebony grandfather clock. Honoria peered into the two tiny rooms opening off the hall then moved, silent on thick cherry-red carpet, towards the kitchen. As she approached she heard a most strange sound – a long, juddering, in-drawn breath as if someone was being severely shaken.

Honoria hesitated, not from nervousness but from an inbred aversion to tangling with any situation not proceeding along smoothly conventional lines. She also had a distaste verging on abhorrence for minding anyone's business but her own.

She decided to open the door just a chink to see if she could discover precisely what was going on. Unfortunately the door creaked. Loudly. Laura, who was sitting at the table, her head resting on her arms, weeping, looked up. The two women stared at each other. It was impossible for Honoria to withdraw.

Laura must have been crying, surely, Honoria thought, for some hours. She was so used to seeing the other woman's skilfully made-up face regarding the world with cool detachment that she hardly recognised her. Eyes so swollen as to be almost invisible, scarlet puffy cheeks, damp hair hanging any-old-how. And still in her dressing gown.

Rigid with mortified disapproval, Honoria struggled

towards speech, for it was plainly impossible to say 'excuse me' and leave. That would have looked appallingly heartless and, although Honoria was appallingly heartless, she had no wish to bandy the fact between all and sundry. Really, she thought crossly, if people choose to behave in such a loose manner they might at least have the decency to do so behind locked doors.

'My dear,' she said, and the endearment sat as awkwardly in her mouth as an ill-fitting tooth, 'what on earth is the matter?'

After a long pause Laura gave the reply people nearly always do in such circumstances. 'Nothing.'

Strongly tempted to reply 'Well, that's all right then' and leave, Honoria descended two glossy stone steps and drew a wheelback chair out over the blue slate tiles. She sat down, saying, 'Is there anything I can do?'

Of all the bloody awful rotten luck. Laura cursed herself for forgetting to put the Yale back down after signing for a registered package. Of all the bloody awful rotten people to walk in. Laura had looked up only briefly, but once had been enough. Honoria's prurient disengagement and passionate wish to be elsewhere were unmistakable.

'No, honestly.' She took a tissue from a nearly empty box, scrubbed her cheeks, blew her nose and dropped the soggy ball into a waste basket. 'I get like this sometimes.'

'Oh.'

'I guess everyone does.'

Honoria stared in disbelief. She had been brought up under the strict understanding that a lady never displayed her emotions. Honoria had never cried, not even when her beloved Rafe had died and she had been split asunder with the pain of it. Not then or at the funeral or at any time afterwards.

'Shall I make you some tea?'

'Tea?' God, she'd be here for the duration. Making it, letting it stand, pouring it out. Milk and sugar. Bloody biscuits. Go away, you horrible old woman. Just go away.

'That's very kind.'

Honoria filled the kettle and got milk, still in its carton, from the fridge. The teapot, a pretty piece of Rockingham covered with blue flowers was, to her relief, sitting on the side. She hated the idea of opening cupboards. Seeming to pry. Which meant doing without a milk jug. The silver-gilt caddie held Earl Grey bags.

'Do you have bis—'

'No.' Laura had stopped crying but her face remained crumpled, this time with incipient crossness. 'I eat them all so don't keep them in the house.'

'I see.' Honoria was unsurprised at this further example of undisciplined dishevelment. 'What a charming pot,' she added, whilst waiting for the tea to brew. 'You have such lovely things. I suppose it's being in trade.'

Laura blew her nose again, this time more loudly, putting the tissue in the pocket of her dressing gown. Actually when the drink came she was glad of it, for she had taken nothing since after dinner the previous evening.

What was it, she wondered, about the making and proffering of this, the English panacea? No matter how appalling the occasion – a devastating accident, incipient bankruptcy or news of bereavement – the shell-shocked survivors were offered a cup of tea. And after all, thought Laura, aren't I newly bereaved? Deprived forever of the hope that once sprang eternal.

She sipped the fragrant, steaming liquid. The deceit of him. *The deceit*. Such rectitude. The lonely widower nursing his loss in pious and dignified silence. Refusing all comfort. His whole life a lie. Laura crashed her cup down into the saucer.

Honoria, sitting bolt upright and already gripping her handbag very firmly, now held it up before her in the manner of a shield. Anxious both to justify her presence and to get away she reminded Laura about the catalogue, concluding, 'Of course it doesn't matter now. I can come back again.'

'Oh! Don't do that.' Laura sprang up with uncomplimentary speed. 'I'm sure I know just where they are.'

She ran upstairs to her second bedroom, which doubled as an office, and started sorting through her in-tray. The catalogue wasn't there. Or in the desk. Or in the Garden (Design) file. About to check her briefcase she remembered that she had been flipping through the thing the previous evening in the sitting room. And that was where she found it, in the magazine rack.

'I've ticked the ones I thought might be suitable.' Laura re-entered the kitchen. 'There's no hurry to bring it back. The sale isn't for six weeks.' She paused. 'Honoria?'

Honoria jerked her head round suddenly as if she had been dreaming. She rose and took the catalogue without looking at Laura. Her lips, always of a censorious set, seemed even more rigidly clamped than usual. Her cheeks were flushed and her eyes burned with a cold puritanical fire. Laura was glad when the front door closed behind her. And it wasn't even as if anything would come of it. This wasn't the first time such an idea had been mooted. Honoria was far too mean to spend five pounds, let alone five hundred.

It was when she was once more sitting at the table wondering whether to start crying again or make some fresh tea that she noticed the photograph. About half an hour before Honoria arrived Laura had removed it from its silver frame beside her bed and dropped it in the waste basket. Since then a certain amount of tear-soaked Kleenex had gone the same way but the picture was not quite concealed. Gerald's face was still visible, smiling through the sog.

Had Honoria seen it? Seen it and filled in the missing links, crossing the 't' in romantic and dotting the 'i' in despair. Laura raged at her own carelessness in forgetting the picture was in there. At Honoria for barging in. And at Gerald for being Gerald. Impelled by a mixture of anger and disgust she tipped the contents of the basket into the Raeburn and was immediately and bitterly sorry.

Rex was on the point of starting work. He had thoroughly masticated some bran and prunes, trotted his dog three times round the houses, taken fifty deep breaths in front of an open window and washed his hands. This last was of vital importance. Rex had seen a television interview once with a famous screenwriter during which the man had expressed great reverence for his hands, repeatedly referring to them as 'the tools of his trade'. They were insured for huge amounts of money, 'like the feet of Fred Astaire', and the screenwriter washed them thoroughly each morning, using only the finest triple-milled honey and glycerine soap. After being carefully rinsed in spring water they would be patted dry with a virginally white, soft, fluffy towel kept pristine until that very moment beneath a sealed wrapper. Only then did the celebrated inkslinger even think of approaching his state-of-the-art computer.

Rex had been terribly impressed by the man's faith in this ritual and straight away claimed it for his own. He knew the importance of routine. All the How To Succeed

As A Writer manuals, of which he had practically every one extant, stressed it. Rex started work at eleven a.m. precisely. Not a minute later, not a minute earlier. There was a transistor on his desk to make sure he got it right. As the pips started he picked up his pen. By the time they finished he had written his first sentence. So vital was this procedure that if anything happened to disrupt it he never really recovered. He completed his two thousand words of course (writers write), but nevertheless felt peculiarly out of sync all day.

Now, at five minutes to eleven, someone knocked at the front door of Borodino. Rex, at that very moment turning into his study, heard them with a mixture of irritation and alarm. Would it be a matter he could handle in five – no, he glanced at his pocket watch, nearer four minutes? Or someone who would want to come in and start going on?

One thing was certain. There was no way he could go into his study and settle down with someone standing on the front step. For a start they would spot him through the window. And he couldn't draw the curtains without giving away the fact that he was in. Botheration take it. He opened the door. It was Gerald.

'Rex – I'm sorry.' He stepped inside. 'I know you start work around now—'

'Yes. At eleven o' clock act—'

'I simply have to talk to you.'

'Is it about the food?' Rex was supplying a tin of glazed pralines, having been dissuaded from preparing one of his famous curries.

'No. Though it is about tonight. In a way.'

To Rex's dismay Gerald walked into his holy of holies. Just strolled in, lifted yesterday's pages from the seat of a tapestry wing chair, dropped them on the floor and sat down. Rex stood and hovered, unable to bring himself to sit behind his desk merely for the purpose of idle banter. He waited, but having moved in the first instance so decisively Gerald now seemed to have difficulty getting to the point.

He stared distractedly out at the garden – not seeing the bird table, a battleground of squabbling starlings and sparrows, or Rex's great hound, Montcalm, absent-mindedly truffling among the frosty cabbage stalks – while Rex stared, covertly, at him.

Gerald looked terrible. He had not shaved and looked as if he hadn't washed either. His eyes were red-rimmed and crusty with sleep. He kept clenching and unclenching his fists while seeming to be unaware of the fact. Rex, genuinely concerned, put all thoughts of *The Night of the Hyena* aside and said, 'Gerald old chap. You look completely done in. Would some coffee help?'

Gerald shook his head. Rex, who had drawn up a companion chair, could smell the other man's breath, sour and stale with more than a hint of liquor. They sat quietly for several minutes and finally Gerald spoke.

'This is going to sound pathetic.' A long pause. 'I don't really know how to put it.' He stared at Rex directly for the first time. Half despairing, half ashamed. 'However described I'm afraid it'll sound very odd.'

'I'm sure it won't,' said Rex, already consoled for his lost day by finding himself in that most pleasant of positions, consumed by a curiosity that was about to be promptly satisfied.

Gerald had put this moment off again and again. Now there was no time left. And, old and garrulous though he might be, it had to be Rex. There was no one else that Gerald could even consider approaching. Yet how to find the words? Even exposing the barest bones of his dilemma must make him look a fool and a coward. For the first time he noticed the working of his hands and spread them on his knees, pressing the fingers hard against the grey flannel, forcing them to be still.

'You said it was about tonight,' said Rex helpfully.

'Yes.' He looked like a non-swimmer forced to the end of the high-dive board. 'The fact is I knew Max Jennings a long time ago. There was some unpleasantness. We parted bad friends.'

'These things happen.' Rex tactfully hid his appreciation of what sounded like a very juicy mystery and tried to sound consoling. This wasn't difficult for he was, at heart, a kind man.

'Quite honestly,' continued Gerald, 'I didn't think for a minute, when he saw my signature on the invitation, that he would come.' That letter, so endlessly worked and reworked and all in vain. 'I don't know what his reasons are. He can be very . . . unpredictable. The thing is, Rex,' his voice was taut with nervousness, 'I don't want to be on my own with him.'

'Say no more,' cried Rex, his eyes shining with excitement. 'But what can I do?'

'It's simple really. Just don't leave until he does.'

'Of course I will. Or rather – of course I won't.' He hesitated. 'I suppose you wouldn't care to tell me—'

'No, I wouldn't.'

'Fair enough.'

'You don't mind, Rex?'

'My dear chap.'

'It might be a bit awkward. Sitting it out, I mean. After all the others have gone.'

'You think that will happen?'

31

'Yes.'

Of course he should never have written at all. That was his big mistake. He should have told the group he had asked and been refused. No one would be surprised. And when they wanted to see the letter, which they always did, he could say that Mr Jennings' secretary had declined the invitation by telephone. It was Brian, suddenly offering to write himself, which had brought on such a panic. Gerald realised Rex was talking again.

'Sorry?'

'I said, what if he turns up before anyone else arrives.'

'He shouldn't. I gave him eight instead of seven thirty. And if he does . . .' Even to Rex, Gerald could not admit that he would then be reduced to hiding, like an animal in its lair when the dogs are scrabbling at the entrance.

'I wish you'd told me earlier, Gerald. We could have changed the venue. Held the meeting somewhere else.'

'Then he would simply have left when I did. No, this way at least I have some sort of control.'

'Would you like to come and sleep over here—'

'For God's sake!' Gerald exploded, screwing up his eyes and clenching his fists again. 'This is how I think it best to handle things – all right?'

'Of course. Sorry.'

'No – I'm sorry.' Gerald got up stiffly and moved towards the door. He added, even while knowing his words would probably be a waste of time, 'I need hardly say—'

'Oh, strictly between friends of course. Would you like me to come over at seven, Gerald? Just in case.'

'Yes. Good idea.' Gerald managed a weak smile. 'And thank you.'

Rex escorted his visitor down the path and through the

gate, enthusiastically attended by Montcalm. Gerald walked heavily, shoulders bowed. He did not even cheer up when Rex pointed out that, by calling when he had, he'd missed a visit from Honoria, who was, even now, pedalling stolidly away from Plover's Rest.

Once more back in the house Rex made some coffee and sat at his desk. Not to work of course. As an object of fascination the Hyena, presently in Baghdad buying information from an anti-Husseinite cell, paled in comparison with this real life drama. Of all people, old Gerald – the last word in boring, perhaps even slightly pompous, respectability – had a past. Who would have thought it?

Rex was tempted to pop out to the phone box, barely a minute's walk away, but hauled temptation firmly back. He must keep his promise, at least till the evening was over. He looked at the clock. Seven and a half hours to go. How on earth was he going to bear it?

Sue had cleared away after supper, stacked the dishes in the sink and was now laying the table for breakfast. Upturned shiny brown cereal bowls, bunny egg cups, ill-matched cutlery and a scruffy plastic tub of home-made muesli with a label designed by herself.

Overhead, music thumped loudly as Amanda supposedly did her homework. Sue always thought of her offspring as Amanda. Allowing her to name the child had been one of the last indulgences that Brian had seen fit to bestow. Even then he had not had the generosity to conceal his displeasure at her choice. Pretentious. Snobbish. Affected. The baby had been 'Mandy' from the day of her birth and, once Brian had really got the hang of high-rise/comprehensive linguistic mores, 'Mand.'

Sue turned on the gas heater over the sink, which popped fiercely. She made a lot of noise washing the dishes, for Brian was in the downstairs loo which opened directly off the kitchen. He never attempted to go about his business quietly, regarding any such discretion as nothing more than middle-class prudishness. Sue, on the other hand, would put toilet paper in the bottom of the bowl if visitors were present, to silence the splash. And as for doing plip-plops, well . . .

Now, after an especially defiant raspberry, she heard the squeak of the transom window opening. Brian emerged, doing up his zip. Crossing to the table, he started to fiddle with some school papers, standing them on end, jigging them into neatness, laying them on one side, tapping them level, turning them upright, jigging them again. Sue, tea towel in hand, bared her teeth in a silent grimace and stared out of the window.

Brian had his back to her. His jeans fell, straight as a yard of tap water, from waist to ankle. Sue remembered a friend at teacher-training college saying 'Never trust a man with no bottom'.

She walked through the sitting room with the bread board, opened the front door and tipped the crumbs into the garden. Gerald's halogen lamp was on. Sue walked down the path and looked out along the pavement. Parked on the forecourt of Plover's Rest was a long, low silvery Mercedes. She rushed back into the kitchen, where Brian had fallen into the only armchair and was tackling the *Guardian* crossword.

'Brian . . . Brian . . .'

'*Now* what are you getting excited about?' He spoke as if she spent her entire life in a ferment of agitation.

'Max Jennings is here.'

'I think not. It's barely ten past seven.'

'Who else could it be?'

'Who else could what be?'

'The car.'

'Your grammar's more bizarre than your cooking, woman. And that's saying something.' Brian had an irritating, snickery little laugh. He gave it now. Hyuf, hyuf.

'If you don't believe me, go and look.'

'I can see I'll have no peace until I do.' Sighing, Brian made a great show of marking the crossword clue as if it was a riveting passage in some vastly long epic, drew on his knitted hat and gloves, which were keeping warm on the Aga, and strode out into the cold dark.

He stared sternly at the German beauty gleaming like pulsing steel in the hard white glare. It struck him as deeply unsatisfactory. Not in any way the sort of vehicle you would expect the child of cruel, poverty-stricken parents with an inclination to suicide to be riding around in. He rushed back in out of the cold.

'He must be pretty insecure to need a car like that.' Brian picked up his paper, sighing and smoothing it carefully, though it had not been touched since he flung it down. 'Now . . . "Friday's child gives one a thrill".'

'Frisson.'

'Do you mind?'

'What?'

'*I* do the crossword.'

'Why can't we both do it?'

'Because you always hold me up.'

Sue dried the last dish and hung the tea towel neatly over the metal arm of the sink heater. 'We'll have to go soon anyway.'

'There's fifteen minutes yet. We don't all drop

everything and jump to it just because someone semi-famous blows a whistle.'

Sue's round moon face flushed. Over her head Take That increased in volume. Amanda clomped down the stairs, in her weighty platform shoes, clomped into the kitchen and over to the fridge.

'Hi, Mand.' Brian immediately put the *Guardian* down and bestowed upon his daughter's back an alert and interested look. 'How's it going?'

'Awri.'

Mandy, having taken some apple juice from the fridge, now thundered over to the cake tin.

'You won't want your supper,' said Sue, nodding towards a tray covered with a clean cloth.

Mandy hated sharing meals with her parents. A couple of years ago she had demanded the right to eat only in her room. Brian and Sue, united for once, refused. Mandy had simply stopped eating altogether and how were they to know that she was buying, begging or stealing food elsewhere. They stuck it out for three days then, terrified of anorexia, gave in. Now she helped herself to three flapjacks.

'You don't need—'

'Leave the girl alone.'

Mandy disappeared next door and switched the television on. Sue mopped the draining board, her thoughts on the evening ahead. She wondered what Max Jennings would be like. She had never met a real writer, though she had been in Dillons once when Maeve Binchy was signing copies of her latest bestseller. Unable to afford the book, Sue had stood on the sidelines while those who could queued up. She watched Maeve smiling as she asked the buyer's name and inscribed a personal message in *The Copper Beech*.

Sue had so wanted to go up to her. To ask how she got started. How it felt the very first time you sold something. Where she got her ideas from. Eventually she was in the shop so long she felt everyone was staring at her. In a flurry of discomfort she bought a paperback, using money she had been saving for some new brushes.

Standing on a pine bench she opened a cupboard over the breakfast niche and took down the iced carrot cake.

'Such a palaver.' Brian would have been horrified had he known how closely his sentiments paralleled Honoria's. 'And for what, basically? Some scribbling hack hardly anyone's heard of.'

'People buy his books.'

'They buy his books because they haven't read them. If they had it'd soon be a different story.'

'Well. Yes.'

'*Now* where are you going?'

'To put some make-up on.'

'We're due there in five minutes – OK?'

'But you said—'

'F.I.V.E., five.'

Brian gazed sourly as the long-boned, stooping figure of his wife left the room. On the stroke of seven thirty, when she hadn't come down, he put on his hat and gloves and left, slamming the door loudly behind him.

When Rex opened the door to Max Jennings he was sure, straight away, that Gerald had nothing to worry about. There was something so warm and appealing, so immediately friendly, about the man. Even when he found himself facing a total stranger and showed a certain amount of surprise the amiable smile remained. Rex introduced himself.

'Gerald's upstairs.' He took the visitor's camel coat, which was both light and soft as silk. 'But I am empowered, as they say, to offer you a drink.'

'How kind.' Max looked across at the tantalus, which had one decanter missing, and at the heavy tray of assorted bottles. 'Tonic water please.'

'With ice and lemon?'

Wondering, indeed hoping, that this choice meant Max was a reformed alcoholic, Rex flourished the tongs. The visitor seemed already quite at home. He was strolling round the room touching things, looking at pictures, bending sideways to read book titles.

Rex noticed, with a little thrill of comprehension, that Gerald's wedding photograph had disappeared. By the time he had found and sliced a lemon a solution for this manoeuvre had been worked out. The unpleasantness in the past to which Gerald had referred was obviously connected with Grace. They had both loved her but, thinking to know the promptings of her heart, she married Gerald. Alas, on accidentally meeting Max again she realised her mistake. But by then, her life tragically ebbing away, it was too late.

As Rex handed over the drink he looked as sympathetic and understanding as he possibly could without actually giving the game away. Max was sitting comfortably in an armchair, gazing at the long, low coffee table covered with food.

'I hope I'm not supposed to eat all this.'

'Good heavens, no,' Rex laughed. 'The others will be here any minute.' Then he remembered that Max had been told the meeting didn't start till eight. How much there was to keep track of, to be sure, when one was playing a part. He felt a fleeting sympathy for the Hyena, which train of thought led him to wonder if it would be discourteous to take advantage of the present situation to ask Max a few questions. Helper's perks and all that. Why not?

'I write spy stories,' he said, sitting on the sofa, 'and I was wondering how much time you think one can decently spend on the details of relevant weaponry. I'm very interested in armoured vehicles – the one-ton Humber Hornet especially. I've written roughly ten pages describing its various functions. Do you think that's too long?'

'I do rather,' said Max. 'I'd've thought your readers will be wanting to get back to the plot long before then.'

'Ah, now.' Rex looked shy and somewhat disconcerted. 'That is something I have a problem with, plot. Plot, characters, dialogue and descriptions of the natural world. Apart from that, I'm fine.'

Max sipped at his drink, seeming to turn this over, then said, 'Have you thought about writing non-fiction, Rex? Perhaps a textbook, as you obviously have such specialised knowledge.'

But then the doorbell rang. It was Laura. And no sooner had she taken off her coat than Honoria and Amy arrived.

Laura was more than a little surprised to find herself at Plover's Rest for, since Honoria's visit, she had changed her mind about the meeting a thousand times. Veering from knowing she could not bear to see Gerald to knowing she could not bear not to see Gerald; from being sure one minute that she knew exactly how she felt (hated him, *hated him*) to being sure the very next that there was no way she could possibly know how she felt till their next meeting. The relief when she realised that he was not actually in the room was so tremendous that she was overcome by dizziness and almost fell. This sensation was re-triggered the moment she sat down, when the door was opened again. But it was only Brian, closely followed by Sue, red-faced and puffing from the effort of trying to catch him up.

Brian gave a curt nod in the direction of the guest's armchair. Sue smiled shyly and shook hands, concealing her surprise, for Max was nothing at all as she had expected. Sue had been picturing a big bluff tweedy man perhaps smoking a pipe. Max Jennings wore tweeds, true, but they were closely woven, beautifully cut and the colour of driftwood and he was smoking slender brown cigars. His heavy linen shirt was the extremely pale shade of green that used to be called eau-de-nil. It was impossible to guess how old he was for, although he had snow-white hair springing back in deep waves from his forehead, his clear, lightly tanned skin was quite unlined. And Sue had never seen such eyes. Brilliant azure. The blue of Moroccan skies. Matisse blue. He was slightly built and not very tall.

Brian, having taken a seat within easy reach of the banquet, flung one baggily trousered leg over its fellow and stared contemptuously around. What a pathetic lot. Dressed up to the nines as if for royalty. Amy wore frills, Rex his dusty pinstriped funeral gear, Honoria a halfway decent Daks skirt and heather-mixture cardigan. Laura had excelled herself in a narrow black dress and Chinese brocade jacket. As for Sue, well . . .

A rainbow-patterned full-length caftan over a badly bobbled limegreen mohair jersey. Hair half plaited, half not (she had panicked on hearing the front door slam) and too much highly coloured make-up. Brian, once he had caught his wife's eye, rolled back his own, registered disbelief and shook his head. Then, satisfied that his state of absolute unimpressedness had been observed by one and all he reached out and helped himself to a sandwich.

'Don't you think,' called Honoria, as loudly as if he were still in his own kitchen next door, 'that it might be courteous to wait until all of us are present? Or, at the very least, until you are asked.'

'Folks uz wait till they're arst,' replied Brian, thinking to speak broadest Yorkshire, 'get nowt.' Then, having shown his independence and provoked the desired response, he crammed the sandwich into his mouth and said, 'Where's Gerald?'

A question no sooner asked than answered. Footsteps were heard running quickly down the stairs and, a moment later, their host came into the room. He went straight across to Max Jennings' corner, holding out his hand and apologising profusely for not being present when Max arrived. He then introduced himself. Twice.

Rex felt gravely let down. One of the ways he had killed time that afternoon was by writing and re-writing this meeting of Gerald and Max in his mind. He had imagined all sorts of permutations. Some quite tame, some funny, others wildly unreasonable. What he had not considered for a moment was that Gerald would simply pretend that they had never met before.

Now Max was getting up, taking the outstretched hand and gracefully turning the apologies aside. Looked as if the play was going to be over before it had even started. Rex's disappointment deepened when it struck him that perhaps Max genuinely did not remember the incident in the past that had caused Gerald such distress. How humiliating. Comforting too, of course. In a way. He indicated the spare place beside him on the sofa and Gerald sat down. Rex smelt brandy and recalled the missing decanter.

Now everyone was present there was a general flutter of anticipation followed, quite quickly, by a rather unnatural stillness. The meeting (Laura and Gerald excepted) gazed at Max Jennings with a constrained vitality that plainly declared a desire for action. He returned a hesitating smile. Sue wondered if he was waiting for some sort of formal introduction, which was surely only proper, but no one seemed moved to give one and eventually he began to speak. His voice was low and musical, with an accent that she could not quite place.

'If I start by saying "unaccustomed as I am" I can assure you it's no more than the truth. I've simply never done this sort of thing before. I haven't prepared anything, I'm afraid. Just come along to see what you wanted. And how, if at all, I can help.'

For a moment there was silence. People looked around uncertainly. It was as if years of rejected invitations had left them unsure they were hearing right. That they were, in fact, sitting in their usual gathering place but this time with the real McCoy – a living, breathing professional writer who had actually offered to help if he could. The sheer novelty of the situation seemed to be about to prove too much for them.

Then Brian uncrossed his legs, leaned forward and, with an expression of great solemnity, cleared his throat—

'I am in the process of writing,' declared Honoria, 'the history of my family, which is to say the history of England. The Lyddiard blood has, without the slightest taint of bastardy . . .'

Brian, irritated almost beyond endurance at being pipped at the post, sat back but in a pouncy, gathered manner as if to warn all present that he would not be cheated a second time. Consumed with resentment, he tried to stop his ears against Honoria's droning recitation. If he had been even halfway actively true to his principles he should, long since, have thrust two fingers right up her high bridged, bonily Roman, aristocratic hooter. The fact that he had never been able to bring himself to do this he blamed on his emasculating parents and their ghastly, toadying enthusiasm for society's upper crust.

Brian had bitter memories of being forced to take his cap off in the village high street every time a member of the fox-and-hounds squirearchy trotted by. He had been cruelly mocked by his peers for these archaic genuflections and had complained in anguish to his parents, only to be told that such little courtesies were the cement that held society together. There would always be a man on horseback and one on foot, his father had explained. It was the natural order of things.

Brian stamped on this sorry drift and tuned back into the present just in time to hear, '. . . in every battle or even the meanest confrontation the Lyddiards always hunted in full steel.'

Honoria then made the mistake of pausing, both for breath and in order to evoke an admiring response. Max immediately obliged. 'It sounds a most worthwhile endeavour. Now,' he smiled encouragingly around the room, 'what about the rest of you? Um. Amy, isn't it?'

'Oh. Yes.' Amy, flustered at being unexpectedly called on, fumbled in her pocket and produced a little square of paper. No need to open it, for she had her first question off by heart. Keenly aware of how very slender her acquaintance was with the world of New York socialites on the razzle, Parisian models on the catwalk and Italian princelings on the make, she said, 'We're always being told, Mr Jennings—'

'Max, please.'

'Max. That we should only write about what we know. Isn't that a bit limiting?'

'I don't think it's meant to be taken in the narrow, literal sense. One can know things – quite wild, fantastic things – to be true in the imagination.'

'You mean like science fiction?'

'Exactly.'

'Also, whenever I'm writing a scene I keep thinking of other ways that might be better. And I never know whether to stop and start again or carry on.'

'I'm afraid that's par for the course. Writers spend their lives haunted by discarded alternatives.'

How tactful he was, Laura thought, glancing briefly at Max's engaged, intelligent profile before turning her attention back to Gerald. Plainly something was wrong there. Very wrong indeed. His body, balanced on the very edge of the sofa, was curved in the shape of a half hoop and taut as a drawn bow. His face was impassive, but Laura sensed, from the knotted cords in his neck, that it was kept thus only by the most tremendous effort. She realised as well that although, like the rest of them, his head was turned in Max's direction his eyes were fixed at a point on the wall beyond Max's shoulder. One of his shoes, Veldschoen, conker-bright with a pattern of punched holes in the toe cap and gingery laces, tapped urgently on the carpet.

Looking at him, loving him, Laura became aware from the familiar churning of her stomach that nothing had changed. Faithless he might be, but she was still in his thrall, as she had been from that first moment. She would just have to accept the blonde. End up probably like the baron's wife in Balzac's *Cousine Bette*, dying in her bed of love starvation while he tumbled the maid downstairs.

Dragging her attention away she saw that Max was, momentarily, watching her. Then knew that this quick bright observance had led him to understand her feelings exactly. Annoyed and resentful she stared hard at him in return, letting her displeasure show.

Amy was asking her final question: what were the most important attributes for an author to have?

'A wayfaring mind. Nothing should be beneath our attention. And stamina. You have to hang on in there.'

'But you were successful straight off,' said Brian, rudely emphasising the personal pronoun.

'I was fortunate. Even then, in a way, one is always back to square one. Each new book is started from scratch. And of course success can antagonise. Critics come gunning for you. My historical novels come in for quite a bit of flack.'

'I was wondering . . .' Although Sue had taken a deep, calming breath her voice still quaked. 'Have you had any experience at all with children's books?'

'I'm afraid not.'

'I paint, you see . . . pictures.'

Pictures eh? How amazing. Brian's thoughts were ruefully plain as he made equalising eye contact with their guest. What can you do with them? He said, 'I suggested she start with a few short stories or poems but she wouldn't have it.'

'How wise. They're almost impossible to sell.' He smiled encouragingly at Sue. 'What are the paintings about?'

'A dragon called Hector.'

'And does he eat people?'

'Only thin ones. He's on a diet.'

'I love it!' Max gave a splendid and apparently quite spontaneous laugh and Sue's confidence was persuaded into a brief florescence. Not that the play group did not

45

regularly fall about when she described Hector's adventures but, as Brian said when she had first told him, what do a bunch of kids know?

She looked across at her husband tapping his chin with his index finger, thin lips moving slightly – a sign that he was polishing up some pithy, controversial dialogue. But as he leaned forward Honoria lumbered into the vertical.

'I don't know about anyone else, but I'm hungry. And I'm sure Mr Jennings must be too.'

There was a swell of apologetic murmuring. Amy took a plate and napkin to their guest. Gerald came to life, murmuring 'coffee, coffee', and almost ran into the kitchen, followed closely by Rex.

Honoria, having quickly constructed for herself a tottering tower of assorted goodies, returned to her seat, saying loudly as she passed Brian, 'Your mouth's open.'

Brian, furious at having been once more cheated of his *moment d'estime* and convinced he heard the words 'common little man' floating back over Honoria's shoulder, snapped his jaws together. The circle broke up. Laura went to help with the coffee and found Gerald and Rex deep in animated conversation. They were patently disturbed when the door opened and Gerald frowned so forcefully that she immediately withdrew.

In the drawing room people had changed seats. Amy and Sue had moved closer to Max, who was nibbling on a cream-cheese wheel, to pose problems they had been too shy to ask about publicly. Laura glanced over what was left of the food. There was nothing she really fancied. In any case she was still experiencing a faint queasiness – a sensation she knew from experience would be with her until she was well away from Plover's Cottage. She cut a fragile slice of Sue's carrot cake and turned away quickly from the sight of Rex's de Montargis pralines. They looked like the varnished brains of tiny mammals and she could not possibly envisage putting one into her mouth.

Brian, far from defeated and biding his time, sat, a well-filled plate on either knee, listening to the oh-so-predictable questions. Did Max work regular hours? (Nine till five.) Did he rewrite much? (Everything. All the time.) Did he start with plot or characters? (Indivisible. The characters are the plot.) Did he do much research? (As little as possible. Preferred an educated guess. Often wrong.)

At this point Gerald and Rex appeared with two cafetières and jugs of milk which they put on the sideboard already laid with cups and saucers. Honoria cried 'At last,' as if the pair were a couple of tardy waiters.

Amy left Max Jennings' side at this point to fetch him some coffee and Brian seized his chance. Slipping into her place, he began to describe his thrice-weekly drama sessions.

'. . . building rather than writing a play, which I regard frankly as a totally passé word. Not to say elitist.'

'Which word?'

'Pardon?'

'"Building", "writing", or "play"?'

'Oh. "Writing".'

'I see.'

'We work in a very loose, inspirational way. Rapping, improvising, free association. We are talking totally knife edge here. You hit the ground running at my rehearsals, believe me, or you are out. O.U.T., out.'

'Tough stuff.'

'I don't know if you've ever heard of Mike Leigh?'

'Of course.'

'What did you think of *Naked*?'

'Deeply patronising and sloppy.'

Brian fell back. One swift movement as if someone had punched him hard in the chest. He seemed bereft of speech and just sat there, aghast.

'Not to mention far too long.'

'Come and help yourself everyone,' called Rex from across the room. They all did. Amy took some back for Honoria, who was by then asking their guest a final question.

'Who do you think' – she leaned forward, heavy legs in peat-brown shooting stockings set sturdily apart – 'would be the best company, once my history is complete, to approach? I don't want it published by just any old firm.'

'I'm afraid I'm not a good person to ask, Miss Lyddiard. My contacts are all in the field of fiction.'

'Really?' Honoria sounded cross and nonplussed. 'But we thought you'd have a much broader range of knowledge than that. Right across the board as it were.' Her eyes bored into the remaining morsel of cheesy wheel on Max's plate as if he had devoured the rest under false pretences.

'I thought that too,' said Brian quickly. Bloody celebrities. He'd had enough. Smug inflated self-important windbags. Who the hell did they think they were? Emptying his second plate by pushing two Florentines into his mouth at once Brian sprang vigorously to his feet. 'Sue?'

'Yes.'

'Come.'

'But I've only just—'

'Very well. Stay here if you wish. Far be it from me—'

'No.' The aftermath would simply not be worth it: 'It's all right.' She put down her barely tasted coffee.

Gerald brought Sue's shawl and Brian's tartan wind-cheater out of the downstairs cloakroom. Then he went back for everyone else's things, whereupon they all felt it was time to go and the meeting was suddenly over.

Laura, aware that Gerald had been completely routed throughout the evening by forces of which she was completely ignorant, now saw that their guest, who had also risen with an air of imminent departure, would leave without as much as a thank you were it left to the group secretary. So she made a brief speech saying how very helpful and entertaining the visit had been and Rex, Sue and Amy echoed the sentiments and clapped loudly.

As Gerald opened the front door an icy blast whistled into the house. Amy and Honoria muffled their faces and hurried away, followed by Brian and Sue. Laura turned on the doorstep, looking up at Gerald, who had his hand on the door's edge as if anxious to push it to. Laura stared hard into his face. Always aware that she had never known him, she now knew, with a terrible daunting certainty, that she never would. It was unbearable. She reached out and seized his arm. It felt like a piece of wood.

'Gerald, what is it? What's the matter?'

'Nothing.' Angrily he snatched his arm away. His eyes were screwed up against the glare of the lamp and his mouth was as narrow as a piece of string.

'There's something wrong.'

'Don't talk such nonsense.'

'You're afraid.'

'Really, Laura. What on earth has got into you tonight?'

'It's true.' He was about to close the door, she could see it. Without a breath of hesitation (it always seemed to Laura afterwards that she had no choice in the matter) she leaned forward and kissed him.

With a look of absolute amazement Gerald stepped quickly backwards and forcefully closed the door. He was still trembling when he returned to the living room.

Max had draped his beautiful camel-hair and cashmere overcoat over the back of a chair and was sitting on the sofa. Rex was stacking the coffee cups. Gerald walked straight through to the kitchen without speaking to either of them.

A few moments later Rex entered with his loaded tray. The two men stared at each other, then Rex, eyes shining, mouthed silently and with gross over-emphasis, *Don't Worry*. Then, aloud and at an equally inappropriate level, 'Shall I help you wash up, Gerald?'

'Mrs Bundy will be here at ten.'

He spoke normally but Rex, reluctant to abandon his new plot line, pointed urgently at the other room, mimed the chore, then indicated the kitchen clock.

Gerald presumed all this to mean that if they took their time over the washing up Max would get tired of waiting and leave. He wished to God they'd both leave. He wished Rex wasn't enjoying himself quite so much. He wished the pain would go away.

'Could I be a terrible nuisance and ask for some more coffee?' Gerald and Rex jumped. They hadn't even heard him get up. 'Just to keep me going for the drive home.'

'Of course.' Gerald painted a smile on his face. Hanging on to the words 'drive home', he emptied the grounds from the smaller of the cafetières. It slipped from his fingers to lie in the sink.

'Instant will do.'

'I don't have instant. One for you, Rex?'

'Definitely.'

They all stood around like figures in an exhibition until

the coffee was made, then took their beakers back to the sitting room. Here, in spite of Max's previous hint of a fairly prompt departure, he began what proved to be a very lengthy conversation about money. The pound against the dollar and why its fluctuations affected his income. How the spread of democracy meant he was now published in the Eastern bloc, although it wasn't always easy or even possible to get the royalties out. The frolicsome lira and the advantage of being paid in Deutschmarks. The nervous yen.

Rex listened, wondering how much longer he would be able to stay conscious. He was usually fast asleep by ten, for he would be awoken by Montcalm, seeking his morning constitutional, on the crack of five thirty. He thought, for the first time, that all this wasn't quite fair of Gerald. Then he became aware that Max had asked Gerald a question and was waiting, with an expression of polite interest, for an answer.

'Short stories mainly.' Gerald studied the drawn curtains behind his interrogator's head. 'Unpublished, before you ask.' His nostrils were pinched, rimmed white with tension.

Feeling he was not pulling his weight, Rex described his own attempts at a series of short stories featuring the adventures of an early Gatling gun. His jaw began to ache and his skin itched with tiredness. Then, just as another lengthy pause seemed to be yawning, Max suddenly got up and said he really must be going.

'It's been a most enjoyable evening.'

'It was good of you to come.' Gerald seemed not to notice the outstretched hand.

In the hall Rex tried to catch Gerald's eye, hoping for a conspiratorial exchange. A significant glance perhaps?

Raised eyebrows. A nod of satisfaction at a job well done. But he was unlucky. Gerald did not even accompany them, but remained at the far end of the hall tapping, then reading, the barometer with close attention as if he was already alone. He did not even say 'goodnight', never mind 'thank you'.

Rex opened the door and stepped over the threshold. Max followed, said, 'My gloves,' turned back into the house and closed the door. A bolt slid into place. In less than a second the very thing that Rex had promised faithfully to prevent had taken place.

Half an hour later and Rex was in his bedroom. Not preparing to sleep, for shock had woken him up entirely, but because the view from his window included the frontage of Plover's Rest. The silver Mercedes was still there. The wind had got up a treat and it was raining.

After the slippy manoeuvre that had left him shut out, Rex had hung around for several minutes not knowing what to do. He had put his ear to the door jamb at one point, listening for he knew not what. Sounds of violence perhaps? Gerald trying to push Max forcibly out? But there was nothing. Not even the murmur of voices.

After a while Rex started to feel foolish. He felt he should have walked off straight away. Perhaps they were waiting for him to do this before starting their conversation. Then he thought, what if someone passed by, saw him hanging round in the porch and reported him. Wasn't loitering an actionable offence? This disquieting recollection, plus the fact that he was desperate to go to the loo, set him striding down the path, shutting the gate loudly to announce his exit.

Now he was wondering guiltily if he had done the

wrong thing. He recalled how vehemently Gerald had spoken when urging his co-operation in the matter of Max's departure. Anyone would think it was a matter of life and death. Rex was quickly coming round to the idea that he had given up too easily.

Hadn't the bolting of the front door been rather . . . well . . . sinister? There was no doubt in Rex's mind that Max had been responsible. It had been so quickly accomplished that Gerald could not have reached the door in time. The conviction that he had made an error grew, soon gripping Rex to a degree where he could no longer stand there and do nothing.

He rushed downstairs, suddenly in a bigger hurry to return to Gerald's cottage than he had ever been to get away. No need to put on a coat, for he had not taken off his British warm. Rex hesitated by the collection of beautifully polished walking sticks in the hall before, feeling absurdly melodramatic, selecting one with a silver buffalo-head handle. Then he put on his cord cap, secured it with a woollen scarf tied under his chin, and strode off.

The gate of Plover's Rest now stood half open. He walked boldly up the path. He had decided to knock on the back door and ask to borrow some milk. Transparent certainly and, like most people unaccustomed to lying, Rex had already reinforced this simple request by an elaborate sub-structure of quite unnecessary detail. When he couldn't sleep only cocoa helped. Made with water it gave him tummy ache. Milk bottle slipped through his fingers when taking it from the fridge and smashed on the floor. Saw Max's car so knew you would still be up.

There was no light in the kitchen but the inner door was open and Rex could see through to the section of room in which Max was sitting. He was talking and gesturing in an open-handed rather appealing way, as if he were offering a present. Then he became silent and his stance changed. He shook his head vigorously and leaned forward, listening. His profile showed a deeply involved attention. He looked – Rex sought for the exact word – concerned. Yes, that was it. Deeply concerned. Like a Samaritan.

Now, if only he could see Gerald. Rex screwed his head sideways, laid his cheek against the glass and squinnied with effort, but all to no avail. He stood upright again, aware of a sharp crick in his neck. Everything seemed all right. It looked, in fact, as if old Gerald had been worrying over nothing. Anticipating a disaster that just wasn't going to happen. On the other hand, he (Rex) had definitely promised . . .

It was precisely then, as he stood hesitating, that Rex became aware of an unpleasant, crawly feeling somewhere between his shoulder blades. After a moment the feeling intensified and changed direction, worming its way coldly down his spine. He swung around.

Behind him barely defined trees gathered, crowding the bare borders, together with dense, black clumps of shrubs. Gripping his stick, telling himself that the kitchen door was a mere few feet away, Rex moved towards the willow fence. Then, staring hard into the massed trunks and tangle of branches, he called out.

'Hullo?' Silence. No leaf rustled. Not a night creature moved. 'Is there anybody there?'

Rex heard only his own breathing. But he knew, as surely as he felt the freezing ground beneath his feet, that someone, or something, was out there. And staring straight back at him.

Midsomer Madness

Tom Barnaby was missing his daughter. Cully was in Eastern Europe with an Arts Council tour of *Much Ado About Nothing*. She was playing Beatrice while Nicholas, her husband of eighteen months, had been cast in the colourful but vastly subordinate role of Don John. This after a year with the Royal Shakespeare Company had failed to offer the kind of parts he spent all his offstage moments dreaming about.

They had visited the Barnabys the night before their departure and Tom, who knew Nicholas well and his daughter very well indeed, could see trouble on the horizon. Nicholas was plainly torn between pride in his wife's success and resentment at the widening gap between their professional fortunes. To rub in the salt, Cully had recently been filming in *The Crucible*, a prestigious production for BBC2 to be shown while they were away.

Of course Nicholas could have turned *Much Ado* down and hung around London waiting for something better, but there was no way, he told his father-in-law on the eve of their departure, that he was letting Cully racket around half Europe in the company of a dozen male actors. He and Barnaby were sitting in the conservatory at the time, drinking Clare Valley Shiraz. Watching his beautiful girl, arm in arm with his wife and on the point of joining them, Barnaby sympathised keenly.

It was not, he was sure, that the lad did not trust his wife. The root of the problem lay in Nicholas's own insecurities. He still could not credit that he had won such a prize. Even on the wedding day, passed in a golden haze of bliss, Barnaby had noticed quite clearly this obverse shadow of disbelief.

They had been away now nearly two weeks and had left behind a memento – an enchanting Russian Blue kitten, Kilmowski, acquired just before the tour was offered. At least, Joyce described it as enchanting. Barnaby regarded the animal as a damn nuisance. He could no longer sit down without remembering to check both chair and cushions or open a door without a warning squeal from his wife. Yesterday the *Independent* had been torn to shreds on the doormat, unreadable even before wee'd on.

And, as if his daughter's absence and the kitten's presence was not enough, Barnaby was now faced with the misery of dieting. Always a big man, he had taken up cooking a couple of years previously, largely in self-defence, for Joyce's food was so spectacularly bad that friends, invited for dinner, had been known to bring it with them.

He had taken to the art like a duck to orange sauce and had discovered, after years of munching on indescribable indefinables chased by antacid tablets, that he had, by nature, the appetite of a king. It was just his luck that the king in question happened to be Henry the Eighth.

Even a man of six foot three cannot healthily carry sixteen stone and he had been warned, at his last check-up, that a minimum of thirty pounds would have to go. And he was trying. He really was. But it was bloody hard. At the moment he was spinning out a slice of toast, having polished off his boiled egg in two scoops.

Joyce, pressing the plunger in the cafetière, was keeping an eye out for the postman. She was hoping for a card or letter from Poland, where *Much Ado* was running for the next fortnight – hoping, she realised, probably in vain, for Cully was a negligent correspondent to put it mildly. Nicholas was the one most likely to keep in touch.

Joyce couldn't help worrying about them both however much common sense pointed out that an august body such as the Arts Council would hardly be sending a company of English actors into danger. But the whole of Eastern Europe seemed to her so volatile that today's safe area could well be tomorrow's war zone. Threatening words and phrases pattered around Joyce's mind – 'unstable government', 'fundamentalist guerrillas', 'racial riots', 'trigger-happy border guards', 'roof-top snipers'.

These unhappy reflections were shattered by an enraged yell. She turned to see her husband grasping the kitten by the scruff of its neck and lifting it into the air.

'What on earth do you think you're doing?' She ran across the room. 'Give him to me. Right now, Tom!' Kilmowski was passed over. 'How could you be so unkind.'

'It's just walked through my marmalade.'

'He doesn't know.' Joyce kissed a grey velvet triangular nose. 'Do you?' The kitten squinted amberly at her. 'Poor little scrap.'

She placed Kilmowski gently on the carpet, whereupon he immediately sought the edge of the tablecloth, dug in his claws and started to climb again.

'Look! Look at that.'

'Leave him alone. D'you want some fresh coffee?'

57

'No thanks.' Barnaby glanced at the clock. It was nearly nine thirty. 'Better be off.' As he was putting on his overcoat the phone rang. 'Would you take that, love? Say I'm on my way.'

'Of course it might just be for me.' Joyce sounded quite huffy. 'I do have a wide circle of friends, some of whom have been known to ring me up from time to time.'

''Course you have.' Barnaby came back wrapped in heavy black and white herringbone tweed and pulling on his gloves. 'And of course they do.' He kissed a coolish cheek. 'Back around six.'

As he turned to leave Barnaby sourly regarded the kitten, now squatting, with great dignity, in the precise centre of his tray. Kilmowski stared straight through him then, crossing his eyes with effort, gave a squeaky little fart.

It was a foul day. Rain during the night followed by an early morning freeze-up had turned the roads to glass. Barnaby drove his blue Orion with great care, taking twice as long over the journey as was usual. An extremely cautious swing through the police station's main gates had his rear wheels skittering sideways. A scene-of-crime Sherpa van, on the point of exit, wheeled into nippy avoidance. He eased gently into his reserved space and walked slowly into the building.

A WPC at the desk looked up. 'Morning, sir. They've been trying to get you at home. Something's come up.'

Barnaby lifted his hand in acknowledgement and made for his office. He was crossing the enclosed walkway that linked the CID block to the station proper when he observed his bag carrier striding smartly towards him. Gavin Troy wore a long, tightly belted black leather coat which flapped and slapped against his boots. A dark cap covered his cropped red hair and he had, in readiness, put on the steel-rimmed glasses he wore when driving. He looked like a storm trooper.

Knowing the pleasure such a comparison would afford, Barnaby immediately put it from his mind. As they drew closer he could see that Troy was scowling with bad temper.

'Morning, sergeant.'

'Chief. We've got a murder.' Troy gave a regimental swivel on his heel and fell into step beside the boss. 'On your desk.'

'Well, there's a novelty.'

'Midsomer Worthy. Just the bare details. Apparently the woman who discovered the body, a Mrs Bundy, was so hysterical nobody's been able to get much sense out of her.' Troy moved ahead quickly to open the office door. 'SOCO have just left.'

'Yes. I barely missed them.'

'And Doc Bullard's there.'

'Already?'

'He lives in the next village. Charlecote Lucy.'

'So he does.' Barnaby sat down behind his desk and picked up the report.

'Victim's male,' said Troy. 'Found in his bed—'

'Thank you. I can read.'

Suit yourself. Troy waited, impatient but concealing it, while Barnaby cleared his desk. This involved two memos and several quite lengthy phone calls delegating work in hand.

The chief inspector had not troubled to remove his coat and this, plus the warmth of the building, made him feel quite snug, but once outside the harsh air snatched all the heat from his body. His lungs cringed as the wind whistled down his windpipe and his lips were so dry and cold they stuck together.

Inside the car Troy drew on his black peccary driving gloves (sliced off at the knuckles and buckled at the wrist), turned the heater full on and negotiated his way into Causton High Street. He was an extremely skilled driver but inclined to be overproud of that skill and to perform on occasion in a very flamboyant manner. At work he never took unnecessary risks, but Barnaby sometimes wondered about his sergeant's off-duty motoring. However at the moment he was easing the car along the A4007 in a manner that was, for him, positively decorous. The bad-tempered scowl, so marked half an hour ago, had died down into mere sullenness.

'What's the matter with you this morning?'

'I'm all right, sir.'

The matter was Troy's cousin Colin. His mother's sister's boy. Colin had been a thorn in Troy's flesh for years. Sailing through exams that Troy had had to sweat blood even to scrape a pass in. Silver-tongued, sarcastic, Colin was always laughing at things his cousin held most dear. He seemed to regard Troy's whole lifestyle as some sort of comedic entertainment, referring to the sergeant more than once as a clockwork Rambo. Last night he had turned up at his Aunty Betty's when Troy was also present and for the same reason – to deliver a birthday gift. Winking at his cousin, Colin had taken off his filthy battered sheepskin jacket to flash the message on his T-shirt: '*When The Going Gets Tough The Smart Bugger Off*'. He had just left university and, to Troy's deep satisfaction, had so far been unable to find a job.

'They make me laugh,' said Troy, with bitter lack of

humour. Barnaby sensibly received this out-of-the-blue remark in silence.

'People who don't reckon the police,' continued his sergeant, signalling and easing on to a slip road. 'Catch them being mugged or burgled or losing their bloody car. They start yelling for us then fast enough.' His grip on the steering wheel tightened till the seams on his gloves looked fit to burst.

Barnaby only half listened. The inclination to tease out the reason for Troy's present petulance had proved fleeting. It could be anything, for Gavin was a walking mass of insecurities. He also had an overwhelming need to be admired which, given the public's current perception of the Force, was in no danger at all of being satisfied.

The chief inspector was also distracted by a keen gnawing in his stomach, which seemed similarly proportioned now to the inside of Jonah's whale – his breakfast slice of toast and solitary boiled egg bounced and fell from wall to hungry wall like a solitary sock in a tumble dryer.

'Over there, chief.'

Troy was crunching around a village green on a surface newly scattered with rough sand. Barnaby could see a Panda, the SOCO van and George Bullard's blue Viva parked in the driveway of an attractive double-fronted cottage with prettily fretworked shutters. Troy pulled up a few feet away.

It was very quiet. There was some moody quacking from the ducks slithering about on their frozen pond and a fair amount of bird song, though what the hell they could find to sing about on a day like this Troy could not even begin to comprehend. He took in the immaculate oval of expensive, beautifully maintained houses. In their gardens trees and shrubs glittered with frost in the hard, bright winter light. Only the prominent display of burglar alarms detracted from a Christmas-calendar image of perfection. As they approached Plover's Rest the footsteps of the two men rang out on the rock-hard road with the clarity of horses' hooves.

At the gate a constable was telling a small gathering of people, who were staring at the house in a hopeful and fascinated way, that there was nothing to see and would they please move along. Stretching his arms wide he moved towards them and, broom-like, swept them away a few feet. He had done this more than once and more than once they had drifted back. Soon the barriers would go up and the containment problem would be solved. There was something officially dissuasive about the holey orange plastic. Once it was pegged in, observers, no matter how half-hearted their previous willingness to toe an invisible line, rarely pushed or climbed beyond it.

A policeman at the cottage door which was standing open, said, 'Upstairs on the left, sir.'

Unnecessary information. Barnaby could smell the carnage even in the hall. As he climbed the stairs the scent became stronger and his stomach, already so cruelly maltreated, revolted further in anticipation.

The small bedroom was full of people. Scenes-of-crime; three men and one woman, their hands and feet encased in polythene. A stills photographer. And the body of a man clad in a towelling robe lying between the bed and the wardrobe. His feet were towards the door, his head, what there was left of it, closer to the overhanging duvet.

'Have we got what did it?' Barnaby stood on the threshold, neither touching the door nor stepping inside. A heavy candlestick smeared with blood and hair and already bagged and ticketed was held up. 'Where's the doc?'

'In the kitchen, chief inspector,' said the photographer – a young man with curly hair and a bright smile that his calling seemed to have done nothing to diminish. 'Nice to see the sun for a change.'

Barnaby no sooner showed his face than George Bullard, sitting with a woman at the table, got up swiftly. He eased Barnaby and Troy back into the hall.

'Can't talk in there. She's in a terrible state.' They stood bunched into an awkward knot in the narrow passage, the knob of the downstairs cloakroom digging into Troy's back. 'Before you ask, between eleven last night and one this morning. Might be a bit later, but that's as close as I can make it right now. Whoever did it was in a hell of a temper. There's a huge blow in the centre of the forehead which may well have finished him but they just went on bashing—'

'Yes, George, I saw. Face to face then?'

'Absolutely. Nothing sneaky about this one.' He was carrying a mug which he now drained and handed to Sergeant Troy. Then he picked up his coat, which was draped over the banisters. 'No fighting either's my guess.'

The tiny hall became even more jammed as the technical services video team arrived and George Bullard tried to squeeze out. Barnaby and Troy backed into the kitchen, where the unfortunate discoverer of the body was being comforted by a policewoman. The air was thick with cigarette smoke and Troy's nostrils twitched in appreciation.

On first hearing the name Bundy, Barnaby's imagination had lazily conjured up a middle-aged dumpling of a woman. A Happy Families playing card. Starched apron, up to her stout dimpled elbows in flour.

Voluble, a bit of a busybody but warm-hearted withal. The sort who would 'do anything' for you.

The person facing him was thin, barely thirty and wore a shiny nylon overall – three-quarters-length, in pink and white check, with tails like a man's shirt – plus leggings and a black polo-necked jumper. Her hands gripped the upper parts of her arms, which were tightly folded against her flattish chest, and her fingernails, quite long, dug fiercely into the flesh. Barnaby suspected that, once released, her whole body would start to vibrate. Her face was in constant motion, eyes blinking, lips twitching, and her head shook rapidly from side to side as if to remove some terrible imprint from her mind. Barnaby sat down at the table. Troy withdrew, leaning his rough notebook on a worktop near the sink and uncapping his Biro.

'Mrs Bundy . . . ?' She stared down into her cup, at the congealing puddle of melting sugar. 'This must have been a terrible shock for you.'

After a very long pause her carefully painted lips formed the soundless word, 'yes'. She coughed, repeated the affirmative then said, in a thready whisper, 'I've never seen a dead person before.'

'I'm sorry,' said Barnaby. He gave it five and then a bit longer. 'Do you feel up to helping me by answering one or two questions?'

'I don't know.' She released her arms and reached with a trembling hand for a gold packet of Benson's Super Kings lying next to a half-full ashtray. She lit up, producing a gas lighter from her pocket, and drew deep, exhaling with her eyes closed. 'I'm not going back upstairs.' Released, her voice ran shrilly up the scale. 'Not in that room.'

Behind her back Troy rolled his eyeballs, mocking such dramatic overkill. He caught the attention of the policewoman and gave a complicitous wink. She stared coldly back.

'No, no. Of course not.' Hastily Barnaby offered reassurance. 'Really I'm more interested in discovering what happened before you found Mr Hadleigh.'

'Oh.' She looked very slightly consoled but also puzzled. 'You mean, on me way here? I come on the bus.'

'More when you first approached the house, Mrs Bundy. Did you notice anything at all unusual?'

'What sort of thing?'

Well, if we knew that ducky, Troy muttered in his head, we wouldn't be asking, would we? They were going to be here all day at this pussyfooting rate. He leered hungrily at the shiny packet of twenty minus seven and decided he could murder the rest.

'Well, the gate was wide open. That means the postman's been. He won't shut it, even after Mr Hadleigh went and put a sign on. So I closed it behind me and walked up the path and – you talking about anything out of the ordinary – I couldn't help noticing the curtains were still closed. Downstairs in the lounge and in Mr Hadleigh's bedroom. And then I go to let meself in—'

'You have your own key?'

'Oh yes.' She added, with rather touching pride, 'All the people I clean for have given me a key. But the door's bolted on the inside. I stood there for a minute not knowing quite what to do, then I went round the back. I tried the kitchen door but not with what you'd call high hopes. It doesn't have a proper Yale but it's got a dead bolt top and bottom. Anyway, I lift the latch and walk right in.'

'It opened straight away?'

'Yes. I went in the hall and shouted "hello"—'

'Did you see any post there, Mrs Bundy?'

'No, I didn't, now you come to mention it.'

'Carry on.'

'I put me apron on—'

'Do you bring it with you?'

'No. That hangs on a peg in the broom cupboard together with a scarf against the dust.' She patted her hair – a straw-coloured airy confection; teased, sprayed, moussed and bleached beyond redemption.

'Then I notice not just that he hadn't had his breakfast, but the table wasn't even laid. So, what with that and the curtains and everything, I wondered if he might've been took bad. I felt a bit embarrassed, to tell you the truth. I didn't like to go upstairs in case he was still in bed – me husband's a bit funny over things like that – on the other hand I couldn't settle down to work not knowing if the house was empty or not. If you get my meaning.'

'I do,' said Barnaby. 'Absolutely.'

'So . . .' Here it was. The dark heart of the tale. She braced herself, incising half moons once more in her arms. 'I went to his room—'

'The door was open?'

'Yes.'

'Light on?'

'*Yes*,' Mrs Bundy shouted, and struck her forehead with her fists, compelled by a fierce hatred of the memory. 'Oh! I could curse myself for going in there. The smell . . . *the smell* . . . that should have told me. Why didn't I just go back downstairs and call somebody? But you don't think, do you?'

''Course you don't, love,' said the policewoman.

'I shall never stop seeing him. I know I shan't. Never. Till the end of my days.'

Barnaby thought that this was probably true. The image

would change, of course, but would inevitably re-create itself a thousand times. A bad day indeed for Mrs Bundy.

She had already mentally fled back to the kitchen. Barnaby, reluctantly but necessarily, took her back upstairs. 'Did you touch anything in the room?'

'Christ! Are you kidding?' For the first time vitality flared. She sounded outraged. 'I come down that bloody fast me feet didn't touch the carpet.'

'Did you see—?'

'I saw him. That's all I saw. One look and I scarpered. All right?' She pushed her face across the table until it was inches from his own. Barnaby could see she was either going to strike out or burst into tears.

'Fine. That's fine, Mrs Bundy. Thank you.' His voice was excessively calm. He looked at the young police-woman. 'I think we could all . . . ?'

While tea was being made Mrs Bundy extended her acquaintance with the Bensons. There were now nine lipsticked butts in the ashtray. Troy looked elsewhere.

The sergeant was a deeply frustrated man. He couldn't smoke in the office. He couldn't smoke in the car. He couldn't smoke on the job. (Not his day job anyway.) And, now that the dangers of passive smoking had been provably demonstrated, he had to be bloody careful when and where he smoked at home. For Talisa Leanne, his heart's delight and the best reason for living a man could ever hope to come across, was only two, and two-year-old lungs were obviously extremely vulnerable. Troy had found himself, only that very morning, not only enjoying his post-breakfast ciggie in the toilet but blowing the smoke out of the window. I'm an endangered species I am, he reflected bitterly now, accepting, in poor substitute, a cup of strong Breakfast Blend.

'So you're back in the kitchen, Mrs Bundy,' said the chief inspector, adopting an easy conversational tone as if they were discussing the weather.

'I am,' said Mrs Bundy firmly.

'And then what?'

'I was sick.' She nodded in Troy's direction. 'Over there.'

Although the sink was by now spotless the sergeant sniffed fastidiously and whisked himself and his notebook some distance away.

'Then I rang Don at work and he got in touch with your lot. He come right over but they won't let him in.'

'No. Sorry about that,' said Barnaby. 'But I won't keep you a minute longer than I have to.' He drank some of his tea, which was delicious. 'That's a lot of crockery on the draining board. Did he entertain much, Mr Hadleigh?'

She shook her head. 'Very rare. Only there's a group in the village meet here regular. Once a month. They do writing together – stories and that.' She sounded faintly apologetic and smiled for the first time. 'Well, it takes all sorts doesn't it?'

'It does indeed.' Barnaby, smiling in return, sensed, on the edge of his vision, that Troy was about to speak and gave a small holding movement with his hand. 'Could you perhaps, Mrs Bundy, give me the names of any of the members?'

'As to who was here last night I wouldn't really know. But Mr and Mrs Clapton next door sometimes come.' She pointed to her left. 'And the Lyddiards from Gresham House. It's about six down on this side of the Green. A big place. Pineapples on the gate. I do for them as well. Just the rough.'

'A married couple?'

'Oh no. Miss Honoria and her sister-in-law. She's sweet,

Mrs L. I feel sorry for her. They haven't even got a telly.'

'Had you worked for Mr Hadleigh long?'

'Nearly ten years. Ever since he bought the cottage. All through once a week and top up Thursday. His washing goes to the laundry.'

'So you'd know him pretty well?'

'I wouldn't say that. He was very reserved. Not like some of my ladies. Often I'll just be getting started and they'll go, "I'm that down today, Carol. Come on - let's have a break and a cuppa." And we'll pull a chair up and they'll tell me all about it. But not Mr Hadleigh. Close was his middle name. Quite honestly I don't think I know him any better now than I did the day I started.'

'What was he like to work for?'

'Very particular. Everything had to be just so. Ornaments and books back exactly where they came from. But at least he left you alone to get on with it. Unlike some.'

'No Mrs Hadleigh then?'

'He was a widower. You'll see their wedding picture on the sideboard in the lounge. Always a vase of fresh flowers nearby, just like a shrine. Very sad. You'd think he'd be getting over it a bit by now.'

'Do you know when Mrs Hadleigh actually died?'

'No idea.'

'Can you think of any reason, Mrs Bundy, why anyone would want to—?'

'No, I can't! And I want to go home now.' She looked at the policewoman in a beseeching way as if the woman had some sort of casting vote. Her voice had started to shake again.

'Almost through,' said Barnaby. 'I'd just like you, if you would, to glance around here and the sitting room and see if anything's missing.'

'Everything's all right in here.' She got up, looking at the policewoman. 'Would you mind . . . ?' They left the room together, returning almost straight away.

'The photograph's gone. Of the wedding.'

'Nothing else?'

'Not that I can see offhand.'

'We'll probably have to talk to you again, I'm afraid—'

'Not here you won't. I'm never coming in this place again as long as I live.'

'Don't worry. It would be at home or at the station, whichever you prefer. And we'd like your fingerprints – just for purposes of elimination.'

The policewoman helped Mrs Bundy on with her coat and opened the kitchen door only to smartly close it again. She took Mrs Bundy's arm, led her to one side and Barnaby heard murmured suggestions of support and possible counselling. One or two addresses and telephone numbers were noted down.

There were heavy footsteps on the narrow stairs and some stumbling and banging as Gerald Hadleigh departed his home for the final time. A few minutes later Mrs Bundy followed and the police were left in sole occupation of Plover's Rest.

'All yours, Tom.' Aubrey Marine stood in the doorway, still encased in protective polythene. 'We're downstairs now.'

The windows in Hadleigh's bedroom were wide open, but the air still stank of mashy flesh and thick, puddling blood. There was a dark, sticky stain on the flowered Axminster, but nothing else to show that violence had been so recently and ferociously meted out. Every splinter of bone, however minute, every smear of grey matter and shred of skin, had been scrupulously tweezered away for close and, with luck, revelatory examination.

The room was sparsely furnished with expensive but dull reproduction pieces. A heavy oak bed and large wardrobe looking vaguely Regency. A pair of bedside cupboards with gilt filigree handles. A walnut chest of drawers, more on the Georgian side, on which stood two mildly-surprised-looking Staffordshire lions, their black-painted, crinkly knitting-wool manes glazed with powdered aluminium, as was every other smooth surface in the room. There was also a single bronze candlestick, twin to the murder weapon. On the bedside cupboard, furthest from where the body had lain, was a carafe of water covered by an upturned glass, a leather travelling alarm clock and a bunch of keys. Barnaby picked them up.

'He drove a Celica.'

'Very nice too.'

Troy, having opened one of the wardrobe doors, now reached up and, slipping his fingers behind the bevelled edge of the other, released the bolt. Two thirds of the space was taken up with clothes on hangers: suits, hacking jackets, a Burberry, neatly pressed trousers, a tie rack. And the rest by a stack of sliding, open-fronted drawers, eight in number, holding shirts in transparent wrappers, underwear, socks and soft, pricey sweaters in cashmere or lamb's wool labelled Pringle and Braemar. Troy removed one of the shirts and regarded its immaculate snowy folds with deep approval. A mark showing some sort of feathered vertebrate admitted that the garment under scrutiny was kept in such pristine nick by the Brown Bird Laundry. The sergeant replaced it carefully and stepped back for a moment looking at the neatly folded stacks of clothes. Their regimental order and cleanliness warmed his heart. He himself left the house each morning a vision of spotless perfection and woe betide Maureen if things were otherwise.

On one of the rare occasions when he and the chief were having an off-duty drink Barnaby had said that he felt sometimes his sergeant objected to murder not so much because it was an outrageous violation against a human soul but because it was chaotic. Troy had been both hurt and angry at this remark and the lack of moral sensibility that it implied. He had dwelt upon it at some length after the two men had parted, which process made him angrier still, for introspection was not his forte and he avoided its dangers whenever possible. He dodged them now by bringing himself back to the present and getting on with the job, slipping his fingers quickly but thoroughly into the pockets of all the clothes on hangers. He discovered nothing more exciting than a clean handkerchief.

'Look at these.'

Barnaby was standing by the bed, stripped bare by the SOCO team. A pair of striped pyjamas lay on the mattress. Troy, having dutifully crossed to the chief's side and looked as instructed, was rather at a loss as to how to respond. Seen one pair of pyjamas and, it struck him, you had seen a multitude.

'Very nice, chief.'

'Why wasn't he wearing them?'

'How d'you mean?'

'He got undressed but instead of getting into these he put a robe on.'

'Probably going to have a bath.'

Barnaby gave a non-committal grunt and wandered into the rather spartan en-suite bathroom. It was like a tiny sauna. The walls, bath enclosure and ceiling were stripped pine. A wooden bowl of shaving soap and an ivory-handled brush were on the shelf over the basin next to a double-sided mirror. Also on the shelf was a Rolex Oyster. He opened the louvred door of the cabinet. It held nothing but the usual complement of pain relievers, plasters, cotton wool, eye drops and deodorant. There was no steam on the glass or droplets of water on the wall but then, after twelve hours and in this temperature, there wouldn't be. The post-mortem would tell them if Hadleigh had had a bath but not, of course, if he had merely intended to.

Troy, who had completed his search by going through a box of cufflinks, studs and other very ordinary bits and pieces, called out, 'Nothing in the wardrobe. I'll try the chest of drawers.'

'Fine,' Barnaby replied, though he knew how necessarily superficial their observations must be in comparison with the forensic reports that would be landing on his desk sometime within the next forty-eight hours.

'Chief?' Barnaby wandered back. 'We've been robbed.'

'So we have.'

Barnaby bent down and peered into the four drawers – two small ones paired over two large. All were lined with gingham-patterned paper which had a slightly waxy surface – not ideal from an investigative point of view. All were empty. He said, 'How strange.'

'Don't see anything strange about stealing clothes in weather like this. A dosser'd be glad of the extra warmth.'

'Maybe the drawers didn't contain clothes. And I'm not sure this crime's opportunistic. There's a Rolex Oyster in the bathroom.' Troy whistled. 'No petty thief leaves a watch behind, whether he knows its real value or not.'

'True, true,' said the sergeant. 'Pity the back door was

unlocked. Means we don't know if the murderer's someone who'd normally have had to break in.'

'Well, whoever it was must have moved very quietly, otherwise Hadleigh would have heard them and come downstairs.'

'Perhaps he was planning to. Picked up a sound when he was half undressed, put the robe on to investigate but they got up here first. Would explain why he wasn't wearing pyjamas.'

Barnaby wandered out on to the landing and into the second bedroom. It was even smaller than the first and used for storage. It held stacked cans of paint, rollers and a ladder. Plus a vacuum cleaner resting against an ironing board. There were also two well-worn brown-leather matching cases. One only slightly larger than a briefcase, the other medium sized. Barnaby made a mental note to check with Mrs Bundy if there had been a third.

He pulled aside the fawn velvet curtain and looked down at the Green. The portable pod had arrived and was setting up near the duck pond. It was a long, pale pre-fabricated building dropped quite literally (and hydraulically) off the back of a lorry. The locals were already departing from the front of the house in droves. Calling out, 'Downstairs,' he moved off.

Troy, trying on the Rolex, turning his wrist this way and that in front of the bathroom mirror, removed it in a hurry and smeared his crisp shirt cuff with grey powder. He cursed silently, knowing it would irritate him for the rest of the day. He wondered how odd it would look if he pushed the cuff out of sight up his coat sleeve. Of course then he'd have to do the same with the other. Snorting with annoyance he joined his boss.

The house was still full of people. More detectives were

working in the kitchen and the second door, leading to the garage, now stood open. Barnaby spotted the flat, reptilian head of Inspector Meredith, his *bête noire*, peering into a segmented wooden box of cutlery. Scenes-of-crime were all over the garden. At the front of the adjoining wood were more spectators. One man had a little boy perched on his shoulders and was pointing something out to him.

Barnaby entered a large room to the right of the front door where, he presumed, the Writers Circle had met. Like the bedroom it was curiously characterless. It contained a long sofa and one much smaller, plus three capacious armchairs. All the furniture had loose chintz covers in wishy-washy pastel shades or insipid flower prints. The curtains were beige velvet and floor length, the walls a dreary cream. More boring pictures, this time in rather ornate frames: pyramids of fruit in pewter dishes flanked by dead game birds, hunting scenes, a print of Salisbury cathedral. There was something somnolent and torpid about the place. It had the air of a gentleman's club, or an elderly solicitor's waiting room.

The chief inspector recalled Mrs Bundy's remarks about Mr Hadleigh giving nothing away. This room certainly supported such a notion. But could Hadleigh, could anyone, be as blandly dull and predictable as these trappings and the clothes upstairs implied? The answer to that was obviously yes but Barnaby was hopeful that subsequent investigations would prove otherwise.

In the far corner a light-oak bureau with a drop-leaf front was being systematically worked over by Detective Sergeant Ian Carpenter, who looked up as Barnaby walked over.

'Good morning, sir.'

'Found anything interesting?'

'Not really. Insurance – car and house. Bank statements. The usual bills – water, phone, electricity. All paid.'

'No letters?'

'Nothing personal at all. Except this.' He picked up a framed photograph which had been lying face down inside the bureau and passed it across. Barnaby took it over to the window.

The happy couple were standing in the doorway of what appeared to be a very old church. She wore a cream dress and a little pill-box hat embroidered with gold thread and tiny pearls. Attached to this was a fluttery shoulder-length veil which she was holding away from her face with a gloved hand that also clutched a nosegay of carnations and mignonette.

Gerald Hadleigh, dark-suited, an apricot rose in his buttonhole, gripped her other hand tightly. She was much shorter than him and had tilted her head back to quite a sharp degree so that she could look into his eyes. She was laughing happily but the groom's profile was serious and intent and the set of his mouth suggested that the prize he was holding on to so firmly would not easily be surrendered.

Barnaby regretted that Hadleigh was not facing the camera. He would have liked to look directly at the man, try to guess his thoughts and imagine his emotions. Hadleigh was certainly attractive. Reconstructed, the battered head proved to be both large and shapely, with a straight nose and strong, square jaw. He could have been a soldier. An explorer, perhaps. Or an extremely determined man of the cloth.

What was really interesting about the picture, of course, was why it was not in its place on the sideboard beside the vase of scented viburnum but hidden away in a bureau.

Barnaby looked forward to finding the answer to this. He was, in fact, looking forward generally.

There was something about the very beginning of a case, when no medical or forensic evidence to speak of was available, that exhilarated him. Marooned in a vast landscape of unknown limits with barely a visual aid in sight, Barnaby remained quite unfazed.

But it had not always been so, which was why he understood, and sympathised with, his sergeant's very different reaction. Troy suffered greatly from what Barnaby always thought of as the 'treading-water syndrome'. Panic at being out of one's depth. Fear that, if a case did not quickly yield up its secrets, it would remain forever impenetrable. Troy craved for something to hang on to, and quickly. A fact, an artefact, a list, a bag, a lighter, a wallet. Anything as long as it was solidly present and clearly visible. Right now he was picking up and sniffing the remains of a cigar. But Barnaby had seen too many wrong conclusions drawn from apparently incorruptible certainties to take easy comfort from their presence.

'This,' said Troy now, rolling the elegant, slim, gold-banded cylinder between his fingers, 'is what I call a stogy. Beautiful.'

'Must be one of the guests,' said Barnaby crossing to an alcove filled with books. 'He's no smoker. You can always smell it.'

The chief inspector bent his head sideways, twisting round to read the titles. All non-fiction. Architecture, travel, food and wine. Several on the craft of writing. The arrangement of the books was in sharp contrast to those in his own household, where volumes would be jumbled up any old how with titles every which way. There was always at least one stack of books on the floor, a pile of new paperbacks by Joyce's chair and at least a couple on her bedside table. Here the spines were aligned like high-kicking chorus girls, tallest at each end, smallest in the middle. Most wore shiny, fresh-looking dust jackets now dulled by SOCO's ministrations. Barnaby reached out and, with a satisfaction which he knew to be pathetically childish even as he indulged it, poked one of the books completely out of line, muttering 'Anal retentive.'

'Was he?' said Troy, abandoning his contemplation of rosy apples and lifeless grouse. 'The dirty devil.'

Barnaby went outside, only to be once more accosted by Aubrey Marine, this time divested of his polythene carapace and carrying a sealed metal container.

'The Celica's missing, Tom.'

'Oh? Garage doors forced?'

'Nope. All nicely locked up. Of course our man could simply have used Hadleigh's keys and replaced them. Or the car could be off somewhere having its MOT. Just another little wrinkle.' He beamed and set off down the path.

The two policemen followed, the cold air smacking them hard in the face. Barnaby shivered and told himself this was due to a grievous lack of solid pabulum. He looked at his watch, convinced he had missed lunch by half a century, but it was barely twelve.

'We'll have time to call next door. What did she say their names were, Mrs Bundy? Crampton?'

'Clapton, chief.'

'What would I do without your memory, sergeant?' It was true. His own got worse every day. 'Maybe she'll come up with a cup of tea.'

'You never know. We could strike lucky.'

'And a biscuit.'

* * *

Outside the cottage the crowd, now untidily straggling behind a barrier, had increased. Young mothers with toddlers in pushchairs, three children of school age. Old men in flat caps and mufflers which crossed their chests to be tied up behind like soldiers' bandoleers. They were blowing on their mittens, flinging their arms backwards and forwards, trying to keep warm. Catching their deaths. Some middle-aged women, hair rollers like pink foam sausages poking from woollen head scarves, were sharing a Thermos. One was bringing a new arrival up to date.

'Basically they have brought him out but he was in this zip-up. You couldn't see a thing.' The tone of her voice was deeply resentful, as if a ticket for a show had been bought and the curtain had failed to rise.

'Our Don hangs his suit up in one of them,' said her companion. 'They're dead useful.'

'Mister, mister.' Two boys, around eight or nine, ran up to Barnaby.

'What do you want?' Troy grimaced fiercely at them and his fingers twitched.

'I want a burger, onions and chips,' said the larger of the lads, jerking his head in the direction of the portable pod, 'and he wants a hot dog.'

'Very funny. Why aren't you at school?'

'I got a bone in me leg,' replied the village wit.

'Well, if you don't want a pain in the arse to go with it you'd better clear off.'

At least a dozen cars had drawn up on the far side of the Green. Every gaze was fixed on to the cottage as if the occupants' heads had been locked into position. Troy stared coolly across at them all and he made his leather coat crack fiercely round his boots as he strode along, basking the while in his authoritative role at the very heart of the drama.

'I say!' Barnaby, his hand on the gate of Trevelyan Villas, was stopped by a girl holding a runny-nosed blue-cheeked baby swaddled in a puce and ultramarine shell suit. 'There's nobody in. He teaches at Causton Comprehensive and Sue's at the local play group.'

'Do you have any idea when Mrs Clapton will be back?'

'Around one usually.'

'Thank you.'

'What do you want to see them for?' asked a tall, thin man wearing a sweater with a snowman on it. He had a dewdrop at the end of his nose.

Ignoring him, the policemen turned their backs and Barnaby set off along the sparkling cold pavement. Troy hurried to keep up.

'You going to try the Lyddiards, chief?'

'Might as well.'

Gresham House's pineapples were in poor condition. One had lost its leaves, the other was crumbling from the base up. The sandstone pillars they surmounted were also in poor shape and the iron gates, some fifteen feet tall and ornately curlicued, were rusty.

The house was a monstrous pile of heavily pitted grey stone, three storeys high with a small, round tower fatly bulging from one corner of the top storey like a warty carbuncle and from which icicles depended like daggers. The door and window frames, once white, were now a dirty grey and flaking fast. Perhaps in the spring and summer, softened by climbers in bloom or pots of bright geraniums on the steps, it might, just, have seemed attractive. But at the moment (thought Sergeant Troy) it looked about as jolly as Castle Dracula.

Barnaby, on the contrary, saw much to admire. His gardener's soul was cheered by the many trees and the shrub borders on each side of the drive. Variegated hollies festooned with damp cobwebs, a shiny sealing-wax-red dogwood. Two flowering wintersweets, the ground beneath them thick with aconites and *Iris stylosa*. Mahonias, their droopy yellow racemes smelling richly of honey, and also several hebes. He recognised the tough and charming 'Mrs Winder', her narrow elliptical leaves gleaming purple in the grey winter light. And . . . could that *Cotoneaster* be? . . . surely not? . . .

'Good grief. It's a Rothschildianus.'

'Is that right?' Troy stared at some creamy yellow balls roughly the size of sheep droppings.

'What a jewel. I've got the Exvuriensis. Nice of course. But not the same.'

'No, well. It wouldn't be.' Troy racked his brains for some intelligent rejoinder, for he hated to be found wanting. Faintly, memory chimed. 'Aren't they rich, chief? The Rothschilds? Millionaries or something?'

'They have this wonderful garden in Hampshire. Exbury. You can buy plants there.'

Troy nodded vaguely and his interest in the creamy balls, never overwhelming, expired, for there was not a spot of horticultural blood in his veins. Almost the first thing he had done after moving into his small 1970s terraced house was see off the front garden and replace it with a tarmacadam parking space.

'Not much point in trying that,' said Barnaby. On the top of a cracked flight of steps was a mass of dried leaves and twiggy bits which the wind had piled against the front door. 'Doesn't look as if it's been opened for years.'

As they made their way down the side of the house Troy

said, only half joking, 'Beggars and tradesmen round the back.'

They found a second opening. Poorly made and ill fitting, the door was the type that usually leads simply to an outhouse, but it was the only one visible so Barnaby rapped on it. Quite loudly, but without result.

He waited for a few moments and was about to try again when Troy stayed his hand. A woman, having made her way through a bareish vegetable garden, was crossing the stone courtyard towards them. A large, middle-aged woman in a shapeless, lumpy woollen skirt, a Barbour almost black with age and a waterproof fisherman's hat. A worn leather pouch hung around her neck, bouncing on the granite shelf of her bosom like a nosebag on a horse. She had a huge face, an expanse of raw red flesh, the features lassoed into a tight, malignant bunch in the centre, dark shaggy eyebrows and a mouth like a gin trap. She was what Troy's dad would have called 'as ugly as sin'.

'I was right about this place,' Troy mumbled just before she hove into earshot. 'Here's Dracula's mother.'

To the men's astonishment she walked straight past them as if they were invisible, lifted the wooden latch in the old door and slammed it in their faces. Barnaby was furious. He raised his fist and thundered on the shaky panels. The door was immediately snatched open.

'How dare you! Can't you read?' She pointed a Fair Isled digit at a weathered metal plate: No Hawkers. No Circulars. 'Go away at once or I shall call the police.'

'We are the police,' replied Barnaby and his helpmate smirked invisibly at the sweet neatness of this riposte. Arrogant, fart-faced old biddy.

'Well, why didn't you say so?'

'We were hardly given an opportunity.' Barnaby

reached inside his overcoat and produced his warrant card. 'Detective Chief Inspector Barnaby. Causton CID.'

'What do you want?'

'To ask a few questions. I take it you are Miss Lyddiard?'

'Questions about what?'

'Could we come inside for a moment?'

She gave an impatient and irritated sigh but stood back, admitting them into what is now called a utility room, though this one had the floor area of a two-bedroomed bungalow. It was full of old furniture, a rubber-rollered mangle, garden tools, jumbled-up sports equipment – croquet mallets, tennis racquets and nets – and bicycles. There was a long workbench covered with dahlia corms, drying bulbs and other gardening paraphernalia.

A family of five could live in this, bridled Sergeant Troy as he made his way silently behind the others though, in truth, he had little concern for either the homeless or the destitute.

At the far end of the room was a second door much more solid and with a wire-mesh glass panel in the top half. Honoria pushed at this and they were in the kitchen. Another vast space – high ceilinged, shabby and extremely cold.

It was not unoccupied. A small, round woman, wearing baggy trousers and several sweaters topped with a cardigan embroidered vividly with butterflies, was making pastry at an ancient deal table. She stopped immediately when they came in, looking embarrassed and a little apprehensive, as if caught out in some foolishness.

Barnaby, uncertain whether this was the sister-in-law, the cook or someone else entirely, waited to be informed, but in vain.

'We're investigating a suspicious death.' He addressed the two of them equally. 'I'm afraid a near neighbour of yours. Mr Hadleigh.'

He observed their twin expressions of incredulity without surprise and wondered how many more times he would be faced with just such a reaction before the day was out. It was always the same. No one could ever believe that someone they had recently seen alive and apparently well was no more. It was impossible. That sort of thing only happened to strangers. An unknown name in the papers. An alien face on the television screen.

The woman in the cardigan had gone deathly pale. She had a sweet face which seemed made for happiness, not the slack-jawed distress that had now overtaken it.

'Gerald . . . But we only . . . oh. Ohhh . . .'

'For heaven's sake, Amy. Remember who you are.' Honoria seized her sister-in-law by the arm and bundled her, none too gently, into the nearest chair. 'There are strangers present.'

'I'm sorry.' Amy trembled and looked around with the air of a child seeking comfort. Barnaby suspected she might be in for a long wait. Honoria spoke.

'There has obviously been some abhorrent mix up,' she said firmly, putting both of them straight once and for all.

Barnaby could imagine her on the seashore forbidding the waves their approach. Or standing in the eye of a storm sending the wind about its business.

'I'm afraid not, Miss Lyddiard. Mr Hadleigh was killed late yesterday.'

'Killed. Are you saying—'

'Murdered. Yes, I'm afraid so.'

Amy burst into a storm of frightened tears. Honoria sat down and became very still. Her face had a stripped quality as if she had suddenly forgotten everything that she had ever known. Eventually she said, 'I see.'

'I understand that there was a meeting at his house last night and that you were both present.'

'How perfectly frightful.'

'Indeed.'

'And in Midsomer Worthy. I warned people again and again, but no one would listen.' Her grey eyes stared directly at him and Barnaby was frigorified. He had never seen such coldness. 'The barbarians are at the gates.'

'I'm sure you would wish to help—'

'What has this dreadful business to do with us? I am a Lyddiard, as is my brother's wife. Our name is woven into the very warp and woof of England and above reproach.'

Oh dear, oh dear, mused Troy. Pardon me while I curtsey. Knowing he was expected to remove it he pushed his cap to the back of his head with his thumb and glanced around with bold derision, taking in cracked gloss paint on walls the colour of dirty custard, free-standing old-fashioned cupboards and a huge Electrolux fridge of the type that was obsolete before Adam went into the cider business. He'd be ashamed to ask Maureen to keep her yoghurts in it. If I couldn't do better than this, reflected Troy, with a deep inner glow of satisfaction, I'd shoot myself. He tuned back in.

'. . . and so, I am sure you would wish to help us in any way you can.' Here Barnaby paused, wondering if, by introducing the word 'duty', he had overstretched his luck but it seemed not.

'Naturally we would wish to do all that we can to bring this miscreant to justice. If justice it can these days be called.'

Barnaby recognised a note of harsh longing and guessed

that Honoria was wistfully recalling the days when a villein could be publicly disembowelled for patting his master's dog. He said, 'Could you perhaps tell us first who was present at your meeting last night and give us their addresses.' Troy wrote the details down. 'And you met, how often?'

'Once a month.'

'And did yesterday follow the usual pattern?'

'No. We had a guest speaker.' Already she was sounding impatient. 'What on earth has our meeting to do with someone breaking in and attacking Gerald?'

'No one broke in, Miss Lyddiard.' Barnaby saw the release of this information as inevitable given the form his questioning would be compelled to take.

'You mean' – Amy was staring in disbelief – 'Gerald just opened the door and let him in?'

'Opening the door' – Honoria separated her words and spoke loudly as if Amy was not only mentally retarded but deaf as well – 'is not the same as letting someone in. People are always calling round,' she turned back to Barnaby, 'delivering rubbishy newspapers, begging for charity or asking for jumble—'

'At that hour of the night?' Troy consciously exaggerated his West of Slough twang, whining his vowels and dropping his T's – emphasising the social divide but on his own terms. He could have saved his breath. Honoria did not even deign to glance in his direction, just stared blankly down her nose, her expression that of someone noticing a fresh and particularly repulsive specimen of doggy doo in the middle of their priceless Aubusson.

'A guest speaker?' reminded Barnaby.

'Grave disappointment. Max Jennings. Some sort of novelist.'

The name sounded vaguely familiar, though Barnaby couldn't think from where. Certainly it would not be from personal experience, for he never read fiction. Indeed hardly read at all, preferring to paint or cook or garden in his spare time.

'Consequently,' concluded Honoria, 'we finished later than usual. Around ten thirty.'

'And did you all leave then?'

'All but Rex St John. And Jennings.'

'To go straight home?'

'Of course,' snapped Honoria, adding, without apparent irony, 'it was a dark and stormy night.'

'And you didn't go out again?' She stared at him as if he were mad. 'Or return to Plover's Rest for any reason?'

Pluvvers is it? noted Troy, who had been rhyming it with Rover's, as in Return.

'Certainly not.'

'And . . .' Barnaby turned to the younger woman. 'I'm sorry, I don't . . .'

'Mrs Lyddiard – Amy. No. I didn't go out either.'

'Did you retire straight away?' Barnaby asked.

'Yes,' replied Honoria. 'I had a headache. The visitor was allowed to smoke. A disgusting habit. He wouldn't have done it here.'

'And you, Mrs Lyddiard?' Barnaby smiled encouragingly.

'Not quite straight away. First I made us a drink – cocoa actually—'

'They don't want to know every little detail of our domestic life.'

'I'm sorry, Honoria.'

'Why don't you tell them how much sugar you put in? Describe the cups and saucers.'

Amy's full lower lip started to quiver and Barnaby gave

87

up. There seemed little point, given Honoria's recent strictures on the spreading of gossip, in persisting. Plenty of other people were yet to be questioned and some, merely by the law of averages, were bound to prove co-operative. And he could always get back to Mrs Lyddiard, preferably when she was alone. But Troy jumped in where his superior had decided not to tread. Touching his tie and ostentatiously displaying nicotined fingertips he said, 'What sort of man was Mr Hadleigh?'

'He was a gentleman.'

And that put paid to that. End of conversation, end of audience. Barnaby explained that their fingerprints would be needed. Honoria retaliated with great vigour. Such a degrading procedure was quite out of the question. As Amy was showing them out she could be heard declaiming loudly, 'Jumped up clowns!'

A gentleman. Troy kicked savagely at the gravel as they made their way back to the rusty gate. Of course we all know what that means. The upper crust on life's farmhouse. He lit a cigarette. A member of the club. Right tie. Right accent. Right attitude. Right sort of money. Right wing. (Troy himself was extremely right wing, but from quite a different jumping-off point, and for quite different reasons.) And, of course, blue balls.

'You can't believe folk like that, can you?' He opened the gate and stood aside to let Barnaby pass through. 'In this D and A. I bet she's never done a stroke of work in her life. Bloody parasite.'

'Now look.' Barnaby, his voice sharp and irritable, stopped in mid-stride. His back ached from standing and he liked being patronised no more than the next man. 'Your prejudices are your own affair, Gavin, unless they interfere with your work, in which case they also become mine. Our job is to extract information and to persuade people to reveal themselves. Anything that hinders this procedure is a time-wasting bloody nuisance. And I don't expect to find it coming from my own side of the fence.'

'Sir.'

'Have you got that?'

'Yeah. Got that.' The sergeant chewed furiously on his high tar. 'It's just they get up my fucking nose.'

'No one's asking you to pretend liking or respect. In any case either attitude would be as inappropriate as the one you're currently wallowing in. Your own feelings are immaterial. Or should be. Self-absorption is fatal in our job. We should be looking out, not in.'

'Yeah,' said Troy again. 'Sorry, chief.'

Trouble was, he knew Barnaby was right. And on the whole he did look out for he loved his work and wanted to do it well. Troy took great pride even in his most modest achievements – of which, it had to be said, there were many. He decided to make a real effort. Politeness to a fault would be the order of the day. After all, civility cost nothing. But there'd be no green-welly licking. Green-welly licking was right out.

By this time they were halfway across the green. Kitty Fosse, a dark, attractive girl, a reporter on the *Causton Echo*, came running to meet them.

'Hi, chief inspector. What's the story?'

'Hullo, Kitty.' He walked on. The reporter, hurrying to keep up, stumbled over a tussock of grass and Troy leapt forward to assist.

'Someone in the crowd said a body had been taken out,' she said, while attempting to retrieve her arm.

'That's the case, yes.'

'And is it the man who lived there? (Thank you,

89

sergeant, I can manage.) A certain,' she checked her spiral notebook, 'Gerald Hadleigh?'

'Mr Hadleigh was found dead early today in suspicious circumstances.'

'Who by? (I said I could manage!)' She wrenched her arm away. 'How was he killed?'

'You know the form, Kitty. There'll be a proper statement later from communications.'

As the chief strode away Troy turned to the girl. 'Why don't we meet up later for a drink? Might have a leak for you by then.'

'You're not catching me on that one twice.' Kitty gave him a look of deep disgust.

'Sorry?'

'Eighteen months ago. The Jolly Cavalier?' She had naively gone along hoping for some sort of scoop, but had received instead several propositions, none of which was fit for a girl to blow her nose on.

'Hey – that's right.' He grinned in belated recognition. 'Another time then?'

'Don't hold your breath.'

Barnaby had a visit to Rex St John next in mind. If he and Jennings had been the last to leave, discovering the time and order of their departure was extremely relevant. They found the weather-beaten clapboard house, almost directly opposite Plover's Rest, without any trouble but, although their approach produced a canine response the like of which neither man had ever heard nor ever wished to hear again, no human soul appeared.

Putting Borodino firmly behind them and making their way back to Hadleigh's cottage Barnaby noticed a woman with a bicycle standing by the gate of the house next door. She had obviously been informed by someone in the crowd that they had been previously seeking her out, for she was looking in a concerned, expectant manner in their direction. Barnaby, fishing for his warrant card, approached.

'Mrs Clapton?'

'Yes. What is it?' Her expression, a little alarmed but plainly anxious to be of help, was a welcome contrast to their last encounter.

'Could we talk inside, do you think?'

'Of course.'

The front door opened on to a tiny square of coconut matting directly behind which reared some steep and narrow stairs. The stairwell was painted Prussian blue and covered with stars. Sue showed them into an untidy sitting room where, after asking permission, Barnaby sank, swiftly and gratefully, into a deep armchair from which, when the time came, he could hardly extricate himself. Troy settled himself at a table affixed to a single barley-sugar-twist leg. The whole thing had such a severe wobble that he ended up balancing his notebook on his knee.

'Is it about Gerald?' She was breathing quickly and her eyes were wide with apprehension. 'People on the pavement were saying all sorts of things. That he'd had an accident. Even that he'd . . . died.'

'I'm afraid that is the case, Mrs Clapton. But it was not an accident. Mr Hadleigh was deliberately killed.'

The colour leached from her face and flooded uncontrollably back, swoosh, a crimson tide. Then she hung her head, her expression invisible behind a fall of hair. After a few moments she sat up, appearing more composed. Her complexion stabilised at a shade resembling pale tea.

'But we were all together – our Writers Circle. We had a lovely time.' She sounded completely bewildered and also slightly resentful, as if the very loveliness of the time should itself have proved an amulet against disaster.

'You met regularly, I believe?'

'Yes. Every month.' She was gazing now at her clogs. Clumsy things painted with little flowers and worn with woollen socks. 'Gerald . . . *Gerald* . . .'

'You can't think of anyone who would wish to harm Mr Hadleigh?'

'What do you mean?' She looked from one man to the other in amazement. 'Surely it was a burglar? A break-in?'

'We are of course considering that possibility.' Barnaby was at his most avuncular. 'How long have you been neighbours?'

'Since we moved here. About five years ago.'

'You'd know Mr Hadleigh quite well, then?'

'I wouldn't say that. He was always polite and helpful. A good sort to live next to – cleared the snow last winter when Brian did his back in. That sort of thing. But he wasn't what you'd call revealing.'

'But you met socially?'

'Only at the group. We didn't mix otherwise. Brian wouldn't have liked it.'

'Why not?'

'He just doesn't care for . . . that class of person.'

Well there's a turn-around, thought Troy. Mindful of the recent ticking-off his voice was politely neutral as he asked, 'What class would that be, Mrs Clapton?'

'"Officer class" was how Brian described it. Not that Gerald had been in the Forces. I got the impression he was a retired civil servant. It's just Brian's way of putting things. He's a socialist.' She squared her shoulders slightly

92

and lifted her chin as if bravely confessing to some shameful peccadillo as, around Midsomer Worthy, it probably was. 'People are pretty good about it on the whole.'

'How did your writers' group get on together?'

'Fine. Mainly.'

'But there must have been likes and dislikes. The occasional disagreements. Jealousy perhaps over a member's success.'

'Oh no. We weren't professionals.'

Touché, thought Barnaby, before realising the remark had been made in all innocence. 'Were you all working on different things?'

'Yes. Gerald wrote short stories, Amy's working on a novel . . .'

As Barnaby listened he took in his surroundings. Two walls were emulsioned a hot, sandy orange, one terracotta, the fourth the same colour as the stairwell, minus the nebulae but with the addition of a stately and rather beautiful palm tree. A black frieze, in a Greek-key pattern, had been painted beneath the picture rail. It all reminded Barnaby of a visit he and Joyce had paid to Knossos. There was a wooden clothes-horse from which depended several bunches of slowly drying flowers and herbs. The carpet was wall-to-wall muesli. Sue continued talking.

'. . . *Night of the Hyena*. I can't relate to it at all. Guns, bombs, rockets – that's men's stuff, isn't it? Just silliness. Except in real life of course, when they go off and kill people.'

'Did you always meet at Mr Hadleigh's?' asked Sergeant Troy.

'Yes. Laura's house is tiny, Rex's a bit of a mess. Brian didn't want them here and Honoria grumbled about it being too much trouble. Actually Amy said it was because she didn't want to have to pay for the coffee and biscuits – oh! You won't tell . . .'

'No worries on that score, Mrs Clapton,' said Troy with a sympathetic smile.

Sue smiled shyly back. She took off her glasses, which she hated, and rested them in her lap. The lenses were thick as the bottoms of milk bottles. Sue dreamed of one day seeing a film where, after first letting her hair down, the hero remove the heroine's glasses and says, 'Hey . . . know what? You look better with them on.'

Barnaby said, 'I understand you had a guest speaker yesterday.'

'A rare treat. You'd be surprised how difficult it is to get people considering we're under an hour from central London.'

'But this time you struck lucky?'

'Yes. Everyone was surprised when he accepted. And he was so nice. Not a bit grand. Gave us all sorts of advice and tips. And he really listened, you know?'

'So the evening was a success?' She nodded vigorously. 'No tensions or cross currents that you noticed?'

'Only Gerald.' Her face changed as she remembered what had momentarily been crowded out. 'He hardly spoke, which was surprising. I thought he'd be asking lots of questions because he so much wanted to succeed. He would work over and over his writing trying to make it better.'

'Was he any good?' asked Troy.

Sue hesitated. Knowing it was wrong to speak ill of the dead she was certain it could not then be right to speak ill of their achievements. On the other hand she always tried to be honest and it wasn't as if, in this case, the truth would hurt anyone. Least of all poor Gerald.

'When Gerald read his stories out they sounded fine. He'd learned how to do it, you see, from all his books. But the minute he'd finished you couldn't remember a word he'd said.' This devastating indictment concluded, she suddenly got up as if remembering her manners.

'I should have made you some tea,' she said, plucking apologetically at the rainbow laces in her waistcoat.

'That's very kind of you, Mrs Clapton.' Barnaby's hope of a biscuit was more than realised. A cake tin arrived with the tea and it was suggested that he helped himself.

'Why are you asking so many questions about us?' said Sue, handing around large mugs.

'Just background. I understand Mr Jennings didn't leave with the rest of you.'

'No – it was funny, that. Brian made the first move, Gerald got the coats and it looked as if there was going to be a general exodus but then, when we were all halfway out the door, Max Jennings sat down again.'

'Did you get the impression that was a deliberate manoeuvre?' asked Troy.

'I don't think so. Just one of those awkward moments.'

'Wouldn't have taken you long to get home,' said Barnaby. She didn't reply but watched him with unnaturally close attention, like a participant in a quiz game expecting a trick question. 'Did you go out again at all?'

'No.'

'Either of you?' She frowned and covered her eyes with her hand as if needing to think. The movement was quick, but not quite quick enough for Barnaby to miss the flare of emotion. Stronger than concern or apprehension. Alarm perhaps. Fear even.

'It was a bit late for that.'

'Walking the dog maybe,' said Troy, leaning forward – for he too sensed they were on fertile ground.

'We haven't got a dog.'

She elaborated quickly, using stiff little sentences looping round each other. Brian had gone up straight away. She had had things to get ready for play group. Plus some washing up from Mandy's supper. Brian was well away by the time she got to bed. She herself couldn't get to sleep. Too excited by the evening. But Brian, he was asleep the minute his head touched the pillow. And so on and tortuously on.

Barnaby listened, not unsympathetically, for he was aware of her dilemma. Unbrazen people who had something, by no means necessarily criminal, to hide either froze into protective stillness or talked non-stop about anything and everything to keep their tongue from alighting on the matter for concealment. Needing to move things along, he interrupted.

'Perhaps, being awake, you heard Mr Jennings drive away?'

'Yes.' It was one long gasp of relief. 'Yes, I did.'

'Do you happen to know when that was?'

'I'm afraid not. You know how it is, lying in the dark. Time passes at a funny rate.'

'Sure it was Mr Jennings' car?' asked Troy.

'I can't imagine who else's it could have been. It had a very powerful engine and seemed to be revving up practically under our window.'

'But you didn't look out?'

'No.'

'Well, Mrs Clapton.' Barnaby now entered upon his marathon struggle to part company from the fierce embrace of the armchair. 'No, no. It's all right. I can manage.'

'We called on Mr St John,' said Troy, averting his eyes for fear of laughter, 'but he was out.'

'Yes. It's market day. He draws his pension and does the shopping and then his research at the library. Goes in at nine and catches the four o'clock bus back. You won't find Laura at home either. She opens her shop at ten so she'd probably have left home before all this was discovered.'

'What shop would that be?' asked Sergeant Troy, closing his notebook.

'The Spinning Wheel. Antiques. In Causton High Street.'

Barnaby, now fully upright, recognised the name. He had bought Joyce an outrageously priced Victorian footstool there for her birthday last year.

'I shall have to ask you for some fingerprints I'm afraid, Mrs Clapton. Purely for purposes of elimination.'

'Oh dear.' Worry shadowed her eyes, which, without the hugely magnifying lenses, were small, blinky and weak as a rabbit's. 'My husband wouldn't like that. He's very into civil liberties.'

'They'll just be on a strip – not filed. And destroyed when our investigations are complete. In your presence, if that is what you would prefer.'

'I see.'

'There's a portable incident room on the Green, as I expect you noticed.' Barnaby spoke firmly, as if her popping in was as good as settled. 'Or you and Mr Clapton might like to come to the station.'

By now they had reached the door. Fastened to one of the stripped wooden panels by Blu-tack was a painting of a dragon. His tail was wrapped around his body, the arrowed tip covering his nostrils and held in place by a wing membrane. Above his head in primary colours were the words: 'Thank You For Not Smoking In Our Home'.

The creature's expression of guilty naughtiness, alarm at being discovered and a lurking, laughing confidence that it would be forgiven was so precisely that of a well-loved child caught in similar defiant circumstances that Troy chuckled silently and Barnaby laughed out loud.

'Who did this?'

'Me. That's Hector.'

'It's very good.'

'Thank you.' Sue blushed with pleasure. 'He's in all my stories.'

'Do you ever sell your paintings, Mrs Clapton?' asked Troy.

'Ohh . . . well . . .' Her face became transfigured.

'Only my little girl, she'd just love him. In her room like.'

'I could . . . I suppose . . . Yes.'

'Fine. I'll be in touch.'

They were all on the step by this time. As Barnaby and Troy left, Kitty Fosse, now in the company of two more reporters, both male, a man with a camera on his shoulder and a woman waving a long cylinder of yellow fluff pushed through the gate and zoomed, like a swarm of hornets, up the path. The policemen stood aside, judging, correctly, that their target was Sue.

'So,' said the chief inspector as they walked away. 'What do you make of all that, sergeant?'

'Covering for him, isn't she?'

'It looks like it. I wonder what Mr C. was actually up to while he was supposed to be "well away" last night.'

'The smart move would be to talk to him before she does.' Barnaby turned for a last look at Trevelyan Villas. The Press had disappeared inside. 'And if you can get us to Causton Comprehensive within the next twenty minutes

I'd say we have a very good chance of doing just that.'

'On these roads?' They had reached the car. Troy struggled to open the door which had frozen to the frame. He grinned. 'No problem.'

In the gymnasium Brian was organising his play-construction group. Everyone but Denzil was spread around on the high-gloss, honey-coloured parquet. They sat cross-legged and back to back or lay acumbent. Denzil hung upside down from the ropes, his hands gripping and squeezing the rubber rings. Veins corded his neck and sweat hung from his lobes like drops of crystal.

'Come along now, Denzil,' called Brian. 'We're ready to start.'

Denzil showed no sign of having heard nor did Brian expect him to, for from the beginning he had made it plain that his *modus operandi* would be one of democratic openness. He knew that to assert the dialectic of belonging they needed to erase the official academic landscape and impose their own. Their meetings were not to be class/teacher confrontations but periods of adventurous exploration during which they would all reach out and spontaneously reveal their dreams, longings and frustrations which Brian would then shape and organise into a full-length drama provisionally entitled *Slangwhang For Five Mute Voices*.

This was scheduled to be seen at the close of the spring term – a fact that was already causing him considerable anxiety. Although the group undoubtedly had a great relish for dramatic expression (once they got going) and threw themselves with vigour and imaginative energy into all the improvisations, they were simply not interested in learning lines. In vain would Brian take home his rehearsal tape, extract the obscenities, massage the rest into some sort of coherent shape and transfer it to Mandy's Amstrad. The group would accept the thin, perforated sheets, stuff them into the pockets of their jeans with discouraging nonchalance and ignore them thereafter.

Now Brian asked if anyone had had time to look over the results of the previous week's work. Denzil, lowering himself slowly, said, 'Yeah.'

'How did it feel?'

'Absorbent, man. Really absorbent.'

He hung an inch from the floor exciting deltoids which bulged like coconuts beneath grey, unhealthy skin, then dropped. Noiselessly. The others applauded. Denzil put a hand mockingly on his chest and dipped his shaven skull. A spider crouched in the very centre, the navy-blue threads of its web woven over his skull and disappearing down the neck of his Guns N' Roses T-shirt. The words 'CUT HERE' were tattooed around the base of his throat. He strolled over to join the others, taking his time. 'I reckon I could've been a trapeze artist – given the luck.'

'Right! Warm-up time, you lot,' cried Brian in a rushy, foolish voice. He started running on the spot, shaking his arms and legs about and rolling his head.

Denzil stood in front of Edie Carter, straddled his legs and mimed playing a guitar, rhythmically thrusting his pelvis into her face. Sluggishly two of the others got up. Collar, so called because he could not bear anything touching his neck, started shadow boxing. Little Boreham, weedily hopeless but dressed like an Olympic athlete, did a few shallow and uncertain press-ups.

Edie and her brother continued to sit, back to back, like a pair of exquisitely carved, beautifully decorated bookends. In profile their faces appeared almost identical (they were born on the same day) but Tom's jaw was a little more prominent and heavier. They had long, thick, curling hair the colour of marmalade, exquisitely shaped noses and high, marbly-white foreheads like the children in Tudor paintings.

Brian looked forward eagerly each day to his first sighting of the Carter twins, for they constantly re-styled and re-invented themselves and never looked the same twice. Their dazzling skins, thick and smooth like cream, seemed, like blank canvases, to be crying out for decoration. They dressed, as small children would if left to themselves, in an assortment of unrelated finery. Today Edie wore a foamy scarlet RaRa topped with shreds of silk and lace and a banana-coloured sweat shirt full of holes. Tom was in jeans resembling pale blue shredded wheat and an American Repro jacket stencilled with midnight hags and burning cities and comic-book expletives.

'Come on you two,' called Brian.

Edie parted her rich carnation lips, flickered out her tongue, drew it in again. And smiled. Brian turned quickly away and began shadow boxing with Collar, much to the latter's resentment.

When the group had first been formed Brian, very heavily into non-verbal communication, had encouraged everyone to sit around in a circle holding hands with their eyes closed. Next had come various physical exercises leading to a full class workout. These had been discontinued when Brian, wrestling on the floor with Collar, had accidentally touched his neck, receiving in return a clout across the ear that had made his head fizz for a week.

'OK. Gather round, earthlings.'

Brian sat down in a single but rapidly accelerating movement. The twins turned towards him and smiled.

Brian, faint with excitement and desire, smiled back. He could never decide which was the more beautiful, for he was equally besotted with them both.

'Now,' he said briskly, 'where had we got to last week?'

No one remembered. Brian held the pause, nodding interrogatively at them all in turn for all the world, as Collar said afterwards, like the daft dog in the back of his mum's Escort.

'Was it . . .' Boreham puckered his brow, 'the bit where Denzil went down the Social and got in that fight with a Paki?'

'No,' said Brian shortly. He was keenly aware of the ethnic imbalance in his group and had tried in vain to remedy the matter. No non-white person was interested in joining, possibly because of Denzil, who could be seen every Saturday in Causton High Street enthusiastically selling the *British Nationalist Magazine* on behalf of the BNP.

'That were good. We could do that one again.'

'No, we couldn't.' Brian was beginning to feel depressed. All the improvisations, no matter how pacific their inception, quickly became confrontational. Everyone it seemed loved rows and while there was no doubt that they were good theatre even Brian, inexperienced director/devisor that he was, could see that each violent highlight needed to be cushioned by a tranquil low light if the whole thing wasn't going to explode in everyone's faces.

'I remember.' Edie swivelled to face him, legs apart, elbows resting on her knees. 'My bit I mean. From last week.'

'She remembers, Bri,' said Tom, taking pride. He winked, lowering an eyelid brilliantly adorned with red and blue flowers. Brian had long been agitatedly concerned over Tom's eyelids. As far as he could see the pattern never varied by as much as a petal's fall. The vivid colours were never smudged. The thought had struck him once that the lids might be tattooed, that this was some test of high machismo that only the greatly brave essayed. He'd never had the nerve to ask.

'Excellent. So what was the situation? Listen everyone.' Brian clapped his hands.

'I were this woman that got really mad at her husband.'

'And do you remember why, Edie?'

'Yeah. 'Cause he were married to me and knocking somebody else about.'

'Ah.'

'So I go: "Eat shit, scumbag. Piss off to the fat old slag. See if I care. And take your stinking dog with you." He had this pit bull, y'see.'

'Bor could be the dog,' said Collar.

'Bloody ain't.' The royal-blue track suit rolled into a tight ball, like a hedgehog.

'He's little enough,' Denzil grinned. 'Trouble is, he'd never bite anybody. 'Cause he's chicken – aincha, Bor?'

'No!' Boreham screwed up his eyes and folded his arms around his head.

'Chicken . . . chicken. Kwaa . . . kwaa . . .' Denzil and Collar began to walk around, arms winged, moving in sharp, quick little jerks. Cast down glances darted everywhere. Feet, booted and sneakered, were slowly lifted and put down again with splayed out, finicky precision. It was very funny and, considering their sole experience of the real thing had been via Iceland's frozen-food cabinet, amazingly accurate.

Brian hugged himself, rocking backwards and forwards

on his non-existent bottom at these inventive and exuberant *ad hoc* measures. Then Denzil pecked Collar, who flapped his arms wildly in response and started to run about in all directions, squawking loudly.

Brian climbed wearily to his feet. Clapping his hands yet again and with much the same effect, he called: 'OK. Kill the impro. That's enough.'

Plainly it was not. The fowl play continued. Boreham, seeing his teasing compatriots were safely engaged elsewhere, decided after all to occupy the role of pit bull. He ran on all fours to where Brian was standing and started savaging his trousers.

'Stop that, Boreham.' Then, thinking a jovial note might restore the status quo, 'Down boy!' Little Bor lifted his leg.

Tom and Edie sat, unnaturally still and self-contained, watching. There was something about the quality of their attention, as they took in Brian's dilemma, that disturbed him. He sensed both pity and relish, in which he was half right.

'Everyone? Listen . . .' He put a friendly chuckle into the words. Bor, encouraged, gave an extra matey nudge and Brian crashed to the floor.

At this point the swing door was pushed open and Miss Panter, the head's secretary, showed in two men. One, tall and heavily built, wore a tweed overcoat. The second, slim as a whip, was wrapped in black leather. Only Brian did not recognise the intruders immediately for what they were.

'Mr Clapton?'

'Yes.'

The older man came over and showed Brian a card with a photograph on. 'Chief Inspector Barnaby, Causton CID. We'd like a word, please.'

'Of course.' Brian scrambled up awkwardly. 'What about?'

'In private.'

The younger man held the door open and Brian followed them out, unaware that his stock had just zoomed from rock bottom to something approaching gilt-edged.

They walked briskly towards the headmaster's office, Brian, who happened to be in the middle, with the air of a squaddie being escorted to the jail house.

Troy had re-entered the portals of his Alma Mater with a certain swagger but no sense of nostalgia or pride. He had hated school. But, knowing from an early age what he wanted to be when he grew up, he had worked hard at the subjects that bored him as well as the few (social studies, computer science) that, just about, held his interest. He also avoided mixing with any hard-line bunking-off troublemakers. His ferocity at games, which kept him off the sports field almost as much as on, also kept him free of the jeering hassle any consistent attempts at serious study would otherwise have provoked. Now, striding over stained brown haircord down well-remembered corridors he muttered, 'God, I loathe this place.'

Barnaby had finished his own schooling in the early fifties, before the local grammar had been integrated, but his daughter had been through the comprehensive system, eventually winning an exhibition to Cambridge. The Barnabys had been members of the PTA during her time at 'this place' and both had been impressed by the dedication of the teachers – often, it had seemed to them, in the face of overwhelming odds.

'Cully came here, didn't she, chief?'

'That's right.' Barnaby spoke abruptly. He had never

become indifferent to the wistful leer in men's voices when they spoke his daughter's name.

The head, Mr Hargreave, had vacated his office for their purposes and Miss Panter showed them in. Brian took the chair behind the desk, although a two-seater settee and large armchair were both empty. Barnaby, mindful of his earlier experience, sat on the edge of the sofa. Miss Panter returned with a tray of tea and some Garibaldi biscuits. Troy poured out, setting a cup in front of Brian.

'There you go, Mr Clapton.'

'What's all this about?'

Barnaby thought the man's bewilderment was probably genuine. The murder had not made the one o'clock news and, according to the main office, Brian had received no telephone calls that morning. Troy was taking advantage of the lull to despatch as many Garibaldis as he was able without appearing to push them non-stop into his mouth. He was starving. Parched too (down went the tea), plus, needless to say, desperate for a fag. He caught the chief's eye and replaced morsel number five on the plate.

'Delicious,' he said, opening his notebook. 'Squashed-fly biscuits we used to call them.'

'I'm afraid,' began Barnaby, when Brian had finished his tea, 'that I have some bad news.'

'Mandy!' The cup clattered into the saucer, spilling the dregs.

'No, no.' Barnaby hastily offered reassurance. 'Nothing to do with your daughter.'

Troy watched as a little colour crept back into Brian's deathly countenance. I shall be like that, he thought, when Talisa Leanne starts school. I shall never have a moment's peace. The insight affected him physically, a cold gripe in the guts. As he struggled to put it aside Barnaby was explaining the reason for their visit.

'*Gerald!*' Amazement had barely registered before excited, almost pleasurable, interest took its place. The word 'gleeful' might have been appropriate. He said, in a crisp, self-satisfied manner, 'I myself was with him only yesterday.'

'We're aware of that, Mr Clapton.' Barnaby, who had no time for false displays of grief, had even less time for naked enjoyment in the face of violent death. 'Could you tell—'

'It was a most peculiar evening.'

'Really? In what way?'

'Tensions. Hidden tensions.' Brian tossed back long but sparse ginger hair. 'Visible none the less to a really perceptive person. Which of course, as a writer, one has to be.'

Barnaby nodded encouragingly and sat back to be a bit more comfy. This one was plainly going to run and run.

'I'm in charge of drama here . . .'

Brian spoke at length and was very frank, as people often are who have little worth concealing. Troy took advantage, resting his Biro, and managed to put away two more squashed-fly biscuits before the chief steered it all back to hidden tensions. Perhaps Mr Clapton could expand?

'Gerald was behaving very oddly. Unnaturally quiet. And couldn't wait to get rid of us.'

'What about the others?'

'Spent the whole time gushing over our visiting "celebrity". What a reactionary fossil he turned out to be. Not a clue about contemporary drama. Not surprising, the stuff he churns out.'

107

'You don't admire Mr Jennings' novels?'

'Never read them. Got better things to do with my time.'

'Can you recall who first suggested inviting him?' Barnaby watched Brian's reaction write itself across his face. He didn't know. He hated to admit he didn't know. But if he made an answer up he might be proved wrong, thus losing face even more notably.

'You'll have to leave that with me, chief inspector.' Brian stroked his beard thoughtfully. He had grown it as soon as he was physically able, to hide the numerous large pink shiny warts on his chin.

Troy, who had got Brian well sussed, curled his lip. He could just see the little squit asking round, finding the answer and phoning in having 'just remembered'. What a piss artist.

'Did you talk to Mr Hadleigh during the course of the evening? Get any idea why he was so withdrawn?'

'Not really. The conversation was general. As I've already explained.' He spoke tersely and glanced at his watch.

'Do you have any idea who might be responsible for Mr Hadleigh's death?'

'Me?' In the centre of his bushy beard Brian's wet, pink lips rounded to a wet, pink O, like the orifice of some tentacular sea creature. 'What do you mean?'

'I'd've thought the question pretty clear, sir,' murmured Troy.

'But you're surely not— I mean . . .'

Here we go, thought Troy, pinching the final biscuit. Altogether now, one, two, three: break-in, break-in. Wasn't it a break-in? Brian did not let him down.

'There was no sign of a forced entry, sir,' replied

Barnaby, omitting for the moment the matter of an unsecured kitchen. 'Would you describe Mr Hadleigh as a cautious person?'

'In what way?'

'Might he for instance be likely to open the door to just anyone late at night?'

'Doubt it. You know what they're like, the professional classes. Piling up more stuff than any person could possibly need in one lifetime then frightened to death someone else might get a bite of their cherry.' Troy snorted at the unconscious *double entendre* then turned his snort into a cough. 'He'd got a door chain, window locks, burglar alarm. They all have round the Green.'

'Given the present climate,' said Barnaby dryly, 'they'd be foolish to do otherwise.'

'But all this hardware's just a challenge to a really enterprising kid,' cried Brian. 'I've tried to explain this but will they listen?' He sighed briefly over the intransigence of the bourgeoisie. 'You should see Laura Hutton's place – been there yet?' Barnaby shook his head. 'Like the Bastille.'

'She's probably got a lot of fancy pieces,' said Troy. 'Being in the trade, like.'

'Some trade. Ripping off pensioners then selling the stuff at fifty times the price.'

'An attractive woman all the same,' murmured Barnaby, recalling his purchase of Joyce's footstool.

'If you like tall redheaded icebergs with more money than they know what to do with.' If? thought Troy. *If?* This man was round the twist. 'Personally I've always found her completely unreal.'

'You were Mr Hadleigh's nearest neighbour—'

'Only geographically. We didn't mix.'

'He was a widower, I understand. Would you happen to

know if he was ... well ... emotionally involved with anyone at the time of his death?'

'If you mean having it off,' said Brian, with forthright contempt, 'why don't you say so? The answer's no. At least not with anyone in Midsomer Worthy.'

'How come you're so sure, Mr Clapton?' asked Troy.

'Easy to see you don't live in a village. Half the people there've got nothing better to do, once they've finished the *Times* crossword and checked their share prices, but stare out of the window. They don't miss a trick, believe me.'

'I wonder if there is anything you could tell us about Mr Hadleigh's background?'

'A civil servant who had taken early retirement. And we all know what that means. A platinum handshake and a fat pension all out of the taxpayer's pocket. I've no time for people of that ilk.' He caught the chief inspector's eye and seemed to read something there that stayed his tongue. He paused, then added, rather awkwardly, 'I'm sorry that he's dead, of course.'

'I'm sure,' said Barnaby. 'Now – if we could get back to yesterday evening. You left Plover's Rest when exactly?'

'Ten fifteen.'

'And then?'

'Home, where else? Marked some essays for the morning and went to bed.'

'Sleep well?'

'Oh yes. Do a *proper* day's work and you have no trouble dropping off.'

The look he gave them underlined the implication in his words. Barnaby, though he had experienced in his long career tiredness so absolute that, waking or sleeping, he seemed to be trudging endlessly down a dark corridor of exhaustion in iron boots, rode this supercilious attack with ease. Troy took it personally, as he did everything, and reacted as if stung.

'So, just to recap,' said Barnaby, 'you went home, did some checking and went to bed.'

'Yes, yes.' Brian shot his cuff and studied his watch. He managed to give the impression that though everyone else in the room might have world enough and time, his own was very tightly structured, crammed with exciting incident and that a plane for LA was standing by even as they spoke.

'In other words, you did not go out at all?'

'No.' After a lengthy pause Brian picked up his cup, put it down again. Coughed. Blew his nose and peered into his hanky before putting it back into his pocket.

'Mrs Clapton, on the other hand,' said Sergeant Troy quietly (almost as if musing to himself), 'seemed to have had a lot of trouble dropping off. She was still awake in the small hours. Heard Max Jennings drive away.'

'Really.'

'Yes. Really.'

There was an even longer pause during which the two policemen exchanged confident, almost amused glances not missed (and not meant to be missed) by the interviewee. They were both enjoying his predicament but Troy more so for he had, by nature, an unkind heart.

Brian removed his glasses and polished them. They were little and round with cruel steel rims. The type that even good-looking people cannot wear to advantage.

'You understand why we are asking this question, Mr Clapton?' Barnaby said eventually.

'Um . . .'

'Mr Hadleigh's murder took place between eleven and the early hours of this morning.'

111

Barnaby eased himself off the sofa and stood, a big broad man, towering over the desk. His expression was paternal. He smiled down at Brian with deep, confidence-inducing expectation and waited. It didn't take long.

'Oh!' Brian struck his forehead with the palm of his hand. 'I did pop out. Just for a quick turn around the Green. To blow the cobwebs away.' He looked up, half wary, half seeking approval, and gave a rather infantile smile.

'See anyone?'

'No,' Brian said, adding, lest there should be the slightest confusion, 'no one at all.'

'Well, I think that's it.' Having got his way Barnaby let his jaws part in a smile. 'For now.'

'Thank you,' said Brian.

As they were leaving the office Miss Panter called out, 'Mr Clapton? Your wife rang just after your meeting started. She said it was urgent. If you'd like to call her back by all means use my phone.'

'I'm that hungry.' Troy, caught up in the Causton one-way system, crept around the market square, which was crammed with stalls covered in bright awnings and traders shouting out impossible never-to-be-repeated bargains.

'You want to rob me, darling?' yelled a man holding a cauliflower in each hand. 'Come and rob me. I'm ready, willing and past it.'

'*You're* hungry?' Barnaby made his irritation plain. His sergeant's capacity to lower endless piles of highly calorific foodstuffs without ever putting the slightest pressure on his belt had long been a sore point. 'You've just seen off half the contents of Huntley and Palmer's warehouse. How on earth can you be hungry?'

'Perhaps we could pop into the canteen for a lash-up.' Troy turned right and pushed aggressively into a traffic jam inching along the High Street. 'After we've seen Mrs Hutton. And speak of the devil . . .'

They had ground to a halt on a level with the Magpie's shop front. A CLOSED sign hung on the door. There was a large tapestry hanging in the window showing a Bruegelesque scene of unbridled merrymaking. Rosy-cheeked burghers banged foaming tankards on rough-hewn planks. Snowy coifed buxoms fell out of their frocks, children in hand-cobbled footwear stuffed their faces with hunks of bread and one man lay flat on his face in the mud. Troy regarded it thoughtfully.

'Bit like our Christmas social.'

No response. Why do I bother? he asked himself. Working my buns off trying to bring a little jollity into the miserable bugger's life and for what? Might as well save my breath. I shall get one of Mrs Clapton's dragons for the back window. Thank You For Not Laughing In Our Car.

'Odd her being closed on a Wednesday. You'd think it'd be the busiest day.'

'She must have heard about Hadleigh. I imagine there's been quite a ring-round going on. She might still be on the premises. There's narrow opening just here . . .'

Troy swung on the wheel.

'I said narrow!'

'OK. OK.' Troy responded sharply as he always did to any adverse comment on his driving. And there was certainly no problem on this occasion. Twice the width of the paint. At least.

He pulled into the large asphalt parking area at the rear of the Magpie which it shared with the Blackbird bookshop next door. A Ford Transit van and a scarlet

Porsche in beautiful condition were parked there. Over the solid rear door of the Magpie was a British Telecom burglar alarm. The door itself was secured by two mortice deadlocks and flanked by long rectangular windows which were heavily barred. Barnaby knocked once and then again more firmly. There was not the slightest reverberation. He could have been rapping a block of concrete. He pressed his ear to the jamb, but could pick up no response. Troy slipped his hands through the iron bars and tapped on the glass.

'Someone in there, chief. I think they're coming.' He took off his headgear, smoothed his hair and replaced the cap at a more rakish angle. Then he turned up his coat collar and rounded off the transformation by allowing a half smile, warm and, he hoped, mysteriously compelling, to play lightly about his lips. A shadow appeared on the glass and a voice, promisingly husky it seemed to Troy, said, 'What is it?'

'Causton CID, Mrs Hutton,' said Barnaby. 'Like a word, please.'

A bolt was withdrawn and then a second, heavier and needing a spot of oil. A chain rattled, a key turned in one of the mortice locks. Troy, holding his breath, realised he had lost his light but compelling smile and hurriedly tacked it on again.

'I shouldn't bother, Gavin.'

'Sir?'

'She's too old for you.'

The smile vanished and Troy looked perturbed. This was not so much at having his mind read – the chief had always been good at that (far too good actually) – but by the heretical suggestion that anyone with more money than they knew what to do with could possibly have a sell-by date.

'Come in.'

Laura Hutton was standing behind the door, covering her face. Barnaby presented his card. She didn't even glance at it, but walked away towards a tiny office of glass and tongue-and-groove boarding which had been made by enclosing a small corner of the large, high-ceilinged space through which she was now leading them.

Barnaby looked around him. He could have been in the props room of Joyce's amateur theatre group. Furniture stacked on top of itself, paintings two or three deep facing the wall. Ornaments. Cardboard boxes, with lot numbers stamped on, crammed with old cutlery and other household junk.

Her office had a tiny antique desk, the surface almost invisible beneath a Macintosh LC, telephone, fax and answering machine. The air was scented by a soapy fragrance. Barnaby guessed that she had probably heard his first knock and had washed her face in the pretty flowered hand basin before coming to the door. If this was in an attempt to conceal the fact that she had been crying it had failed, one could say miserably.

Her face was screwed up with distress and, even as Barnaby apologised for the intrusion, her eyes shimmered and brimmed with fresh moisture. At last, he thought, someone is weeping for Gerald Hadleigh.

'I'm sorry.' She caught the tears, now pouring down her cheeks, with the brightly coloured silk square in her hand. 'It's the shock . . .'

Oh, more than that. The chief inspector watched her mouth, once speech had stopped, fall into a slack, grief-stricken curve. Much more than that.

'Then you know why we're here, Mrs Hutton?'

'Yes. I can't believe it. Can't . . .' Her narrow shoulders

shook and she covered her eyes with her hands. She said 'sorry' again.

'I shouldn't have let you in. I thought I could cope.'

Barnaby hesitated, unsure whether to continue. Not out of sensitivity. He was a sensitive man but it had never stopped him doing extremely insensitive things if he had to. But because he could see that she might, in all probability, go to pieces. He'd get nowhere and next time her memories of the present encounter could well make questioning her that much more difficult. He said, 'Would you like us to come back another time?'

'No. Not now you're here.' Laura reached out and switched off the desk light. In the dimness that ensued she seemed slightly more comfortable. She sat down in a padded swivel chair, the only seating in the room. Troy rested his notebook on the filing cabinet and only hoped he could read his writing. Barnaby leaned against the door. 'Though I don't quite understand what you want.'

'Just a word about last night, Mrs Hutton.'

'I see.' She obviously didn't see and her dull, lifeless voice indicated that neither did she care.

'How your meeting went, for instance.'

'The meeting? But what has that to do with . . .' She appeared not to be able to say his name.

'Did you notice anything different about Mr Hadleigh at all?'

'Yes. He barely spoke to anyone, which was unlike him. He was never a garrulous man, but he enjoyed talking about writing. I expected him to seize the opportunity to ask lots of questions.'

'Did you get the impression that this withdrawal was in any way connected with the visiting speaker?'

'No, not really. Although . . . it's strange you should say

that. Because when Max Jennings' name first came up he—'

'You mean Mr Hadleigh?'

'Yes, he was very put out. He actually dropped his coffee. You can still see the stain.'

'He was opposed to the idea?'

'I wouldn't put it as strongly as that. He just seemed to think it was a waste of time. We're always asking well-known authors to come and talk to us and they never do. But in the end he agreed to ask.'

'Why was it down to him, Mrs Hutton?' asked Sergeant Troy.

'He was the group's secretary.'

'A lonely business, writing,' said the chief inspector, as people always do who've never done it. 'What's your line exactly?'

'I'm transcribing a mass of papers I came by at a sale in Aylesbury. A lot of recipes – or "receipts" as they were called then – plus notes on running a Tudor household, animal husbandry, herbal medicines . . .' Laura hesitated then stopped at the realisation that this fiction was no longer necessary. Would never be necessary again.

'Another *Diary of an Edwardian Lady* perhaps?' She shrugged. 'Did you all leave together yesterday evening?'

'Except for Rex, which was a bit odd.'

'In what way, Mrs Hutton?' asked Troy. He smiled, but without calculation, for he could see, even in this light, that she was indeed not only too old for him but consumed by an utterly private wretchedness in which any flirtatious gesture would be grotesquely ill placed.

'He usually dashes straight off. Sometimes before the rest of us. Worries about his dog.'

Troy nodded understandingly. He loved dogs and had a

magnificent young German Shepherd, brindled cream and grey, an ex-police dog wounded during a stake-out and consequently of no further use to the Force. He asked Mrs Hutton if she had gone straight home after the meeting and she said yes.

'And you got home when?' asked Barnaby.

'Just before half past ten. I only live a short distance away.'

'And you didn't go out again?' She shook her head. 'Mr Hadleigh . . . would you say he was popular in the village?'

'I've really no idea. I'm not involved in parish-pump matters.'

'He was a widower I understand?'

'That's right – a grieving widower.' Her harsh voice cracked. Barnaby saw her hands clench into fists as she fought for control. She stared hard at the computer screen. 'I have to be in Gerrards Cross in half an hour to look at some furniture. I'm sorry, but I'm afraid I'll have to ask you to leave now.'

'More to that than meets the eye,' said Troy, never one to mint a new phrase when an old one still had mileage. 'My mum's mad on that Edwardian Diary stuff. Every Christmas, every birthday, that's all she's on about. Tea towel, chopping board, egg cups, tea cosy – she's got the lot. The family's getting desperate. Soon there'll only be the book left.'

'That is desperate,' said Barnaby.

'Lunch then, chief?'

'God, yes please.'

It was nearly three and the station canteen was half empty. Barnaby, mindful of his five-hundred-calorie allowance, took a lean beef and salad sandwich with slimmer's mayonnaise to a separate table, unable to bear the sight of his sergeant's robust scoffing.

Afterwards they drove back to Midsomer Worthy, beating the four o'clock bus by five minutes. It was almost dark when they parked once more outside the gates of Borodino. The bus stopped a few yards away and several people got off. Some crossed the Green, others disappeared in the opposite direction. Only three people advanced towards the policemen – a young girl with a child in a pushchair and an immensely tall, very thin elderly man who loped along in a slack, disjointed manner, long legs quite out of concordance, each apparently quite unaware of the other's existence. He was festooned with shopping, most prominently an old-fashioned string bag stuffed with bloody parcels wrapped in newspaper. He also carried several books encircled by a tightly buckled belt, the strap of which was looped through his braces. His silver hair was in constant movement, flowing softly around his head like a shining puffball. As he came closer they could see that he was smiling, happily but inwardly, in an appreciative, reminiscent sort of way. As he opened the gate Barnaby got out of the car and crossed towards him.

'Mr St John?'

'Yes.' He looked from one to the other. The smile became hopeful and interested. 'Hullo.'

'We're police officers.' Barnaby proffered his wallet. 'Could we have a word, sir?'

'Good heavens. Come in, come in.'

They were all on the path when Rex, turning to close the gate, spotted the portable pod. 'Just look at that. Honoria will be quite enraged. She hates the gypsies. I myself feel one should live and let live. Is that why you're here?'

Barnaby replied with a simple negative. He felt bad news could keep until they were at least inside the house. Rex produced a large, iron key from beneath a well-worn doormat and slid it into the equally large keyhole. A ceramic plate, painted with the words CAVE CANEM, was screwed to the door. As he opened it, and just before he stepped inside, Rex shouted, 'Stand back' over his shoulder.

As they entered there was a tremendous series of deep, thunderous barks and a shuddering bump as of a great weight hitting the floor overhead. Then a heavy pounding and a huge grey beast appeared, tumbling and rolling down the stairs before galloping to where Rex stood and rearing up on its back legs to embrace him.

Troy was impressed. He'd seen some dogs. Thought he had a dog and a half himself. But this one was really something. It had the size and bulk of a rough-haired, bantam-weight donkey. A generous length of rosy-pink felt unrolled itself from the animal's mouth and, after first courteously sloshing all over Rex's face and clothing, came to rest on its real objective, the string bag.

'It's the bones.' Rex looked apologetic. 'I'll have to give him one otherwise we'll have no peace.'

Troy nodded understandingly. Barnaby did not. As has been previously explained he had no interest in animals unless they were arranged in tender, nicely sauced portions around the edge of a dinner plate.

Rex opened a door, deeply scored with scratches, on their left and indicated that they should enter before he disappeared, the dog, drooling and snorting, at his heels.

Barnaby sat down on an elderly leather chaise-longue which prickled even through his overcoat. Troy, interested immediately in the contents of the room, wandered round.

Three walls were lined with open shelves containing model figures of soldiers standing to attention or displaying their skill with musket and cannon. Little trays overflowed with badges and buttons. On the fourth wall were glass cases of medals, two gas masks and recruiting posters from the First and Second World Wars. Barnaby faced an angry-looking man with a walrus moustache who pointed a stern finger over the command: Kitchener Wants You! Hanging over the back of a chair was a short braided cape and pill-box hat. The hat had a narrow leather chin strap.

On a table covered with green baize, which took up most of the room, a battle was in progress. A phalanx of dark-skinned soldiers wearing tasselled hats and strange robes advanced in waves of historical caricature towards a large grey wall, pushing heavy cannon from the mouths of which depended tiny balls of fluffed-out cotton wool. Everything was rather dusty.

Rex entered holding a bottle of Tizer and three plastic tumblers stacked inside each other. He kicked the door to behind him, saying, 'Best shut the noise out.'

And indeed the noise was formidable. Great crunchings and splinterings accompanied all the while by mumbling growls. A sort of canine fee-fi-fo-fum. With his free hand Rex let down the flap of an ugly, dark-stained bureau. Inside was an assortment of snack food; crisps, chocolate bars, cheesy biscuits, boiled sweets. There was even a jar of pickled onions. He poured out the Tizer and handed it round.

'Now,' he indicated his schoolboy hoard with a trembly, liver-spotted hand. 'What can I offer you?'

'Nothing, thank you,' said the chief inspector.

'There's a fine selection here.' He waved it into focus again. 'Sweet or savoury. Ice cream if you prefer. A fridge full. Strawberry or vanilla. I'm afraid the macadamia brittle's run out.'

'No, honestly.'

'Or I've got some posh nuts.' This offer also being refused Rex made his way to a worn, old armchair, pausing briefly to adjust the folds of the cape and the tilt of the little round hat.

'These are Montcalm's. He wears them at the onset of every fresh manoeuvre. In his role as regimental mascot you know.'

The minds of both policemen boggled.

Rex waved at the table. 'The Siege of Constantinople. A thrilling confrontation though, of course, with dreadful odds. The end of the Byzantine empire. Only four thousand dead but fifty thousand sold into slavery. Ahh . . .' he included both men in his sweet, pacific smile, 'they knew how to do it in those glory days. I ask you, where's the fun in just pressing a button? Well,' he lowered himself, slowly and with considerable care, into his seat, 'I expect you're waiting to tell me why you're here.'

Barnaby told him why they were there. Sitting in the room of pantomimic warfare and toy soldiers and explosions made of cotton wool, he described Gerald Hadleigh's real, true death in plain language.

The effect on Rex St John was extraordinary. He stared blankly at the wall for a long moment, his mouth agape, then flung his hands over his ears as if it were possible to shut out what he had already heard. His head shook violently to and fro and he shouted, 'It isn't true, it isn't true . . .' He was shaking like a leaf in the wind.

Barnaby crossed the room and touched the old man on the shoulder. 'Are you all right, sir?'

'I did it. Oh God – it was me—'

'Just a moment, Mr St John.' Barnaby removed his hand. Troy got quickly to his feet. 'Are you confessing to the murder of Gerald Hadleigh? If so it is my duty to warn you that anything—'

'It was my *fault*. He asked me to protect him and I let him down.' Rex's fingers were twisted around each other like a lattice of freckled twigs. 'What have I done? Gerald . . . ohh . . .'

Barnaby carried one of the wooden dining chairs up closer to the armchair, sat down and said, 'I think you'd better tell us all about it. And take your time, there's no hurry. No hurry at all.'

But Rex started talking straight away. It was as if he couldn't wait to get rid of the terrible words in his mouth. They tumbled out, like the evil spirits in Pandora's box, telling the story. How Gerald had begged not to be left alone with Max Jennings. How Rex had promised to stay till the man had left and been tricked into leaving. How he'd gone home, come back and hung around in the rain. Felt afraid, believed himself to be observed and returned home again. By the time he had finished he was crying.

'Try and calm down a bit, sir. It's early days to take all this on your shoulders. For all we know Mr Jennings may have nothing to do with the matter at all.'

'Oh but surely . . .' Rex produced a large khaki square decorated with a bear and a ragged staff, the insignia of the Royal Warwickshires, and rubbed his eyes.

'This conversation you've just described with Mr Hadleigh, when did it take place?'

'Yesterday morning. He was very embarrassed. I got the impression he'd put it off till the last moment.'

'Did he give you any idea why he didn't want to be left alone with Jennings?'

'Not really. Just that they'd known each other several years ago and there had been some sort of upset. "A certain amount of unpleasantness" was how Gerald put it. He admitted he'd written the invitation in such a way as to discourage a visit.'

'So why write at all?' asked Troy.

'Brian got all Bolshie when Gerald demurred and said he'd do it himself. I suppose he – Gerald I mean – thought at least this way matters remained in his own hands.'

'Do you remember who first suggested asking Mr Jennings?'

'I'm afraid not.'

'Did you get the feeling that Hadleigh was actually afraid of such a meeting?'

Rex frowned so deeply he seemed to be in pain. 'It's tempting, isn't it, to be wise after the event? But, to be honest, although he seemed apprehensive, I wouldn't have put it as strongly as "afraid".'

'And he didn't appear to be so during the course of the evening?'

'Not really. Quiet and very withdrawn. I must say Max was a most affable and friendly person. Of course he may have said things, unkind things I mean, that only Gerald would have understood the meaning of.'

'You've described what happened when you left the house. What makes you so sure it was Jennings who bolted the door?'

'Because Gerald couldn't possibly have reached it in time. He was at the far end of the hall.'

'And then you went home?'

'Yes,' whispered Rex, hanging his flossy head.

'What time was that?'

'I'm afraid I didn't notice. But I do know what time I

went back. Twelve five ack emma. That was when I saw Brian – Mr Clapton.'

'Oh yes?'

'Coming back from the village.'

'You sure about that, Mr St John?' asked Sergeant Troy. 'That he was coming back from that direction and not from a walk round the Green?'

'Quite sure. Then I went round the back of the house—'

'Where you felt someone was watching you?'

'They were standing in the trees on the edge of the wood. I got this awful creepy crawling down my backbone. It was dark. I became frightened and ... deserted my post.'

'I shouldn't be too hard on yourself, Mr St John,' said Barnaby, knowing he was wasting his breath.

'But to be so ... so womanish.'

Womanish, thought Troy. He wants to meet some of the women I've come across. They'd have his legs for breakfast. He said, 'Why do you think Mr Hadleigh chose you to help him in this matter?'

'I'm not really sure.' A blush of shame mantled Rex's still damp cheeks as he recalled the excitement and happy curiosity that had consumed him after Gerald had left.

'You weren't especially friendly then?'

'Gerald didn't seem to have any close friends. Neither do I, of course, now. They've all become casualties of time. I asked him round when he first moved in. That was 1983. The year that bomb in the Lebanon destroyed an embassy. Just courtesy, you know. He turned up and was nicely civil but nothing came of it. I expect I bored him with my war games.'

'Did he speak about his past at all?'

'Not really. But he did tell me he was a widower and that he moved here because he couldn't bear to go on living where his wife had died.'

'Did he say what part of the world that was?'

'Somewhere in Kent I think. He took early retirement from the Civil Service.'

'Any idea what branch? Or where?'

'I got the feeling it was the Min of Ag and Fish, although I don't suppose they call it that nowadays. And it was in London I know because he said what a terrible fag the journey was.'

'Do you have any idea when his wife died?'

'Just before he moved here so that would be nine – no, ten years ago.'

'And do you know if Mr Hadleigh has been involved with anyone else since then?'

'Involved?' Rex looked completely baffled.

'An affair,' said Troy. Poor old devil. Probably been so long he'd forgotten what he'd got it for. You had to make allowances. 'Another woman?'

'Oh, I'm sure not. Although—'

At this point they were interrupted by a fierce scratching at the door. The noise was so loud the policemen half expected to see claws splintering through the wood.

'It's Montcalm. He's finished his tea.' Barnaby experienced a risible representation of the dog sitting up, a napkin round its neck, tucking daintily into a plate of cucumber sandwiches. 'I'll have to let him in.'

'We're almost finished, Mr St John.'

'But he doesn't like—' Rex broke off, head cocked. It had gone quiet outside. Montcalm padded away. Then, after a brief pause, they heard him return at a gallop which culminated in a tremendous crash. The door panels shivered mightily under the impact.

Rex said 'Sorry' and let the dog in, prudently closing up the tuck shop first. It trotted twice around the room, happily wagging its plumed tail, and knocking several soldiers flying. Then it scrambled up on to the chaise-longue beside its master, transferred itself to his knees and rested its great head against his cheek.

'We were discussing . . .' Barnaby broke off in some confusion. He found himself facing a pair of trousered legs, five feet of rough, grey, hairy hound and two intelligent, enquiring faces. It was like questioning some fabled beast from the realms of mythology.

'Emotional friendships.' Sergeant Troy came to the rescue. 'I think you were about to have second thoughts, sir.'

'Was I?'

'You said "although",' the chief inspector reminded him.

'Although what?'

Barnaby prayed for patience. Troy winked at the dog. It gave a cavernous yawn, its lolling tongue and sharp pointed teeth scarlet with bone juice.

'Ah yes,' remembered Rex. 'I used to wonder if Laura didn't have rather a pash.'

'Any special reason for thinking so?'

Barnaby asked the question while his sergeant relished 'pash' and vowed to try it out on WPC Brierley.

'Just that she was always watching him,' said Rex. 'With a certain expression. Rather like Montcalm when I'm about to open the Winalot.'

They talked for a while longer but Rex had little of note to add. Barnaby offered his thanks, then explained that it would be necessary for Rex to come to the mobile incident room or, after tomorrow, to the police station to have his fingerprints taken. On hearing this Rex perked up slightly, as if a visit to the pod was a sort of treat. Something to look forward to. Perhaps it was. Poor devil.

'Who'd be old,' said Barnaby, as they made their way back down the garden path.

'He's all right,' replied Troy. 'Got the soldiers. All those medals. Not to mention his posh nuts.'

'What the hell sort of dog do you call that anyway?'

'Irish wolfhound.'

'Make a great rug.' He strode across the Green (the grass was greyish-orange now in the sodium lighting) and climbed into the incident room. It was cosy inside and there was coffee on the go. A middle-aged couple, no doubt the last of many, were offering information which might or might not prove helpful.

Barnaby rang Amersham police station, asked them to check their electoral register for Max Jennings' address then, while he was waiting, helped himself to a warm drink. They rang back in just under ten minutes.

'Trouble is after a murder,' said Sergeant Troy, picking up the A413, 'people describe things differently from what they might have done otherwise.'

'You mean the way they talk about the victim?'

'That, yes. But their own experiences as well. Take St John – there he is, hanging around in Hadleigh's back yard, supposedly keeping an eye. Now he says there was someone in the woods watching him. But did he genuinely think so at the time?'

'Could be he's trying to persuade himself,' said the chief inspector, 'to excuse the fact that he cleared off.'

'Not much chance of proving it, what with the rain and Joe Public trampling all over the place.'

Barnaby did not reply. He was having a brief, silent rail at the malignant fates who had organised Gerald Hadleigh's murder the night before Causton's market day. If he had only talked to Rex earlier. Had got to know of the connection between the dead man and the visiting author. Naturally he had planned to talk to Jennings, but had presumed this would involve a few brief questions dealing mainly with the time of his departure. Bugger. In a word.

However, regret being a time-wasting and sterile occupation, Barnaby soon gave it up and turned his attention to Laura Hutton. In the light of her display of grief, Rex's suggestion of a pash seemed to be putting it mildly. It seemed to Barnaby that she must have loved the man – and fruitlessly, or why that rasping cry, 'That's right – a grieving widower'?

She had fought for control afterwards, plainly regretting the slip, and so determined to make no further revelation that she had turned her back on them to end the interview. And the remark had not only been bitter but shot through with sarcasm. Was this fuelled merely by the angry resentment of a woman scorned? Or did she know something about Hadleigh's private life that made a mockery of the man's public sorrow over the death of his wife? When she was calmer, if it still proved necessary, he would question her again. This conclusion returned him to the present and the realisation that they had stopped driving and had started flying.

'For God's sake! Do you want to spread us both over the tarmac?'

'Roads are fine now, sir.'

But Troy came down to fifty-five and forbore to comment on this further example of unjust criticism. He had never had an accident nor caused one to be had. Sailed through Police Advanced, than which there is no harder, with comparative ease. Practising his skills gave him immense pleasure. The fluid connection of clutch and gear change and finely balanced play of the wheel, the open landscape sweeping, tearing by or, conversely, the constant observation and eye for detail needed when negotiating town hazards. But he had no patience, which would forever stop him being quite as good as he thought he was. Especially he had no patience with what he thought of as his chief's excessive caution. But then, what could you expect of a man who drove an automatic? Not that 'drove' was in any way the appropriate term. You just sat in the thing and it trundled you about like an old cart horse. Troy had never heard of the Frenchman who thought the servants could do his living for him but would have immediately recognised, in the idle sod, your typical automatic driver.

Mirror, signal, manoeuvre and their headlights had swallowed up the Chalfonts and were already sweeping the pretty lanes of Warren d'Evercy. Troy cruised, checking right. Barnaby, taking the other side, was the one to spot the gates. As tall and elaborate as the ones at Gresham House but in a much more elegant state. A golden M in the centre of each was held in place by a wreath of acanthus leaves. The gates were flanked by sandstone pillars atop which were a pair of well-worn and aloof-looking griffins. Discreetly set into the side of the nearest pillar was a push button and grille. Barnaby pushed and spoke. After a crackling exchange with a deeply masculine foreign accent the gates swung open.

The drive was quite long and brightly lit by what appeared to be original Victorian street lamps. There were flower beds, presently full of winter pansies and rather formal groupings of shrubs. It was attractive enough but impersonal. A bit like a public park.

The house, whilst quite grand, was also markedly unoriginal in design. Styled after the manner of a Southern ante-bellum mansion, it was fronted by six white columns and grandly positioned behind an approach of marble steps. Troy sucked his teeth with admiration. Barnaby was less impressed. The building called to his mind the shrink-wrapped Parthenon of Pearl and Dean.

As he was looking over the carved wooden lintels for a bell one of the doors swung open and a short, swarthy man stepped out. He had naked feet and was wearing tight white 501s, a loose flower-patterned shirt and several gilt chains. His dark, curly hair was wet.

Troy flashed his warrant card, saying, 'Mr Jennings?'

'Stavros, I am butler.'

'Causton CID. We'd like a word with your employer, please.'

Stavros stepped back into the house and beckoned. The policemen found themselves in a large, circular hall with a domed ceiling from which depended a glittering and very lovely Venetian chandelier.

The butler set off down a corridor, leaving a trail of damp footprints. The walls of the corridor were lined with watermarked ivory silk and hung with ormolu mirrors and many original but unremarkable paintings. Overhead, at regular intervals, were more chandeliers, tiny spears of light, which shivered and tinkled as the three men walked beneath. They had passed several doors before Stavros halted in front of a mirrored wall some thirty feet in length. He pressed a button and, with a sweet, almost silent, click-clickety-click, the entire wall slowly started to fold up like a screen.

They stepped into what appeared to be a large orangery with a high, arched roof made of ribbed steel and shadowy apple-green glass. The place was crammed with exotic flora – palm trees in tubs, plants with huge fleshy leaves and Day-glo flowers the size of dinner plates, bananas and pineapples, climbers with hairy stems as thick as conger eels, giant cacti, hanging swags of richly perfumed orchids. All of this stuff dripping with moisture in the thick, steaming air.

Stavros having vanished, Barnaby and Troy crunched forward over grass of such a sizzling emerald hue it could only be fake. Discreetly dispersed amongst all this lush exuberance were various pieces of gleaming sports equipment that peered through the foliage like shy jungle creatures. Invisible speakers introduced the mellow Herb Alpert's Tijuana Brass.

Barnaby and his sergeant made their way around various artificially raised beds, avoiding (or in Troy's case tripping over) snaking hoses, before finally coming up against a filmy curtain of delicate fern. Close to they could hear rhythmical splashing. Troy pushed the curtain aside. Stepped forward. Caught his breath.

A long, narrow pool lined with turquoise tiles of such brilliance that the water shone like liquid lapis lazuli. The flowers and trees came to the very edge of the pool so that the woman, slowly swimming up and down, seemed not to be in a man-made environment at all but in some hidden grotto on a tropical island. Her coppery limbs emerged, dark and glowing, from a white one-piece swimsuit. She turned on her back and her hair streamed softly about her head.

Troy stood and stared, entranced. Surely this was Hollywood. Hollywood and Beverly Hills and Dallas,

Texas. He let out his breath in a long, satiated sigh of pleasure. The woman got out and stood for a moment, water streaming from her wide bronzed shoulders and endless elegance of legs. As she turned and walked away, her neck, wrists and ankles flashed fire and Troy thought: my God – she's swimming in her jewels. *Swimming in her jewels.*

He mopped his forehead before slipping off his jacket and carrying it in such a way as to conceal his own fireworks. Then he followed the boss, who was picking his way carefully over the ersatz turf.

They caught up with her in a clearing containing several loungers and wicker armchairs, none of which they were invited to occupy during the conversation that followed. There was also a drinks cart. She started to shovel shavings of ice into a tumbler with a little silver trowel, added a huge slug of gin and a quick squirt of juice from a plastic lemon. Barnaby said:

'Mrs Jennings?'

'Yes.'

'We were hoping to speak to your husband.'

'Oh?' She threw the gin down her throat and picked up the bottle again. 'What about?'

A hiccupy grunt, 'Whabah?' She climbed up on to a bar stool with some difficulty and regarded them with singular lack of interest.

'Is he here?' asked the chief inspector. He was wondering how old she was. The flesh on her face seemed unnaturally taut compared to that on her calves and inner thighs. The backs of her hands were veiny and her eyes, though set in wrinkle-free surroundings, were knowing and exhausted.

'No.' She did not elaborate. Just carried on sipping.

'When do you expect him back, Mrs Jennings?' Troy's excitement subsided as he noticed the neat roll of fat around his goddess's middle and those tired, knowledge-able eyes.

'Haven't the foggiest.'

'Perhaps you could tell us what time he arrived home last night?'

'Took three dream-easies. Wouldn't know if the end of the world arrived last night.'

'This meeting he attended – at Midsomer Worthy?' She didn't reply. Just peered at Barnaby intently as if he was slowly becoming invisible. 'Had he discussed it with you at all?'

'No.' She trowelled in more icy slush, drowned it in Beefeaters, gave it a mere flirtation with the plastic lemon. Glug-glug-glug.

'It didn't, did it?'

'I'm sorry?'

'Turn up last night.'

'What's that, Mrs Jennings?'

'The end of the world.'

'No.'

'Just my fucking luck.'

'Any idea where we might catch up with your husband?' said Troy. She didn't seem to understand the question at all. Impatience followed disenchantment. He said, extra loudly, 'Where has he gone?'

'Finland.'

'*Finland!*'

'Signing books.'

'How long for?'

'Ask his so-called secretary. Bouncing Barbara. They're thick as thieves.'

'Do you know what time he left?'

'Better talk to Stavros. He runs everything. Hot breakfasts, nice clean clothes, perfect pool maintenance. Pity he's such a rotten lay.'

She presented her back to them. Barnaby thanked her, turned on his heel (snapping the head off a crimson blossom) and withdrew.

'No wonder he's shoved off,' said Troy as they went to look for the butler. The sergeant had no time for neurotic women. To be fair he had no time for neurotic men either. Troy liked people to be simple and uncomplicated, which was how he saw himself.

'That sort of caper though' – he meant the book signing – 'funny way to do a runner. A bit high profile isn't it?'

'Well at least he's gone somewhere we can extradite him.' Sweat was pouring down Barnaby's face. His clothes were sticking to his skin. 'God I'm glad to get out of that swamp.'

They found the butler in the kitchen, an area so dazzlingly comprehensive in its display of unusual and inventive equipment that it was hard to believe the place existed merely for the preparation of food. Stavros was sitting at a stainless steel table reading *Taxythromos*.

'Mr Stavros?' said Troy.

'Stavro.'

'Pardon me?'

'I am Stavros Stavro.'

'Oh. Right. Well Mr Stavro, we'd like a word.'

'I am all legal.' The Greek got hurriedly to his feet, folding up his magazine. 'Visa, papers, everything, for six months. I show you—' He started to leave in some agitation.

'Nothing to do with that,' said Barnaby. 'Just a few

questions about Mr Jennings. For instance, were you around when he got home last night?'

'I always wait up. The gates are opened from inside.'

'What time would that have been?'

'About one o'clock.'

'And what sort of spirits would you say he was in?' Stavros looked puzzled. 'Happy? Sad?'

'Ah – sad, yes. Quite and sad.'

'Did he say anything about the evening? How it had all gone?'

Stavros shook his head. 'We don't talk like . . . like . . .'

'Friends?' suggested Troy.

'*Neh – e filos*, friend. He just say the time to be called, then go to bed.'

'What sort of bloke is he? All right to work for?' Stavros shrugged.

'What about Mrs Jennings?'

Troy could not resist the question nor could he keep a knot of resentment from his voice. Whilst his own fancy for the lady had been fleeting, to say the least, he loathed the thought of this oily little tosser getting his end away between those cinnamon loins. He said:

'Tell us about this morning, Mr Stavro.'

'What about?'

'All about.'

'I wake Mr Jennings, six half with tea and run the bath. Then I pack for him—'

'What sort of things?'

'Country things, warm tops, shirts. He wear his favourite suit.'

'That wouldn't be the same one he had on last night by any chance?' asked Barnaby.

'Yes.' Stavros looked anxious at the chief inspector's sudden dark frown. 'Is there a mistake?'

'What time did he leave?'

'Nine and a half.'

'Did he say for where?'

'Heathrow.'

'And what did he actually take with him?'

'Two big cases and a handbag.'

'You what?' Troy's eyes widened with surprise.

'Briefcase, sergeant. Don't be obtuse.' Barnaby was getting more bad-tempered by the minute. 'Did Mr Jennings say when he'd be back?'

'No. Just he would telephone.'

'Where are the rest of the things he was wearing last night? Shirt, socks, underwear?'

'In the machine.'

'Washed?'

'Yes.'

'Brilliant.'

'*Then katalava* . . .'

Stavros was beginning to look most apprehensive.

'Did Mr Jennings ask you to wash the things straight away?'

'No. I always do in the morning.'

'Was there blood on them?' asked Troy.

'Blood! *Mitera tou theo* . . .'

'All right sir, calm down. Calm down.' Bloody foreigners. It was like being in the middle of an opera. Any minute now it'd be 'Nessun Dorma' and time for the kick-off.

'We shall need the washed clothes, Mr Stavro,' said Barnaby. 'Also the shoes and tie Mr Jennings wore last night if they're available. I trust the shoes have not been cleaned.'

'No.' Stavros looked even more apprehensive. 'I don't think to get into trouble.'

'You don't know what trouble is, sunshine,' said Sergeant Troy, 'until you refuse to help the police with their enquiries.'

Troy would have liked to reassure the butler further by suggesting that a refusal to comply might well mean the precious visa being shredded and flushed down the swanny, but thought better of it. The chief was strongly against threats for the sake of threats, preferring to save them for really tight corners from whence he had been known to fire such devices with the force of a howitzer.

'Someone will come along tomorrow from our scene-of-crime department to collect the stuff,' he was explaining now. 'Just point it all out to them. Don't handle anything yourself – all right? There's one more thing . . .'

Troy took down a detailed description of Max Jennings' Mercedes and the registration number.

Stavros saw them off the premises, perspiring with relief. As they climbed into the car he rose on the balls of his feet as if preparing for flight.

'Imagine living in that.' Barnaby, looking back at the house, spoke with a certain scorn. He wound the window down slightly, letting in a rush of pneumonia-bearing night air. 'Talk about medallion man writ large.'

Not knowing what to say, for he had loved the house and everything in it, Troy shivered and kept silent.

At roughly the time that Barnaby and Troy were speeding towards Warren d'Evercy, Sue Clapton, having washed up and cleared away, was preparing the next day's lunch boxes. Chopping celery and red cabbage for fibre, adding raisins for energy before mixing in walnuts (lineolic acid and vitamin B). Adding her own special lemon dressing in a little glass jar. Taking endless trouble as always, quite unaware that Mandy swapped the fresh salad and home-made bap each day for crisps, Coke and a Mars bar.

Sue's husband and daughter had both been late home. Brian had been whisked off by two of his colleagues for a drink after school where, quite misunderstanding their requests that he should tell them all about the drama, he had bored them both rigid with a mercilessly detailed update of *Slangwhang For Five Mute Voices*.

Amanda, casually mentioning that she'd only been fast asleep while a murder was going on next door, that's all, found her company, for the first time in her life, in great demand. The absolute superlative was when Haze Stitchley, who was well wicked and had her own gang, asked Mandy round after school for a takeaway and video (*Vampire Sex Slaves*).

Neither of them thought to ring Sue who, by the time they finally did arrive home, was frantic with worry. Mandy, smelling strongly of wine, was unrepentant. Brian, perhaps recalling his own moment of fear in the head's office, felt guilty. Guilt made him bluster and shout. Neither wanted any supper, a delicious steamed onion pudding with ginger sauce, so Sue ate alone, forcing food down a throat closed tight with anger. Now she added a Cox's pippin to Brian's box and fitted a ripe banana around Mandy's salad bowl.

Next door the television blared. Brian was laughing in the enforced, unnaturally loud way he had when he was not at all amused but desperate to take part in whatever Mandy was enjoying. Sue listened to them chortling away. Daddy and his little girl. She didn't understand how they could. Not when someone living so close had just died. And in such a terrible manner.

With so much noise her head was splitting. Funny how the children at play school never affected her like this, no matter how much racket they kicked up. Sue wrapped herself in a shawl, stepped outside into the back yard and closed the door behind her. In the windless dark a blackbird chirruped, sounding as if he were in the old apple tree. The contrast between the sweetness of his song and the ugly cacophony in her sitting room made her want to weep.

Eventually it was turned off and Mandy came into the bathroom to clean her teeth. Sue could see her formless shape behind the thick, wavy glass. After she had spat her final spit Mandy slammed off and, moments later, Nirvana came blasting through her bedroom window. The blackbird gave up. Brian came out.

He said sternly, 'We have to talk,' and held the kitchen door open for her to enter. Feeling like a child reporting for punishment Sue went back inside.

Once there and seated Brian, wound up like a spring, seemed unable to get going. He drummed a little on the edge of the fridge and fiddled with the plastic letters, turning 'Hello' into 'Holel'. Then he sucked the insides of his cheeks and played with his beard. Sue was familiar with this mood of evasive punchiness. It meant he was going to attack her but was not sure where best to begin. She began her calming routine. Inhale to a count of ten, exhale twelve, hands linked loosely in lap. Visualise landscape of tranquil beauty, e.g. the Bounty Bar island.

'I couldn't believe it. Just Simply Could Not Believe It.'

'What's that, Brian?'

'Gerald was discovered first thing this morning? Correct me if I'm wrong.'

'Yes. Poor Mrs Bundy found him.' One of these days I *will* correct you and you'll die of shock.

'Something like ten o'clock?'

'Around then.' And so shall I, probably.

'And . . . And . . .' But it was no good, disbelief had become too much for Brian. He had to break off and wag his head about before being able to continue. 'You actually let me know at *three*.'

'I explained that—' The island had white sands and curling, creamy ocean waves, all beneath a shimmering sky.

'Five hours later!'

'Yes. I was—' Plus a beautiful bird of paradise with a furled rainbow tail.

'But surely there's a telephone here? I distinctly recall paying several extremely large bills.'

And who runs those up? 'I didn't get back from play school until one, Brian. The police came and explained what had happened and then the reporters arrived . . .' Sue's voice quavered. A cloud hung over the brazen meridian. 'They just pushed past.'

'They wouldn't have pushed past me,' cried Brian, fiddling up Llohe. 'Licensed manipulators of populist greed.'

'I rang as soon as they'd gone but—'

'But, but. But by then that Morse clone and his fascist sidekick were at the school acting as if they were in some cretinous telly series. God – I could have written better dialogue in my sleep.'

I didn't think he was a fascist. I thought he was sweet. He's got a little girl who would just love a picture of Hector.

'They must have burned up the road getting there. Banking on us not having time to talk. Trying to trick me.'

'Trick you, Brian?' Momentarily Sue was so surprised she forgot her ironic counterpoint. 'Trick you into what?'

'Well . . .' Brian stared hard at his wife as if testing her ingenuousness. There was a long pause. The problem was a tricky one. How to find out what a person knows without asking them, in so many words, how much they know. Oh hell.

'I mean – take for instance all those asinine questions. What time did we get home and go to bed? Did we go out again? Did we hear the car leave? I don't know what you told them.'

'That I went up around quarter to eleven, that I couldn't get off to sleep and that I did hear the car leave.' Sue looked up from her quietly folded hands. 'What did you tell them, Brian?'

'What d'you mean, you couldn't sleep? You were well away when I came up. Snoring your head off.'

Sue, who always pretended to be well away whenever Brian was in the bedroom, lifted her wide, earth-mother shoulders in a resigned sort of way.

'You didn't say I'd gone out for a bit of a walk then?'

'No. Did you?'

'After I'd finished checking the homework. Round the Green. Just to blow—' Brian restored the letters on the fridge to their most popularly accepted distribution. 'God – that's typical of you, that is. Bloody typical.'

Sue started to cry. Brian picked up the *Guardian*, came across a Make This The Year You Learn To Write advertisement and vented his wrath by cutting it out and sending it to Jeffrey Archer.

* * *

That night Midsomer Worthy was slow to settle. The Old Dun Cow was packed with professional journalists and morbid nosy parkers jostling for the locals' attention. The air was shot through with sparkling dialogue along the lines of: I suppose, living here, you must have known him – Oh, sorry, what are you drinking by the way?

And not a manjack among the villagers was found wanting. Lowering doubles and triples at the speed of light, they told what they knew, then conjured from the ripe atmosphere what they did not. And although none of them got it even remotely right, the dead man would still have been astonished at the luxurious complexity of their imaginings. All left the hostelry at closing time, tired and emotional, aware of nothing so much as value given and a job well done.

Several of them staggered past Plover's Rest which, though now sealed, still showed a police presence. And the pod was still there. Troy had gone home, but Detective Chief Inspector Barnaby was inside reading through information which had come in during the day, drinking coffee and waiting for the airport police at Heathrow to return his call. He was whacked and on the point of giving up when the telephone rang.

They were sorry for the delay. There had been several flights to Finland on the eighth but at this hour the relevant offices were locked so it had taken some time to raise the information he required. But they were now in a position to inform him that none of the flights in question had carried a passenger travelling under the name of Max Jennings.

The Woman in Black

Barnaby was in the incident room early next morning, bad-tempered, greatly disturbed by his own anxieties and unrefreshed. He had spent the night drifting in and out of sleep and bad dreams. He couldn't remember what the dreams were but woke fighting for breath and wrestling with the duvet, which seemed to be pressing itself over his nose and mouth.

He had got up at six in the winter's dark, switched off the alarm and made himself some tea. Then later, as Joyce slept on, followed this with a delicious and deeply un-healthy fried breakfast, sneering at a wistful-looking kitten as he turned the bacon. The postman came while he was eating. Two gardening catalogues and the phone bill.

Barnaby put the dishes in the sink, made some fresh tea and took a cup to Joyce. By the time he came down again there was a tight squeezing between his shoulder blades that presaged indigestion and Kilmowski was sitting by the fridge mewing anxiously.

'Hasn't taken you long to suss where the nosh is, has it?' He put on his coat and scarf. 'Well you needn't get your feet under the table. They'll be back in two weeks.'

Troy approached his boss treading on eggshells, for he knew the old man in this mood. No matter what the sergeant said or did nothing would be right. And if he just stood there saying or doing nothing then his thoughts would be for it. Or his choice of clothing. Or the way he combed his hair. Or the shape of his left leg. Might as well go and stick his head in a bucket and have done with it. He put the cup and saucer down with extreme caution.

'What d'you call this?'

'Coffee, sir.'

'It's cold.'

'But I've only just—'

'Don't argue with me.'

'No, sir.' Troy hesitated. 'Shall I get some more?' A brown bottle was being unscrewed and tablets that he recognised tipped out. Two were swilled down with the scalding coffee. Barnaby's eyes bulged and sweat broke out across his forehead.

'Would you like some water, chief?' Troy received a glance to strip his teeth of their enamel.

'Are you trying to be funny?'

'Of course not. I just—' The air was cleft by a furious gesture with a bunched fist and the sergeant tiptoed off.

But in the corridor his oppression was lightened with miraculous suddenness for, if life at Causton police station left a lot to be desired, one of the things it left most to be desired was now walking straight towards him. The delectably blonde Audrey Brierley. A source of grievous bodily pleasure if ever there was one.

Troy indicated the door through which he had just passed, gave a warning grimace and drew his thumbnail graphically across his throat. Audrey narrowed her baby blues, said, 'Promises, promises!' and walked on by.

Barnaby closed his eyes and rested his head in his hands, withdrawing from the clattering keys, shrilling phones and murmurs of conversation into a dark interior quietness and ordering his thoughts for the day's briefing, which he had convened for nine thirty. He stayed like this for ten minutes, made a few notes and got up from his desk.

The chief inspector attempted to run, given the rigid police hierarchy, a democratic incident room. Time permitting, he would listen and talk to anyone, aware that intelligent insights could as well be present in the minds of the lowly ranked as elsewhere. And, should that prove to be the case, he would frequently give credit where it was due. This by no means common attitude meant that he was respected (if not always liked) by the majority under his command.

There would be two enquiry teams. The first, which would include several civilian machine operators, stayed in the incident room manning the telephones and computers, searching for and collating information. The second, the foot sloggers, went out and about, looking, listening, asking questions. Thirty people fell silent and paid attention as Barnaby made his way to the far end of the room.

He stood before a wall of aerated panels that strongly resembled grey Ryvita. On these were pinned still photographs plus enlarged freeze frames from the video made at the scene of the crime and when Barnaby opened by describing the case as a very messy one it was only too clear what he meant. A blow-up of Hadleigh's wedding picture was also displayed, along with photographs of the murder weapon. Barnaby recapped only briefly on the information gathered so far, for they all had notes on yesterday's interviews.

'We now know that Jennings hasn't flown to Finland, or

anywhere else come to that, from Heathrow. We're checking other airports today. We've also telexed the seaports and might pick up something there. Obviously the fact that he's cleared off after lying about where he's going is a cause for some concern. On the other hand we must remember that after leaving Hadleigh's he drove home, went to bed and this morning had his valet pack for him and ate breakfast before leaving. This does not indicate a man in a hurry.

'If he killed Hadleigh there was no way he could know that the body had not been found. Rex St John seems to have made his role as minder very plain so, for all Jennings knew, the minute his car drove off St John was back round there. The murder would have been discovered, the police notified, St John's story told and Jennings easily apprehended. We also have to take into account the nature of the attack. This sort of severe bludgeoning indicates someone in a fit of rage, which argues against premeditation. I wouldn't wish to push this suggestion too far. A murder can, of course, be coldly planned and still emotionally carried out, but I'd like you to bear this in mind.

'The house was not secure, which means we can't discount the possibility of some opportunist or vagrant nipping in. Aggravated burglary happens, as we all know, but I feel here the odds are against it. The cleaning lady is sure nothing was taken from downstairs. Unfortunately, upstairs she will not go. I had a further word with her last night however and it seems that, as I suspected, a large brown case is missing from the small bedroom. It was there the previous week when she cleaned through and I think it not unreasonable to assume that whoever emptied the chest of drawers used it to carry the contents away. I'm hoping SOCO will be able to give us some idea what they were.'

'So are we looking at robbery as a motive after all then, sir?' asked a young detective constable, shiningly alert and crisp as a biscuit.

'Hard to say at this stage, Willoughby. The theft might have been an afterthought, yet I can't help thinking, as a hugely expensive watch was left behind, that it was also quite specific. Mrs Bundy says the drawers were always kept locked.'

Inspector Meredith, who had so far sat in a distant silence picking his thoughts over (for all the world, Barnaby commented later, like unclaimed jewels), spoke up: 'Using the suitcase as the means to hand would surely indicate that matey-boy did not expect to find what he did or he would have come prepared to take the clobber away. After all, you can hardly conceal that much stuff about your person.'

'Indeed you can't, Ian,' replied Barnaby and heard, just behind his left shoulder, a sharp intake of breath and intuited, indeed positively shared, his sergeant's antagonism.

Inspector Ian Meredith, heading the outdoor team, had been the object of Troy's resentful envy since the day of his arrival. One of the short-cutters. A Bramshill flyer. Out of Oxbridge with his degree round his neck like an Olympic gold. Made up to sergeant before he'd taken his stripey scarf off, inspector in four years, plus, most galling of the lot, connections in high places. And without the grace to wear this largesse lightly.

'Nevertheless,' continued Barnaby, 'it's an odd house that doesn't contain a couple of cases or travelling bags, so I don't think we can read too much into the fact that he came apparently unprepared.'

That's told him, said Troy's supercilious mask. 'Matey-boy' indeed! Jesus. He smirked at Inspector Meredith and was disconcerted to discover that the man was nodding his head in agreement. Some people just didn't seem to know when they were being put down.

'We'll keep the search going on both cars, but I imagine you'll find Hadleigh's in some local garage having a checkup. It's the Mercedes that I suspect we shall find elusive.'

'What sort is it?'

'In your notes, Inspector Meredith.'

'A 500 SL sir,' said Detective Constable Willoughby, simultaneously.

'Oh, yes.'

Meredith's acknowledgement was of a casualness to imply that all his friends and relatives had one. Trouble was, thought Barnaby sourly, they probably did. He said: 'I want you to find out all there is to know about Hadleigh. Gossip and hearsay as well as what's officially on record. We're told that he was married to a woman called Grace, surname unknown, and that they lived in Kent, where she died of leukaemia. He worked for the Civil Service, supposedly in the Ministry of Agriculture. Once all this has been verified we can start building on it. The video of the crime scene is now available. I shall expect you all to make yourselves familiar. That's all.'

The outdoor team disappeared. The rest swung away from him on their swivelchairs involving themselves in the glint and dazzle of their VDUs. Barnaby strode off to his office, where he could use the telephone in reasonable peace and quiet.

He had the number of Max Jennings' publishers and had already rung twice without reply. It was now nine forty-five. He picked up the receiver and tried again. Nothing. Barnaby sucked his teeth with a rather self-righteous click, for he had the early riser's puritanical disdain for slugabeds. At last a Sloaney female accent responded.

He stated his business and was put through to publicity where, neatly fielding considerable curiosity, he asked if it was the case that Mr Jennings was currently on a book-signing tour in Finland. This remark was repeated aloud at the other end, causing much merriment.

'We're in stitches here,' said his contact, unnecessarily. 'We can't get Max into his local bookshop under cover of darkness to sign as much as a paperback. Let alone the full cheese and wine at Waterstones. Someone's been pulling your leg.'

'So it seems.' Barnaby sounded very regretful. 'I wonder . . . would there be any details about Mr Jennings you could perhaps let me have? Publicity handouts – that sort of thing?'

'Well.' She turned away from the phone and he heard a quiet exchange. 'There's a biog. we send out. It's pretty up to date. I could fax you that.' As he gave the number there was more murmuring and his contact said, 'We think you should talk to Talent.'

'Who?'

'Talent Levine, his agent. Have you got a pen?' Barnaby wrote the details down. 'They'll be able to help you much more than us. He's been on their books from the year dot.'

Barnaby thanked her, hung up and sat back in his chair. The tensions of the briefing over, and his indigestion almost entirely abated, he discovered to his surprise that he was hungry. Or at least (for breakfast was only two hours gone) that he fancied a little something. Telling himself that he could always cut out lunch he wandered into the corridor to see what was available in the automat.

Like most of its kind it offered only garishly wrapped and highly calorific items. Barnaby selected a whirly Danish studded with glacé cherries and put his money in.

Further down the corridor Sergeant Troy emerged from the Gents reeking of nicotine. Smoking had, from January first, been banned in the station under a Thames Valley ruling and was now allowed only in the toilets. These, by the end of the day, resembled Dante's Inferno with the shades of uniformed or plain-clothed sinners diving in and out of swirling clouds of smoke.

Troy moved on light, quick feet. Spring-heeled Jack. Exciting times were in the offing. The case was opening up and, whichever way the next few hours crumbled, they seemed to be fairly full of Eastern promise and relatively short on paperwork. Then he spotted the boss and wiped the pleasure from his countenance. Just to be on the safe side.

'I'd like some coffee with this.' Holding up the cellophane packet. Walking away.

'Right, chief.'

When Troy produced the coffee, Barnaby was on the blower. The sergeant put the cup down, less warily this time, for he could see things were looking up. And he was actually thanked. Just one raised finger. Which made a nice change.

Barnaby listened, relishing the voice. Cigar rich. Garrick Club fruity. Port and nuts and Armagnac. The brazen clash of money, with a wheeler-dealer edge.

'The only things Max Jennings signs are contracts,' rumbled Talent Levine. 'Why exactly do you want to speak to him?'

'We are investigating a sudden death. Mr Jennings was one of several people who spent time with the deceased yesterday evening.' Barnaby explained the circumstances in some detail.

'Talking to some scribbling amateurs in the back of beyond? I don't believe it.'

Barnaby gave assurances that such was indeed the case even as he wondered how the inhabitants of Midsomer Worthy would regard being reassigned to the polar ice caps.

'He wouldn't even talk to Lynn Barbour,' continued Talent. 'Mind you, that was on my advice.'

'We're fairly sure that Mr Jennings knew the man who issued the invitation quite well. Did he ever mention the name Gerald Hadleigh to you?'

'Not that I recall.'

'It would be going back a few years.'

'No. Sorry.'

'We're getting some background material on Mr Jennings from his publishers—'

'Why?' Barnaby was momentarily silenced. 'I want to know much more than you're telling me, chief inspector, before I start answering questions about my client without his permission.'

'Very well. The facts are these. Mr Hadleigh was murdered late last night. As far as we know your client was the last person to see him alive. Now Mr Jennings, after giving false information about his destination, seems to have disappeared.'

There are pauses and pauses. You would have needed a wrecker's ball to dent this one. Eventually Max's agent said, 'Christ almighty.'

'Do you have any idea at all where he might be?'

'Absolutely none.'

'If he gets in touch—'

'I need to take advice on this one, chief inspector. I'll get back to you. Perhaps later today.'

'I'd appreciate that, Mr Levine.' An interruptive growl. 'Oh, I beg your pardon. Ms Levine.'

He hung up, murmuring to himself, 'Curiouser and curiouser.'

Troy remained silent. Even if he had the chutzpah this was no time to correct the chief's grammar. Barnaby once more turned his attention to the pastry. The cherries, so glossy and seductive under wraps, proved to be as hard as wine gums. He took a bite, felt a savage twinge in his tooth and flung the remains down in disgust.

'There's something rotten in the state of Denmark, Gavin.'

'It's the same everywhere.' Troy removed the empty, coffee-stained polystyrene beaker and dropped it, together with the pastry, in the bin. 'Maureen's stopped putting the news on.'

He produced a snowy handkerchief, smoothed the rest of the crumbs into his hand and disposed of them. Then he wiped his palms and fingers carefully.

'When you've finished dusting,' said Barnaby, long familiar with his sergeant's obsessively meticulous behaviour but still capable of being entertained, 'I want you to go and see Clapton again. Lean a bit. Find out just what he was up to on Tuesday night when he was supposed to be taking this quick turn round the Green.'

'I'm so glad you could come round.'

'We were lucky. Me with a break. You on afternoons.'

Sue dunked tea bags in stone mugs. Camomile for

herself, Sainsbury's Red Label for Amy. There was a home-made oat and carob slice each, too. All on a tray balanced on the cracked old Rexine pouffe in front of the fire.

Amy took her tea, murmuring, and by no means for the first time, 'A terrible day.'

'Oh, yes – terrible. Terrible.'

They had talked about it and talked about it. Amy starting even before she had taken her coat off.

It was twenty-four hours now since the police had called at Gresham House. After their visit, and the dreadful revelations they had left behind, Amy had naturally expected that she and Honoria would sit down and slacken their disbelief together. Absorb the shock (as she and Sue were doing now) over a warm, comforting drink. But Honoria had appeared satisfied merely to deliver a run-of-the-mill diatribe describing the sociological forces that had combined to bring the criminal element so firmly into their midst. These, though varied, were neither wide ranging nor original.

Ignorant and indulgent parents, lax teachers, spoon-feedings by the state from the cradle to the grave and easy access to the depravities of television. Contempt for authority came next, closely followed by the abandonment of corporal and capital punishment and the deliberately malicious council policy of siting municipal dwellings a mere thieving's distance from the homes of decent, tax-paying citizens. All or any of these heinous components could, it seemed, be permed any which way to produce the thing that had killed Gerald Hadleigh – for that he came from the dregs of society went without saying. Foolishly, Amy had argued.

'Aristocrats killed people. Elizabeth the first was always chopping heads off.'

'Royalty is different.' Honoria had stared at Amy with

her round, hard pebbly eyes. 'If you're so interested you should have asked that turnip-faced hobnail of a policeman if you could go over and have a look.'

'Honoria! What an awful— As if I would ever— *Ohhhh*.'

Amy's fingers trembled anew as she broke off a piece of her carob slice. To be made to feel like a morbid snooper, like those awful people parked on the Green. She didn't want to see anything. Indeed felt quite ill at the thought. But surely (and she had said so) it was no more than human to wish to discuss such an appalling incident on one's own doorstep.

'In that case,' Honoria had replied, 'I'm glad I'm not human.'

'Tell us something we don't know,' said Sue, as Amy passed this on.

They had cried a little together, as they had separately the previous day. Sue had wept when the news hawks had finally left her in peace, Amy during the brief moments she had spent in St Chad's after visiting Ralph's grave.

Not knowing if Gerald had been religious, and not being especially religious herself, she had kept her prayer simple, merely asking that his soul should be accepted in heaven and there find peace. Of course all this sort of thing would be properly and officially attended to at the funeral, but Amy had a vague notion that time was thought to be relevant in these matters and that there should not be too much delay.

Sue spooned thick meadow-flower honey into her tea. 'I got in touch with Laura and Rex,' she said, 'when I knew you were coming, in case they wanted to join us. She was really short with me and Rex seemed to be out when I went round.'

'Oh well.' Amy was not really disappointed. She loved sitting in this room with Sue, the fire crackling, throwing shadows on the dark red walls. It was like being in a snug cave.

They had become friends almost by default – drawn together as two English people might be if marooned in a foreign country, reaching out in their isolation, sensing immediately a kindred spirit. Without words each understood the other's situation. They never needed to ask, as outsiders might (and frequently did), why on earth do you put up with it?

Instead they offered comfort, encouragement and advice. Sometimes they would let off steam, angrily berating their oppressor's behaviour. But, in the main, they struggled to remain humorous and detached. What else could you do?

Neither allowed the other to slide into self-pity, or take unnecessary blame. When they had first started meeting Sue had done a lot of that, explaining that Brian only acted the way he did because she was slow and not very bright. Amy had knocked that notion severely on the head.

They had an escape plan, of course. Sue was to become a famous illustrator of children's books and buy a little cottage with room for just herself and Mandy, if she wanted to come. There would be a garden with space for ducks and chickens. Amy would sell her block-buster and get a house not too far away. It would be spacious, airy and modern, for she had had enough of clanking radiators and stone floors and smelly, mildewed cupboards.

And when they met they would have slow, thoughtful conversations with breathing spaces. Not like now, when they talked and laughed and interrupted each other non-stop but always with one eye on the clock. Amy said they were like two nuns from a silent order vouchsafed a once-a-year speaking day.

'I keep wishing,' said Sue – they were still discussing the murder – 'that I'd looked at my clock when I heard Max drive away.'

'How were you to know? Anyway I don't see that it would help the police that much.'

'It would give them a time when Gerald was still alive.'

'I thought post-mortems sorted all that out.'

The phrase struck them both with a deep chill and they looked at each other in some distress.

'I expect they'll have to talk to him – Max I mean. It's so embarrassing. Us mixing him up in something like this.'

'Could be worse.'

'I don't see how.'

'Could have been Alan Bennett.'

They burst into nervous giggles, ashamed at such levity yet also knowing relief. Then, acknowledging that the time had come to put their reflections on death aside, Sue said, 'Something nice happened yesterday. Did you have the policeman with red hair?'

'Yes.'

'"Fox" I called him at first,' said Sue, for she anthropomorphised everyone. 'But then I had second thoughts. His lips were so thin and his teeth so sharp that I decided he should be "Ferret". And the bulky one's "Badger".'

'Oh yes, I agree with "Badger",' said Amy. She agreed with 'Ferret' as well, for she hadn't liked Troy much at all. 'What about him?'

'He wants to buy a painting of Hector. For his little girl.'

'That's brilliant! How much will you ask?'

'Heavens, I don't know.'

'Twenty pounds.' Sue squealed her disbelief. 'At least. He's getting an original Clapton. Tell him one day it'll be worth a fortune.'

Amy knew she was wasting her breath. Sue would probably just mumble, 'Oh, that's all right' when the time came. Or shake her Greenpeace collecting tin, with soft timidity, in Ferret's general direction. She was saying something else.

'I still haven't heard from Methuen.'

'But that's good news.' Sue had submitted some paintings and a story nearly three months ago. 'If they hadn't wanted your book they'd have sent it back straight away.'

'Would they?'

'Of course. It's being passed round to get lots of opinions. Depend upon it.'

'Amy.' Sue smiled across at her friend. 'What would I do without you?'

'Likewise.'

'How is *Rompers*?' asked Sue. 'Have you managed to do any more?'

She did not ask out of mere politeness. The immensely baroque structure of Amy's book impressed Sue enormously and she followed every twist and turn of the narrative with the deepest interest. It seemed to her wonderfully gripping and she was sure that, should Amy ever snatch enough secret moments to finish it, *Rompers* would be a great success.

'Well, believe it or not, after such shattering news, I did six pages last night.'

Amy had been quite perturbed on their completion unsure whether writing under such circumstances meant she was a true professional or an amateur with a heart of stone.

'Has Rokesby,' Sue was continuing eagerly, 'discovered that Araminta has the same surname as the Duke of Molina because she is his sister and not, as Rokesby believed when he rejected her, his wife?'

'He has, yes.'

'Well?'

'Too late. Hurt almost beyond human endurance she has fled to the Corsican Riviera with Black Rufus.'

'The notorious drug baron!'

'She believes him to be a Save the Children representative.'

'And Burgo?' Burgoyne was Sue's favourite. Ebony-haired and pantherine, he spoke twelve languages, often simultaneously. He had violet eyes, an olive skin the beauty of which was enhanced rather than disfigured by a zigger zagger duelling scar, and a name respected and feared on the world's international espionage circuit.

'Suspended from his heels in a rat-infested bauxite mill somewhere on the Caymans.'

'Ohhh . . .' Sue's eyes shone and she clapped her hands at the sheer extravagance of it all. 'How absolutely wonderful!'

'It's not at all wonderful. That isn't supposed to happen till page three hundred and something.'

'Where are you now, then?'

'Forty-two. I've got a riot of plot and nothing else.'

'But Amy, that's what bestsellers are.'

'Really?'

'You won't give up?'

'Good heavens, no. And neither must you.'

Amy got up and looked out of the window, something she had done several times since her arrival. Honoria had gone to the post office to collect a parcel of books from the London Library. She had gone in person this time as the need to harangue Mr and Mrs Sandell had yet again become paramount. A letter was recently delivered to Gresham House with a slight tear in the envelope and the flap barely secure. This could mean a ten-minute trounce or a lecture lasting half an hour and the length of the queue behind Honoria would have no bearing on the matter.

Even as she watched, Amy told herself what nonsense this surveillance was. After all she was not, technically, a prisoner. On the contrary she seemed to be out of the house as often as she was in. Running errands, delivering messages (or rather edicts), fetching and carrying. But always conscious that the time used was not her own.

And Honoria seemed to have a built-in radar that kept a most accurate track of her minion's movements. If Amy went swiftly and efficiently about her business, looking neither to right nor left, deliberately depriving herself of the warmth of human contact, all would be well. But let her so much as stop briefly to comment on the weather, pat an animal or ask after someone's health and before she had even stepped across the threshold on her return there would ring out, 'Where have you *been*?'

Honoria knew nothing of Amy's meetings with Sue. If she found out they would be stopped. How, Amy could not even begin to guess, but she was sure that it would be so. Even if Honoria knew they were a lifeline. Especially if she knew they were a lifeline.

'There she is!'

Amy jumped away from the window, suddenly pale. Sue scrambled to her feet, catching the alarm, hating it when Amy so vividly demonstrated her subservience, uneasily aware that in the quick, dismayed movements lay a mirror image of her own.

As Amy moved quickly to the door, Sue shouted, 'Wood! Wood!'

'Gosh – I nearly forgot.'

Sue ran into the back yard, where a bundle of branches always lay ready. Amy's excuse for her walk. They hugged goodbye on the step and Sue watched Amy race down the path and speed away, as if stapled to the wind.

She turned back into the house. It was not until she was packing her box for play school that she recalled the one thing above all others that had been worrying her and that she had meant to talk to Amy about. How could she have forgotten something that had occupied her mind so constantly? Now the question once more possessed her. Why, when Brian had simply walked briskly once round the Green on the night of Gerald's murder, had he been absent from the house for well over three quarters of an hour?

Brian's drama class had reconvened but was not going well. He had spent the first fifteen minutes trying to get them off the subject of murder. Starting with questions about Gerald the conversation had expanded rapidly to cover serial killers, the chain-saw massacre, vampirism and necrophilia – the latter dead boring, according to Collar.

In vain he had dragged them through a warm-up, got them pinching their cheeks to promote alertness, rolling their heads ('let those cannon balls *go*') and pretending to be clowns on unicycles to fire their imaginations. The minute it was over they were back on the same subject.

'You being his friend, I reckon the filth would've let you see him.'

'I didn't want to—'

'They say his head were well bashed in.' Boreham's eyes shone. 'I bet his brains fell out.'

'Different from you then,' said Collar. 'Bash you from here till Christmas your brains wouldn't fall out.'

'Why's that then, Collar?' asked little Bor, knowing his place and, for once, his lines.

''Cause you keep them up your arse.'

'All right you lot,' Brian bleated. He clapped his hands and adopted his 'lost in the magical world of theatre' expression. 'Let's go on. Have you all brought your scripts?'

They stared at him in deep incomprehension. He sighed, recognising the moment, for there had been many such. And yet, how rosy it had all seemed on day one. There they were, his raw material. There he was, a gifted Svengali ready to unlock talent and enthusiasm that a plodding, authoritarian educational system had all but vanquished Under his concerned tutelage they would expand and flower. Eventually their lives, immeasurably enriched, would intermingle with his own. Then they would be not teacher and pupils but friends. Lately, by some indulgently tortuous manoeuvre of his mind, Brian had seen one of them – preferably Edie or Tom – becoming famous and adopting his mentor's surname in gratitude. Like Richard Burton.

Brian acknowledged no multiplicity of motives in all this. He gave, they took. He chose not to admit the charge he got in return. Those heady, fearful moments when an improvisation got out of hand and violence scented the air. (Brian had a warmly sentimental attitude towards violence, largely because he had never been around when any was being dished out. He referred to it sometimes as grace under pressure, tossing the phrase as casually into a conversation as if it had been his own.)

But the truth was that these moments reflected uncomfortably similar disturbances in his own heart.

Repressed, they fuelled his dreams, spawning lubricious disorder. Why only last night—

Brian, struggling to quell these torrid recollections, found the Carter twins in his direct line of vision. Today Tom was in a Confederate Army greatcoat and tight snakeskin trousers. He sported a button showing a police helmet over the slogan 'DESTROY THE HUMPBACKED PIGS'.

Edie rose from a circle of unseamed felt like a flower from a grubby black calyx. The skirt was slashed to the waist and worn over a tiny pair of striped fur shorts. Brian's skin darkened still further at his first glimpse of these raffish tormentors. He took a deep breath, got down on his haunches and said, 'What I'd really like is to end this play with what is known in the business as a coo dee tayartray.'

'We had one of them,' said little Bor, 'but the wheel came off.'

'A dazzling effect to stun and amaze.'

'Sounds lovely,' said Edie.

'But one does have to work up to this sort of thing and, quite frankly, I'm not at all sure we're in a recruitment mode in every sphere.'

'Fact is Bri,' said Denzil, '100% British Made' according to the stencil across his forehead, 'what we'd really like to do is something by ourselves.'

'Yeah.' Collar was enthusiastic. 'I bet we'd be real good.'

'I hardly think so.' Brian felt shut out and rather hurt that they could even think of such a thing. 'You'd never have the discipline for a start.'

There was a chorus of 'oh yes we woulds.'

'OK, where are the computer print-outs you promised to learn DLP at our last rehearsal?'

'What's DLP?' asked little Bor.

'Dick-licking pervo,' said Denzil, quickly rewarded by a full house of guffaws. He pushed his tongue out as far as it would go and wagged it about, spraying the air with spittle.

'We could try though, Brian,' said Edie, 'couldn't we?'

'If you insist.' He could refuse her nothing. 'But I must remind you that we're running very short of time. I know yesterday's interruption wasn't your fault, but even before the police arrived we'd got nowhere. Messing about being chickens does not help us produce a text.'

'I don't see why chickens shouldn't be in a play,' said Collar. 'People gotta eat.'

'Wotcha think of Gavin Troy, Brian?' asked Denzil.

'Who?'

'The red-headed git in the leathers.'

'He seemed all right.'

'He's a bastard,' continued Collar.

'Nearly broke Denzil's arm.'

'Goodness.'

'Have you as soon as look at you, Troy would,' said Denzil, adding, not without a certain pride, 'Missed me by a hare's breath last week.'

'What were you—?'

'He had our Duane,' said Collar. 'And he weren't doing nothing neither. Just happened to be standing by this chippie on the market square—'

'Fat Leslie?'

'Yeah – anyway this fight broke out. Duane climbed in the van to try and calm things down – p'raps make a citizen's arrest like – when ratarse comes on the scene shopping with his missus. Straight over the counter wasn't he? Poor old Duane ended up with his face on the hotplate.'

Brian stared, thrilled and aghast in equal measure, wondering how much of it was true.

'Did he try and make you confess, Bri?'

'Of course not. I haven't done anything.'

'That wouldn't bother them,' said Edie. She parted her legs, affording Brian a much clearer and more devastating glimpse of furry tiger markings. She plonked her eighteen-hole Doc Martens firmly on the parquet and rested her hands on her knees. 'Keep after you. Wear you down.'

'They were perfectly civil.'

'Yeah, to you. Tame-o.'

'Tame-o,' repeated little Bor shyly.

'Should see'm round our estate,' said Denzil. 'Any excuse, stop and search.'

'After a feel half the time,' said Edie and Brian's heart jerked with excitement. She winked at him, lowering an eyelid the colour of ripe damsons spangled with silver. 'You gotta go down the station?'

'I don't know.' Brian was sharply aware of his complete ignorance as to the functioning of the humblest traffic unit, let alone the CID. 'Do they usually say if they want to see you again?'

'No,' said Tom. 'Not usually. They just turn up.'

And, at that very moment, the swing doors parted and Sergeant Troy appeared.

They talked this time, without the aid of refreshments, in a small room leading off the science lab. It was unheated and there was a faint but distinctly unpleasant smell coming from an old-fashioned sink in the far corner. The chill struck Brian keenly in spite of his thick lumberjack shirt, reindeer sweater and string vest.

Troy stood by the window, which was deeply

embrasured. He had put his Biro on the stone shelf and was now taking out a notebook in a leisurely manner. He turned to the place he wanted and laid the book down next to the pen. He tugged his belt through the buckle and let his coat hang loose. Then he took off his cap and his hair sprang up, crisp and sparkling like a fox's brush. Only then did he turn and speak to Brian, who was perched on a laboratory stool behind a bench of instruments and retorts.

'Sorry to take you out of your rehearsals for the second time, Mr Clapton.'

'That's all right.'

'Going well are they?'

'Oh yes – very.'

'What play is it you're putting on again?'

'*Slangwhang For Five Mute Voices*.'

Troy nodded and looked deeply interested without responding verbally.

'A very demanding project. I ask a great deal of them. And of myself too, naturally.' Brian relaxed a little, unwinding his legs, which had been locked around the struts of the high stool. 'They're a great bunch. Especially the Carter twins.' He had to say her name. Just once. 'Edie. And Tom. They really are remarkable.'

'They are indeed, sir,' replied Troy, who had come across Edie for the first time five years previously. She had been brought into the station when her mother, accompanied by the child, had been caught shoplifting. Edie had been wearing a full-length Teddy Bear coat with every inch of the cunningly pocketed lining stuffed with enough fags and sweeties to open a corner shop. A harmful little armful, to put it mildly.

'So talented. And with life stacked completely against them. Yet they never give up.'

166

'Certainly agree with you on that score, Mr Clapton,' said Troy. Thinking – stone the crows, this bloke doesn't know the difference between arsehole time and breakfast time. They must be running bloody rings round him.

'The girl seems to me especially bright.' That really must be the last time, Brian told himself. The very last. Not that he'd repeated her name, but still. Best stop while he was safe.

Troy merely smiled, but he had noticed the swoopy Adam's apple and slightly quickened breath and he caught the sexual drift. Oh yes. Brian fancied a jump there all right. A little flutter. An apple for the teacher. And under age too. Naughty, naughty.

Admitting to recent fatherhood, Troy asked a couple of questions about teaching generally. Brian responded by talking about himself in particular and in great detail and Troy let him run on for a bit. This was the chief's way when he had something nasty up his sleeve. He called it giving them a bit of margin.

First, isolate your rodent. Let him unwind, become expansive and off guard. Show him the prime Stilton. Have him sniff around a bit. Enjoy a nibble and then—

Brian, now so relaxed he was putting his slippers on, was explaining how he had rejected Cambridge as too elitist choosing instead Teacher Training College in Uttoxeter. His pale eyes shone behind his Schubert glasses. Even his dingy bottle-brush moustache bristled, with satisfaction at this sweet unrolling of his prideful narrative.

Troy, whose mum had always dinned it into him that self-praise was no recommendation, found it as boring as tears.

'All this is very interesting, Mr Clapton,' he lied pleasantly, 'but perhaps now we'd better get down to the matter in hand.'

'Oh.' Brian had almost forgotten why they were there. 'Yes, all right.'

'Just a small point.' Troy rustled the pages of his notebook in the pretence of finding a reference. 'The night of Mr Hadleigh's death, you told us' – more rustling, this time at greater length – 'that you left the house somewhere about . . . let's see . . . quarter to eleven. Turning right, you walked once around the Green to, I believe the phrase was "blow the cobwebs away".'

'Yes,' said Brian, though not without a pause.

'And that is correct?'

'Indeed it is. My yea is my yea, sergeant, and my nay my nay, as all who know me will confirm.'

'Well, I'm afraid we have a witness, Mr Clapton, who says they saw you return at just gone midnight. And what's more approaching your house from the entirely opposite direction.'

The expression on Brian's face was that of someone suddenly savaged by a dove. He stared at the man who, only seconds ago, had been listening to the story of his life with such courteous interest. Troy smiled. Or at least parted his lips slightly. His sharp teeth gleamed.

'Ahhh . . . really . . . ? I don't know who this person is supposed to be, but perhaps it might be in order to ask them a few questions. Such as what they were doing, hiding in hedges at that hour of the night, spying on people.'

'Hiding in hedges?'

'Well, I didn't see anyone.'

'That is strange. Because you would certainly have passed him had you, in fact, been coming back from a walk around the Green.'

Silence. Brian, moisture prettily pearling his brow,

closed his eyes. Immediately he lost thirty years. Aged three, he picked up a Victoria plum on a neighbour's lawn and took it home. His parents, greatly alarmed at this early example of their only offspring 'getting into trouble', dragged him, crying, next door to apologise and return the booty. After that, forewarned, they laboured ceaselessly to protect Brian from his baser instincts.

He was taught that speaking to strange children or even trying to share his sweets would get him into trouble, as would bringing friends home or going to their houses. Cheeking grown-ups, especially those with even the slightest shred of authority, would, more than any other misdemeanour, bring disaster on them all. Brian cursed their cringing servility from the bottom of his heart. They had eviscerated him. Taken out his guts and left him defenceless.

'You are aware, sir, that this is a murder investigation?'

'Oh yes, yes. And anything I can do to help. Anything at all.'

Troy was standing very still, one arm lying across his notebook on the stone window shelf, the other resting at his side. Behind him the sun caught his hair, which glowed, an aureole of fiery quills. There was something concealed behind his blank expression that hinted at great deter- mination. He looked like a rigorously disciplined monk. Or enthusiastic inquisitor.

Brian could, with no trouble at all, see him applying some troublemaker's face to a hotplate.

'So. The other night. He may be correct, your witness. Or she of course. If it was a she. I don't know.' Hyuf, hyuf.

'Go on, sir.' Troy clicked his Biro and smoothed out the paper.

'Possibly I walked into the village. In fact, now you

come to mention it, I remember passing the letter box, so I must have done. Walked into the village that is.' Pause. 'I can't imagine why I said I'd gone round the Green. I can only assume that, as you'd only just that minute told me about Gerald, I was picturing Plover's Rest and had sort of tangled the two things up in my mind.'

'Perfectly understandable, Mr Clapton.'

'Yes, it is. Isn't it?' A wisp of colour returned to Brian's cheeks.

'See anyone on your walk?'

'Not a soul. It was a filthy night.'

'So I understand. I'd've wanted a jolly good reason to go out on a night like that, myself.'

'I did explain—'

'I would have thought a couple of minutes in the back yard would have been quite long enough to blow a whole lorryload of cobwebs away. Myself.'

Troy wrote for a moment then said, 'How long would you say you were out, sir? Altogether?'

'Ohh . . . about an hour.'

'In that weather?'

'Yes.'

'For no reason?'

The sergeant lowered his head and the sun hit Brian full in the face. He clambered down from his stool, caught his foot on a low cross strut and stumbled away from the blinding light, dragging the stool with him.

'You weren't perhaps,' continued Troy, 'on your way to some sort of tryst?' He was glad of a chance to use this word, which he had picked up from a chocolate commercial on the telly.

'*Tryst?*' The faint blush of colour on Brian's cheeks deepened and spread like an ugly naevus. A tic doloreux danced beneath his left eye. He croaked, 'Of course not.'

'In that case, Mr Clapton, let me put my own theory on the table. I think you left the house intending to turn right – which was how you came to make the slip in your earlier statement – but saw that someone nearby had observed you. So you turned left and walked off, returning later when the coast was clear.'

'Clear? Clear for what?'

'For you to re-enter Plover's Rest of course.'

'Talk about Jemima Puddleduck,' said Sergeant Troy, who had recently taken on the sweet pleasures of reading to his daughter. 'Another five minutes I'd've had to mop the floor.'

He was sitting in the incident room rejigging the scene in the science cupboard for Barnaby's benefit, twirling with satisfaction on a tweedy swivel chair and nicely relaxed after a spaghetti bolognese, double chips, Bakewell tart and custard and several cups of tea in the staff canteen. All this consumed in time unofficially included in the visit to Causton Comprehensive.

'He admitted he'd gone in the opposite direction from what he'd told us. Gave me some rigmarole about getting confused. Still insists he just went for a walk to clear his mind. I suggested that he had in fact left his house intending to return to Plover's Rest, seen someone hanging around and been forced to depart elsewhere until they'd gone, whereupon he made his way back there, presumably to get on with the dirty deed.'

'Did you now?' said Barnaby, entertaining himself by fleshing out the scene. 'And how did he react?'

'Nearly passed out.'

'You must have enjoyed that, sergeant.'

'Just doing my job, sir.'

'Quite. Did you believe him?'

'I did actually,' said Troy. 'I shouldn't think he's got the guts to crack a flea let alone do a bloke's head in. He looked dead guilty but he's the sort who'd look guilty if a copper asked him for a light.'

'He took the trouble to lie though, which means he wasn't simply out for a constitutional.'

'My bet is he was hanging around Quarry Cottages.'

'The Carters' place?'

Troy nodded. 'Came over all hot and bothered talking about them. And he's just the sort of pathetic sod to peer through bedroom windows jerking off.'

'I agree,' said the chief inspector, for Brian had struck him as a sad case – the sort of man whose personality was out of print before the ink was dry on his birth certificate. 'He'd be well advised to keep his distance. They'll have his balls in the shredder.'

'Got to find them first,' said Troy, recalling Brian's limp cords. Hard to believe they held as much as a tin whistle let alone two fun bags and a hot dog.

'But what really made his day,' continued the sergeant, chortling happily, 'was when I said I thought his wife's paintings were so good I'd decided to commission one. That did for him good and proper.'

'So now we know of two people at the meeting who went out again that night. St John I feel has been honest with us. Certainly his remorse strikes me as totally genuine. Clapton's something else. You might well be right about the Carters but I don't want to leave it there. Give him a breathing space to get nice and comfy then try again. We got his prints yet?'

'Coming in today on his way home.' Troy laughed.

'Couldn't wait to oblige. Much arrive this end while I was out?'

'Several things. Ms Levine rang back unable to help us further, which didn't surprise me. Uxbridge had a call from Hadleigh at ten thirty p.m. the night before the murder reporting his car stolen. It had been parked in Silver Street. No luck tracing it so far. The inquest on Hadleigh is convened for next Tuesday. His GP has agreed to identify the body. And the PM report's come in. Unfortunately there's nothing unexpected or revelatory. He was killed, as George Bullard suggested, by a single massive blow to the forehead, probably the first one struck. Whether the murderer knew this and couldn't stop, or didn't and thought he was making sure, we can only guess at this stage. Hadleigh had eaten next to nothing but drunk quite a lot of whisky, which bears out what we were told. He was killed between eleven at night and two a.m. and, mingled with the blood and mucous, were found heavy traces of lachrymal fluid.'

'Come again?'

'He was crying, sergeant.'

'What – you mean as he . . .'

'Then or directly before.'

Troy took this in, staring firmly out of the window. He had no brief for men who cried. Men were supposed to die bravely, not weeping and begging for mercy. Wasn't that what it was all about? Why hadn't Hadleigh put up a fight? I would, thought Troy. God – I'd murder the fucker. Yet, for some reason, he could not bring himself whole-heartedly to despise the dead man. Always uncomfortable with ambiguity of feeling he shifted awkwardly on his seat.

Like Troy, Barnaby had been touched at reading this detail, so clinically described in two lines of type. Strange as it may seem, more touched than by the incident room's gallery of hideous photographs now facing him. Unlike Troy he had no trouble accommodating this, or in recognising and accepting the feelings of pity and anger that prompted such a response.

Barnaby was not afraid of emotion and would say, without hesitation, what was in his heart as well as what was in his mind if he thought the occasion warranted it. But, like all policemen, he tried not to get personally involved in an investigation, recognising the need for a clear and disinterested viewpoint. Sometimes (when the victim was a child, for instance) you couldn't help it. None of them could.

The phone rang and Barnaby saw his sergeant, who had briefly disappeared into some shadowy inner space, become engaged again.

'DCI Barnaby.' He listened. 'Yes, put them on.'

'Are you the gentleman in charge of poor Mr Hadleigh?'

'That's right, sir. I understand you have some information for us. Perhaps I could start by taking your name?'

Troy snatched up a pad and started writing, for the phone was the hands-off variety and the speaker clearly audible.

'I wasn't sure whether to bother you because when they came to the door they only wanted to know about the Monday and this was the night before but I talked it over with Elsie, that's my wife, and she said, "If you don't go, Harold, you'll be dwelling and dwelling and end up with one of your heads." So here I am.'

'Very good of you, Mr Lilley.'

'It was quite late, coming up to midnight I'd say, and I was taking Buffy, that's our collie cross, out for his final trot. Passing Plover's Rest I saw someone in the front garden.'

'What – you mean hiding?'

'No. That bright light he's got were on and she was standing right close up to the window. Looking in.'

'She?'

'That antique woman. Lives down by the Old Dun Cow.'

'Are you sure?'

'I'd know that hair anywhere. She didn't seem to notice me. After I'd walked by I turned and had another look. It was her all right.'

Barnaby waited, but Mr Lilley seemed to have had his say. The chief inspector thanked him and hung up.

'You're not surprised, chief,' said Troy.

'I can't say I am entirely. It was obvious from her reaction yesterday that she's passionately involved with him on some level or other.'

'Ah,' said Troy, tapping his nose with his finger, 'but was he involved with her?'

'The general opinion seems to be not. And unrequited love . . .'

'Can turn extremely nasty.'

'If, as looks to be the case, she was spying on him, was it simply because he was the object of her adoration? Or was she hoping to catch him out?'

'Maybe she's already caught him out. There was that crack about the grieving widower.'

'Do you remember what St John said?' Troy frowned. 'That, on the night of the murder, there was someone in the trees behind the garden watching him.'

'Oh, yes.'

'If that was not imaginative fright but a true perception it opens matters up somewhat.'

'You mean, it could have been Laura Hutton?'

'Indeed. And if so, did she wait there till Jennings left? And then approach the cottage?'

'And if she didn't she might perhaps have seen who did.'

'Just so.' Barnaby heaved himself up and made his way towards the curly-pegged hat stand. 'We'll talk to her again this afternoon.'

'Shall I ring first?'

'I think not. Well, I'm for lunch. Coming?'

'No, that's all right.' Troy straightened his shoulders in a self-sacrificing sort of way. 'I'll stay here. See what comes in.'

The chief inspector, buttoning his black and white herringbone, stared disbelieving at his bag carrier. 'You've been skiving off down there already, haven't you?'

'Me?' Troy stared back, the picture of puzzlement.

'Yes, you. You bloody gannet.' He pulled on his gloves. 'I shall ask them.'

He would too. The mean old devil. 'Just a quick sarnie.'

Barnaby closed the door behind him, saying, 'And the rest.'

Laura bent her head forward and blew her nose gently. Her sinuses were raw and her throat ached. Give or take the briefest of intervals she felt she had been weeping for days. First in anguish at Gerald's perfidy then with grief at his demise. And whoever said tears were healing was talking through their hat. She felt worse now than when she'd started.

She swung her legs to the side of the bed and stood up, stroking smooth the bright woollen Aztec cover. All her bones ached as if they had been broken by a hammer and clumsily reassembled. The knowledge that she would not see him again flared anew.

Never again. Not buying oranges in the village shop. Or stumbling through his instantly forgettable stories. Or smiling as he crossed her path, murmuring a greeting, tilting his grey trilby with the peacock feather. She said the words aloud, 'Never, ever again' and felt the flesh on her face shrink as if in anticipation of a wound.

The doorbell. Laura cursed, remembering that she had left her car outside. She had actually driven to Causton that morning, stupidly thinking she would be able to do some work, if it meant only getting off a few catalogues. She had been home within the hour, back in bed with a sleeping tablet. Pilled days now as well as nights. Another imperious ring.

Laura crossed to the window. Although it was almost dusk she could still make out a strange blue car parked between the gate posts of the drive. She dragged herself downstairs, put the chain on the door and opened it.

'Good afternoon, Mrs Hutton.'

'Oh. It's you.'

'I wonder if I might take up a little more of your time? Something's come up which I think you might be able to clarify for us.'

'I suppose you'd better come in.'

Barnaby entered first, looking round him. The cottage was exquisite, like a jewel box. All the doors, skirting boards and banisters gleamed with thick, white paint. Deep-piled carpets covered the floors and stairs. She showed them into a tiny sitting room with rich yellow silk-covered walls and switched on a lamp in the form of a Chinese dragon with a coolie shade.

Invited to sit, Barnaby lowered himself with immense care on to a Regency cane sofa. Beside him was a papier-mâché card table inlaid with mother-of-pearl on which were a swansdown waistcoat under a glass dome and a jasper chess set. Troy sat on what looked to him like a section of some old choir stalls and marvelled that he should ever see the day.

Laura asked if they would care for a drink then, the offer being refused, poured herself half a tumbler from a Georgian decanter. The warm, peaty smell of excellent whisky pervaded the room. She started to drink it immediately. No casual sipping here. Or pretence that she was indulging merely to be sociable.

Barnaby was reminded of Mrs Jennings. Expensive cut-glass misery was apparently fashionable everywhere. Not that the present situation was without its satisfactions, for nothing loosened the tongue like a drop of the hard stuff and she was already pouring a second.

'I can't imagine how I can help you any further, chief inspector.' She had put her tumbler down on the marble mantelpiece and picked up an enamelled vinaigrette which she handled nervously, fiddling with the stopper and the fine-linked chain. 'I told you what little I knew yesterday.'

'Not quite, perhaps.'

'What do you mean?'

She sounded aggressive, which was bad news so early in the interview. What he was after was alcoholic reminiscence and careless recollection, not boozy defiance.

'Please don't misunderstand me, Mrs Hutton. I'm not at all suggesting that you've concealed anything that has a bearing on the case. What I'd like to ask you about, if I may, is your connection with Gerald Hadleigh.'

'There was no connection! I told you yesterday. We only met at the writers' group. How many more times.' She seized the glass again and the golden liquid slopped and trembled.

'Perhaps I should have said,' Barnaby's voice was softly apologetic, 'your feelings for Mr Hadleigh.'

A pause. She looked everywhere but at him. Her glances, swift as the flight of birds, darted to every corner of the room, glanced off the ceiling.

'You were seen, Mrs Hutton,' said Troy. 'Late at night, loitering in his garden.'

He caught the almost imperceptible shake of his superior's head a second too late and retreated into a cross silence. He was always doing that, the chief. Did it yesterday with that cleaning woman in the kitchen. It was a bit much. Any distressed females to be interviewed and Troy was judged surplus to requirements. He found it deeply offensive. As if he had no compassion. As if delicacy and sensitivity had somehow been missed out of his make-up. Hit the spot with this one all right though. She was looking as if someone had clouted her round the chops with a brick.

'Oh, God.' Laura's expression, by no means calmly ordered in the first place, became even more disturbed. 'It'll be all around the bloody village. At least Honoria never gossips.'

'Miss Lyddiard is aware—?'

'She barged in here the day of the murder. Quite disgusted to find me in my dressing gown at eleven a.m. Not to mention bawling my head off. Who is this other person . . . ?'

'Someone walking their dog. We didn't get a name,' he lied.

'So you follow up anonymous rumours? Charming.' But the hostility had gone from her. She looked tired, slightly bewildered and in dire need of further recourse to the grain.

'It was the night before Mr Hadleigh died, Mrs Hutton. Quite late.'

'Oh, yes.'

Barnaby stretched his legs out over the smoke-blue carpet. Another couple of feet and his boots would be touching the opposite wall. He waited and felt like Alice, growing.

'I'm divorced, you know.' She sounded defensive, as if he had accused her of old-maid deprivation. 'Got married, stayed married, got unmarried. All with no more discomfort than a mild toothache. I didn't know what love was until I saw Gerald. I curse the day I came to live here.'

She poured slightly less this time. Barnaby, concerned, sympathetic, kept his glance fixed on her face. He could see she wanted to talk and suspected that, once started, there'd be no stopping her, but she was not yet irrevocably set upon that path. He caught her eye and smiled encouragingly but she seemed to have forgotten he was there. All to the good.

'I fell totally and absolutely. At first sight, like a teenager. I thought of nothing else. Saw his face everywhere. Lay on my bed and dreamt about him. Wrote long mad letters which I burned. He said once, casually, that he liked yellow. I went out and bought masses of yellow clothes that I look hideous in. I even had this room done in case he ever came to the house. When I discovered he was a widower I was so happy. I could see he was reserved but I thought I could easily overcome that. I'm not used to failure in these matters.'

Barnaby could believe that. Even now, wretchedly miserable and unmade-up, the face beneath the tousled mass of burnished hair was very attractive.

'I wangled an invitation for a meal, *à deux* as I thought,

at his house. Went along, all dressed up like the dog's dinner. Half the street was there.' She laughed, an ugly, tearing sound. 'Even then I didn't give up. Told myself that on that first occasion he had needed people round him. That he was shy. So, a few weeks later, I tried again. He'd mentioned once that he was fond of Victorian paintings. I had a small oil in the shop – a rather sentimental fireside scene, late 19th century. I wrapped it up and took it round one afternoon. Tea time.

'I knew, as soon as he opened the door, that I'd made a mistake. He showed me into the kitchen, looked at the picture and admired it but said he didn't really have the wall space. We staggered through a bit of quite artificial conversation, then someone came to the door. It was Honoria, wanting some smilax for the church. Gerald was so relieved at the interruption. If it hadn't been so painful it would have been funny. He went off with her into the garden and started snipping at green stuff. They seemed to be good for a few minutes.

'I didn't plan to run upstairs, yet suddenly I was there. I suppose I must have seen it as a chance to find out more about him. Where he slept, what sort of soap he used – stupid things like that. I remember I took his pyjamas from under the pillow and held them against my face. Opened the wardrobe, ran my hands over his clothes. All the while going back and forth to the window checking they were still busy outside. In a chest of drawers I found a shoe box full of photographs. I lifted them up and took one. From the bottom, thinking he'd be less likely to notice. As I was putting it down my bra I heard their voices coming closer to the house. I ran downstairs, bundled up my painting, called goodbye through the kitchen door and left.' She paused, rolling her glass between the palms of her hands, swilling the liquid.

'I gave up then. Not loving him – would that I could! But trying to force any sort of intimacy. I was afraid if I pushed things too far he might leave the group and then I'd never see him at all. So that's how things were for months, then, gradually, human nature being what it is I suppose, hope returned. I knew about Grace of course, how happy they'd been, but nobody can mourn forever. And I was greatly consoled and comforted by the fact that, if he didn't want me, at least he didn't appear to want anyone else. Or so I thought.'

The ensuing silence went on for a long time, yet Barnaby was loath to break it. She had withdrawn totally and was staring into the speckled but extremely grand Venetian mirror over the fireplace, frowningly perturbed, as if the person looking back at her was a stranger. He hoped all these painful recollections had not brought some immovable portcullis clanging down in her mind leaving her beyond the reach of his questions and immune to all persuasion. He was on the point of interrogatively reprising her final remark when she started to speak again.

'I'd started haunting the house. It was a compulsion. A drug, I'd go there after dark hoping to catch sight of him through the window. I knew it was only a matter of time before someone saw me, but I couldn't stop. I felt there must be another side to him – no one could be that starchy and formal all the time. I thought if I could discover what it was it would help me reach him. Well, I got more than I bargained for.' The nearness of revelation stretched her flat, colourless voice taut as a drumskin.

'I was looking into the kitchen, loathing myself for the awful indignity of it, as I always did, when I heard a car draw up at the front of the house. I ran into the trees at the side of the house and saw a woman getting out of a taxi. She paid off the cab then knocked at the door. It opened and she went inside. I was devastated. I saw her through the sitting-room curtains. Very elegant, black suit, long fair hair. He'd given her some wine and she was lifting her glass to him, *lifting it* . . .'

Laura swung her own glass high and whisky flew about, splashing the looking glass. Some droplets fell on her face. She stared around the room. Her eyes were vague and dull with rings beneath them the colour of fresh bruises. Seeing that she was on the point of passing out, Barnaby got up quickly and took her arm.

'Come and sit down, Mrs Hutton.' He had to put his arm around her once she had released the mantelpiece. She was a dead weight. He guided her to a low nursing chair. 'Would you like us to make you some coffee?'

'. . . coffee . . .'

Barnaby nodded at his sergeant and Troy went off reluctantly to find the kitchen. Once there he searched for a jar of instant in vain but did discover a box of Sainsbury's individual filters. This was a relief, for he did not relish messing about with some complicated and no doubt expensive equipment, with perhaps disastrous results.

Common or garden mugs seemed to be at a premium, but there were some cups hanging from the shelves of the dresser. Troy took them down with great care. The handles were shaped like harps and there were apricots and walnuts and pale green, delicately veined leaves painted on the bottom. The cups were translucent and shallow, more like dishes really. Troy held one up to the light, squinting appreciatively before putting it tenderly down on the matching saucer and filling the kettle.

Even before the coffee came Laura Hutton was recovering. Barnaby watched her in the glow of the lamp dredging up the energy to reassemble her wits and gather her diffused attention. He could see she already regretted her rash revelations. The baring of her romantic soul. People always did. When he put another question (Did she see the visitor leave?) she replied, tartly, 'What do you think? I couldn't get home fast enough.'

'And did you go out again, Mrs Hutton?'

'Absolutely not.'

He let things ride for a few minutes after that, sitting silently, looking around the room at the books and ornaments. It was all so perfect, like an expertly assembled set for a period drama. Only the clothes were wrong. She should have been in high button boots and leg-of-mutton braided sleeves, he in a celluloid wing collar with a curly brimmed bowler balanced on his knee. She was talking again.

'I cheered myself up briefly by deciding she was a pro. An escort, as I believe they now call themselves. Or is it masseuse? I mean – turning up in a taxi at that hour.'

'More than likely, Mrs Hutton.'

'Oh – do you think so?' The note of dull fatalism had vanished. She sounded hopeful, even excited. As if it could possibly matter now. 'Actually, I know this'll sound unlikely – but she seemed to remind me of someone.'

'Oh?' Barnaby looked up sharply. 'Who was that?'

'I couldn't think at first. The feeling was so certain but though I went over and over it in my mind the answer escaped me. I ran back to the house – obviously sleep was out of the question – and was sitting in here bawling my head off when it came to me. And it wasn't a person at all.' She smiled for the first time and pointed over Barnaby's left shoulder. 'It was that.'

184

He got up and turned round. Hanging behind him on the wall was a painting – a large portrait, ornately framed, of a boy who appeared, from the elaborate richness of his apparel, to be a fifteenth-century princeling. A heavy velvet cloak of russet and silver was folded over one slim shoulder and secured with some sort of papal decoration. His slashed doublet was thickly embroidered with pearls and golden thread. There were pearl drops in his ears too, and he wore a russet velvet cap which had a speckled feather curving across his cheek.

Beside him was a table holding an astrolabe and an exquisitely painted mask on a stick. In the background was a dark landscape of wooded hills cleanly divided by a silken waterfall. An angel, bright-winged, posed rather stiffly in the air and looked sternly down in the rather directorial way that angels have. A ray of grace beamed from its hand. The whole scene was bathed in a soft, feathery light. In the bottom right-hand corner were the initials 'H.C.'.

'I bought it twelve years ago in Dublin,' said Laura. 'A sale of country house furniture. Cost me all I had, but I told myself I'd eventually make a profit, or at least get my money back. In the event I could never bring myself to part with him.'

She had moved to stand beside Barnaby during this speech and reached out now, laying the tips of her fingers on the heavily beringed hand of the boy. The whole painting was crazed and spidery cracks ran over the ivory skin.

'Doesn't he look sad?'

'Terribly sad, yes.'

The boy carried the weight of his heavy robes with sweet dignity but the wide-apart green eyes were dreamily mournful and the lovely curve of his mouth inclined more to sorrow than to joy. Barnaby had the sudden, deeply fanciful notion that his pallor could have come from recent tears.

'How old do you think he is?' asked Laura.

'I would have said fifteen or so, except for these.' He pointed to the delicate, well-shaped hands. 'They belong to a young man.'

'Yes. I wonder about him and because I'll never know I make things up. That his parents are insisting on a dynastic marriage with someone he hates. That he reigns over a kingdom struck down by plague. That the court necromancer has him in thrall. Whatever the reason, I feel sure his heart is breaking.'

And that, thought the chief inspector, as his ears picked up the sound of a delicate crash, as of many falling china fragments, is not all. Mrs Hutton appeared not to have noticed. Moments later Troy eased open the door with his foot and came in with a tray.

The coffee was delicious, though lukewarm as the filters would not fit the dish-like cups and Troy had had to hold them over the cups one at a time while the stuff dripped through. He gave Mrs Hutton the freshest.

As they sat sipping Barnaby sought to bring the conversation back to that summer afternoon when she had called on Hadleigh and stolen (although of course he did not describe it so) his likeness. But she got more upset and started shouting that she had had enough.

'Please I'm almost through—'

'*You're* almost through?'

'Surely you want to help us discover—'

'How can you ask me that? Me of all people.' Her face was white with outrage. She threw back the heavy mane of

186

tangled hair and glared at him, then made as if to rise, appeared overcome by giddiness and fell back into her seat.

'Are you all right, Mrs Hutton?'

'I've taken a pill. You woke me.'

'I'm sorry.'

'Are you allowed to do this? Just turn up at someone's house and . . . browbeat them?'

'I've no wish at all to distress you—'

'Then go away. That's the simple bloody answer to that. Just go away.'

Laura covered her face with her hands. Although there were three people, one of them extremely large, in the tiny room she appeared physically isolated, as if her misery had thrown up an invisible barrier.

Barnaby, in a quiet explanatory tone, said, 'The point is that you, more than anyone else, are in a unique position to be able to assist us.'

'Oh?' She looked at him with grudging interest. 'In what way?'

'The chest of drawers where you found the photograph was always kept locked. Whoever killed him took everything that was in it away. Obviously to discover someone who has actually seen what was inside—'

'But I didn't. I'd only just opened the drawer when I heard them coming back. I grabbed the picture and ran.'

'Wasn't there anything else in there apart from the shoe box?'

'Some plastic boxes with fitted lids. The sort you keep salad in. Or left-over food.'

'Did you notice any of the other photographs? The one on top, for instance?'

'No.'

'Could I see the one you do have?'

'I burned it the morning after I saw his . . . girlfriend. Threw it in the Raeburn with a basket of soggy tissues. I regret it now, of course.' Slowly she put the coffee down and her face in the shadows was distraught. 'Dreadfully. It was all I had of him.'

'It would assist us if you could describe it.'

'I can't possibly imagine how.'

'We're trying to discover all we can about Mr Hadleigh. The smallest details help.'

'It was just a holiday snap, in a restaurant or night club. There were three or four men dancing in a line, the Greek way. A woman was there as well but I cut her off.'

'Was it the person in the wedding photograph?'

'No. He was younger in the picture . . . laughing . . . happy. I wish I'd known him then.'

Although the words were clear enough her expression was becoming muddled and confused and she swayed on the edge of her seat with exhaustion, plainly at the end of her tether. Barnaby nodded to his sergeant and they both got up to leave. Laura made no attempt to see them out.

As he was being driven back to the station Barnaby re-ran the scene over and over in his mind. He recalled her tears and had no doubt that they were genuine. But tears could mean pain and anger as well as grief. Or even that most wasteful and bitter of emotions, remorse.

He wondered again if Laura Hutton, after the discovery that she was not only a woman scorned but a woman scorned in favour of another, had returned to Plover's Rest after the writers' meeting, confronted Gerald Hadleigh with his perfidy and struck him full in the face with the nearest means to hand?

That love could turn to hatred was hardly news to any

policeman, for the majority of murders they were called upon to investigate were simple domestics. And crimes of passion, in the heat of occurrence, were simple, pared down to the emotional bone. It was only afterwards, in wretched recollection and, sometimes, regret, that even the most crude analysis could begin to take place.

So far she was the only person in his sights with a definite motive, for Jennings, circumstantially leading the field, was still an unknown quantity. And for that reason alone suspicion of her involvement could not be put aside.

Back in the incident room Barnaby immediately asked for a trace on the driver who had taken Hadleigh's visitor to Plover's Rest. She may well have been, as Laura Hutton hopefully suggested, a lady of the night but this did not necessarily mean that Hadleigh had not discussed with her what was on his mind. Lonely, buttoned-up types often found it easier to talk to strangers.

'At least now we know,' Troy was tapping at a keyboard, bringing up the report of the stolen Celica, 'why she had to take a cab.'

'He may not have given her a lift even if he had the car.'

'Yeah. Him being so ultra-ultra.' Troy absorbed details slowly and carefully then said, with a wink in his voice, 'Maybe he picked her up at that new club. It's not far from where he seems to have parked.'

'What new club?' Barnaby got up to read over his sergeant's shoulder.

'Latimer Road. The girls wear long ears and fluffy tails.'

'Bit old-fashioned.'

'Called "The Buck Stops Here".'

'You're joking.'

'Straight up.'

'I'll bet they are.' Barnaby laughed, checked the screen again and said, 'Odd.'

'What's that, chief?'

'He finds the car missing at ten p.m. and phones to report it at ten thirty.'

'So?'

'Silver Street, where he left it, is all of two minutes from the station. Why not go straight there? For all he knew it had only that second been nicked. Half an hour could have made all the difference.'

'Maybe he was walking around looking for it.'

'No time. Finding a cab, being driven home, which is where' – Barnaby pointed to the dazzling emerald letters – 'he said he was calling from, would take all of half an hour.'

Troy frowned and was plainly uncomfortable. Ten years in the force and he was still ill at ease when faced with unpredictable behaviour. Villainy, aggression, out-and-out lies, nil problemo. Routine. But when people did not do the obviously sensible thing that any given set of circumstances logically dictated they should then the sergeant found himself on shifting sands. And he didn't like it. Pondering at some length on the general cussedness of human nature he came round to find the chief focusing strongly in his direction.

'You have the gift of hearing, sergeant?'

'Far as I know, sir.'

'Milk and no sugar.'

'Right.' Troy turned smoothly on his heel. 'Then is it all right if I take five?'

'I thought you just did.'

Barnaby turned his attention to the messages and print-outs on his desk. Like many older officers he missed the circular card indexes and regular flow of action forms through his hands. But new tricks had to be learned and there was no denying the tremendous speed and efficiency of computers. Information that might once have taken days to obtain could now be displayed on a screen in as many minutes. Only a fool would wish the clock turned back.

Thoughts about Jennings, always on a quiet, sub-terranean bubble, surfaced. He hoped it was not too long before the missing fish was in their net. Barnaby hoped to avoid if possible a police-would-like-to-interview press release. And not only because any advantage of surprise would then be lost. A hell of a lot of time would also be wasted sifting the odd grain of possible fact from the outpourings of genuine nutters, self-aggrandising morons and fraudsters who liked nothing better than sending police cars, ambulances or fire engines on pointless errands of mercy.

He rustled through more flimsies. The results of the previous evening's house to house were, as expected, of little positive use. Few people had been out and about on that filthy February night. Dun Cow habitués had either walked or driven quickly home. And the net-curtain brigade, those invaluable peepers at life's rich pageant, seemed all to have drawn the blinds and gone to bed. Perhaps more helpful facts might be discovered today, when officers had a wider brief.

They were now moving into the evening of the second day. Still close to the beginning of the case. The time when the scene, if properly protected and assessed, was at its most fertile, most willing to yield up its secrets. Unfortunately this was also usually the time when the information needed to make sense of these secrets was simply not available.

Barnaby walked over to one of the three television sets concealed behind a plywood partition, rewound the scenes-of-crime video and pressed 'play'. Troy turned up with the coffee just as a slow zoom brought the battered cranium of Gerald Hadleigh into focus.

'He just didn't know when to stop, did he?'

'He certainly didn't,' said the chief inspector, taking the beaker and swallowing with some relish, for the days were long gone when such sights could put him off his victuals. 'And I must say it makes me uneasy.'

'How's that, sir?'

'Beating someone to this degree argues great calculation or great rage.'

'I'd go for the second myself.'

'Why?'

'Um . . . not sure.'

Troy knew that this would not be considered an acceptable response and he was right. To say, truthfully, that he spoke from a gut feeling would also not be acceptable. Not that the chief didn't have gut feelings but, in his case, they were called perceptions and treated with cautious respect. When Troy had perceptions he was told he was being sloppy-minded and to think things through. So now he thought, quite hard, eventually coming up with:

'I suppose the only reason I can think of for a calculated battering is to conceal identity. And we know that wasn't the case here.'

'But, assuming pro tem it's Jennings we're after, he didn't appear angry when St John saw him through the kitchen window.'

'Rows can blow up in seconds. Had one this morning on my way out.' Troy's eyes narrowed at the recollection. 'Halfway through the door when she started—'

'Let's stick to the point. I get the feeling,' continued Barnaby, 'that Hadleigh wasn't so much physically as emotionally afraid of this man. That he dreaded, perhaps, being compelled to relive painful memories.'

Troy would have loved to ask on what his superior officer based this 'feeling' and if it might not perhaps be a good idea if he thought the matter logically through. And wondered if the day would ever come when he would be brave enough to put this observation into words. Dream on, Gavin. He said:

'So what if such a thing actually came about, chief. Jennings putting Hadleigh through it – taunting him about the old days and that – Hadleigh becomes enraged, picks up the candlestick and goes for him. Jennings turns the tables in self-defence.'

'Which makes the murder unpremeditated.'

'Right.'

'So where does Jennings' clearly preplanned escape scheme come in? And where was this taunting supposed to be going on?'

'Could have been anywhere.'

'Hadleigh was killed upstairs.'

'But if they were arguing and one stormed off the other would follow. Rows go from room to room. Or say Hadleigh went up to get his keys to lock up once Jennings had left when the bloke happened to be using the bathroom.'

'Won't work. Hadleigh was undressed.'

'OK. So maybe this "past" involved a touch of the other.' Here Troy dropped his wrist in an insultingly coy gesture. 'And they were going to have a final bash for old times' sake.'

'And what evidence do you base that notion on?'

193

Barnaby watched Troy's jaw tighten in mulish resentment as he stared sullenly at his gleaming boots. 'I'm not trying to catch you out, sergeant.'

'No, sir.' Not much.

'But it's important not to come to over-quick decisions. Also to hold any theories lightly. Especially one that you've set your heart on.'

Troy did not reply, but the curve of his mouth hardened.

'You must learn to argue against yourself. If you're right it can only make your case stronger. If you're wrong it can stop you looking foolish later on.'

'Yes.' Troy looked up and his expression lightened. 'I know that really, but with Jennings . . . You must admit it does look completely open and shut.'

'And the chances are it is,' replied the chief inspector. 'But I'm always wary of anything handed to me on a plate. What do we keep, sergeant?'

'Our options open.' Troy tried to look respectful and only succeeded in looking desperate for a fag.

'The outdoor lot all back?'

'Bar Flash Harry and partner. And they're on their way.'

'Inspector Meredith to you, sergeant.'

'I'll try to remember,' said Troy, grinning. 'Sir.'

'Debriefing in half an hour then.'

Rex sat in front of his bureau looking down into the open space where his iron rations had been. Crisps, biscuits (sweet and savoury), chocolate, boiled sweets, pickled onions – he had devoured them all. Well, Montcalm had helped.

There were three tubes of Smarties left. Rex prised out the little white plastic disc with a yellow, horny nail. The dog's drooling jaws gaped wide. Rex poured the sweets in.

The jaws closed. A single incisive mashing was followed by a noisy swallow and they were open again. It really was extraordinary. Like standing by a factory bench feeding a machine. Open, crunch, gulp, close. Open, crunch, gulp, close. Open . . .

Rex, his spherical frizz of hair now drooping sadly, picked up a second tube then stood distractedly staring at the closed curtains. The truth was he did not know what to do with himself. He had no heart for the downfall of Byzantium. Or for map reading. Nor making out mock orders for bully beef and hard tack on his faded pink pad of quartermaster's forms before polishing his medals. Even his *Dictionary of Weapons and Military Terms* for the first time ever failed to enthral. For Rex was gripped by the most devastating remorse.

If only, he moaned silently, I had hammered on the front door the moment it was closed, and kept hammering. Or gone round to the kitchen and got in that way. Anything would have been better than running away like a frightened rabbit. Ten-year-old drummer boys under fire had shown more courage. Rex recalled with shame the feelings of embarrassment that had kept him from persisting. For the sake of mere self-consciousness a man had died.

And if only, once back in Borodino, he had talked to someone. Anyone. For Gerald would surely have understood that it was only concern for his well-being that had forced Rex to break his promise. Or he could have rung Gerald up himself from the box. And why, when he finally did return, had he not taken Montcalm? Instructed, the dog would have barked and thundered and skittered his claws till someone had responded. He would not have slunk away, at the first little set-back, to the safety of his own bunker.

But the hardest question of all, the sharpest lance, was why he (Rex) had been so quickly seduced into complacency by the sight of a relaxed Max smiling, sipping a drink and chatting, with apparent amiability, to Gerald.

Oh! that word 'apparently'. For, with hindsight, it seemed to Rex that Max could well have sensed that he was being observed and was merely faking benevolence. Maybe by that time poor Gerald was already disabled in some way, lying wounded, or gagged and bound, just beyond Rex's line of vision, praying that someone would break in and save him from the *coup de grâce*.

Last night Rex had had a dreadful dream. He had been staring through the kitchen window at Plover's Rest, obsessed with a fearful knowledge that something terrible was about to happen. Inside, Gerald was making a sandwich. He had lain down a slice of white bread the size of a dinner plate then taken down his mortar and pestle and emptied into it a large brown bottle of tablets that Rex understood to be lethal. Grinding them slowly into powder he had then shaken this on the bread and folded it over. Pacing up and down the room, he started to eat very fast, pushing the sandwich at his mouth, knuckling in the edges. Rex pounded on the window but the glass simply gave way under his hand then sprang back, smoothly undented, making no sound. Gradually, as Gerald ate, his skin became all red and shiny, like wet paint.

Rex shivered. He was very cold. It was bedtime but he had forgotten to fill his hot-water bottle or switch on the tiny electric fire in his bedroom. He felt Montcalm's head, the beard still damp with salivary gratitude, nudging his knee.

He unplugged the last two tubes of Smarties and shared them out, thinking what a relief it would have been to have spoken all these bitterly regretful musings aloud. But you could not burden a simple canine mind with such concerns. Montcalm would just have become depressed both over the sad facts of the case and his inability to be of any solid, practical use.

There was another reason too. (Here Rex got slowly and stiffly to his feet.) The heart of the matter was that he could not bear the dog to discover he had a master of whom he should be ashamed.

Amy was sitting beside a grate holding nothing for her comfort but a dusty, accordion-pleated, crimson parchment fan. Honoria, sitting upright as if bolted into position, was behind her desk studying a page of four heraldic plates by the light of an ancient cream Anglepoise. The book had been in the parcel from the London Library. Membership was expensive but, because of the importance of the work, not regarded as an extravagance, unlike Amy's Biro and copying paper. This last cost two pound sixty-five a packet and, such was the amount of time she had to spare, lasted forever.

Honoria also used the reference library in Uxbridge, wearing white cotton gloves bought specifically for that purpose from the pharmaceutical section at Boots. She never took books out for fear of where they'd been. (Marie Corelli's notion that the working classes should be denied access to such institutions to stop them spreading their filthy germs would have found great favour with Honoria.) Amy's polluting volumes were kept safely tethered in her room.

'Look at this,' Honoria hissed, baring camel-like teeth the colour of old piano keys.

She appeared to be talking to herself but, just to be on

the safe side and also for a chance to get near the warm, Amy went and stood behind the carved, throne-like chair. In the centre of the page, which Honoria had just spanked severely, was a very faint brown ring.

'Would you believe it?' she now cried.

'Yes I would,' replied Amy. 'I took out an Iris Murdoch once and someone had inked commas in between all her adjectives.'

'You expect no more from the users of public libraries.'

She was wrong; there was quite a lot more. The counter assistant had told Amy of a book returned with a fried egg used as a marker. When remonstrated with, the subscriber had said she'd been brought up never to turn the pages down.

'What are you standing there for?'

Amy returned to her seat, where she also was doing research. Behind the protective shield of *Art and Architecture: English Country Houses in the Eighteenth Century* was concealed Penny Vincenzi's *Old Sins*. Amy was analysing as she went along, seeing when hares were started and how various plot lines finally meshed, noting how the dialogue both carried the story and revealed character.

As it was a tenpenny bargain from the church jumble she was able to make notes discreetly in the margin. Of course she would rather be working on her own book. Amy had been astonished when Max Jennings, asked for a definition of writing, had said, 'Looking for something else to do.' She could never wait to get back to *Rompers*.

The problem was, although it had never been said in so many words, that her time was not really her own until she retired. And Amy could not retire before bedtime drinks were made. She could sit all evening with – or rather in the

198

same room as – Honoria, or potter about in the freezing kitchen, with never a demand being made. But should she disappear upstairs, within minutes there would be a call for a fact to be verified, a pencil to be sharpened or perhaps merely a cup of Ridgeway's Orange Pekoe to be infused.

Amy peered over the edge of her pages at the formidable bulk of her sister-in-law, noting the massive shoulders and unyielding cliff of a bosom. Impossible to imagine Ralph's downy infant head resting comfortably there. Yet rest it must have done. There was an oval photograph of them both on the washstand in Honoria's room. She was wearing a brightly patterned dress over a froth of petticoats and shoes with little Louis heels. She had been a big girl even then, with beefy shoulders and a strong jaw. But she looked so happy, holding the baby high in the air, arms straight, head thrown back and laughing with joy into his face.

Amy looked at the picture often. Knowing that Honoria had loved and cared for Ralph every day of his young life made the miseries of Gresham House a bit easier to bear. And this devotion had been a sacrifice in more ways than one. Ralph had told Amy that his sister had been on the point of getting engaged, to a farmer from Hertford, when their parents were killed. He had refused to accept the child and severed the relationship. Amy sometimes wondered if this story was true and not only because the idea of anyone being romantically interested in Honoria seemed so totally preposterous. Amy would not put it past her to make something like this up in an attempt to bind Ralph with chains of guilt.

Yet surely Honoria had not believed her brother would never marry, that she could somehow 'mother' him to the end of his days? How against nature this would be. Amy imagined Ralph, handsome, light of heart, slowly transformed into a sad middle-aged bachelor looking after a crabby old woman seventeen years his senior. But perhaps, if he had stayed at home, she would not have become crabby.

Amy had really looked forward to meeting her beloved's only relative. She had imagined many visits of quiet happiness when they would go through family albums together while Honoria filled in the background, repeating old jokes and Ralph's infant malapropisms – scenes such as Ralph enjoyed when he visited Amy's parents. But the reality had been quite different. Honoria had greedily taken over Amy's husband the minute they arrived, sucking him into 'do you remember' conversations with an insatiable and, it seemed to Amy, rather unhealthy relish. She had been reminded of those doting parents who say of their infant 'Couldn't you just eat him?'

She saw why Ralph had to get away. And stay away if he was to survive and grow. Before she had got to know Honoria Amy had urged Ralph to see more of his sister. Write more frequently. But sometimes, when they came to England, Ralph would not even let Honoria know they were in the country. Amy had never told her sister-in-law this. She had an unwillingness to inflict pain that Honoria said was the sure sign of a weakling.

The springs of the grandmother clock, coughing softly, recalled Amy to an unhappy present. It was ten o'clock, time for the news.

Honoria got up clumsily, jarring the chair back and almost overturning the lamp and switched on something that could only be called a wireless. A maple bird's-eye cabinet with bakelite knobs, fawn silk fretted panels and valves that had to be let warm up. Honoria always stared at it fiercely when it was animate as if listening alone would not give full value. Amy closed *Old Sins*, slipped the book under her jumper and went to make the cocoa.

She measured two cups of liquid and put the pan on. It had to be half and half for there were only two pints of milk a day and she had made some queen cakes that morning. Honoria was so mean. Yesterday, after Amy had scraped the very last smear of Marmite from the jar to make lunch-time sandwiches, Honoria had filled it with hot water, swilled it round and put the residue aside for gravy.

Ralph had said it was because she remembered the war, but Amy didn't believe that for a minute. Her own mother had lived through the same period and had been the most profligate of women, hurling butter and cream into her cooking, leaving soap to dissolve in the bath and tossing left-overs straight into the bin.

At Gresham House even a single uneaten sprout would be placed in the cavernous Electrolux and covered with a saucer, to be usefully incorporated in some future repast. It would turn up, sometimes days later, squatting next to a Welsh rarebit like a soft little green boulder or bulking out a pilchard omelette.

Amy snatched at the pan just in time and made the drinks. She was tempted to a queen cake, but Honoria might have counted them, as she had the Butter Osbornes last week.

Amy's fingers strayed to the locket with Ralph's picture that always hung around her neck. She wished with hopeless, helpless longing that he was beside her. Then all the penny-pinching would have been merely a lark and the rambling, stone-cold barn of a house filled with warmth and light and sunshine. But Ralph lay beneath the yew trees in his grave and oh! might Amy have cried, had she been at all familiar with the phrase, the difference to me.

Barnaby once more made his way to the table at the far end of the incident room, taking all its attention with him. Those seated turned aside from their computers, rolling their heads and hunching their shoulders to relieve tension. Footsloggers perched on the ends of desks or leant against the wall, talking amongst themselves and popping cans from the automat. Inspector Meredith, sleek in his Tommy Nutter tweeds and moleskin waistcoat, had found himself a nice-looking chair and positioned it prominently.

Barnaby opened with a brief summary of the post-mortem. He then recapped on his interview with Laura as did Troy on his with Brian Clapton. Then Barnaby spoke again.

'We had news a short time ago about Hadleigh's car. No surprises. A straight TDA. Good and wrecked and dumped in the river. We should have the SOCO report on Plover's Rest first thing in the morning and there's been a fax from Jennings' publishers, which I've condensed, giving details of his background. Sergeant?'

Troy cleared his throat. 'Born and brought up in Scotland in the early fifties. State educated. Degree in eng . . . um . . . ing . . .'

'Eng. Lit. I think you'll find, sergeant,' said Meredith.

'Yeah. Right.' Troy's near-transparent skin reddened. 'From Birmingham. Returned home, got a job on the local newspaper subbing and writing features. Moved to London and wrote copy for various advertising agencies while working on his first novel, *Far Away Hills*. Following its success became a writer full time. Married to dancer Ava June. One child, died in infancy.'

'No luck so far,' Barnaby moved on quickly, seeing that Inspector Meredith was about to chime in, 'on finding Hadleigh's marriage certificate, will or even National Insurance number, but we have traced the estate agent who sold him the cottage and hope to have, by tomorrow, the name of the solicitor who did the conveyancing. There's just a chance he may have handled other business for Hadleigh as well. So . . .' He stared questioningly at his outside team.

Detective Constable Willoughby, still, to everyone's annoyance, looking as cookie crisp and fresh from the cleaner's as he had nearly ten footslogging hours ago, spoke up.

'This blonde Mrs Hutton mentions, sir. Doesn't tie in at all with what we've been picking up—'

'Yes. Thank you, constable,' interrupted Inspector Meredith. After a commanding check around the room to see that all were attending, he continued, 'I'm afraid, in spite of a most comprehensive and pertinent series of interviews, with a wide range of villagers, we've had more success finding out what Mr Hadleigh didn't do than what he did. With the exception of the Writers Circle he joined in no aspect of rural life and this includes going to church. No one can recall friends staying overnight or even day visitors and the house is perfectly placed for these sorts of comings and goings to be observed. His car was serviced regularly by the Cross Keys garage at Charlecote Lucy. He paid promptly by cheque and, though civil, was never forthcoming. He didn't use the pub but did frequent the village store. Mrs Miggs, the owner, always thought of him as an ex-military man because he sometimes wore a blue blazer with brass buttons.'

Here the humorous condescension in Inspector Meredith's voice knew no bounds and he gave a little laugh not a million miles removed from Brian's hyuf, hyuf, at the foibles of the ignorati.

'Hadleigh always gave at the door, but not over-generously, although he was thought to be comfortably off. He employed a domestic help and did his own gardening. Moved into Plover's Rest in 1983 and was thought to have been widowed not long before. The village respected his wish for privacy and, as he never did anything to draw attention to himself, seems to have more or less lost interest in him.'

Barnaby absorbed this pompously delivered deposition in impassive silence. If he was disappointed that it told him little he did not know already he gave no sign. But Inspector Meredith had still not finished.

'During my peregrinations, Tom,' (*Tom!* Troy was not alone in his pleasurable anticipation of the chief's response to this uninvited familiarity) 'I've been giving this matter of Jennings' and Hadleigh's previous connection considerable thought.'

'Have you indeed, Ian,' said Barnaby. 'And what conclusions, if any, have you reached?'

'What if,' posited the inspector, 'this past unpleasant-ness we've heard about was not some picayune little squabble but a really serious matter. Let's say one of them had committed a criminal offence.'

'And?'

'And we have an excellent opportunity for blackmail.' The 'of course' was silent but nonetheless perfectly audible.

'Why wait till now?'

'Because now Jennings is rich and successful.'

'He's been rich and successful for ten years.'

'What makes you think, inspector,' interjected Troy, 'that it was Hadleigh who had the power to carry out blackmail?'

'He instigated the meeting.' By now Meredith was visibly constraining his impatience.

'Under duress.'

'Oh – I don't believe that. He could have got out of sending the invitation if he'd really wanted to.'

Here Barnaby made a small rumble of assent, for the words mirrored his own opinions exactly. It had struck him from the beginning that the dead man's feelings about the meeting must have been much more ambivalent than he had admitted to St John. Or perhaps even to himself. Meredith was off again.

'Jennings had a hell of a lot to lose—'

'That depends on the offence,' said Barnaby. 'In today's climate almost anything except the sexual abuse of children, animals and possibly musical instruments can only increase an author's standing. And, presumably, his sales.'

'So you think,' Troy asked Inspector Meredith, 'that Hadleigh attempted blackmail and Jennings, rather than risk exposure, killed him?'

'I think it's possible, sergeant, yes.'

'Then why,' continued Troy, wary of triumphalism yet not quite able totally to conceal a victorious lilt to his voice, 'did he ask St John on no account to leave them alone together?'

'To deliberately mislead.' Again the unspoken 'of course'. 'It was a red herring.'

'A what?' Barnaby's face showed mirth and incredulity. The room, given permission from the top, fell modestly about. 'You seem to have come down with a touch of the Agatha's, Ian. Been watching Poirot, have you? On the telly?

'Right,' he continued, 'if there are no more fanciful or entertaining insights I think we'll call it a day. Briefing tomorrow nine a.m. unless something unforeseen arises. Before you go, Meredith – a word.'

The room emptied and the night-duty shift moved in. Troy took himself off to the chief's office to collect his coat, where a few minutes later Barnaby, teeth still bared with satisfaction, joined him. They buttoned up against the weather and set off for the car park. Troy said, 'I dunno what he's on about half the time. I thought peregrinations were birds.'

'Means "walking about".'

'Why can't he say so then?'

'Ah – that's the beauty of higher education, sergeant. Never use two simple words when one really complicated one will do.'

'What's he got a degree for, anyway?'

'Earth sciences, I believe.'

'Oh well,' said Troy, obscurely comforted, 'earth sciences.' He held open the main door and Barnaby passed through. 'Tell you what, chief.'

'What?'

'He's got a terrible boil at the back of his neck.'

'Has he?' Barnaby and his bag carrier exchanged smiles of complicitous pleasure.

'Goodnight, sir.'

'Gavin.'

Barnaby paused for a moment at the door of the Orion and gazed up at a sky full of cold, savage stars. The sort of stars you could tell at a glance had got it in for you. By the time he got home to Arbury Crescent it had begun to snow.

Between the Lines

Joyce Barnaby stood over the gas stove, warmly wrapped in a candlewick dressing gown, splashing fat over an egg in the frying pan, netting the bright orange yolk with threads of white. All wrong of course – it should have been boiled, then shelled, but he had been too tired for dinner last night so she felt he was entitled to a little treat. The grilled bacon was very lean and he had already had his porridge – oats and bran mixed to lower the cholesterol and shoot him full of B vitamins.

'Oh, cat!' Attracted by the smell, Kilmowski, having already breakfasted exceedingly well, had rolled across the kitchen floor, dug his claws into Joyce's robe and started to climb towards the source.

'Get down ... Ow! That hurt.' She unhooked the kitten, assembled the food on a warm plate and took it over to her husband.

'We're off the front page, thank goodness,' he said, refolding the *Independent*. 'If it hadn't been for Jennings we'd never have been on it in the first place.'

'He must have seen a paper by now. Perhaps he'll get in touch today.'

Barnaby did not reply. He sat, regarding his breakfast, with deep dismay. 'Isn't it sausage this morning?'

'Sausage Sunday.' Joyce tapped her list of menus on the peg top notice board. 'And you shouldn't really have one then.'

'One!'

'If you're lucky.'

He regarded her sternly. 'Nobody's indispensable, Joyce.'

'Is that right?' His wife picked up the coffee pot.

'In Ancient Greece you could get a female slave for two spears.'

'In Arbury Crescent wives who aren't appreciated join the Open University And run off with their tutors.'

'I hate this stuff.' He scratched some mealy, wheyish paste across his toast. 'No wonder they call it "virtually fat free". You feel like a saint if you manage to keep it down.'

'Stop moaning.'

'Cough mixture, bicycle oil and fish paste.'

'Kiki?' Joyce clicked her tongue as she sat down and jiggled the pingpong ball tied with string to the back of her chair. 'Ki-ki-ki . . .'

'Five minutes ago you were telling it off.'

'Oh look, Tom.' Joyce clapped her hands with pleasure. 'Look at him play.'

'Just keep it away from my bacon.'

'He's purring.'

'Of course he's purring – he's a cat. What do you expect him to do? Break into a chorus from *Rigoletto*?' Barnaby watched his wife sourly. 'It's only here till they get back – all right?'

'I know that.' Joyce poured the coffee. 'Why are you being so horrid? It's not my fault you can't stop eating.'

'Thanks.' Barnaby took his cup. 'Where's your breakfast?'

'I'll have something later.' She stirred her drink

awkwardly, the spoon in her left hand. Kilmowski, wide eyed, was clinging to her right arm like a small alarmed muff. His grey silk belly, engorged with milk, bulged.

'Look at that. Stuffed to the gills.'

'Tom?'

'Mm.' He munched morosely on his final crust.

'You are sticking to your diet?'

'Yes.'

'At work I mean.'

'Oh God, Joycey – don't nag.'

'It's important. You know what they said at your medical.'

'Mmm.' He drained his coffee and wheezed to his feet. 'What are we having tonight again?'

'Lamb's liver with herbs and mushrooms.'

'Don't forget to buy fresh marjoram.' In the hall Barnaby's daughter gazed up at him, gravely beautiful in white bonnet and severe dress, from the doormat. He picked up the *Radio Times* took it in to his wife and kissed her goodbye.

'Take care driving, love.'

'Yes. I think I'll put the chains on.'

'Make sure you're well wrapped up. It's snowing.'

Sue hovered around her daughter like a bird with a single fledgling. Amanda was propped up against the sink, chewing one of her mother's bran and walnut cookies and wishing it was a Dime bar. Today everything was black – skirts, tights, sneakers, eye liner, nails. Her hair, unwashed for many a long day, was piled into a dry pyramid.

'It's not snowing. These things are so shitty.' She walked over to the waste bin and emptied her mouth. 'Why can't we have proper cake like everyone else?'

Two reasons actually. One: they were full of suspicious substances, many listed in Sue's *E for Additives* book. Two: cash. There was never enough. Although Brian always seemed to be able to drum up money for his own indulgences, the latest being a director's chair along the back of which he was now stencilling his name, he was very tight indeed when it came to the housekeeping. Expecting a hot meal every evening and a roast for Sunday lunch, he gave his wife barely enough for a week of cooked breakfasts.

All Sue's play-group wages, such as they were, disappeared into the fund and still she could barely manage. She had asked for more, of course, but Brian had refused, saying she was as incompetent at handling his hard-earned salary as she was at everything else and that any increase would simply be frittered away. At the last time of asking he had lost his temper and vowed to solve the problem 'once and for all'.

That weekend she had handed over her thirty pounds and Brian had gone shopping with her, marching up and down the aisle at Causton's main supermarket and throwing stuff into a trolley to the running accompaniment of a grandiloquent directive.

'See? This is an excellent buy – three for the price of two. And here's rump steak on special offer – why don't we ever have steak if it's this cheap? Melon down again. And grapes. And look – Bulgarian Merlot only two forty-five . . .'

At the checkout the bill came to fifty-three pounds. Brian, so sure of his ability to balance the books that he had not brought his credit card, had to stand, crimson with rage and humiliation, while a supervisor was called. A second trolley was wheeled alongside to take all the things that Brian could not afford back to the shelves. The very long queue had not been sympathetic. In the car park he had really let rip.

'Why didn't you *tell* me? You know how much things cost.' He stowed the cardboard boxes in the boot and slammed it. 'God knows how people on the Social manage to eat and smoke as well.'

'They live on cardboard pizzas, oven chips and tins past their sell-by date,' replied Sue, not quite managing to keep the satisfaction from her voice and being made to regret it all the way home.

'Mandy? Mand?' He was calling now from the front step. The door was wide open, transforming the cosy kitchen into an ice box. 'Time for the bus.'

'Awri.' Mandy shrouded herself in a funereal horse blanket, flung the dark, dreary folds about a bit and picked up her Snoopy lunch box.

'Make sure you have a hot drink with that. Not just pop.'

'I might go to my nan's after school.'

'Oh. Thank you for letting me know.' Sue gave the smile that constant disparagement had made a little foolish. 'Bye-bye then.'

The door banged and they were gone. Sue felt, as she always did at such moments, immense relief slightly tinged with guilt. She put a few bits of coal into the greedy Aga, *in situ* when they had bought the place and always on the point of being given its marching orders, and drew the old armchair up close.

The house settled round her, silent and comforting. She breathed in and out slowly, calming down, letting go of the miserable sense of oppression that never left her when the family were present.

Family! What a misnomer that was. Whilst Sue was not foolish enough to be taken in by the sickly radiance of the cereal-crunching simpletons in television commercials, she was sure that, between their phoney jollity and the isolating and loveless desolation pervading Trevelyan Villas, there must somewhere exist a golden mean. Mothers and fathers and children who both argued with and supported each other, loved and hated each other, helped each other out in times of trouble and united fiercely at the merest hint of outside criticism.

She wondered, as she frequently did even when telling herself not to, if there had been a point somewhere in the past where she could have chosen a different path. She had got pregnant – so what? It had been 1982 – not the thirties when single mothers were practically stoned in the street. She could have resisted her parents' pressure and that of the Claptons, terrified lest the neighbours discover that their son had got his 'fiancée' into trouble. Brian, newly in lust (for Sue had 'fallen' for Amanda the first time they had gone to bed), seemed very keen and, of course, an abortion was out of the question.

Sue had always loved children and had hoped one day to have at least four. When Amanda was a baby Sue had been as close to perfect happiness as she had ever known. Bathing and dressing her daughter, playing with her, teaching her to walk. Simply loving her. Even Brian's rapidly souring demeanour and the start of his assertions that she had deliberately trapped him into marriage were rendered harmless by this golden centre to her life.

But then, gradually, everything had changed. Brian's parents, only five miles away and doting on their only grandchild, demanded more and more of her time. Brian would drive over there every weekend, sometimes leaving

Amanda for the whole two days. She would always return with an armful of presents, tired, fretful and sick from too many sweets.

At first, loving her daughter more than she feared her husband's displeasure, Sue had argued against the duration and frequency of these visits. Perhaps one trip a month would be more suitable, just for the afternoon? And why shouldn't they all go?

These suggestions had provoked endless rows, with Mrs Clapton insisting that Susan was trying to turn little Mandy against them and Mr Clapton begging everyone to keep their voices down as noise travelled in the summer even over the sound of lawn mowers. Amanda had screamed and yelled and kicked to demonstrate her own preference and, once having got the hang of the telephone, screamed and sobbed down that as well, leaving her devoted nanna quite heartbroken over the poor mite's cruel deprivations.

Of course Sue gave way. It wasn't hard, for the three of them had so firmly annexed the child that she sensed the battle lost before it was even properly engaged. Also she had, by then, started the village play group and was surrounded every day by toddlers with tears that needed mopping, grazes to be kissed better, tempers that had to be restrained and, most satisfying of all, ears yearning for stories.

This reflection brought Sue back to the present with a start. She jumped up to turn the clock round but it was all right, there was half an hour yet. She opened the cupboard under the stairs where she kept her paints and fabric trimmings, stuffing and glue. The night before she had completed ten finger puppets made from Tampax cylinders – brilliantly coloured monkeys and hobgoblins, witches and dinosaurs. She fixed an anteater, insolently sneering down an endless snout, to her little finger, waggled him about and imagined the children's faces when all ten magically appeared as if from nowhere, nodding and chattering to them all.

Having packed her box Sue sat down again and ran through her check list. Pick up squash from village shop. Remind Mrs Harris she was on biscuits next week. Ask Marie Bennet if her husband would have a look at the electric kettle. Contact Rex.

She had called at the house again yesterday evening and was sure that he was in, for she heard Montcalm bark, but no one came to the door. This was not at all like Rex for, apart from his precious writing period, he was always delighted to see people, sometimes to a degree where it was hard to get away.

Post! Begging aloud, 'Methuen, Methuen, let it be Methuen', Sue ran into the hall. But it was only a notice of a coming sale from the shop where Brian had bought his camcorder.

By nine thirty a.m. Barnaby, having absorbed the scenes-of-crime report, was once more in the incident room passing on its disappointing conclusions to his investigative team.

'The only prints on the murder weapon are those of the cleaner, Mrs Bundy. One quite clear, the rest smudged, presumably by whoever picked it up and used it to batter Hadleigh's head in. They wore gloves, leather rather than a knitted fabric. SOCO can't tell us about rogue prints yet. They're still eliminating. We've now got everyone's dabs except those of Mrs Lyddiard, who's too cowed to defy her sister-in-law, and Honoria herself who has flatly refused.'

'Someone should tell her just how important this is,' said Inspector Meredith, adding, with quick prudence, 'sir.'

'Indeed,' replied Barnaby, letting slip a wintry smile. 'Perhaps, as you are in the village, that is something you could take upon yourself, inspector?'

'I'd be glad to, chief inspector.'

'Unfortunately,' Barnaby, his smile now containing rather more satisfaction, returned to the matter in hand, 'there's no result from Hadleigh's nails at all. Neither skin, hair, nor fibres, so it appears that at no point did he fight back. It's difficult to believe that he deliberately chose not to, so I think we can assume that Doctor Bullard was right and that first blow which, presumably, was totally unexpected, either killed him outright or left him helpless.

'Slightly more luck with the chest of drawers. They were lined with a waxy paper, which didn't help matters, but there was a small amount of dust containing particles of cashmere, pale blue in colour, which seems to indicate it was used to store sweaters or cardigans. Hardly a thrilling revelation I'm afraid. The results on Jennings' shoes are completely negative. No footprints in the garden. Even the ones we might have expected to find from Laura Hutton have been washed away, thanks to the weather.

'No luck with the ports telex. Jennings has not left the country, either with or without his Mercedes, via any of them. At least not under that name. But we have a result on the taxi. A Mr' – he glanced down at his notes – 'Winston Mogani was in the rank on the evening of the sixth when, just before ten thirty, a woman got in and asked him to drive to Midsomer Worthy. She didn't give him an address. Just told him the way as they entered the village. They didn't talk. She made no effort; he had his two-way radio on. Asked to describe the woman, Mr

Mogani said he had people in and out of his cab all day and unless they looked like Whitney Houston he gave them no mind. This woman was fair and middle-aged although, as Mr Mogani is still in his teens, that could mean anything over thirty.

'So far we haven't been able to trace the driver who took her back, so you'll have to move out from Uxbridge proper and cover the villages between there and Midsomer. It's likely that Hadleigh would have called someone nearby. Try the Yellow Pages and, on the offchance that this woman may have been a prostitute, I'd like a thorough check on and behind the streets. Clubs, massage parlours, small ads, the lot.

'I would also like questions asked around the village to see if anyone recalls the name of the company who moved Hadleigh. It's a long shot but you never know.'

'Wouldn't be local would it, chief inspector?' asked DC Willoughby, looking even more crackly crisp than he had yesterday. Even his smile was freshly ironed. 'More likely someone from the Kent end.'

'As I say, constable, a long shot. I'm hoping today, if the electoral register coughs up, we shall discover exactly where he did originally live. To end on a slightly jollier note, we've struck lucky with the conveyancing solicitor, who does seem to have handled other business for the dead man. I shall be seeing Mr Jocelyne later this morning. He may be keeping the documents that one would normally have expected to find at Plover's Rest and with a bit of luck these might include the marriage certificate.'

'How do you see that as relevant, sir?' asked WPC Brierley. 'Do you think there might be a link between the two deaths?'

'I have no idea at this stage,' replied Barnaby. 'But

guessing at unknown connections and possibilities is an important part of any investigative process. Or should be.'

'Oh absolutely, sir.'

'And Grace's demise can be said to have given us the opportunity to observe Hadleigh behaving in a very unusual way.' Barnaby paused and worked his bushy eyebrows, canvassing a response.

Sergeant Troy, assessing, with an accuracy born of long practice, his chances of toughing out the answer to this subtle suggestion, gave up before he started and amused himself by watching the others. Especially Meredith of the Yard, furiously chewing his lips and tuckering his forehead. Barnaby pointed his interrogative gaze directly at the inspector and waited for what could have been construed as an insultingly long time before continuing:

'Hadleigh has been described by everyone we have spoken to, without exception, as a very reserved person. Rex St John has explained how desperately embarrassed he was when compelled to ask for help over this Jennings business. So why did this self-protecting, exceptionally private, buttoned-up man tell so many people about the most painful and intimate event in his life. An event so distressing that he could no longer bear to live in that part of the country where it occurred.'

'You mean his wife's death, sir?' asked Troy.

'I do, yes.'

'Well,' Inspector Meredith said, determined not to lose out twice. 'I suppose because he wanted them to know.'

'Oh, it's more than that,' replied Barnaby. 'If we take into account what the revelation must have cost a man of his temperament I would say that he *needed* them to know. And what we must now ask ourselves, Inspector Meredith, is why?'

* * *

As Sue was buying her orange squash and Barnaby and Troy were about to set off for the solicitor's office, Laura was squinting dully at her Filofax and realising that, in less than an hour, she was due to open the Spinning Wheel to receive a double-fronted Irish linen cupboard. She had bought this several days ago and it had been too wide to go into her van. The previous owner was bringing it across from Lacey Green in his Land Rover. There was still time to put him off. Without thought she reached for the phone, dialled half the number, then put her finger on the rest.

If she didn't go in, what else would she do? Wander distractedly through her doll's house, unable to sit down for more than five minutes at a stretch, unable to read. She would certainly not switch on the television, for watching in the daytime had always struck her as depressingly seedy. She had no wish to join what she had always assumed was an audience composed of the elderly, house-bound mums or the long-term unemployed.

She had switched the radio on and off a dozen times. Radio Three played music that was either totally insipid or so rowdy it hurt her head. Radio Four offered rising young lunatics from Westminster swearing eternal fealty to the electorate with their hands on their wallets. When the unctuous pieties of *Thought for the Day* started she had almost thrown the transistor across the kitchen.

She had never appreciated before that it was possible to believe and disbelieve something at the same time. She knew Gerald was dead. The police had told her so. There was to be an inquest. The funeral, though yet to be arranged, would assuredly be taking place in the not too distant future. Only yesterday she had wretchedly accepted the fact herself.

So why was she now compellingly convinced that if she walked round to Plover's Rest he would still be there to open the door and greet her in the same sad, stiff, over-courteous way he always had. Laura wondered, and not for the first time, if she would have loved him so much, and so persistently, had he not, from the very beginning, been wearing a Keep Off The Grass sign. Pointless to speculate.

These reflections drove her into the bathroom, where she showered, wrapped herself in a robe and looked for something to wear, but without any great enthusiasm. Baggy cossack trousers of sage wool, a mustard silk shirt, a capacious padded coat of ivory wool and leather. Knee high chestnut boots, amber beads, hair pulled through a black velvet chignon. A quick and skilful make-up followed by a spray of Cabochard. And all the while marvelling at herself and at the absolute ineradicability of routine.

She breakfasted on an ice-cold Fernet Branca. She still wasn't hungry and was beginning to feel light-headed. She wondered if there was still alcohol in her blood and if it was safe to drive. She had eaten no solid food for three days, sure that, even if she prepared something, she would not be able to swallow. There was a permanent obstruction in her throat that only liquids over forty per cent proof seemed able to bypass.

She put the empty glass next to several shards of delicate china that had been placed carefully in the sink by that clodhopping policeman. What did he expect her to do with them? Get out the Araldite? God knows why he had chosen to make coffee in soup bowls. And Sèvres at that.

About to leave, Laura suddenly turned back and opened the door of the yellow-silk sitting room. It was full of winter colour, iron grey, cold. For the first time she saw the room as others – Barnaby for instance – might have done. Scaled down, so neatly arranged, prim really. Only the portrait had the quickness of life in it. The heavy folds of velvet at the young boy's hip glowed even without the benefit of the gilded picture light. Moved by an impulse she could not understand Laura leaned forwards and laid her hand over the mournfully disturbed green eyes.

The telephone went. She let it be. It was probably only Sue. She had rung every day since the murder, inviting Laura round for coffee. Wishing to be kind no doubt, but there was something in Laura's fastidious nature that jibed at picking over what would be, for her, extremely emotional pieces. Rehashing the evening that had ended with Gerald's death, worrying away at the whys and wherefores. She was also afraid she would be unable to control her feelings and start weeping publicly for him.

It struck her that she would no longer have to go to the Writers Circle. She could never remember what she had said about her work from one meeting to the next and always expected someone to pick her up, but everyone was so interested in their own stuff this had never happened.

Stepping outside, she winced as the skin on her face contracted in the cold air. In the bird bath a wren, having quite misjudged the temperature, had leapt in for a quick splash and was now frantically skidding around on the ice in circles. Making a mental note to thaw the water when she got back, Laura creaked across the splintering puddles to unlock the garage.

The law firm of Jocelyne, Tibbles and Delaney occupied the ground floor of an elegant eighteenth-century town house. Part of a row of six and situated almost in the town centre, their backs pressed hard by St Bartholomew's parish church. The door, painted liquorice and flanked by tubs of crocuses, shone like black glass. Some heritage-conscious soul had had the bright idea of restoring the approach to the house to its original surface of cobbles embedded in cement. They were hell on the feet and must have been responsible for many a turned ankle. Or so the chief inspector thought as he stumbled over them to mount the highly polished, and equally treacherous, front steps.

They were expected, and asked to wait by a stout middle-aged lady, also rather cobbly in appearance but with a warm, if slightly distracted, smile. She showed them into an ante-room. Very confidence-inducing with panelled walls, solid furniture and low tables holding heavy glass ashtrays and copies of the *Law Quarterly Review*. On one of the close-buttoned and tightly padded chairs a striped cat lay curled up fast asleep, its ears occasionally twitching. Troy nodded in its direction.

'Must be Tibbles.'

'Don't mention cats to me.'

'D'you think I've got time for a ciggie?'

'No'.

Barnaby was right. Even as he spoke a section of the panels vanished inwards and Mr Jocelyne, a short man with a markedly pouty chest and tiny hands and feet, came towards them. Barnaby was reminded of a pigeon. Everything about the solicitor was grey – his pin-striped arms and legs, the soft, sparsely distributed curls of hair upon his head and the more wiry tufts springing from his ears. Even his nails had a blue-grey tinge. He looked bone dry, as if all his essential juices had recently been drained off, and rustled as he walked.

'Ah – here you are!' he cried, as if it had been them who

were keeping him waiting. 'Come along. Come along.'

Once they were seated, in an office almost as stuffy and boring as the anteroom, Mr Jocelyne settled himself behind a desk the size of a rugger pitch and almost disappeared. He said, 'Appalling, appalling.'

Barnaby hoped the man wasn't going to say everything twice or they'd be there till the cows came home. He assumed that Mr Jocelyne was referring to the murder of his client.

'Good of you to dispense with the formalities, Mr Jocelyne.'

'In a murder case, chief inspector. In a case of murder.'

Mr Jocelyne drew towards him a mottled box file that he had placed earlier roughly scrum half. He opened it and took out an envelope containing the will. As he unfolded the sheets of heavy parchment they crackled as sharply as if they were on fire. Smoothing them out, the solicitor began to read.

'Mr Hadleigh's instructions are that any properties that he should own at the time of his death plus all other monies accruing from his estate are to go equally to Emmanuel College, Cambridge and the Central St Martin's School of Art and Design there to endow two scholarships in literature and art respectively for young people of outstanding talent but limited means. The will makes it plain that both these establishments have already been approached regarding this matter.'

'Quite a lot of money involved then?'

'Indeed yes. Mr Hadleigh spread his investments wisely. Global Unit Trusts, Fidelity Cash Accounts, Woolwich Tessa and Treasury Bonds. All in all around eight hundred thousand pounds. Excluding the value of the house of course.'

Barnaby, concealing his surprise, asked the date of the will.

'February the thirteenth 1982. The only amendment has been a change of executor. When Mr Hadleigh moved to Midsomer Worthy he needed a local solicitor for the conveyancing and asked if we would handle his affairs in the event of his death.'

'Who were the previous executors?'

'The firm who drew up the will.'

'Might I have their details please? And the address Mr Hadleigh gave at that time.'

Mr Jocelyne produced a pewter-coloured fountain pen from an inside pocket. He unscrewed the top, fitted it neatly but firmly on to the other end and produced a piece of scrap paper from a neat folder. After checking that it had already been used on one side he cleared his throat as if preparing to speak rather than write and scribbled a few lines. Then he doubled the note, doubled it again and handed the tiny square over.

'Could I ask, Mr Jocelyne, how well you knew your client?'

'I didn't. He was here for the business I have just described and I haven't seen him since.'

'I see. His investments make up quite an elaborate portfolio. Do you happen to know if he used a financial adviser?'

'No idea.' Mr Jocelyne, apparently pleased with this unhelpful response, looked kindly on them both.

'We understand, from what Mr Hadleigh himself gave out, that he moved here from Kent—'

'Hardly my business where he came from, chief inspector,' responded Mr Jocelyne happily. Then, in case there should be the slightest doubt, 'No concern of mine.'

The less helpful he was able to be the warmer the solicitor's manner became. After being compelled to answer several further questions with a brief negative he bordered almost upon the radiant. When the time came to bid farewell he positively beamed and a flash of silver, bright but well within Mr Jocelyne's chosen colour range, sparkled between his front teeth.

As Barnaby opened the door he noticed a large framed photograph of three youngsters, two boys and a girl, dressed in vivid colours, laughing, full of beans. The girl was swinging upside down. They were so obviously having such a wonderful time that the chief inspector took a moment to look, for the sheer pleasure of it.

'Your grandchildren, Mr Jocelyne?'

'No.' A trace of colour finally showed itself, a delicate bloom upon the bloodless cheeks. 'That is my family. Taken on my daughter's fifth birthday. Last month.'

'What a goer.' Troy was chuckling as the two men once more hobbled across the slush-covered pavement. 'No wonder he looks as old as the century. Back to the car now is it?'

'I could do with a warm-up. Let's grab some coffee at Bunter's.'

'Bunter's?' Troy stared in surprise.

'Why not?'

He knew why not but went just the same. They sat down in the genteel snug surrounded by copper kettles and hunting horns and horse brasses suspended from leather straps. The waitresses wore mid-calf length black dresses with aprons like white exclamation points and pleated, pie-crust headbands low on the forehead. But their faces were young and skilfully painted and they moved with just as much speed and efficiency as their confrères at McDonald's.

The room was crowded and very warm, smelling of damp clothes, toast and freshly ground coffee. There was no truck in Bunter's with all that fluffed-up nonsense sprinkled with grated chocolate. Proper EPNS pots, milk jugs and sugar basins with flowered cups and saucers and apostle spoons.

Troy poured for them both, adding three sugars to his cup before warming his fingers round it. Then he sat back, glancing with deep satisfaction over the pleated, half-mast cretonne curtains into the street. For what could be nicer than sitting comfortably in the warm and dry watching one's fellows trudge, pinched and shivering, on their weary way. Not much, Troy conceded, though driving past a bus queue in torrential rain came pretty near. Especially if you could get really close to the gutter.

The waitress came up, said ''kyew', placed an old-fashioned three-tier china cakestand on their table and departed. Barnaby closed his eyes, realised at once that he could hardly stay that way for the duration of his visit and opened them again, swearing he wouldn't look.

Cakes. Great fat profiteroles oozing cream. Slices of neat chocolate, alternately white and dark, held together with the merest scattering of liqueur-soaked ratafia crumbs. Cauliflowers of green marzipan, the curd made from ground almonds bound with honey and rose water. Squares of rich shortbread studded with almonds and smothered with fudge. Millefeuilles layered with freshly puréed raspberries instead of jam, and crème pâtissière. Lemon and orange jumbles drenched in powdered sugar. Vanilla meringues supreme, moist little curls of chestnut purée peeping out. Frangipanes.

'Yum, yum,' said Sergeant Troy. He helped himself to what looked like a small raft of shiny pastry coated with coffee icing and supporting two large swirls of soft, toffee nougat. 'Do you want some more coffee, chief?'

'Um . . .' Barnaby was studying the top plate, the smallest ring on this ziggurat of divine temptation. He figured things should be less fattening on this level. For a start they had to be . . . well . . . smaller. The thing to do was not look down.

Troy assumed the 'um' meant yes, and poured. Barnaby helped himself to two thinnish circles of biscuit sandwiched together by a fawn-coloured paste.

'That doesn't look very interesting.'

'It's interesting enough for me,' said the chief inspector, biting into it. Oh, God – pure butter. And pure praline. Ah well – too late to put it back. He could always cut down on lunch. And it wasn't as if he hadn't known exactly what he was about when he came in.

'Had a look at that address yet, chief?' Barnaby unfolded the tight little square and passed it over. Troy read out, 'Thirty-two Cavendish Buildings, South West One. That's Victoria, isn't it?'

'Yes. Probably a mansion block.'

'So if he lived there in 1982, and moved to Midsomer Worthy in 1983, when did he live in Kent?'

'Search me.'

'At least we know that Grace died before February 1982.'

'Not necessarily. People have made wills before now cutting out their nearest and dearest. Quick—' Barnaby picked up the cakestand. 'Those two women are moving. Put this on their table.'

'But what if we want—'

'We won't'.

'I might.'

'Just do as you're told.'

Grinning, Troy removed the cakestand and returned to find Barnaby chasing a final crumb around his plate with a broad finger and muttering to himself.

'What was that, sir?'

'I was thinking about the money. It's a hell of a lot. When you add on the house – what would that be worth? One fifty?'

'Minimum. Tray posh out there. And only half an hour from the West End.'

'So we're talking about nearly a million pounds.' Barnaby found it rather touching that a man who longed to write and couldn't and, if the paintings in his sitting room were anything to go by, had absolutely no appreciation of art, should leave his money in such a generous manner.

'We are. Lucky devil. Well,' added the sergeant, for he was a fair man, 'up to a point'.

'Hadleigh was obviously much higher in the Civil Service than we pictured him.'

'Not necessarily. Could've been lucky with investments. If you're prepared to take a few risks you can really divvy up.' Troy spoke with the authority of a British Gas and Telecom shareholder.

At this point their waitress came back.

'More coffee, gentlemen?'

'No,' replied Barnaby, quickly. 'Thank you.' He described what they had eaten and she hauled up a little pad dangling from a string tied around her belt.

'That's one *biscuit du beurre de praline* plus,' smiling at Troy, '*a deux jeunes filles sur la bateau*.'

'What's that then when it's at home?' asked the sergeant, smiling broadly.

'Two young girls on a raft.'

'My lucky day then.'

'Seven pounds twenty.' She tore off a slip and the chief inspector reached for his wallet. 'Pay at the till please.'

She cleared the table, stacked everything on a tray, lifted it as if it weighed no more than a feather and swanned off. Barnaby watched her go. She had lovely hair, a long shining fall almost to her waist. He thought of Cully, wondered how she was faring and if it would enter her mind to send a postcard before the tour ended. Probably not.

He reached out to pick up the bill, which his sergeant was regarding with some incredulity.

'What on earth's the matter with you?'

'We could have had double sausage, egg and chips, double Bakewell, soup and tea in the canteen for this.'

'Ah,' said Barnaby, getting into his coat. 'But could you have had it in French?'

They queued up at the till, an elaborate, highly wrought metal contraption that went ping! when the total jumped up in old-fashioned, strictly non-digital style. Troy was still looking deeply disconcerted.

'It's on the house, Gavin.'

'Very nice of you, chief.'

'Not at all. I shall use our eight quid drinks allowance.'

'From now on,' said little Bor, 'I want all my friends to call me "Rebel".'

'You ain't got no friends.'

'Yes I have.' Though Boreham sounded certain his expression was somewhat confused. 'I just don't know who they are yet.'

'You're thick as a nun's whatsit,' said Denzil.

At the moment of speaking he seemed to be the holder

of Brian's perpetually usurped authority. The group was hot-seating the notion of power versus popularity and, unsurprisingly, popularity came nowhere.

'What you have to do,' Collar said, illustrating their number-one choice, 'is get your retaliation in first.'

'Speed plus surprise and no holes barred,' said Tom, making a swift karate chop. 'But especially speed.'

'Exactly,' agreed Denzil. 'Never fuck anybody over tomorrow you can fuck over today.'

'Then,' said Edie, tossing back her wild mane of tangerine hair, 'you got respect.'

Brian shivered and felt deliciously afraid at the thought of all that proximate, barbarian energy on the loose – swift and irrational, roaring round the precinct of a Saturday night smashing bottles, spraying cars, sinking its steel-capped boots into soft, unprotected flesh. And all the while he was lying, snug and safe, tucked up in the warm at home.

'Hating people,' Denzil was saying, with the smile that never reached his mouth, 'is good for you. Gives you a purpose in life.'

'Yeah,' said Collar. 'I could hate for centuries, me.'

Brian knew that, in his role as teacher, he had an ethical imperative to protest against these attitudes of destructive amorality, to offer a little homily along uplifting lines. You only hurt yourselves by this attitude. (Patently untrue.) What would happen if we did just as we liked? (It'd be a damn sight more interesting world, that's what.) He said nothing.

'Wonder what it's like to kill somebody.'

'I been near that. Very near.'

'And me.' Little Bor dodged a swipe from the back of Denzil's hand.

'My dad's brother did a job on a bookie that wouldn't pay out. He's inside now. Detained during Her Majesty's pleasure. Dead good that is.' Collar explained why it was dead good.

'You're talking absolute nonsense.' Finally, Brian was moved to protest. 'You don't even get to meet the Queen. Now – we absolutely must get on. There's less than ten minutes left.'

'They got anywhere with your murder, Brian?' asked Edie.

'Not as far as I know.'

'Did they ask you what you were doing while it was happening? For an alibi, like.'

'They asked all of us.'

'Imagine being next door.'

'Did you hear him screaming?'

'No!'

Brian, pale with queasy imaginings, struggled to retrieve the conversational reins. He almost threatened to walk out, then remembered that the last time he had done so it was they who had vanished, almost before he had finished speaking. It took him three weeks to coax them back.

'What were you doing, then?'

Brian stared at Edie. In spite of the jumps in conversation he knew exactly what she meant. He frowned as if he genuinely could not remember. As if it was not branded on his heart. 'Marking papers. Fast asleep. One or the other.'

'Hope you can prove it,' said Denzil.

'His wife'd back him up. Wouldn't she?'

'They'd back each other up.'

'Wouldn't surprise me,' said Tom, wetting his finger and smoothing down the silky hairs on his forearm, 'if they weren't in it together.'

'Why d'you do it, Bri?' asked Denzil. 'Money?'

'Love,' said Edie, and she hugged her knees and smiled and pouted. 'I bet he did it for love.'

'Yeah. Having it off were they – this bloke and your missus?'

'All right. A joke's a joke.' When she smiled, even unkindly, the angels sang. Brian indicated the gymnasium clock. 'As you can see, our time is up yet again. We don't meet Friday so that gives you three whole days to study your parts.'

Sniggers all round. They left in a bunch, but the swing doors had hardly closed before Edie re-entered. She was looking cast down and apprehensive. He couldn't remember seeing her completely on her own before. She appeared smaller and was standing in a slightly knock-kneed way, her heavy boots pointing inwards.

'Brian – I'm dead worried.'

'And why is that, Edie?' His heart thundered in his breast. How incredibly sweet she looked. And so vulnerable – like a naughty little girl.

'Can I talk to you?'

'That's what I'm here for.'

'I'm in terrible trouble, Brian. You simply gotta help me. I don't know what to do.'

Sue stood, her hand resting on the garden gate, looking anxiously at Rex's house. All the curtains were drawn. Those on the left caused her special concern, for she knew it would take the four horsemen themselves to stop Rex working on his *magnum opus* at eleven a.m. and it was now nearly one. No smoke curled from the chimney and yesterday's milk, together with today's, was on the front step. The cream emerged from the bottles in two frozen columns topped with caps of red and silver foil.

This alone would have given a concerned neighbour pause for thought, but Rex was unlucky in this respect, being placed between a holiday home and a pair of young go-getters. They worked all hours in the city and all the weekend exuberantly entertained other young go-getters, also at all hours. They had hardly spoken to Rex since the day they moved in.

She pushed open the iron gate and walked up the path, her clogs making quite a clatter. Normally any footsteps brought an immediate response from Montcalm, but today there was only silence. She tapped the brass-cannon door knocker gently and waited.

After a couple of minutes, hesitating to knock again she made her way round to the back of the house. Rex's garden – two narrow strips of raggedy grass, some ancient roses that had long since reverted to briar and a few fruit bushes in a broken cage – was marked in several places by Montcalm's recent passing. She remembered again that she had not seen the dog and his master loping around the Green for two – no, three days. Her breath quickened in agitation.

She lifted the latch and stepped into the kitchen, where she was met by a powerful smell of distinctly gone-off meat. Enough light came through the thickly grimed window panes to see that there were several bowls and plates scattered around the rather sticky lino. Lots of milk bottles stood by the sink, which was full of dirty dishes. The bottles were dirty too. One of them was still half-full and had a pale, greenish-grey shape curled up inside, like a small humunculus. The draining board was invisible beneath a mountain of empty dog-food tins. As Sue advanced something scuttled out of a corner and vanished behind the stove.

She called out, 'Hello-o-o!'

Montcalm appeared at the end of the hall. Sue braced her legs and shoulders, for she had long been familiar with his customary greeting and had no wish to find herself flat on her back on the tacky floor. But the dog seemed not at all to be picking up speed. He trotted rather, in a measured way, his claws ticking lightly on the linoleum.

He entered the kitchen and stood, frowning most urgently up at her. Then he turned and retraced his steps, pausing once to look over his shoulder to see that she was following.

There was even less light in the War Room, just a lemony strip of sunshine where the curtains did not quite join. As Sue walked further in she became aware of bumps under her feet. She bent down and picked up a cardboard tube. There seemed to be several of them, together with some empty transparent bags and torn pieces of shiny paper.

She had only been in the room a few times and couldn't remember where the switch was. Groping around she knocked a dish of medals off a shelf. There was a cry, roughly querulous, practically in her ear. Sue jumped, crying out in her turn.

She saw then a shrouded shape, huddled in a wing chair, facing the empty grate. Two shapes actually, for Montcalm was now crouching there too.

'Rex?'

'Who's that?'

'It's Sue.'

'Go away. *Go away*.'

As Sue moved closer she became aware of a most

unpleasant closeness, as if all the air had been sucked from the place, leaving it dense and foetid, like a stopped-up lair.

There was an old army lamp of metal and wood with a canvas shade. She switched it on and Rex's never-ending limbs gave a violent jerk as if receiving an electric shock. Turning away his head he burrowed further into the chair. Even so part of his face remained visible and a sorry sight it was. Every fall and fold of the papery skin was enseamed with dirt and shone with a combination of tears and mucous. The jaw and dependent wattles were covered with white stubble.

Rex's hair, that shining snowy floss that wafted in the air when he walked as if enjoying a lively and separate existence of its own, was plastered against his skull and glued, in flat, darkened patches, to his neck. Sue could not believe the appalling change in him. She said again, 'Rex?'

'Leave me alone.'

'What is it? What's the matter?'

'Nothing.'

'Are you ill?'

'*Go away.*'

'Oh, don't be so silly.' Worry made Sue speak more sharply than she intended. She added, gently, 'How can I possibly go away and leave you in this state?'

She knelt and laid her hand tentatively on his knee, felt that this was perhaps a bit forward, got up again and, leaning awkwardly half across the chair, attempted to put an arm around his shoulder. It could have been carved from marble. She felt so frustrated. If he had been a child she could have given him a good cuddle. The dog sniffed, listened, waited.

They stayed like this for several minutes, then Sue's arm started to ache. She became aware of a dull grating noise.

It was Rex, grinding his teeth. After a moment Montcalm began to do the same, shifting his jaw clumsily from side to side as if working over one of his giant bones.

Sue stood up and began to silently lecture herself – a habit she had found helpful at times when feeling threatened or when the world started to behave in a hostile or incomprehensive manner.

Now, come on. You're a capable person. All right, this is a situation you haven't come across before but that doesn't mean you can't handle it. So – first things first.

There was at least no argument about what that first step should be. Sue retrieved the milk from outside, returned to the kitchen and put the kettle on. This was a large, iron thing which she half filled to do the washing up. A small saucepan would do for tea. She made a lot of noise while doing this. Taps full on, kettle banged down hard on the gas, hoping to discourage whatever had nipped behind the stove on her arrival from nipping out again.

The tea, cheap and rather powdery, was in a tin caddie celebrating the coronation of George VI. The procession covered every side – a golden coach, an open landau, stiff-legged toy soldiers and red-coated horsemen with fire buckets on their heads.

While the tea brewed Sue braced herself to sniff at the various dishes on the floor to see what could stay and what must go into the bin. In the event she decided they should all go and took them out into the back yard together with the empty tins. She could always run down to the shop and get more dog food.

Rex's few pieces of cutlery were laid out in a neat row on old newspapers. The bone handles were yellow with age and knife blades rattled loosely. Sue selected the least discoloured teaspoon, found a tin mug in the cupboard, sliced off a section of the frozen cream and poured out. She took the mug, a bag of sugar and a saucer next door.

Rex seemed not to have moved. Sue sat down opposite him and said, 'How many sugars is it?'

When there was no reply she tried to remember from the Writers Group evenings. As she recalled it, quite a lot. She put in three spoonfuls, stirred and held out the mug until the metal handle started to burn her fingers. She put it down in the hearth. She poured a little tea into the saucer and put that down too but, though Montcalm approached and lowered his rough, grey muzzle to the dish, he did not drink.

'Do have some tea, Rex,' said Sue. 'Please.' Then, suddenly understanding, 'He won't drink until you do.'

Rex turned at this and stared directly at her. And, if Sue had been previously distressed at his appearance, she was now even more so. For there was no recognition in his eyes at all. He looked at her quite wildly as if she was a stranger.

Once more she held the mug out, this time putting it into his hands and guiding it to his lips. Saying 'please' again, and 'for Sue', like she did with her little ones. Rex drank a little and Montcalm immediately started lapping, his huge tongue sloshing the liquid in all directions. It was gone in an instant. Rex got down a couple more swallows then put the tea aside.

Sue asked again if he was ill. There was no response until she added, 'Would you like me to ring the doctor?' Rex shook his head violently.

'But I've got to do something.'

'I'm all right.'

'And what about Montcalm?' said Sue. 'He's not all right.'

Rex started shifting about at this, rocking in his old red-velvet chair, slipping backwards and forwards, his arms locked across his chest.

'You know he hasn't eaten any of the food you put down.'

Rex shouted then, the dull vacancy in his eyes banished by a flare of wretched comprehension. He started to struggle to his feet, hanging on to the mantelpiece. But once up he pitched forward and would have fallen had not Sue taken his weight. Although his frame was fragile there was a lot of it and she staggered as she tried, with one arm around his waist and the other across his chest, to persuade him back into the chair.

In the kitchen the big iron kettle boiled over. Sue could hear the lid dancing and clattering, water hissing everywhere. Probably putting the gas out.

'Oh God . . . Rex . . . please sit down . . .' She lugged him another step backwards towards the seat. 'Please? Sit . . . down . . .'

Montcalm sat. Rex wrenched himself free, moved in the direction of the door and tumbled, saving himself by grabbing at the edge of the games table. Sue left him hanging there and ran into the kitchen.

She found a cloth, so stiff with dirt it was practically standing on edge, and mopped around in front of the stove. She wrung the water out in the filthy sink and thought: I can't cope with this. No matter how firmly I talk to myself. I just can't. As soon as I get home I shall ring the Social Services.

A figure materialised in the doorway, leaning on the architrave. Sue caught her breath. Distracted by anxiety she had not heard him shuffling down the hall, nor the accompanying click of Montcalm's claws.

'Sue. So sorry. Be a bother.'

'Ohhh . . .' She ran across to him. 'Don't say that, Rex. You're not a bother. I'm just at a loss to know what to do.'

'You're very kind.'

'No I'm not,' protested Sue and believed it, as genuinely kind people often do.

They looked at each other and Sue felt a great wash of relief for Rex's eyes, though filled with painful tears, were lucid and intelligent. He made his way, almost unaided, to the table and sat down looking round.

'His food? The dishes?'

'They're in the sink.'

She poured what was left of the hot water over them and looked in vain for some washing-up liquid. She discovered a tiny wire-mesh basket attached to a long handle and containing scraps of soap and whisked this vigorously around the bowl, drumming up a few bubbles.

'I threw the meat away. It was starting to smell. Don't worry if you've run out. I can easily get more.'

'That's all right. There's some in the cupboard.'

She washed up quickly, constantly looking over her shoulder and smiling, anxious not to break the contact between them. Then she mopped things dry with a near-transparent tea towel. She found the dog food, plus a single tin of winter-vegetable soup, rather rusty and with a faded label. She heated this in the saucepan she had used to make the tea. All this while she kept up a murmurous stream of chatter, seemingly to herself but loud enough for Rex to hear. Now and then, to reinforce the link, she would ask a question, appearing unconcerned as to whether or not he responded.

When the soup was warm she looked around in vain for a non-canine bowl. In the end she poured it into a Pyrex casserole, placing this, together with a spoon, on the table.

Rex said, 'I feel very strange.'

'I should think you do. I'll bet you haven't eaten for days.'

'No.' Rex avoided looking at Montcalm. Just spooned some of the soup into his mouth.

Immediately the dog barked, a deep, rumbling woof, and lolloped across to where Sue was forking out some meat. He rose on his back legs, easily reaching the draining board, where he rested his huge paws and waited, slobbering with excitement, as she topped up the pile with some biscuits. She put the dish on the floor. A blink and it had vanished. This procedure was repeated twice more.

A lead was hanging over the banisters in the hall and Sue picked it up. Almost knocked flat by a delirious dog who had seen immediately which way the wind was blowing, she struggled to hook the lead to his collar.

'I'm going to take him for a run now.' Even as she spoke she guessed that the ordering of her pronouns might prove to be extremely optimistic.

'Yes, oh yes,' cried Rex. 'Thank you. Thank you very much, Sue.'

'Try and finish your soup,' said Sue. Wrapping the lead several times around her wrist she opened the kitchen door. As she turned to leave she added, 'And when I get back we must talk.'

Amy was draping greyish sheets over an old clothes-horse in the outhouse. She had just fed them through the rubber mangle, which had got a lot of the water out but by no means all. Even on lovely summer days she was not allowed to hang the washing in the garden. Honoria said it was common.

Amy straightened the second sheet, smoothing out as

239

many wrinkles as she could, for they were very old, a linen/cotton mixture, and absolute hell to iron. Then she carried the old wicker basket back into the kitchen and started to think about food, for it was nearly one fifteen. There was an unopened tin of luncheon meat and, in the fridge, some cooked cauliflower and a heel of hard cheddar. She took down a packet of rice and thought about a risotto. The watery Marmite plus an Oxo cube would do for stock. If she could just find an onion . . . God, it was all so depressing.

It was strange how, if you were warm and happy, the smallest amount of the plainest food satisfied. She and Ralph had sat together on the sun-baked steps of their tiny house in the Spanish mountains and eaten bread and olives and drunk rough red wine and it had been enough.

Sometimes Amy could still feel his arm around her waist. The weight of it; the way his wrist rested on her hip, the light pressure from the palm of his hand. And she remembered how round and firm his shoulder had felt when she rested her head there. And how sweet the line of his neck before the flesh had fallen away from his poor bones.

She found an onion in a twist of old newspaper. A bit on the soft side and sprouting green, shiny shoots, but it would have to do. Amy took out the chopping board and got down to it. The juice made her cry. At least, if her sister-in-law came in, she would have a good excuse.

Honoria hated blubbing. Hated any sort of weakness. In the terrible final days of Ralph's life, when anguish and despair had affected Amy to such a degree that she had become temporarily deranged and had had to be sedated, Honoria had not faltered. Day and night she had sat with her dying brother, pointlessly spooning sustenance into his mouth, closing her eyes when he slept and waking, as if by magic, the moment his opened.

It was Honoria who had talked to the doctors, arranged for the body to be transported, organised the funeral, chosen the stone. Amy simply stumbled after in a druggy, pain-filled haze. If she had not been so totally incapable she surely would not have ended up at Gresham House. Perhaps it was then, thought Amy, scraping the onion into a saucepan, that Honoria had begun to truly despise her. Not that Honoria ever evinced the slightest surprise at the lack of backbone and moral fibre displayed by her brother's wife. It was, she silently implied, no more than one would expect from a person of inferior pedigree, for the only true nobility was the nobility of the blood. When Amy had first been introduced Honoria had behaved like an Edwardian duchess whose son had got secretly engaged to a base-born Gaiety girl.

Apparently (or so Ralph had said) their father had been even worse – a great admirer, like more than one upper-class Englishman in the thirties, of Adolf Hitler and his pursuit of racial purity. Before she had properly understood the strength and virulence of Honoria's ruling passion, Amy had foolishly taken issue when the idea of marriage between different races was being vilified, had spoken of melting pots and world harmony and how, whatever our colour and creed, we were all human beings.

Honoria had explained at length, with cold patience, that such an attitude was not only sentimental and ill-informed but completely against the will of God. Eagles and ostriches and sparrows were all birds, but you never saw them being so foolish and ill-disciplined as to try and mate with each other. Nature had organised matters to perfection so that each feather, eye, beak and claw was repeated to perfection *ad infinitum*. Only man thought he could improve on this flawless system. After all this it was a mere hop, skip and a jump to how efficient Nature was at disposing of the weak, lame, halt and those who had somehow not managed to repeat themselves to perfection. At this point Amy had switched off.

'What are you doing?'

'Oh!' She almost dropped the pan. 'You made me jump.' Aware that she sounded nervous and uncertain, Amy then became resentful. 'I didn't hear you come in.'

Honoria stood in the doorway. Indeed, it would not be too much to say that she occupied the doorway. She stared at Amy with unbroken concentration, then repeated herself.

'Lunch.' Amy hated being stared at. 'I'm making lunch.' She seized a wooden spoon and started agitating the slivers of onion. 'Won't be long.'

'It's quarter past already,' said Honoria.'You're late.'

Amy never knew why it was that moment she chose to rebel. Afterwards it seemed rather that the moment had chosen her. That all the months of skivvydom and endless, niggling humiliations coalesced into a thrust of aggravation so powerful that her jaws opened of their own accord and the words just tumbled out.

'I'm late, Honoria, because I've done the washing. This took a long time as there is no machine. Before I did the washing I cleaned the bedrooms. In between those tasks, if you recall, I was verifying certain facts on your index cards and taking letters to the post. The miracle to me, Honoria, is not that lunch is late but that I've breath to spare to get any lunch at all.'

During this speech Amy did not look at her sister-in-law. And when she had finished she forced herself not to pick up the wooden spoon or relight the gas or make any move along the lines of domestic servitude. The room had gone immensely quiet. Into this vacuum, now that she had said her say, Amy's apprehension started to seep.

And yet, what could Honoria actually do? Throw me out, decided Amy, that's what. But would that be so terrible? Surely she could not be any worse off. There were always people wanting help. She had come across a genteel magazine in the library full of advertisements. Any one of them must surely reveal someone kinder than Honoria, with a warmer home and a more generous purse.

What was it Ralph had said when his illness had first been diagnosed and they had clung to each other's hands in disbelieving terror? *Courage, mon brave.* Surely facing an unknown future must be a trifle in comparison. As these thoughts raced through Amy's mind the glimpse of freedom they engendered was so exhilarating that she felt almost elated.

Blinking her way back to the present she became aware that Honoria was speaking and picked up the words '. . . weren't so slow . . .'

'If I am slow,' Amy said sharply, 'it is because I am cold. My fingers are frozen stiff half the time.' She turned back to the sink and tossed the wooden spoon in with a clatter. 'I can't stay here any longer.'

'What are you saying?'

'I'd've thought that quite plain, Honoria.' Amy's stomach churned. She was beginning to feel sick. 'I want to – I'm going to – leave.'

'You can't do that.'

'Why not?' In spite of the chill Amy's hair was damp

with perspiration. Struggling to brace herself against the tyranny of the past, she slowly looked up.

Honoria appeared stunned. Her stony grey eyes, in which Amy could not recall ever having seen a single flash of emotion, shone with what seemed very much like panic.

'You must stay here. Where I can . . .'

Honoria running out of verbal steam? Another first. Amy, cautiously testing the temperature of this unfamiliar atmosphere, said, 'Where you can work me half to death for nothing.'

'No, no,' replied Honoria quickly. 'Where I can . . . keep an eye on you. I promised Ralph I would.'

There was such an improvisational air about the last few words that Amy felt sure they were false. And yet what was more natural than that Ralph would have commended his poverty-stricken wife into the care of his only living relative? Amy tried to believe it, wanted to believe it. But wanting, she discovered, was not enough.

'I hope you will reconsider,' said Honoria. Her mouth went into some sort of strange spasm. It was as if it held a square obstacle that was trying to force its way past the tight round O of her thin lips. Eventually it succeeded. 'Please.'

Amy was conscious of a great dismay. She had actually screwed her courage to the sticking place. Had seen the door that led to freedom standing ajar. Must it now be slammed forever in her face?

'I've been thoughtless.' Honoria compounded her mysterious felony. 'So used to the cold I don't notice. We must light a fire. And I'll sort out that boiler. Order some coke and really get it going.'

She was moving away as if the matter was settled. Amy couldn't bear it. She wanted to stop her. To cry out that the boiler didn't matter nor the lighting of fires. That it was all too late and her mind was made up. Tomorrow she would be packing and by the next day, gone.

But even as she called, 'Honoria?' the library door closed and she was once more alone.

Barnaby sat behind his desk, rumbling. Mindful of his starter at Bunter's he had consumed only a ham salad in the canteen at lunchtime, cutting the pink and white meat, already paper thin, into even smaller portions and carving up the tomatoes – finding himself in the ridiculous position of eating something he didn't really want while at the same time trying to make it last.

Troy, sitting opposite, had lowered cottage pie, peas, double chips, apricot crumble, two Kit Kats and a huge beaker of Coke which must have given the two young girls on a boat some stick.

'I don't know where you put it all. You must have hollow legs.'

Troy regarded the extremely large figure facing him with some sympathy. It was all that cooking that had started it. The sergeant had been quite perturbed when he first discovered the governor's new hobby, for it had struck him as more than a touch on the bendy side. But then he discovered, via a new sitcom, that all the world's greatest chefs were men, which not only figured but went a considerable way towards allaying his suspicions. For it stood to reason they couldn't all be poofters.

Now he watched as Barnaby got up and started prowling around, staring at screens over their operatives' shoulders, snatching up any phone within an arm's length the second it rang, chatting to the statements reader, interrogating researchers. Keeping busy not just because that was his nature but because he hoped, by so doing, to banish from his mind the image of the calorifically engorged automat squatting a mere few yards away.

'Water's very good,' said Troy.

'What?'

'Maureen drinks a lot of water. When she's trying to lose weight.'

'Just mind your own bloody business – all right?'

Barnaby turned and walked back to his patch and Troy, quite unoffended, followed. He perched on the edge of the desk and said, 'I've had a thought.'

'Well treat it gently. It's in a strange place.'

'About this visit of Max Jennings. I was wondering if it wasn't a coincidence that his name came up at that writers' meeting. We know now about Laura Hutton's feelings. What if – even before she knew he wasn't Mr Spotless – she was getting cheesed off at being rejected. And invited Jennings out of spite.'

'That presupposes she knew the man. Or at least was aware of the effect his visit might have on Hadleigh.'

'Stranger things have happened. You've said yourself, if we put all the coincidences we come across in a book no one'd ever believe it.'

'True.'

'Like for instance the whole lot of them being writers.'

'Not entirely, Laura Hutton was just faking it to make sure she saw him once a month.'

'Seems to me they're all faking it. Nobody seems to have sold anything.'

'I suppose we ought to be grateful they're not writing detective fiction. Remember Lucy Bellringer?'

'Who?'

'That old woman at Badger's Drift whose friend was murdered.'

'God, yes.' Troy laughed. 'Totally looped she was.'

'What is it, Owen?' This was addressed to a uniformed constable coming up to the desk.

'I'm afraid we've had a negative result for 1979 on the trace for Hadleigh's marriage, sir.' He paused, then, noting Barnaby's dismay, said, 'Do you want us to try 1978 or 1980?'

'Not at the moment.'

Dismissed, the man returned to his machine. Barnaby sat back and closed his eyes. Troy watched in silence, thinking how tired his boss looked. His eyelids were droopy and wizened, and the skin on his face looked stiff and pale. Eventually the sergeant said, 'I shouldn't be too cast down, chief. After all we didn't know for certain it was '79. Just worked it out from what Hadleigh put about. Why don't you give the year before a whirl?'

'We're not wasting more time and money following up what I'm beginning to suspect is a load of false information. We already know he was far from being the heartbroken celibate he pretended. And that when he was supposed to have a place in Kent he was actually shacked up in Victoria.' Barnaby got up and turned to face the map on the wall behind him. A blown-up aerial plan of Midsomer Worthy.

'I'm afraid all the people we're currently interviewing only know what Hadleigh wanted them to know. To find out anything really useful we need to talk to someone from the past.'

Barnaby rested the tip of his index finger on the headed pins marking Plover's Rest and thought of the visiting celebrity roaring away, to use Mrs Clapton's term, on the night of the murder. Where was he now?

Although there had been no official call put out, the

author's newsworthy presence on the fatal evening had been well reported. It struck the chief inspector as highly unlikely that Jennings had neither seen these reports nor had them drawn to his attention.

In which case, why had he not got in touch? The answer 'because he was guilty' was obvious enough. Yet there was also a deeply disturbing alternative. Might it not be the case that Jennings had not come forward because he was unable to do so? In other words were they all looking, not for a prime suspect, but for a second victim?

Sue sat, biting her nails, in the cramped untidy sitting room whose glowing terracotta walls still vibrated from the violent slamming of the front door. She was left alone, consumed with a need to talk to someone, anyone, anyone at all, about her visit to Rex's house and their subsequent extraordinary conversation.

She had made innumerable attempts to tell Brian, but he had been behaving so oddly from the moment he arrived home that eventually, out of sheer exasperation, she had given up.

Shouting, 'Ah, tea – tea!' he had dashed to sit down, only to push and pull his food vigorously about without eating it. He kept looking at the clock and flicking the end of the table with his nails.

After eating he cleaned his teeth then, half an hour later, Sue heard him scrubbing at them again, swilling and spitting in seemingly endless repetition. He emerged blowing into his cupped hands and inhaling with a deeply suspicious frown.

He disappeared upstairs and she heard drawers open and close and the forceful clack and rattle of manipulated coat hangers. Coming down, he vanished once more into the bathroom, carrying a pile of shirts over his arm. This time his reappearance was marked by soaking wet hair hanging in a skinny plait and a complexion rosy from friction. Then, after checking the clock yet again, he sat down on the sofa with his bulldog-clipped sheets and began to peruse his play.

All this time Sue had been hovering around submitting conversational openings along 'you'll never guess . . . the most amazing thing . . .' lines that she herself would have found instantly irresistible.

Brian behaved as if she wasn't there apart from once, at the moment of his departure, when, reaching for his scarf, he moved her, none too carefully, out of the way.

When she asked what all this hustle and bustle was in aid of he had said brusquely, 'I've had to call an extra rehearsal. We've barely a fortnight to go.'

Time was when Sue would have extracted comfort from such a statement. Seized upon it as an excuse for her husband's boorish behaviour. It's not his fault. He's tired, worried, under pressure. Now she not only scorned these false consolations but was even beginning to recognise, in this process of rejection, a certain flinty satisfaction. It would not have occurred to her to define this growing awareness as the beginnings of self-respect. But that was what it was.

After Brian had left Sue made a quick call to his parents to say goodnight to her daughter, who was staying over. Mandy did this quite frequently, sleeping an exhausted sleep in her constantly redecorated room after staying up as long as she liked, watching whatever she liked on the box.

Mrs Clapton greeted Sue frigidly and called Amanda to the phone. There was a certain amount of wrangling to get her to do so. Mrs Clapton, who had not covered the mouthpiece as people usually do on such occasions, said happily:

'We're being a naughty girl, mummy, I'm afraid. A very naughty girl indeed. But we're not going to be allowed to get away with it.'

The receiver was laid on its side and Mrs Clapton's sensible Cuban heels stomped off. Sue heard the sound of jovial conversation and Amanda laughing. Now the heels were stomping, triumphantly unaccompanied, on their way back. Before Mrs Clapton had a chance to speak Sue hung up.

Unable to settle she wandered around tidying up after Brian. Clothes were strewn all over the bedroom floor and there was a jumble of sweaters on the bed. She untangled them and folded each one quickly in a beautifully precise way. She had had a weekend job in a haberdasher's when she was fifteen and had never lost the knack.

Downstairs she mopped up the bathroom, which reeked of Brian's Christmas cologne and aftershave, and flung three sopping towels in the washing machine. Then she swished the clippings from his beard down the plughole and cleaned the toothpaste-streaked spittle from the basin. A rub over the tiles and glass shelf, which were also liberally spattered with water, a quick squirt from the Toilet Duck, and Sue was back in the kitchen looking vaguely round for something else to do.

This was totally unlike her. Usually, whenever she had the house to herself, she whipped out her paints and portfolio and got to grips with Hector, but tonight she knew she would not be able to concentrate. The events of the day crowded her mind to the exclusion of all else.

It was at times like this that she missed Amy most, for

there was no one else in the village whom she could really call a friend. True, she knew all the play-group mums fairly well but these relationships were purely of a domestic nature. There was not one that she could contact to discuss what was now weighing so heavily on her mind. They would think it most odd.

Momentarily Sue was tempted to ring up Amy anyway, on some pretext or other, and just pour it out. But that would be very unfair. She had done this once or twice just after they first met, but Honoria had either interrupted, demanding that Amy find or fetch something or other 'at once', or been coldly critical at great length when Sue had hung up.

But, sooner or later, the opportunity would arise and, to have her thoughts in order for when it did, Sue closed her eyes and went over the events of the afternoon, starting from the moment when she had gone flying back through Rex's door on the end of Montcalm's lead.

She found Rex in the kitchen, slumped wretchedly in exactly the same position as when she left. To her great distress, as she approached she realised he had been weeping. The thin, fragile skin on his face was wet through and looked about to dissolve. Before she had a chance to speak he cried out, 'I killed him, Sue! It was me. I did it . . . I *did it* . . .'

Sue had sat down carefully and calmly. She knew, of course, just what he meant – knew that he was not describing an imaginary confrontation in one of his war games or re-running, in his disturbed fancy, an historically famous fight to the death.

It did not occur to her to be frightened, largely because she was quite sure there had been some barmy mistake. For this was Rex, who carried an encyclopaedic knowledge of

251

the world's most devastating weapons of destruction in his head and could not bring himself to swat a fly. But that he believed this wild declaration was obvious, for lines of agony were carved deeply across his brow and his eyes brimmed with hot, fresh tears.

'I don't understand, Rex,' said Sue quietly. 'Please tell me what all this is about.'

He told her, starting with Gerald's visit and finishing with a description of his own shameful conduct.

Sue listened and found herself, despite the seriousness of the occasion, enthralled. Her imagination fleshed out the narrative. She saw Gerald, red-faced and awkward, perched on the study window-sill and Rex, alight with a willingness to help, waving his hands about in gestures of reassurance. She heard the wind in the dark trees at the death of the day and felt, crawling down her spine, the eyes of an unseen observer.

After a rather garbled conclusion, punitively laced with such phrases as 'court martial' and 'shot at dawn', there arose a miserable interval during which Rex gazed wretchedly at his shabby tartan slippers.

Sue did not make the mistake of underestimating the depths of his despair. He had been lying in a pit of it for days and would be crouched there still if she had not happened to drop by. She felt the burden of her responsibility and found herself wishing, but only briefly, that she had called in the Social Services after all and handed things over to them.

She turned over various responses in her mind, but each seemed less adequate than the one before. Her normal response to the crises which happened, with exuberant regularity, in the play-group was one of kind, mildly bossy nannyism. Worse than useless here. Inadvertently Sue sighed, exasperated by her own inadequacy, and her heart quickened with the fear of making a mistake, of choosing words so hopelessly inept that instead of effecting a rescue they would push Rex even deeper into the shadows. But speak she must, for it looked as if, any minute now, he was going to start crying again. She said, with great determination, 'Rex – I am absolutely sure you have got this absolutely wrong.'

The forcefulness of this approach certainly seemed to impress. Rex sat up on the old kitchen chair looking almost alarmed. 'Wrong?'

'Yes.'

'Why are you so sure?'

'Because it's quite impossible.' Why was she so sure? Heaven send me a reason. Please. Any reason. Oh – if only Rex didn't looked so pitifully hopeful. 'Because . . . Because he's a famous writer.'

'I don't see—'

'Famous writers don't murder people. They simply don't.'

'. . . Well . . .'

'Name one. Name me one famous murdering writer.' Sue waited, but not too long. No point in tempting fate. 'You can't, can you?'

'Not off the top of my head,' admitted Rex.

'That's because murderers are always nobodies. That's why they do them. So they can get in the papers and be somebodies.'

'But everything that happened. Gerald—'

'I'm not saying you've got that wrong. Where your mistake lies is in the conclusions you've drawn.'

'Oh?'

'Which you have come to not for logical reasons but because you're consumed with guilt.'

'God, I am. Yes. God, yes.'

'So you're not thinking straight. For instance, haven't you asked yourself why someone should be in the woods at that hour of the night, in such appalling weather, watching Gerald's house?'

'You mean ... that person could have been the murderer?'

'I'm convinced of it. And what's more (out of sight Sue crossed her fingers tightly) the police are too. In fact only yesterday they were back there. Testing for footprints and ... um ... measuring. If you hadn't been shut away here being so silly you'd have seen them.'

She hoped this wasn't too bracing. Rex was looking infinitesimally less crumbly but still far from convinced, as his next words underlined.

'But there's no escaping the fact that Gerald was afraid to be left alone with Jennings.'

'I've some ideas on that situation as well,' said Sue, thinking on her toes and lying in her teeth. 'I've been wondering if we haven't been in danger of taking Gerald's words too literally.'

'I don't quite understand.'

'Not wanting to be left alone with someone doesn't necessarily mean physical fear of that person. Gerald could have wanted to avoid Max's company for all sorts of reasons.'

'Such as?'

He was beginning to sound genuinely interested. Sue cast frantically around for sensible-sounding reasons whilst her face remained calm behind a smile of quiet optimism. Finally one of the more florid convolutions in *Rompers* came to her rescue.

'I would like to suggest,' she began, with a trace of the

swagger that lawyers assume preparatory to hooking their thumbs in their waistcoats and uttering the words 'your honour', 'an intelligence connection. I think we should be asking ourselves why Gerald was so secretive about his past.'

'But he wasn't—'

'Pardon me, Rex,' (objection overruled) 'but he most certainly was. How on earth do you think a low-grade clerk in the Ministry of Agriculture could retire in his early forties, buy a house like Plover's Rest and an expensive car and live, apparently in comfort, without ever doing a stroke of work again?'

'Good heavens!' Rex stared hard at Sue, his mouth hanging slightly open. 'He couldn't possibly.'

'I put it to you that the section of the Civil Service that Gerald worked for was not Agriculture but MI5. And that Max was either a fellow conspirator or, more likely, Gerald's control. They went through hell together – maybe saved each other's lives – but eventually Gerald just couldn't take any more. He became a burnt-out case. No further use to the government. So they cast him aside.'

'What absolute bastards.'

'It's the name of the game, Rex.'

'Poor devil!'

'Forever after he felt the disgrace of it.'

'He would, of course.'

'Naturally the last thing he wanted was to have all this painfully revived.'

'Why didn't he say? I would have understood. It is my field after all.'

'They take an oath.'

'Ah.'

'So you see—'

'Hang on. Jennings. Isn't that an Irish name?'

'I think he comes from—'

'By Jiminy!' And then a softly muttered soldier's curse. 'I believe we're fingering the IRA here.'

'I shouldn't jump—'

'We must ring the police.' Briefly his attorney rested her head in her hands. 'The Terrorist Squad. New Scotland Yard.'

Sue spent the next quarter of an hour dissuading Rex from immediate action before she felt it safe to transfer her attention to practical matters. These included bathing his face and hands and talking him into shaving. She made some fresh tea and drew up a short list of things he needed from the shop.

'I'll get them in the morning.'

'Thank you.'

'I'm going to switch the immersion on now. Promise me you'll have a hot bath and a lovely long rest.'

Rex agreed and meant it, for combined exhaustion and unhappiness had left him feeling he could sleep forever.

'In the morning you can put on some nice clean things and I'll take these grotty ones for a whizz in my machine. Now.' She leaned forward and kissed the deep ridges across his white, dry forehead. 'You're going to be all right, aren't you?'

Rex just trapped a yawn and Montcalm, who had been sitting at his master's feet throughout, smiled in the strange way that dogs have, stretching his blackish-grey top lip, wrinkling back his nostrils and slightly opening his mouth.

And it was on that positive note that Sue had left them. Sitting side by side in the dim, squalid little kitchen, not nearly so distraught as when she arrived but still, she feared, capable in an instant of tumbling back into remorseful sorrow.

Now, back in her own front room, Sue stopped biting her nails, sprang up from the sofa and started pacing about. She had to dream up a method of keeping them happy. And also find a way to stop Rex racing all around the village with tales of Republican mayhem.

Oh, it was all too much for one person to handle. She needed to share this new responsibility. Obtain assurance that she had done the right thing. Perhaps get some advice on what her best course of future action should be.

Then, stopping almost in mid-stride, it came to her. There was someone. Not a person with whom she was especially friendly or had anything in common with, but a member of the Circle nevertheless. And, as such, bound to be interested in Rex's revelations.

Sue sat down again, pulled the phone on to her lap and dialled Laura's number.

Laura was glad, after all, that she had gone into work. Several nice things had happened and, while before last Monday most would have barely registered, today, cumulatively, they had almost cheered her up. She had decided to treat these incidents as omens; small signposts indicating possible ways out of the morass of misery in which she was so helplessly floundering.

First, there were two cheques in the post. One, for over three thousand pounds, from a couple who had ignored all her previous letters and invoices and proved persistently evasive on the telephone. Laura had been finally compelled to threaten them with a summons.

Then Adrian McLaren, the man who had brought the linen cupboard over in his Land Rover, had asked her out for a drink. She had said no, naturally, but had recognised, even at the moment of refusal, a faint but surely healthy glimmer of satisfaction.

But best of all had been lunch. Laura had always had a friendly relationship with the owners of the Blackbird bookshop. They occasionally took in each other's parcels and kept an eye generally if one or the other was absent. Every now and again Avery Phillips would ask Laura round for what he called 'soup and bits' and she always went, for he was a wonderful cook.

Today she had said she really didn't feel up to it which was true, for by one o'clock the nearly imperceptible buzz given by the drinks invitation had worn off and she was feeling utterly dreary again. But Avery had insisted and she had had neither the will nor the energy to argue.

It was not as if, she told herself climbing the steep unvarnished stairs, she would have to make conversation. Avery always talked a blue streak, never waiting for a response or listening if one came.

The somewhat dusty room over the shop was mainly used for storage, over half the space being taken up by boxes and brown-paper parcels of books. Obsolete posters urgently hyping past bestsellers were stuck to the walls. One corner held a small sink and a Baby Belling. In the window bay a small, round table was beautifully laid for three. Stiff white cloth and napkins, plain but elegant wine glasses, bistro cutlery. A bottle of wine, Wolf Blass Cabernet Sauvignon, was uncorked and breathing.

Tim Young, Avery's partner, pulled out a chair for Laura and Avery served, on basic white china, thick curried parsnip soup with nan bread, tiny filo parcels of melting goat's cheese and slices of raw, marinaded fennel. He poured the wine, and its fragrance mingled divinely with the spicy food.

Laura lifted a soup spoon to her lips, then put it down again. Directly facing her was a spectacularly gruesome poster. A yawning grave surrounded by rotting maggoty skulls was giving up its ghost in the form of a massive scaly creature with two heads, each of which held a huge molten eye. Inside these spitting furnaces many tiny creatures were being burnt to a frazzle.

'I'm afraid . . .' Laura averted her head and made a repulsed movement with her hand. Avery looked over his shoulder and immediately got up.

'My dear, I'm so sorry.' He bustled round to her side of the table and changed seats, grumbling to Tim as he sat down. 'What were you thinking of?'

'What I'm always thinking of,' replied Tim. 'My wild nights with Simon Callow.'

'Take no notice,' said Avery, resettling himself. 'He's never even met Simon Callow. I shall take that dreadful thing down after lunch.'

'Oh, don't do that,' protested Tim. 'I like it. It reminds me of your ex.'

Laura listened to them happily prattling on. At first she ate automatically, distracted by melancholy, but nobody could eat Avery's food automatically for long. As her nose and taste buds became entranced by the soft but vibrant impact of the wine and the piquant, buttery soup, Laura's attention was claimed completely.

When she next tuned into the conversation the talk was of VAT returns, the property market and the general bloody-mindedness of bank managers.

'It's not even as if it's their money,' complained Avery, very loudly.

'Calm down,' said Tim.

'I'm perfectly calm!'

'You're shouting.'

'I'm not shouting. Am I shouting, Laura? I mean, truly, am I?'

Laura, nibbling a fat Greek olive that smelled of coriander, did not reply. Now that the meal was almost over she felt the paralysis of loneliness starting to creep back. Isolated, unintentionally withdrawn, she drained her glass in one quick movement.

'What is it, love?' said Tim. 'What's the matter?'

She looked across at the lean, dark face intently regarding her. His eyes – unlike his partner's, which were always inquisitive and glossy with excitement at the merest whiff of another's sorrows – were grave and concerned. Perhaps it was this that made Laura answer honestly. Perhaps it was the wine.

'Someone's died. A friend.'

'Oh, Laura.' Tim reached across the table and took her hand. 'I'm so sorry.'

'And here we were,' said Avery, 'blathering on.' He refilled her glass. 'Drink up, heart.'

'Do you want to talk about it?'

To her surprise, for she had already talked about it to a degree that had left her quite wrung out, Laura found that she did. That previous outpouring to the chief inspector, such an anguished, angry flux, had left her sore and miserable. The whole process had been so untimely – provoked not by a need on her part to speak but by pressure from an impersonal inquisitor.

'The man who died – he was killed actually – lived in our village.'

'Not the one in the papers!' gasped Avery. There was a

sharp movement under the table. He winced and said, 'Sorry.'

'Yes. I loved him,' said Laura simply. And after that it was easy. She started at the very beginning, when she had trodden on Gerald's foot in the village store, and went on until the end, when she had kissed him goodnight (and, unwittingly, goodbye) on the last night of his life.

'I always used to think,' she concluded sadly, 'that if you loved someone hard enough and for long enough eventually they wouldn't be able to help loving you back. Very . . . very foolish . . .'

'Oh darling, don't take on.' Avery produced a large silk Paisley square from his breast pocket and passed it over with a flourish. 'Have a blotette.' Laura blew her nose. 'All due respects, but he must have been blind as a bat. Heavens – if I weren't gay I'd spend my entire life panting through your letter box. Wouldn't you, Tim?'

'Absolutely.' Tim stood up and rested his hand lightly on Laura's shoulder. 'Some coffee?'

'Yes, please.' Her head was heavy from the wine. She looked at her watch. 'Good grief – it's half past three.'

'So?' He plugged in the grinder.

'You'll be losing customers.'

'On a day like this?' said Avery. Hailstones were bouncing off the window. When the coffee arrived he mused aloud on the possibility of there being any choccies. Tim produced a dish of Godiva Manon Blanc and Avery said, 'Ooohh – I shouldn't.'

'Why ask then, you ninny?'

The conversation reverted to the tragedy. Tim told Laura she knew where they were and if there was anything they could do, anything at all . . . Avery said she must come to dinner at the flat very soon, then asked what Max

261

Jennings was really like. Tim spoke again and wondered if she'd thought about moving.

'Moving? You mean the shop?'

'No, no. From the village. You seem to have been terribly unhappy there,' he continued, 'since you fell for this chap. And if you stay you'll just be endlessly reminded.'

And that was how Laura came to be sitting on her pretty little turquoise love seat five hours later surrounded by bumf from Causton's many estate agents, one of whom was coming at ten in the morning to value her house. The speed with which she had accepted Tim's suggestion left Laura with the feeling that she must have, eventually, come to just such a conclusion by herself.

She felt – not light-hearted, that would be going too far – but as if some sort of corner had been turned. Now that Gerald was no longer present, would never be present again, she would try to love him in a less tormented way. Grieve cleanly, as if for an old friend. And perhaps, eventually, resignation at her loss would transform itself into release.

As Brian approached the rusty railings encircling 13 Quarry Cottages he found a moment, even in the midst of extreme physical and emotional turmoil, to wonder at their nomenclature, for they were not only a mere two in number, but a hell of a stone's throw from the nearest quarry.

He stood motionless beneath the sugary laden branches of a slender tree, doubly drained of colour by ice and moonlight. Frost nibbled at his vitals. He kept swallowing very fast in a futile attempt to slow down his heart rate and remain calm. He had stood precisely thus many times, including the night of Gerald's murder, but never before by appointment.

To pass the time he ran through the three scenes he had, after much rewriting, finally completed. They were not entirely satisfactory. Rather like blancmange their outline was tremulous and their content hard to define.

The problem was that Brian, having been compelled to weigh freedom of expression – the ripe invention of his actors' movement and dialogue – against his own future as a schoolmaster, had come down, quite unequivocally, in favour of the latter. Of course he was well aware that all his cuts could be reinstated 'on the night' or even (he fainted at the thought) improved upon. Nothing he could do about that but trust to luck.

It would be all right. Basically, at the end of the day, they were good kids. On his side. Like all ignored, neglected youngsters – and grown-ups too come to that – they only wanted admiration and respect. To be somebody. He understood that, oh yes. With all his heart and soul.

Brian pushed back his cuff and consulted his Kronograff Cosmopolitan. Numerals the colour of phosporescent mushy peas glowed up at him. It showed the time in London, Paris and New York and was water resistant to a hundred metres. Brian rubbed the glass admiringly with the back of his glove and, boldly risking radon poisoning, peered closely at the dial. It was good to know that whatever the occasion, whether strolling down the Boulevard Haussman or snorkelling in the Hudson, should a casual passer-by happen to be in need of the hour they would not ask in vain.

Brian became aware that the tip of his nose was frozen. Without a doubt the shirt he had finally decided on was not warm enough, even under his mother's hand-knitted

Aran cardie. He had decided to abandon his string vest. His baseball cap, through the back slot of which his plait had been pulled, did not really keep the warm in.

Edie had said nine o'clock. One minute to go. Trained up into precise punctuality since babyhood he could not bring himself to knock on the door a second earlier.

When she had come back after rehearsal to ask for help with her script his pleasure had been tempered by a certain scepticism. In fact he had gone so far as to check the corridor, half expecting to discover the rest of them snorting and giggling behind the swing doors. But it had been quite empty. And his suspicions had been completely vanquished when, as they were parting, she had said, 'Don't tell the others.'

At this remark an upsetting little thrill had rippled through Brian's slender frame. Agreeable yet alarming. For the words seemed to him to add a definitely clandestine gloss to Edie's request. Hoiked it out of the simple teacher/pupil category into something quite different. He had been both relieved and disappointed when she had added, 'They'd only laugh.'

Even so the fact remained that he would, presumably, be alone with her and since their brief exchange his imagination had run lubriciously riot. In vain did he argue that the aim of the visit was basically pastoral. Inventive and spicy images still seethed.

She sat, hands on her wide-apart knees, revealing those absurdly brief, terribly tight, furry knickers. What Tom called her pom-pom shorts. Alternatively, Brian zoomed in on her ears. One a transparent spiralling unblemished shell of exquisite delicacy, the other brutally hammered by bronze and iron-like shapes – studs and pins and rings and dependent, trembling corkscrews of silver wire. He pulled a comb from her hair and it tumbled, like glowing lava, over bare shoulders.

An owl hooted. He glanced again at his wrist. Half a minute past! Thirty whole, deeply precious seconds wasted. He looked for a gate, could not find one and climbed over the railings.

By the light of a brand-new carriage lamp he could see a scrubby bit of grass littered with domestic detritus. A rusty fridge, part of a sideboard, some smashed-up tea chests and a disembowelled armchair piled with old car tyres. Next to the chair was a beer barrel lying on its side.

As Brian approached the house he heard a rattling shake then, with a terrific snarling and snapping, a dog leapt out of the barrel and flew at him. Brian yelped with fear and shot up into the air like a rocket. At once the dog doubled up on the vocal pyrotechnics, tugging on its metal chain and growling with great ferocity.

'Sabre!' A rectangle of golden light and Edie stood in the doorway. 'Shut that bloody row.' She held the door wider, smiling at Brian as he approached with admirable speed. 'He won't hurt you.'

'Goodness.' Brian gave vent to a costive chuckle. 'Dogs don't bother me. Quite the reverse in fact.' Boldly he made as if to reverse his steps. 'Here boy . . .'

'I shouldn't pat him, all the same.'

'Oh. Right.'

She did not make way for him to enter the house. Brian had to squeeze by, holding his breath apologetically, giddily aware of her lovely face, a mere kiss away from his own.

They were immediately in what Brian assumed must be the sitting room, though there wasn't a lot of space to sit. One of the walls had almost vanished behind stacks of cardboard boxes labelled Sharp and Hitachi. The black-vinyl settee, disgorging foam chippings from various gashes and splits, looked as if it had been playfully gored by a bull. In the corner was the largest television set that Brian had ever seen. Vast, matt black, state-of-the-art Technic. On top of it was a wicker basket full of plastic flowers in violent shades of red and orange, and underneath, a video. A handsome ghetto blaster played pop music, very loudly. Clothes were lying about in untidy piles and a couple of dresses hung from the picture rail on wire hangers.

Edie did not even refer to the state of the place, let alone offer excuses, and Brian could not help but be impressed. His mother would apologise for the mess if one of her quilted salmon-velour scatter cushions, Velcroed into position across the back of the chesterfield, was an eighth of an inch out of true.

'Make yourself at home then.'

'Thank you.' It was extremely warm. Brian unzipped his anorak, folded it carefully , laid it on the settee and sat on it. He was touched to notice one of the computer print-outs that he had handed out, heavily notated with Biro. He coughed nervously and looked around, searching for something to say. His eye fell on the boxes.

'You . . . er . . . go in for hi-fis then, Edie?'

'We're collecting them. For the Multiple Scrolosis.'

'Excellent.' Brian was careful to keep the surprise from his voice. 'Keep up the good work.' Hyuf, hyuf.

'You wanna drink?'

'Thank you.'

She crossed over to an old, heavily carved 1950s sideboard covered with ornaments, glasses, more plastic flowers and birthday cards and opened it, producing a totally unfamiliar bottle.

'To whom do I wish many happy returns, Edie?'

'Me mum. Thirty-one yesterday.'

'Good heavens.' Younger than me. 'Is she . . . er . . . around at this moment in time?'

'No. It's her weight-lifting night.'

He wanted to ask where Tom was, but feared seeming too obvious. He knew where her father was. Doing ten years for armed robbery in Albany.

'Put the wood in the hole, Bri.'

At a loss he stared around then noticed a door standing open in the far corner, leading to some stairs. He closed it and leaned against the panels, raising his eyebrows whimsically. Then it struck him that this stance might look a bit threatening, so he moved back into the centre where he was given his drink.

'Bottoms up, then,' said Edie as he stood awkwardly clutching the smeary tumbler.

'What is it?'

'Thunderbirds Mixed Wine.' She grinned. 'It's fruity. Apples and lemons and that.'

'Aren't you having any?'

'Got to keep me head clear, haven't I?'

'Of course. Sorry.'

'You'll be leading me in wicked ways, Brian.'

More to smother this wondrous notion at birth than because he was thirsty Brian took a large gulp of the liquid, which exploded between his ears.

'All right?'

'Absolutely.' He clutched the back of a chair. 'Thunderbirds are go.'

'You what?'

Of course she would be too young for the first TV series and too old to bother with the repeats. What a stupid thing to say. She'd think he was an absolute cretin.

Eyes closed, Edie was swaying now to the music, the arch of her back as strong, slender and supple as a steel spring, balancing gracefully on spiky, high-heeled shoes of patent leather that seemed slightly too big for her. Brian wondered if they belonged to her mother and the thought impelled feelings of excited tenderness. He boldly joined in, shifting clumsily from one foot to the other and clicking his fingers – off the beat, his ear for music being even worse than his ear for dialogue.

'You wannanother drink?' She had stopped dancing.

'Better not. Thank you.'

'Sit down then.'

Brian looked about him. The single armchair held video and audio tapes, freebie newspapers, some tights and a plate streaked with tomato sauce and dried egg yolk. He gravitated back to the settee.

This also held a certain amount of debris. Edie threw it all over the back. This move involved both kneeling and reaching and the narrow band of Lycra posing as a skirt was so tautly stretched that Brian could clearly see the cleft between her buttocks. He broke out into a warm glow, which he put down to the excessive heat from a three-bar electric fire.

'So, young Edie.' Keep it light and jocular. 'How can I help?' She bounced down beside him.

Well, fair enough. There was nothing in that. In fact, looking at it from a purely practical viewpoint, it was the only sensible place to choose. Not a lot of point in her sitting miles away in that cumbersome old armchair. If this was going to be a counselling session – and all the signs indicated that it was – then proximity was of the essence. He only hoped he would be able to hear what she was saying over the music. The driving, chopping beat was splintering his skull. He would have liked to ask that it be turned down, or even off, but was afraid she would think him square and middle-aged.

Edie settled, tucking her legs beneath her. Her shiny black tights had a single run, starting at the left knee and disappearing inside her leopard-spotted bandeau of a skirt. Somehow Brian dragged his eyes from the ladder and ordered his frenzied imagination to stop picturing its final resting place. Then he asked once more what he could do to allay her anxieties.

He spoke softly, knowing she would not be able to hear him, and, to his relief, the ploy worked. Edie got up and switched off the ghetto blaster at the plug. The fiery blooms on the television set also ceased their dazzle, wilting immediately into a tired bunch of dusty grey plastic.

'Thing is Brian,' she sat down again, surely fractionally closer than before? 'I'm never going to be able to stand up in front of all them people.'

'Of course you are. Once you step on-stage all those nerves will vanish. Believe me, I know.'

'Then there's my accent. I reckon she should talk better. More like a receptionist.'

'Your accent's perfect for the part.'

Even as he spoke it struck Brian that the remark might have been better phrased, for the character in question was a sluttish, foul-mouthed drug-addicted scrubber, on the dole and on the make when she wasn't on the game. A type in fact not a million miles removed from Denzil's deceased auntie, who made medical history, according to her nephew, by producing a death rattle in the vagina.

'Actually,' the fingers of her right hand, resting lightly

on the edge of her skirt, curled inwards. Disappeared. 'I find her whole personality difficult. She's the sort that really gets on my tits. Know what I mean?'

'Errkk . . .' Brian, mesmerised by the shifting movements beneath her skirt (was she stroking? scratching?), croaked, 'Let's hot-seat this one Edie, OK? Now – no pause for thought – one, two, three – why?'

'The way she keeps pretending she don't fancy Mick when it's dead obvious she's dying for it. Me – I'd come right up front and tell him.'

'Ah – but that's the fun of acting.' He got the words out, though his voice had knots in. 'Living the life, just for a while, of someone quite unlike yourself. You see, Edie, that's the whole point of art. To sublimate brute facts.'

'You're really deep, Brian.'

Brian, about as deep as clingfilm but not nearly so useful, gave a falsely deprecating shrug.

'But,' continued Edie, 'when you've finished sublimating, aren't you just back where you started?'

Faced with this shattering perception Brian found himself lost for words. Edie looked at him hopefully for a moment then, with an air of disappointment, turned sadly away.

Shame that he had failed her jostled in Brian's mind with a ravenous hunger as he studied that exquisite profile. Tiny parrots swung from golden perches in her ears. Wooden, brilliantly painted birds. Above one of them a question mark composed of punctures where all the studs and screws and pins had been. Observing this he became aware of a disturbing longing. A need to fondle, bite and kiss the grubby lobe. He put his hands together, trapping them firmly beneath his denimed knees.

'Your wife know you're round here, Brian?'

'No.' He arranged his features into a deep puzzlement, making it clear just how incomprehensible he found such a question. 'She wasn't in when I left. But I'm often out on school business. I don't always give chapter and verse.'

'Must be lovely to be married. Have your own little house and family.'

'Don't you believe it.' Brian produced an arch but slightly anaemic hyuf, hyuf. 'A man can die of domesticity.'

'You're not dead.'

'I am inside.'

He regretted the words instantly. It was one thing for him and Edie to be equal when rehearsing. Be a hundred per cent open, there for each other and so forth. Quite another for him to reveal intimate and, worse, deeply unflattering aspects of his private life. It never occurred to Brian that displaying a deeply discontented and envious state of mind would endear him far more quickly to his group than the patronising jollity he familiarly employed.

'Ohh Bri . . .' Edie sighed and rested her hand, laden with rings, sympathetically on his knee. 'I'm ever so sorry.'

Brian flinched. His mouth was dry as sand. He stared down, almost cross-eyed with tension, at the badly chipped cyclamen nails.

'All that was strictly *entre nous*, Edie.'

'You what?'

'I wouldn't want you to tell anyone.'

'What sort of person do you think I am?' As quickly as she had leaned towards him she jerked away, her young face cold and hard. 'You got a funny idea about friendship, you have.'

'Oh – forgive me. I didn't mean – Edie? Don't go . . .'

But she was already walking away. He watched her swaying across the sculptured whorls of purple carpet, watched the high, deliciously rounded leopardy buttocks jostling sweetly, cheek by cheek, against each other and thought that any minute he might well pass out. Now she was at the sideboard uncorking the Thunderbirds.

'Wannanother?'

'Yes! Yes, please. Thank you, Edie.' He didn't, but if it brought her back to his side perhaps he could . . . Could what?

'Then we can do my lines, if you like.'

She seemed to be pouring one for herself as well this time, looking across at him and smiling as sociably as if their sharp little exchange had never happened. This rapid and seemingly irrational change of mood, which was common to them all, was one of the things that Brian found hardest to understand. He himself was much given to sulking and withheld forgiveness relentlessly.

'I gotta get them DLP,' said Edie. 'That right?'

'Spot on.'

'Remember what Denzil said it stood for?'

'No.' A lie, for even now, in fantasy, her lips and tongue nuzzled inside his jeans.

She put another tape in the ghetto blaster, this time disconnecting the florist's lament. The music was slow, sweet and quiet.

'Like it?'

'Very much.'

'So . . .' She gave him his drink, sat next to him and said, 'Link up, then.'

'I'm sorry?'

'Like friends do.'

She slipped her arm through his then lifted her glass to her mouth, which movement drew their faces close. Her breath smelt of cigarette smoke and salt and vinegar crisps and an underlying pungency that reminded him of the science lab and that he recognised later as pear drops. Locked together thus, struggling and laughing, they drank. In his excitement and nervousness Brian spilled most of his.

'Fuck,' said Edie. 'All down me jumper.'

'Sorry.'

'It'll dry.'

She drew away and, once more, her face came into focus. Mango lips, damp now with gleaming wine, huge violet-shadowed eyes, the lashes so thickly mascara'd they stuck out like tiny thorns. Her wonderful marmalade hair had been pinned up carelessly and several frondy, twisting curls escaped. She sat facing him, cross-legged, swallowing deeply and with languid relish.

Brian, bemooned, gazed back. He strove to come up with an innocuous remark, one that would neutralise the conversation and steer it firmly into strictly platonic channels. The only one that occurred (and recurred) was hopelessly inappropriate and much more likely to inflame than douse the situation. Tension clicking in his mind like a turnstile he delivered it anyway.

'I'd have thought someone like you would have a boyfriend to come round and hear your lines.'

'Him?' Edie jeered. Brian felt a stab of disappointment that he had been proved right, tempered by a certain satisfaction at the scorn in her voice. 'He's useless.'

'In what way?'

'Every sodding way. He's the original non-fattening centre. Know what I mean?'

Brian stared, uncomprehending. He was beginning to feel slightly zonked, what with the Thunderbirds, a surfeit of body warmth and the rampant excitement in his underwear. Certainly his brain must be addled because, for the life of him, he could not spot any causal link between an unsatisfactory suitor and a box of Maltesers. Unless she meant he never brought her any.

'I bet your wife don't have no problems in that department.'

Edie winked, but Brian missed it for his glance, having roamed across the curve of her belly and climbed that unbearably sexy ladder, had now come to rest on the thin, wraparound top, the damp sections of which were clinging very closely indeed.

'That can't be very comfortable.' He spoke through stiff lips and, although nothing in her expression changed, he knew that some invisible barrier had been crossed. That he would no longer be able to get up and walk away. Even so he was completely unprepared for the speed of the next development.

'You're right,' murmured Edie. 'I'll catch me death.'

Without taking her eyes off his face she pulled at the securing ties behind her back. The garment fell apart, revealing beautiful, blue veined, pearly-white breasts with raspberry tips. Brian stared, dumbstruck with exhilaration and fear. Then she leaned forward, uncoiled a tongue like a humming bird's and slid it into his ear.

Brian panted and groaned. He felt so dizzy he thought he might lose consciousness.

'Touch me Bri . . . come on . . . *quick* . . .'

'Ohhh . . . Edie . . .'

'Give us your hand . . .'

'They're so beautiful.'

'Harder . . . between your fingertips . . . rub . . .'

'I've dreamed of this.'

'Yeah. Me an all.'

'I picture you, Edie, every time I'm having it.'

'Naughty.'

'Makes me . . . you know . . .'

'He's all wired up – arncha, Brian?'

'Yes,' cried Brian, not knowing what it meant but knowing that he was.

'Fancy moving down a bit?'

'Mmm.'

'I saw you. Looking at my legs.'

'Such pretty legs.'

'Want to climb my little ladder, don't you?'

'Yes, *yes* . . .'

'Go on then.'

'Eeny, meeny, miny . . .'

'You're ever so good with your hands, aren't you, Brian?'

'No complaints so far.'

'Shelves and that.'

'Nnnnggghhh!'

'Got to Mo have you?'

'Ohh Edie.' Suddenly her tights were round her ankles and her fingers were tugging at his shirt. 'What are you doing?'

'Taking this off. Fair's fair.'

'I'm . . . a bit thin. Never had time to work out.'

'Not thin down here though, are you, Brian?'

'Yipes!'

'Not thin where it matters.'

'That hurt, actually.'

'Now your jeans.'

'Are you sure the door's—'

'Can't screw with your jeans on.' Edie canted up her skirt, then reached out and tickled his beard.

'Don't do that.'

'What are all them bumps?'

'Could we have the light off?'

'More fun with it on.'

'Nuff said.'

'I don't half want it, Brian.'

'Um . . . I've never been— I've never done—'

'Well, now's the time to start. That's it. Oooh – lovely. Off you go then.'

And off Brian went but not, alas, for long. In what Denzil would have called a hare's breath it was all over. They uncoupled with a sad squelch. Edie swung her legs sideways and rested on the edge of the settee. Brian hovered apologetically. On the wall the light carved out their silhouettes. Brian said, 'Sorry. I'm afraid it was the excitement.'

'What excitement?'

Then, as quickly as she had slithered out of her tights, she was dressed again and walking away. Brian sat gloomily down on the gummy vinyl and watched as Edie lifted up the egg-streaked plate in the armchair and retrieved a shiny packet of Rothman's King Size together with a match folder. She put a cigarette in her mouth and flicked a match against her thumbnail.

'Wanna fag?'

'I don't, thank you, Edie.'

Brian became uncomfortably aware of a broken spring sticking into his bottom. One side of him, closely adjacent to the fiercely glowing bars of the electric fire, was crackling nicely. The other goose-pimpled fast. Surreptitiously he watched Edie. Her cheeks were sucked into hollows by vigorous inhalation. Smoke poured from her nostrils. She was as totally and utterly separate from him as if their conjoining had never been. He had a terrible headache from the wine and was wondering if he might ask for a cup of tea. About to speak he realised that she was, in fact, speaking to him.

'Sorry – I didn't get that.'

'I said me mum'll be back any minute.'

'Bloody hell!' Brian nearly fell off the settee. He scrambled up, seizing his clothes. 'Why didn't you tell me?'

'I am telling you.'

'Come on . . . *come on* . . .' He started swearing at his shirt, punching the flapping folds with his fist, searching for the armholes, finding them, ramming his arms in.

'That's inside out.'

'Shit.'

'More haste less speed, eh, Bri?'

He tore at the sleeves with fingers like huge, sweating sausages, pulled them through to the right side and buttoned the shirt up, skew-whiff.

'You've got the wrong—'

'Yes, I am aware of that. Thank you.'

She shrugged and, picking up a pair of tights from the pile on the armchair, went over to the settee and started mopping up the traces.

'Where are my underpants?' shouted Brian, only half to himself.

'How should I know?' She threw the tights over the back of the settee.

Brian gave up looking. He pulled on the He Man jeans, stuffing his slippery genitals inside. He got them safely past the zip only to catch them on the semi-upright prongs of a row of copper rivets. Tears sprang to his eyes and he howled in fury and distress.

'Not your night, is it?'

Somehow he got into his windcheater. By now his mind had become swamped by images of gigantism. He saw Mrs Carter, muscles engorged with newly pumped blood, bestriding the threshold like a colossus, preventing his escape. Tossing him about the room like a shuttlecock. Eating him alive.

Edie was holding the door open. Drowning in appalled anticipation, Brian shot through and out into the freezing cold.

By twenty-two hundred hours the outside team had all returned to the station and debriefing began. Like many a Christmas morning it held quite a few unwelcome surprises as various items of information were offered that no one had expected to find in their stocking and did not quite know what to make of now they had.

Extensive and thorough questioning of prostitutes on the streets and around the clubs of Uxbridge had, so far, produced no lead on the blonde in the taxi. However, many of the girls did not show themselves until late evening, so enquiries would continue throughout the night and into the next day if necessary.

No luck either in finding the driver who had picked her up at Plover's Rest and taken her wherever she wished to go. All freelance cabbies within a twelve-mile radius of the village had been followed up, as well as every one in Causton. Luck though, of a sort, with Hadleigh's removal van.

'Came across an old biddy,' said Inspector Meredith, 'who actually recalls not only the day itself but the name of the firm.' He ruffled his pages and continued, abandoning his natural drawl for what he appeared to regard as a South Bucks working-class accent.

'Oi remember thaat corz thaat was Beech Hams and moy maam used to give uz Beech Hams pills.' He chortled, no doubt at the quaintness of old peasant biddydom in general and this crusty old example in particular.

Nobody joined in. Barnaby watched the inspector sourly. He was closing his notebook now, no doubt after memorising the fragment of folklore to entertain his chums. They'd be pissing themselves at the Athenaeum over that one.

'Her name I believe,' concluded Meredith, 'was Mrs Staggles.'

'Well, whatever her name is,' replied the chief inspector, 'she's certainly a long way from her native Norfolk. I trust,' he carried on quickly over the laughter, which he perceived to derive as much from pleasure at Meredith's displacement as at his own wit, 'you didn't leave the matter there?'

'Naturally not.' Skin extremely tight around the eyes. 'The firm, it appears, was taken over a year ago by a much larger company. Cox's of Slough. They didn't keep any of the staff – there were only half a dozen – but did take their names and addresses in case there were vacancies sometime in the future. I plan to talk to any who are still living locally, tomorrow.'

'I shall be interested to hear the result,' said Barnaby. 'I think you may well find that they did not move Hadleigh's stuff from Kent, as we've been led to believe, after all.'

'Really, sir? What makes you say that?'

Barnaby briefly described his visit to the solicitor's and the reading of the will, which filled the room with some surprise and quite a few whistles of envy.

'The more we seem to discover about Hadleigh,' continued the chief inspector, 'the more we find ourselves on shifting sands. We've been unable to find any record of his marriage in the year that he implied it had taken place. We're trying to trace an insurance number but the name is not all that uncommon and we have no date of birth to go on. The Department of Agriculture at Whitehall are checking their records but, quite frankly, I've little hope in that direction either. It's becoming plain, I'm afraid, that Hadleigh was a man bent on concealment. At this stage we can only guess at whether what he took such pains to conceal was connected with his death.'

Barnaby sat back, watching his team take all this in. Personally he found these conclusions totally depressing. He was not a man to relish complication for the sake of complication, as Nicholas had discovered while trying to teach his father-in-law to play chess.

Policewoman Audrey Brierley started smoothing her neat cap of shining hair, a nervous habit she indulged when speaking in front of a group. 'But why would anyone make up a whole set of lies about themselves, sir?'

'A good question.'

'Have we checked if he's got form?' asked Inspector Meredith.

'Yes, we have,' said Barnaby crisply. 'And no, he hasn't.'

'Not under that name,' said Audrey.

'Precisely. The fact that it's proving so difficult to pin him down suggests that the name is false. And it may not be the only alias.'

'Maybe he's a cut and runner,' said Troy. 'Wife and kids all too much – buggers off. Or a bigamist.'

'I wonder if you've considered the possibility . . .' Inspector Meredith, who had not waited for the previous speaker to finish, leaned back in his chair. He crossed one elegant tweed leg over the other and lowered his narrow head as if thanking his muse for this, the latest in a long line of inspiration. If he puts the tips of his fingers together, thought Barnaby, and rests his chin on them, I will personally go over there and bash his head on the floor till his brains rattle.

'The possibility,' reprised the inspector, 'that what we may have here is an official make-over. If Hadleigh had been some kind of supergrass a complete change of location, totally new background and identity could have been part of a deal. I have a connection in the Home Office and would be glad—'

'I'll keep that in mind.'

Barnaby, having a rough idea what such transformations could cost, suspected they were very rare indeed. He also knew how close the Home Office played such matters to its chest. Still, the suggestion could not be entirely discounted. He only wished someone else had made it.

'Maybe Jennings will be able to fill in some of the blanks, sir,' said Detective Constable Willoughby. 'Are you going to be putting out a press release about him soon?'

'I thought we'd give it another twenty-four hours, but if there's no trace by then of the man or his car, I'm afraid we'll have to.' Barnaby rose to his feet, saying, 'Right. If that's it . . . ?'

Glancing about he noticed Inspector Meredith's sudden frown and look of increased concentration, as if some perception or other had occurred. The man looked alert within himself. Barnaby said, 'Well, inspector?'

'Sir?'

'The little grey cells working overtime again?' There were a few toadying snickers and Barnaby chided himself for such petty spite. It was hardly Meredith's fault that the system upgraded graduates to inspector in four years whilst making hard-working, foot-slogging, intelligent constables hang around for fifteen. He drained the acid from his voice before continuing.

'You've had an idea, I think?'

'No, sir.'

At that point the night shift arrived. Barnaby checked his desk over and made for the door, his mind already closing on the anticipatory pleasures of the kitchen. Herbs and mushrooms to be chopped, liver to be thinly sliced. A glass of the '90 Crozes-Hermitage while he worked. What could be nicer?

As he passed the windows of the incident room on his way to the car park he noticed that Inspector Meredith was still there. Utterly engrossed, his fingers were tapping busily at a computer keyboard as his snaky head, quite still and urgently attentive, studied the screen.

Hector Pulls it Off

Brian pushed his muesli and grated apple sullenly around its homely dish. He had had a rotten night and was now looking at a rotten, filthy day. Rain beat in a rattling crescendo on the white-framed kitchen windows and, in the garden, trees and shrubs bent this way and that in the force of a driving wind.

Sluggardised by wakefulness and bad dreams Brian sat on the fake pine breakfast bench attached to the table. Actually he did not so much sit as lurch, semi-upright. A posture that, should anyone else in the family have adopted it, would have brought about an immediate lecture on slovenly behaviour.

Brian was going over, as he had done more or less constantly since hobbling away from Quarry Cottages, the complete turn of events that had taken place there. His imagination had already largely rewritten several crucial moments, but enough were left inviolate to make his memories of the occasion somewhat disagreeable.

But he tried not to dwell on those. And it wasn't as if matters could not be put right. It had, after all, been the first time. A certain amount of awkwardness was only to be expected. But now that he knew what Edie wanted, what turned her on, things would be very different.

Looking at the already brown fruit mincings in front of him Brian reassembled the apple in his mind's eye. Immediately it transformed itself into a creamily perfect, pink-tipped breast.

Keenly fraught with lust, he shifted uneasily back and forth, staring sourly across the room at his earnest shambles of a wife. He wished her moon face far away. And her saggy, russet-aureoled boobs and big feet. Christ, how was it possible for a woman with legs like Olive Oyl to take size eights? He'd thrown himself away there all right, by God he had. Casting the pearls of his intellect and talent before such an unpractised simpleton.

There was little doubt in Brian's mind where the main responsibility for last night's shortcomings lay. Why, when finally holding the girl who had fired his red-hot imaginings for so long in his arms, he had reacted like a puritanical schoolboy.

A more sensitive partner, a more perceptive, caring partner, would have found ways to develop her husband's sensuality. Made him wise in the paths of carnal knowledge, for were not the skills of the harem in every woman's blood?

Oh! Why had he ever let his parents persuade him into 'doing the right thing'? Why hadn't he had the courage to just clear off and leave Sue and her infant to fend for themselves? Other men did. Tom Carter probably would have. Collar and Denzil, no question.

It wasn't even as if his family appreciated the sacrifice. Sue took him totally for granted and spent money as if he had a printing press in the garden shed. Mand, quite sweet when she was little, now hardly spoke unless it was to moaningly compare him to someone called Trixie's dad who apparently let his daughter stay out all hours, drove an open-topped Jaguar and looked like Jason Priestley.

Brian tucked a cushion beneath the vacuum in the seat of his trousers and tried to wriggle into a comfier position. He was fraught with anxiety at the thought of meeting Edie again. There was no rehearsal, and no English class either today so unless he sought her out, or unless, miracle of miracles, she sought him out, they would not see each other till after the weekend. He didn't think he could bear that.

Brian wondered how it would be when they did meet. Perhaps she would be shy and unable to bring herself to talk about the matter. Or eager, like she was last night, already angling for another date? He'd take her somewhere really plush next time. Maybe a hotel on the river for a drink and a meal afterwards . . .

Already the negative aspects of their encounter (squalid environs, uncontrollable spillage of the Clapton seed, genitals that felt as if they were gift-wrapped in barbed wire) were fading fast. And Edie's post-coital coldness, wounding at the time, was, on reflection, totally understandable. How she must have been looking forward to that first conjugation. Naturally, after his inadequate performance she had withdrawn, no doubt needing to protect herself from further hurt and humiliation.

If only she hadn't touched his beard.

Brian emerged from this reverie to find himself gazing at a residue of black sludge in the bottom of his cup.

'What the hell's all this?'

'All what?'

'This mud.'

'It's filter coffee.'

'But we don't have a filter.' He spoke slowly and loudly. 'We use a coffee pot.' A. Coffee. Pot. For extra emphasis he held it up.

'You won't drink anything but Costa Rican. And Sainsbury's only had it in filter grind.'

Patience, Brian, patience. She can't help it. Count to ten.

'It's all right if you don't stir it.'

'How on earth you ever got through teacher-training college beats me.' He poured the thick, dark stuff over his muesli and pushed the lot aside.

There was a rattling from the front door and Sue said, 'I think that's the post.'

Brian did not move. Sue hesitated. As head of the house he always picked up the post. It might be something important. But to her surprise he said, 'Well, go on then. No doubt it'll be more bills. You eat me out of house and home the pair of you.'

Forbearing to mention that invoices for provisions rarely arrived via the Royal Mail, Sue went into the hall. There was one letter – a long, white envelope, immaculately typed. She took it into the kitchen and Brian held out his hand, murmuring wearily. 'Let's have it, then. Might as well hear the worst.'

'It's for me.'

'What?'

'From London.'

Sue, sick with anticipation, stood holding the envelope. It was not big enough, not nearly big enough, to contain her drawings and manuscript. She eased up the flap with trembling fingers, drew out a sheet of stiff, headed paper and read, frowning. And read again. Then, with one swift collapsing movement, she fell into the armchair.

'*Now* what?'

'It's from Methuen.'

'Who?'

'Methuen – children's books.' Brian looked cross and

bewildered. 'I sent them a story and drawings – "Hector's New Pony".'

'You didn't tell me that.'

'They want to publish it. Ohh Brian . . .'

'Let's have a look.'

Reluctantly, as if letting the piece of paper out of her possession even momentarily might instantly devalue its contents or, worse, render them null and void, Sue passed it over.

After a quick, efficient scan Brian handed it back, saying, 'As I thought. Trust you to get the wrong end of the stick. It doesn't mention publishing at all.'

'What?' His wife studied a letter suddenly, mysteriously, bereft of promise. 'But the editor says—'

'She merely suggests a meeting.'

'Lunch.' Sue sounded surprisingly firm.

'OK, lunch,' said Brian snappily. 'They obviously see some vague merit in the sketches and are offering some encouragement. I think you'd be very foolish to read more into it than that.'

Sue went over the letter for the fourth time. It was true that it did not actually contain the word 'publication'. Even so . . .

'I'm only saying that,' continued Brian, 'because I hate to see you getting all worked up only to be disappointed.'

Sue did not reply.

'They must do this sort of thing all the time. Keep tabs on people they think might have a bit of talent.'

'I see.'

Sue saw exactly. She lowered eyes brimming with excitement, so as not to annoy him further but could do nothing about her joyful countenance.

'No wonder this place looks like a squat,' Brian

squeezed himself out from behind the narrow table, 'if all you're doing all day is messing around painting.'

Sue watched him in the sitting room struggling into his tartan lumberjacket and checking his Puma bag before making for the front door.

'Brian?'

Grunt.

'Why are you walking like that?'

'Like what?'

'As if your knees are tied together.'

'Don't be so bloody rude.' Brian turned and glared at his wife; the tips of his ears burned fiercely.

'Well. You are.'

'I hit my knee on the car door, if you must know.'

When he had slammed off Sue sat motionless until she had heard the VW drive away, then she stood up, flung her arms open wide and let out a great cry. Jumping out of her heavy clogs she began to dance. Around the kitchen, into and out of each corner of the sitting room, up and down the stairs, to and fro between the bedrooms.

And as she danced, she sang. Nonsense words, old songs, new songs, bits from Hector's story, jingles from commercials, half-remembered poems and nursery rhymes, snatches of operatic arias. She sang her Methuen letter and the *Guardian* headlines and all the ingredients for a Leek and Potato Soubise.

Sue's old brown skirt whirled around, her hair flew and when, physically exhausted, she fell into the old kitchen armchair, her mind danced on.

What am I going to *do*. I can't just sit here, quietly, inside my skin. Not on a day like this. Within minutes, once more full of energy, she jumped up and went to stare out of the window.

She had never in her life seen such an utterly beautiful day. Rain, like rods of silver light, hammered on the glass. The sun had started to shine. There were even a couple of Watteau-ish clouds, snowy and scallop-edged, all puffed up like inflated bloomers. Moving away, Sue caught sight of herself in the mirror and stopped still.

Her cheeks glowed like peaches and her eyes shone. Her long, milk-chocolate hair, usually so stringily forlorn, was a polished curtain of shot silk.

'What nonsense,' she said, laughing. 'It's nonsense.'

She moved away from the lying glass and sat quietly down again, trying to be sensible. She was strangely certain of a momentous difference in herself. What it was she could not fathom for she had completely lost touch with any ability to analyse. But that it had occurred she had not the slightest doubt.

The nine a.m. briefing, though short, was packed with interest. The outside second shift, swigging coffee and looking blearily pleased with itself, had come up with a real result.

Several highly priced companions of the night, working only from their apartments ('Very concerned I got that straight they were,' said Detective Sergeant Johnson), would, if requested by telephone, visit lonely businessmen in their criminally expensive suites at the Golden Fleece Hotel to offer all the comforts of home.

Most of these canny professionals knew each other, at least by sight, and kept a wary eye out for anything new in the way of competition. A couple of them had seen the woman described by their interrogators on several occasions.

'How can you be sure it's the same person?' asked Barnaby.

'She fits the description very closely, sir,' said Johnson, producing a slim roll of statement forms from his jacket pocket. 'Even down to the little hat with the veil. Always wears black, apparently. A Mrs . . .' – he unrolled a form – 'Fionnula Dobbs admits to seeing her at least half a dozen times covering a period of some months. Each instance in the hotel lobby. I don't know if you've ever been in the Fleece, sir?'

'Only if someone else is paying.'

'Quite. Well, the lobby's very plush. Lots of deep sofas and armchairs, tables with newspapers and magazines and a posh bar opening off. The lady was usually sitting quietly, reading something or other and drinking coffee. Minding her own business as you might say.'

'Smoking?'

'Um.' He blushed. 'Didn't think to ask that, sir.'

'Go on.'

'The girls seem to have thought her, though quite attractive, a bit long in the tooth to be any sort of serious competition. In any case the Fleece keeps a very sharp eye out for prostitutes trying to work the premises. The barman's convinced she wasn't on the game. Says she approached no one, and if a man spoke to her he was politely rebuffed. The staff change over at ten this morning, though I shouldn't think,' concluded the sergeant, 'the new lot'll have anything more interesting to add.'

'None of the women you interviewed actually spoke to her?'

'No. There's an acknowledged drill to their visits which the hotel's very strict about. Once on the premises the girls go straight to the clients' rooms then, having done the business, it's straight out again. Any attempt to fraternise and they know they'll be banned.'

Having completed his input Sergeant Johnson placed the statement forms in a neat stack beside the nearest computer.

'Is that it?' asked Barnaby. Seemingly it was. 'Nobody knows anything about her? Where she comes from? Goes to?'

'I'm afraid not, sir.'

'Well, we can't leave it there. You'll have to keep after the bar staff. Ask around. People always know more than they think they do. Right,' he looked around the room, 'anything else?'

If he was disappointed in the resulting silence it didn't show. However all was not lost, for barely had he drawn breath ready to discuss the occupations of the day when Inspector Meredith spoke.

'Actually, sir . . .'

Barnaby looked sharply across the room. He was not fooled by the modest curve into which Inspector Meredith's slender form had settled. Or by the falsely hesitant verbals and unassuming downward tilt of the reptilian head. He studied the immaculate line of Meredith's parting with distaste. The man's hair was plastered to his skull like some thirties' gigolo.

'Yes,' said Barnaby tersely. 'What is it?'

'Merely an idea—'

'Would that be the idea you had last night when I asked you if you'd just had an idea and you said "No, sir"?'

'Well . . .' Meredith smiled and shrugged his elegant shoulders. 'I thought it best to check my facts first. I needed to re-read Mrs Jennings' statement. And work on from there.'

'Work on?' Barnaby spoke softly but there were few present who did not feel the wind of change. An ominous tightening of the atmosphere. Inspector Meredith was one of that few. Sublime in his ignorance, he continued.

'Yes. You were cursing the elusive Jennings and the fact that all the information we had picked up led nowhere. But I had this niggling feeling that there was a name somewhere that had been overlooked and I was right. That name was – Barbara!'

At this triumphant conclusion he glanced smugly round the room as if expecting, at the very least, a round of applause. Then, stimulating the silence with a jaunty back flip, he explained, 'The secretary.

'Unfortunately I only had her Christian name. Tried to get the rest from Mrs Jennings, who wouldn't play, then from the servant, who didn't know. So I thought of his publisher. Seemed to me they were bound to have had dealings. I was lucky. Though it was late they had a book-launch party on and people were still around. Her surname, Cockaigne, was an unusual one and they were able to tell me she lived in North London. From then on it was a piece of cake. I rang and got an answerphone. Now, and this is where it gets really interesting—'

'I hope you're not going to give the entire plot away, Inspector Meredith,' said Barnaby in a voice that reverberated like a hammer striking frozen steel.

The general assembly was by now slipping into its moon boots and ear muffs. Troy, leaning against the Ryvita panels, closed his eyes with pleasure as Meredith went bombasting on and thought, What a scrote!

'The drill on the tape is that she's away for five days, OK? And I don't believe that is a coincidence. She'll have left an address with someone – a friend or neighbour – in case of an emergency. People always do. Find her, chief inspector, and it's my belief you'll find Jennings.'

The silence which followed this improvisation went on for quite some time. Barnaby appeared almost distracted. Frowning, he moved his papers to and fro in an aimless heap. Eventually he said, in a matter-of-fact tone:

'Let me try and explain to you, inspector, how we work here.' He directed a glance of freezing disdain in Meredith's direction. 'We work as a team. I cannot over-emphasise the importance of this. Indeed you will find it a common element throughout the Force and I must say I'm amazed it was not drawn to your attention at Bramshill. It makes for speed and efficiency, you see. Often it saves lives. Of course we are all individuals, some perhaps more so than others, but when we have a little insight we don't run off and hug it to ourselves, follow up on our clever little tod without telling anyone and then produce our conclusion while hogging centre stage like some spoiled kid at a party.'

'I was only try—'

'I haven't finished!'

'Oh.'

'Dissemination of knowledge at every level and between every authority is vital. You only have to look at the Sutcliffe cock-up to see what happens when men of a rank to know better start playing Hooray For Our Gang instead of Pass The Parcel.' He paused. 'You're looking somewhat perplexed, Meredith. Didn't you get to hear about the Yorkshire Ripper in your ivory tower? Your intellectual eyrie in the sky?'

'Of course I did.'

'Then you'll know that women died unnecessarily because information was not quickly and properly conveyed.'

'I thought that was a technical mix-up. Incompatible computers.'

'Not entirely, by a long chalk.'

'Still it's not as if . . .' Meredith tailed off, shrugged and said, 'They were tarts, weren't they?'

Barnaby stared across the room, his face momentarily distorted with disgust and disbelief. He said, 'I'm not quite sure I heard you correctly, inspector.'

'Prostitutes.' Meredith looked around for confirmation. 'Isn't that right?'

The chief inspector's large, grizzled head sank a little between his heavy shoulders. His neck all but disappeared.

'Just remember what I said. All information, all ideas and insights, however slight, however cock-eyed, get tossed into the pool. That's what briefings are all about.'

'If you say so, sir.'

'I do say so, inspector. And you'd better believe I'm saying so or you'll find yourself off this case and back on a six a.m. shift for the rest of your stay here, which, I can assure you, we all hope will be extremely brief.' He stood, very suddenly for such a heavy man, then, propelled by anger and abhorrence, quickly left the room.

Troy followed, catching up with his boss in the corridor.

'Bloody fascist.'

The sergeant responded, with some hesitation, 'He is the chief constable's nephew, sir.'

'I don't care if he's the smile on the queen's backside. He starts that caper here I'll cauterise him.'

Barnaby slammed into his office. Troy took the door in his face, stilled the shivering glass panels with the palm of his hand then entered, as unobtrusively as he knew how. He gave it five hundred before clearing his throat.

'Want me to have another go at Clapton this morning, sir?'

'No. He'll keep. We still haven't talked to Amy Lyddiard. It's hopeless at the house with that Dobermann of a sister-in-law. Go and collect her, would you? Gently does it. Tell her it's for fingerprints.'

After Troy had left he sat staring at the wall wondering how he had come to miss Barbara. There was a time when he missed nothing. Certainly nothing as clearly under his nose as this had been. It was not even a matter of sloppy reading. Christ, he had done the interview where her name had come up himself. Thick as thieves, Ava Jennings had said they were. He remembered the exact words. Thick as thieves.

Barnaby cursed Meredith with his sharp eyes and sharp mind and sharp, upmarket connections, then cursed himself for meanness of spirit. He felt old and heavy and tired. Not to mention in dire need of further sustenance.

Sue, still pneumatically propelled on waves of exhilaration, floated between the twin pineappled pillars of Gresham House, up the drive and round to the servants' entrance. In her excitement she tugged the old-fashioned bell extremely hard and rather a lot of wire came out, refusing to return when she released the engraved metal pull.

Sue let it dangle. She waited, smiling, while the sodden leaves from the wisteria dripped on to her uncovered head. Her arms still ached slightly from delivering Rex's shopping, which had included quite a lot of heavy tins. She had been relieved to find him in improved spirits. Still fretting over the possibility that he may have played some unwitting part in Gerald's death, but determined not to be overwhelmed by the suggestion. He was even talking about going back to work.

Amy, wearing rubber gloves and with a head scarf over

295

her curls, opened the door. Sue stepped inside. The two women stood looking at each other.

'What is it?' Amy cried. '*What is it?*' Then, seizing her friend's hands, 'You've heard from Methuen!'

'Yes.'

'Sue – how marvellous!'

'They want me to go to lunch.'

'Lunch! Ohhh . . .'

'I've been dancing all morning. Up and down the stairs, all round the house, in the street.'

'Of course you have.' Amy beamed, said 'Ohhh' again, gave Sue a great hug and dragged her by the arm towards the kitchen steps. 'You must come in.'

'But what about . . . ?'

'Taking a catalogue back to Laura's.'

Amy had been polishing silver, which lay, in a heavy box lined with frayed green baize, on the old deal table. There was a saucer of rosy paste and several black-stained cloths. The air had a sweet chemical scent.

Sue sat down and started laughing in a rather delirious way, breaking off now and again to say, 'I don't know what to do with myself' and 'I think I'm going mad.'

Caught up in all this exhilaration, Amy, crying 'Don't set me off', was promptly set off. Covering her mouth with her hand and choking with gaiety she gasped, 'If you don't look at me . . . I'll be all right . . .'

And that was how they eventually calmed down, by staring determinedly at a point beyond each other's shoulders. Amy wiped her face and said, 'We should celebrate. But there's nothing to drink in this place. Not even cooking sherry.'

'Funny you should say that . . .' Sue produced from her shopping bag a white cardboard box, a bottle wrapped in tissue paper the colour of methylated spirits and a corkscrew. 'Voila!'

She slipped a rubber band off the box and lifted the lid to reveal a large, gooey chocolate gateau. The bottle contained white wine from the Côte de Gascogne. Sue attacked the green plastic seal with the tip of the corkscrew.

'It's to share around the play group really. After all, if it wasn't for them there'd be no Hector.'

'Poor little mites. They'll be paralytic.'

'The mothers, silly. There's squash for the kids.' Sue reached out for a knife.

'Not that one. It's still got polish on.'

Amy assembled a bread knife, two plates and two forks and fetched a couple of wine glasses from a cabinet in the drawing room. They were thick with dust so she rinsed them in tepid water under the tap.

The village store did not go in for top-flight patisserie. The cake tasted pretty synthetic and the wine slightly warm, yet every mouthful was ambrosial. Amy, chasing a final flaked almond around the margin of her plate, said, 'That was wonderful. I hope it all didn't cost too much.'

'Nearly six pounds.'

'Sue.' Horrified, Amy laid down her fork. She understood only too well the gaping hole such an amount would leave in a skin-tight budget. 'How are you going to manage?'

'Don't know. Don't care actually.'

'But it's your Sainsbury's shop tomorrow. Look.' She laid slightly chocolately fingers on Sue's arm. 'Let me treat you. I've still got some money left from—'

'No, Amy. Why should you?'

'Because I'm your friend.' Sue stubbornly shook her head. 'A loan then. And when you're R and F you can pay me back.'

'I don't think it's an unreasonable amount to spend. Not to celebrate such a brilliant piece of news.'

'Of course it isn't.'

'Some men would have taken their wives out for champagne and a slap-up meal.'

'Indeed.' Amy hesitated as to how to continue. She had no wish to carry on a conversation along unhappy lines. On the other hand Sue seemed to be, quite justifiably in Amy's opinion, somewhat aggrieved. She also sensed a wish to dwell further on the subject of domestic injustice.

'What did Brian say when you told him?'

'That they had no intention of publishing. They had perhaps seen some slight merit in my sketches and were keeping vague tabs in case I came up with something worthwhile in the future.'

'What absolute and utter rubbish!' Amy was so angry her face had gone bright red.

'It is,' said Sue. Then, after a slight pause, 'Isn't it?'

'The mean-spirited little toad.'

'I didn't believe him.'

'I should jolly well hope not. If that was all, they'd have sent the drawings back with an encouraging letter asking you to keep in touch.' Sensing a slight diminution of the radiance opposite she followed through with an interrogative clincher. 'Right?'

'Right.'

'That's settled then. Now – what are you going to wear?'

'God knows. Everything I've got's held together with Sellotape and willpower.'

'We'll go round the charity shops. They have some lovely things. And this time it's a loan and no argument. You must look nice.'

'Thank you.'

'After all, she might take you to the Ritz.'

'W-e-l-l.' Unaccustomed as she was to literary lunches this did strike Sue as flying a trifle high. 'Probably not the first time.'

'You must tell me every single thing about it. From the minute you set foot in the restaurant till the minute you leave. What the place is like, everything you eat and drink, what the waiters are like and the other diners—'

Sue started laughing again. 'I'll never remember all that.'

'Right up to the time you help her into a taxi.'

'Why will I have to do that?'

'Oh, she'll be well away by then,' explained Amy airily. 'They all drink like whales.'

Sue regarded Amy's amused, animated, totally involved expression and warm brown eyes with feelings of deep affection and gratitude. The old saw which promised that when in trouble you soon found out who your friends were had never struck her as all that profound. Of course, in a crisis, people rallied round, sometimes out of genuine concern, more often perhaps because they welcomed the opportunity to become briefly involved in lives crammed with more dramatic incident than their own. But how much harder was it to truly rejoice in another's good fortune, especially when your own had been so savagely cut short.

'It'll be you next time.' Sue stretched out her hand, slipping it, for comfort, into Amy's. 'Once you've finished *Rompers* they'll all be fighting over it.'

For a moment Amy did not reply. She appeared withdrawn and a little sad. Sue wondered if Ralph had come into her mind. If Amy was thinking how pleased he would be to know that she was writing a book. She went on quickly, 'And I'll be able to help. I'll get an agent – you always can once you've signed a contract – and I shall insist they take you on as well.'

'Oh, Sue . . .'

They both fell silent, acknowledging the splendour of the new situation. The glorious difference between yesterday and today. And when I wake up tomorrow, thought Sue, it will still be real. No one can take it away from me.

'Gosh – I've been so carried away I've not told you what else has happened.'

'Something happened here, too.'

'Amy – what?'

'You first.'

'OK. I've been really worried about Rex. I rang two or three times and got no reply, so I went round and discovered him in an appalling state.'

Sue described her visit. Amy listened closely to the very end then said, 'But surely it can't be true. I mean – that Max Jennings murdered Gerald.'

'That's what I said. Famous people just don't do such things.'

'For a start the police would have arrested him. It would have been in all the papers.'

'I tried to convince Rex there must be a rational explanation. He was . . . dying, Amy. Actually dying of shame. It was dreadful.'

'You must have worked a miracle. I saw him on the Green this morning with Montcalm.'

'Yes. And he's going to try writing again, which will help. But he won't be his old self till they find out who really did it.'

'Mrs Bundy said yesterday they were looking for a suitcase.'

'What, one of Gerald's?'

'Yes. Brown leather. Apparently whoever killed him took it away.'

'That definitely points to a burglar. I must tell Rex. It will cheer him up.'

Sue began repacking the cake. Amy tried to stuff the cork back into the wine bottle.

'Do they know what was in it?'

'The entire contents of a chest of drawers,' replied Amy, 'according to Mrs B. She went on about it at great length.'

'I'm surprised Honoria didn't shut her up.'

'Reading her runes elsewhere. Got it!' Amy spoke too soon. The cork popped straight out again, shot across the room and rolled under the cooker. As she bent to fish it out she spoke again, this time with her voice all squeezy. 'I'll give a hand with Rex. Visit him, I mean. And maybe we could ask Laura.'

'Ah – that's the other thing I meant to tell you. She's moving'

'Moving?' Amy was washing the cork under the tap. 'Moving where?'

'Doesn't know yet. I went round last night. I was so worried about Rex and desperately needed to talk to somebody. I could have saved myself the trouble. She was in ever such a funny mood. To tell you the truth, I think she'd been drinking.'

'I'm not surprised. This awful business is enough to drive anyone to drink.'

'Don't worry about that Amy,' (the cork was proving twice as awkward the second time) 'tell me your news. I have to go in a sec.'

301

'Well, it was yesterday. Just gone one.' Amy spoke so seriously and looked so perturbed that Sue, who had got up after packing her basket, sat straight down again. 'Honoria came in complaining that lunch was late. And maybe because I was extra cold or lonely or unhappy or hungry or depressed I finally told her I'd had enough.'

'*Amy!*'

'And that I was going to leave.'

'You didn't.' Sue gazed at her friend in deep consternation, as if surprised to find her still alive. 'What did she say?'

'It was awful. She started going on about how she'd get the heating fixed and give me more money for food. Then she said I couldn't go because she had promised Ralph she'd look after me.'

'Oh, deep dread.'

'Exactly. And it was so weird because I could see it wasn't the truth. I don't know why she really wants me here—'

'Unpaid slavery—'

'No. Well, perhaps, but that's not the main reason. I've got a feeling that I have something she wants. I can sense her watching me. Sometimes, when I'm working in the house or in the garden, she'll come up so quietly, like she did yesterday, and I won't know she's there. It's really frightening. She's waiting for something, Sue. And she doesn't want me to go until it's happened.'

'But you must go.'

'Yes. I have plans. Remember those ads I told you about – in *The Lady*? I'm going to start replying. Thing is, can I give your address? I don't want her to know.'

'Of course you can.' A vista of loneliness opened suddenly in front of Sue and desolation briefly marked her face.

'Don't look like that, love. We'll write. All the time.'

'Yes.'

'And I'll need to come back often. To visit Ralph.'

A couple of hours later, Barnaby, awaiting the arrival of Mrs Lyddiard, was jotting down a few notes. Pointers to questions rather then the questions themselves for, although he could be relentlessly inflexible when the need to pin down was urgent, he preferred to work in an open-ended, even slightly meandering way, casting his net wide. Visitors often left his office after having been quite shrewdly interviewed feeling they'd enjoyed nothing more than a pleasant conversation.

Barnaby was patient in the way an animal squatting silently outside the lair of its prey is patient. And he was genuinely curious about people, unlike Troy, who was not interested in anyone for their own sake, but merely for what they could contribute to the matter in hand. Barnaby's method got results. People told him things they hadn't meant to tell him. Sometimes they told him things they didn't even know they knew.

Audrey Brierley looked around the door and asked if he would like a drink of something. Almost at the same time Sergeant Troy arrived with Mrs Lyddiard. Barnaby ordered two cups of tea and put his calls on hold. Troy quickly worked out that he was *de trop* and took himself off to the incident room.

The chief inspector hung up Amy's coat, offered her the most comfortable chair and came out from behind his desk to sit on the settee. They stirred their drinks in silence, Amy looking round the room with shy interest.

'This is just an informal chat, Mrs Lyddiard. As we were not able to talk the other day.'

'Yes, I'm afraid Honoria—' Amy broke off, realising she was about to be disloyal in front of strangers. She swallowed some tea. 'This is delicious. Thank you.'

'What I really wanted to ask about,' continued Barnaby, when both their cups were empty, 'were your impressions of that last evening at Plover's Rest. If you enjoyed it, for instance.'

'Oh I did,' exclaimed Amy. 'It was great to meet a real writer.'

She enthused, as he remembered Mrs Clapton had done, over Jennings' courtesy, helpfulness and apparently genuine interest in his audience's accomplishments.

'I was really sorry when it was over. I think we all felt inspired.'

'Did you get the impression that Mr Hadleigh enjoyed it?'

'It's hard to say. He was very quiet.' Amy put her cup and saucer carefully on the carpet. 'Poor man.'

'Are you aware that he and Max Jennings already knew each other?'

'Yes. Rex told Sue. He's been terribly depressed about it all. Feels responsible. Ermm . . . have you . . . ? That is . . . if you've exonerated Max – if he's in the clear – it would help Rex so much. To know, I mean . . .' Amy tailed off, hoping she had not committed some misdemeanour by asking.

'I'm sure the problem will be resolved.' Barnaby smiled to soften any suggestion of a rebuff and moved on. 'After the meeting I understand you and Miss Lyddiard went straight home.'

'Yes. I made us some hot drinks then went upstairs to work on my book. Honoria took hers into the study.'

'What's your book about?'

'Oh.' Amy flushed with embarrassment and pleasure at being asked. 'What isn't it about? High finance, drug smuggling, lovers lost and found, a priceless black Russian pearl, a kidnapped foundling.'

'It sounds irresistible.'

'I'm banking on it.'

Amy, more relaxed now, was sitting back in her chair. Barnaby noticed she was wearing the same shabby trousers and butterfly cardigan that she had had on the other day. Her boots were very worn and one of the seams was splitting. He wondered what her financial position was. Pretty parlous, surely, to be prepared to live at Gresham House.

'Do you find the writing group a help?'

'Up to a point. We read our stuff out but then, none of us being very experienced, we're at a bit of a loss to know what to do next.'

'What did you think of Hadleigh's writing?'

'A bit thin. He worked very hard on his stories but, even after several drafts, there didn't seem to be anything much in them.'

'And your impressions of him as a person?'

'I can't tell you anything definite, inspector. I just didn't know him well enough.'

'Indefinite will do.'

This time Amy paused for so long that Barnaby thought she had decided not to answer. When she did speak it was plainly with great reluctance.

'He reminded me of a character I saw in a film, a long time ago. An elderly man – the film was in flashback – who had been traumatised as a boy. He had been used by two grown-ups of quite different social classes – this was in Edwardian times – to pass love letters between them and the discovery of this, plus the dreadful aftermath, ruined his whole life. His face, all his movements, had a dreadful, frozen lifelessness. As if every bit of him was mortally impaired.' Amy frowned deeply, her pretty face marred by pity and distress. 'Gerald was like that.'

'How very sad,' said the chief inspector, meaning it. Then, risking alienation, 'But how interesting.'

'Yes,' agreed Amy, looking somewhat shamefaced. 'I used to wonder about him a lot. Writers are awful. So nosy. I'd make up different pasts for him. Different histories.'

'But he was quite forthcoming about his background, I understand.'

'Oh, I didn't believe any of that.'

'Really?' said Barnaby, leaning very slightly forward.

'It was so sparse. Like one of his stories. True life's all muddle and mess, isn't it? You can't just list a few neat things and say, "This is who I am". It was as if' – Amy tuckered her brows again – 'as if he'd learnt it.'

Even as Barnaby smiled and nodded he wondered why he was feeling quite so pleased with this conversation, for there was little new in it. He decided it was because he enjoyed looking at, and listening to, Mrs Lyddiard. Her sweet round face and mop of curly hair reminded him of his wife, though Amy was ingenuously friendly where Joyce was tartly subtle.

Amy got up to put her cup and saucer on the desk and noticed the large, leather-framed photograph with its back to her.

'Do you mind if . . . ?'

Barnaby said, 'Of course not.'

She turned the frame round and said, as everyone, without exception always did, 'Good heavens. What an absolutely beautiful child.'

'She's grown up now.'

'And that's your wife?'

'Yes.'

'Easy to see which side—' Amy broke off, crimsoned and covered her mouth with her hand. 'Gosh, how rude. I'm so sorry. What must you . . . Oh dear. I don't know where to . . . Ohh . . .'

Barnaby burst out laughing. He couldn't help it. Her confusion was so overwhelmingly complete it was comical. Then he stopped, for she was clearly genuinely upset.

'Please, Mrs Lyddiard, don't be put out. If I had a fiver for every time I've heard that remark I could retire tomorrow.'

'You're just saying that to make me feel better.'

'Not at all. The first occasion was the midwife.'

Amy seemed almost about to smile, changed her mind and went back to her chair. More to ease the moment than because he was really interested, Barnaby asked if she had children. Amy shook her head.

'For a time it didn't seem important. We were very happy and it seemed enough. Then, when I was in my late thirties, I started having second thoughts. But Ralph dissuaded me.' She pressed her hands together, the fingers interlocking with tension, tugging against each other. 'I thought afterwards he must have had some sort of premonition. Perhaps knew, even then, how ill he was and didn't want to leave me with a young child. But he was wrong. I'd give anything now – anything – to have a part of him still with me.'

Barnaby nodded with a sympathy that was far from feigned. He could not imagine, could not bear to imagine, life without his daughter. They might not see, or even hear from her, for weeks on end, but he had to know that she was out there somewhere. Living, breathing, breaking hearts.

'He had cancer.' Amy sounded introspective and so distant she might have been talking to herself. 'That is, he had chronic hepatitis that wasn't diagnosed and treated in time. We were so far away from a hospital you see. Or a good doctor.'

'I'm so sorry.'

'All the awful people who live forever. Murderers and terrorists. Army generals who won't let food trucks through, while Ralph . . .' Tears started from Amy's eyes and she brushed them fiercely away. 'The dearest man. It's so unfair. Honoria blamed me.'

Barnaby released a sound of demurring protest reinforced by a disbelieving movement of his head.

'It's true. She said the most terrible thing, the cruellest thing. I've never told anyone – not even Sue. He'd been unconscious for days in that hospital in Spain and we'd been taking turns to sit with him. I'd been resting and I was going back along the corridor towards his room when Honoria came out of the doctor's office. She gripped my arms – I had the marks for days – and screamed in my face. "If you'd loved him enough he wouldn't have died." It was the most dreadful shock. I didn't know he'd gone, you see. It happened while I was asleep. It was the only time I've ever seen her show any emotion.

'She's taken him back now. The headstone has his name and a single space for hers. His room with all his childhood things is permanently locked. She's always in there. I hear her sometimes reading out his letters or school reports. But none of that matters really. I sit by his grave and talk to him and we're as close as we ever were. All the rest is trimmings.'

After she had finished speaking Amy sat in silence for a

while. There was an almost inaudible click as the minute hand on the clock jumped round and a faint humming from the overhead fluorescent light. But in spite of the brightness of the room and the constant shrilling of telephones and the human clatter just beyond the thin walls, Amy was aware that she felt very much at ease.

'I can't imagine why I told you all that.'

'Sometimes it's easier to talk to a stranger.'

'That depends on the stranger, surely. You seem to have a gift for it, inspector. Perhaps you should join the Samaritans.'

'No patience. They'd be jumping off high buildings in droves.'

Amy was surprised. He had seemed to her endlessly patient and attentive. But perhaps that was just part of his technique. An enforced physical stillness to encourage revelation. Certainly he seemed to have taken rather a lot of notes. She began to feel slightly ill at ease and was quite relieved when he buzzed for the nice policewoman with the shining hair.

'We would like, Mrs Lyddiard,' said Barnaby, unhooking her coat from the curly hat stand, 'some fingerprints from you. Purely for purposes of elimination. They will not be put on file or kept longer than is absolutely necessary.'

'That's fine,' said Amy.

'What do you think our chances are of obtaining your sister-in-law's?'

'Absolutely nil. She's a law unto herself, Honoria.'

Barnaby shook hands. As WPC Brierley and she were leaving he said, 'Take Mrs Lyddiard out via the incident room.' He smiled at Amy. 'You might be interested to see how the wheels go round.'

'Indeed I would.'

Amy followed the policewoman down the corridor determined to make a mental note of everything she saw. She would buy a folder and mark it Police Research. Readers were said to love authentic detail and already Amy's mind was conjuring a scene in which Araminta – after many tortuous travails – finally collapses on the steps of a station not a million miles removed from Causton CID. There, after being comforted and refreshed, she would pour out her incredible story. Probably to a large, burly man who would hear her out in close and sympathetic silence.

The telephone call from the day-shift barman at the Golden Fleece came shortly after one of the mingiest, stingiest lunches Tom Barnaby had ever eaten. He had been frightened into this austere reckoning when, tired of waiting for the lift, he had wheezed his way up a single flight of stairs to reach the canteen. Having attained the final step he found himself overwhelmed by a terrible choking sensation as if his windpipe had been clamped. There was a zinging in his ears and the hand that gripped the stair rail was not only curiously numb but – he squinted, trying to bring it into focus – curiously on the move.

Though these extraordinary physical sensations lasted only a few seconds it had been long enough to concentrate his mind marvellously on the virtuous section of the menu. Consequently an egg salad now nestled in his stomach alongside a slimmer's yogurt and a cube of fatless cheese that had looked and tasted like yellow india rubber. (At least he now knew what to give up for Lent.) All this plus two slices of crispbread. Not that these had been crisp any more than they even remotely resembled bread.

More like soggy sawdust held together by pockets of air. A clear case for prosecution under the Trades Description Act.

'Are you all right, chief?' Troy prised himself away from Audrey Brierley's desk and sauntered over. His eyebrows were raised in mild inquiry, which was as near as he ever came to demonstrating concern.

'Don't be stupid.'

'Indigestion, is it?'

'You have to have eaten something to get indigestion, sergeant.'

Troy laughed in the careless way young, healthy, slender people have. 'That's very good. I must remember that. Tell Mor.'

'She must really look forward to your return, Gavin.'

'Yeah, I think she does. Usually has a go at me, though, about not going straight home.' Like most of the men, and some of the women, Troy unwound after his shift with a few jars in the Police Club.

'You'd think she'd be grateful. I've tried to explain it's for her that I do it. If I took all the stresses and strains of this job back to 18 Russell Avenue she'd complain fast enough. I dunno . . .' He swivelled a chair round and sat down more comfortably. 'Women. No sooner am I in the door than she starts. Jobs usually. When am I going to fix the bathroom tap, kitchen cupboard, landing light? I'm bloody wacked on my day off. All I want to do is kip. After I've cleaned and polished the car.

'You daren't open your eyes. The second the old lids roll back she's off. Latest thing is, why don't I ever talk to her. I said, I never talk to you, Maureen, because I can never get a bloody word in.'

Sensing a lack of interest from the far side of the desk,

Troy asked if anything helpful had come out of the interview with Mrs Lyddiard.

'Nothing I latched on to at the time. But I had the feeling after she'd left that something was said that rang false. I don't necessarily mean that she was lying – just that there was some discrepancy. I'm just about to read through it again.'

But, almost before he had finished speaking, the phone rang and the resulting conversation put all thoughts of Amy's interview from his head.

Garry Briggs, the day barman, was unsure whether the scrap of information he could add to that of his colleagues was worth passing on, but he had seen the woman they were all being asked about leaving the hotel car park, on more than one occasion, in a black Celica. Barnaby asked Mr Briggs if he had noticed who was driving at the time.

'She was.'

'Are you sure? If this is the vehicle I'm thinking of the windows would be dark.'

'Positive. Saw her getting in and out. Always on her own.' When these remarks were received in silence he added regretfully, 'I did say it wasn't much.'

The chief inspector thanked him and hung up. Sergeant Troy, quietly attentive, was leaning forward, hands resting lightly on his knees. He said, 'So she had the use of his car. Which means she wasn't a casual pick-up.'

'Find Laura Hutton's statement, would you?'

Looking slightly puzzled, Troy did so. Barnaby read it quickly through while punching out her number. She picked up the phone immediately but asked if he would ring back.

'I'm showing an estate agent round at the moment.'

'It won't take a second, Mrs Hutton. It's about the night

you saw this woman arrive at Plover's Rest. Do you remember—'

'Good God, man, of course I remember.'

'What I'm asking is,' he glanced down at the form, 'you said she knocked at the door.'

'That's right.'

'Did you see anyone open it?'

'Well . . . Gerald.'

'But did you *see*?'

'No. The porch is in the way.'

'Did you hear the chain being taken off, perhaps?'

'Not really. The taxi's engine was running.'

'Just one more thing. When you looked through the window—'

'I'm not discussing this matter any more. I've told you – there's someone here.' She banged the phone down.

It didn't really signify. Barnaby, mentally transported to the cottage, stood precisely where Laura Hutton had stood, in the soft earth of the flower border, and peered through an imaginary gap in the velvet curtains. He recalled the shape and furnishings of the room.

'What's all this in aid of, chief?'

Barnaby did not reply for some time. Just sat, his eyes focused on the past, tapping at the statement absently.

'We've been taking things at face value, sergeant.'

'How's that then?'

'Obviously one has to do this at the beginning of a case, but I have foolishly let things run on.'

'You mean in respect of this woman?'

'Yes.'

'I wouldn't say that, chief. We've followed the usual procedures. We already know a little bit more about her. I'm sure it's only a matter of time before she's found.'

'I doubt if she will ever be "found", Gavin. I doubt, in fact, if she exists at all.'

'But all these people have seen her.'

'I believe that what they have seen is Gerald Hadleigh.'

'*Hadleigh?*'

'That's right.'

There was complete silence after this. Troy searched for the correct response. Or at least one that would not make him look an absolute prat. But the truth was that this bizarre possibility had simply not occurred to him and, far from now appearing quite likely, the more he thought about the idea the barmier it seemed. In the end he said, simply, 'What makes you so sure, sir?'

'Various things, but primarily aspects of Hadleigh's character. This immense reserve, for instance, that everyone who has met him comments on. His secrecy. I'm obviously guessing blind here, but he may have regarded this woman as his true self and the suave, retired civil servant as a false persona. This would make all the lies he seems to have told comprehensible.'

'Freaky deaky.' Troy flashed his Glad To Be Normal button. 'Just a tarty old drag queen then.'

'I was thinking of transvestism, which is a much more complicated business. The majority are heteros, often with wives and families. The condition is a psychological one and may not affect their sex lives at all.'

'It'd bloody affect mine,' said Troy. 'Maureen came to bed in pit boots, Y-fronts and a jokey moustache I'd be right out the window.' He paused, shocked into temporary silence by the very thought. 'So what do they get out of it then? I mean – queers dressing up, OK, it's sick,' – he pulled a face of grotesquely exaggerated repulsion – 'but if they're playing the girly part in these gruesome fuckarounds, well . . . there you go. But for a straight bloke to do it just to sit around in a hotel lobby – what's the point?'

'Simply to be accepted in public as a woman.'

Simply? What was simple about stapling your balls together and calling yourself Doris?

'They have their own clubs as well. Places where they can meet. But the real challenge is to walk down the street without anyone having the faintest idea that you aren't exactly what you appear to be.'

'You seem to know all about it, chief,' said Troy. Then, watching his back, 'No offence.'

'Cully had a friend that way inclined. At Cambridge. She talked about him a lot.'

'Right.' The sergeant erased, with some difficulty, a lovely face from his mind's eye. 'He certainly seemed to have kept it under his saucy black hat. Not easy in a sharp-eyed place like Midsomer Worthy.'

'I presume the way it worked was, he'd get all togged up then into the garage via the kitchen and drive straight off.'

'Having first opened the garage doors.'

'Well, as the general idea was to avoid drawing attention to himself, Gavin, I think we can safely assume he would have first opened the garage doors, yes.'

'So, when the car was stolen, he'd be right up shit creek.'

'Which is why he didn't go to Uxbridge station to report the theft.'

'But didn't Laura Hutton say this woman knocked and someone let her in?'

'I see that as an extra precaution. Although it was late, and the taxi had taken him right up to the house, at the moment he alighted he must have felt extremely vulnerable. Those halogen lamps are hellish bright. What if someone had chosen that moment to walk by? Or been peeping out from their net curtains?'

'Or, as things turned out, hiding behind a bush.'

'It's common sense to assume that, if you see a person knock on a door and then disappear inside a house, the door has been opened from the inside. But we now know that Mrs Hutton did not see that actually happen.'

'Hang on though . . .' Troy screwed up his face again, this time in concentration. 'Didn't she see this woman and Hadleigh through the window? Drinking wine or something.'

'No. She saw only the woman.'

'But Hadleigh'd hardly be drinking a toast to himself.'

'I think that's just what he was doing. There's a mirror over the fireplace. Why shouldn't he be raising a glass in self-congratulation after having made it safely back?'

'Yeah. Actually . . .' Troy abandoned the sentence but nodded, indicating that he understood completely. Tell the truth, he himself had more than once, whilst waxing and buffing his newly-bought, secondhand Ford Sierra Cossie, raised a can of ice-cold Carling's and winked at the drop-dead stud reflected in the wing mirror. A thought displaced this attractive recollection.

'No wonder Laura Hutton thought the woman reminded her of somebody. It was Hadleigh, not that painting. But if all this happened the night before the murder, where's the kinky gear?'

'Presumably in the suitcase.'

'Wow.' Troy barely breathed the exclamation. His mind was running every which way. 'That's why the chest of drawers was always kept locked.'

'I should imagine so.'

'But – not at the time of the murder?'

'One of the things I discovered from Cully is that this need for cross-dressing often coincides with periods of extreme stress. And we know that Hadleigh was suffering in just such a way directly before he died.'

'So – about to slip into the frillies, he was interrupted . . .' The words tumbled over each other. Troy got up and started walking around, as drawn to this new scenario now as he had previously been wary. 'Which would explain why he had got undressed but not into his pyjamas. Hang about, though – would he even think of doing this while someone was still in the house?'

'I would have said not. But we must remember that he and Jennings go back a long way. For all we know the "unpleasantness in the past" that Hadleigh referred to might have to do with this very thing.'

'Perhaps Jennings was threatening exposure?'

'Unlikely. What would be the point? It's not as if Hadleigh's breaking the law.'

'True. The worse that could happen is a few funny looks from the locals. All he'd have to do then is pack his stuff and go back to the Smoke. Nobody cares up there if you're buggering the goldfish on your night off. Even so,' Troy stopped his pacing and sat down again, 'must be relevant, all this clobber. Otherwise why would the murderer take it away?'

'If it was the murderer.'

Troy stared at his boss in puzzled disbelief. 'Who on earth else could it have been?'

'Someone perhaps who loved him.'

'Not with you.'

'And didn't want him mocked and jeered at, even in death.'

'Laura?'

317

'It's the only name that springs to mind. It's not entirely out of the question that, seeing how strangely he behaved throughout the evening, she may, in spite of her denials, have gone back to the cottage to see if he was all right.'

'Found him dead, stuff spread about everywhere . . . Could be. Jesus.'

Troy ran his fingers through his hair several times and with such vigour it stood on end. 'Every time we discover something on this case it leaves us worse off than we were before. Now we've got at least two Hadleighs, both of which look to be completely unreal. Do you think he's a headcase?'

'I really don't know.'

'It happens. I saw this movie – woman had three separate personalities. None of them clocked what the others were up to.'

'I know exactly how they felt,' said Barnaby.

When Sue got back to the house after play group a hand delivered envelope was lying on the mat. It was not very clean and the torn flap had been stuck down with Sellotape. The pencilled words 'For Brian' were scrawled across the front. She put it on the kitchen table, propped up against the sauce bottle, where he couldn't miss it.

Mandy got in first. Once upon a time, in the days when she had been daddy's pet, she'd have waited for him and they would have driven home together. Now, even though she hated being the odd one out, she preferred to travel on the school bus. Packed in like lively sardines; wriggling, screaming, giggling, smoking, sitting on each other's laps. Mandy, always on the very edge of the shoal, would laugh at all the jokes until her lips and throat ached, whether she got them or not. Sometimes she laughed too soon and they'd know she was putting it on.

Tonight, rather than laughing with them, they had been laughing at her. Three or four of the bigger girls, halfway down the bus, kept turning and staring in Mandy's direction, whispering to each other, then cracking up. Edie Carter leading them on.

Mandy hated Edie worse than anyone. Hated her sly, white triangular face and piled-up tangle of flaming hair and slanty eyes. And Tom was worse. Always making dirty remarks in a very soft, curling voice that made them sound even dirtier than they were already.

The *status quo* apropos Mandy's previous position in class had now been quite restored. Her connection with the murder having been examined and milked dry she was of no further interest to anyone. Even the most unpopular girls in the class barely spoke and Haze Stitchley had gone back to ignoring her completely.

A dozen got off the bus at the Green, linked up in twos and threes and hurried off. Though only four o'clock it was nearly dark and there was a cutting edge to the wind. Mandy raced up the garden path and into the house, banging the door behind her. She dropped her bag and coat on the sitting-room floor and switched on the telly. The fire was a depressing heap of smouldering paper and twiggy sticks beneath a tottering pyramid of coal.

Mandy remembered this time yesterday, when she had been sitting in a big, soft armchair in her nan's cosy lounge. She had barely fallen into its downy embrace before a tray containing a monster iced Coke, buttered crumpets and chocolate-fudge Swiss roll had been placed in her lap together with the TV remote control.

Her nan and grandad didn't drone away about school, asking dreary questions about her day and how she was getting on. Just let her eat and drink and zap through programmes to her heart's content. Unlike her parents they really seemed to want her to be happy. Mandy wished she was there now.

Barging into the kitchen she said, 'What's the matter with the fire?'

'It's sulking.'

'But you know I get home at four.'

'I do, Amanda,' Sue lowered her *Guardian*, 'but I don't think the fire has quite got the message.'

Mandy stood gaping at her mother. Instead of being on the flit, hovering somewhere between the cooker, sink and table, as was usual whenever anyone entered the kitchen, Sue was sitting by the Aga with her legs up at an angle. Her ankles were crossed and her feet, in their thick, felted fisherman's socks, were perkily tilted in the air.

Mandy went to the table. At her place was the usual home-made gravelly finger of oaty molasses-flavoured goodness, a piece of fruit and a glass of apple-juice concentrate diluted one to twenty.

'I got chocolate cake yesterday,' said Mandy.

'I had chocolate cake myself, this morning.'

'Great! Where is it?'

'I've eaten it. I bought it to share with the play group. We were celebrating.'

Sue waited, to give the lines, Oh, really, mum? Gosh, how interesting. What were you celebrating? Do tell me all about it, plenty of time to waste their sweetness on the desert air. Then she took her feet down and turned to face her daughter.

'I heard from Methuen this morning.'

'Who?'

'They publish children's books. I sent them my story

about Hector. The editor wants me to have lunch with her. In London.'

'Big deal,' said Amanda.

'I think so,' replied her mother.

Sue got up, opened the fridge and got out a wine bottle. There wasn't much left, but what little there was she poured into a tumbler that had been resting on the floor beside her chair. Then she threw the bottle into the pedal bin, returned to her seat and disappeared behind the arts page of the newspaper.

Her eyes prickled and the print was definitely on the swimmy side. In fact one feature heading ('A Hundred and One Dalmatians; the Influence of Pointillisme on Dodie Smith') actually seemed about to dissolve. But Sue scrunched up her eyelids and swilled the tears back into her head by sheer force of will. It was nothing but foolishness to be cast down. After all, Amanda's response was no more than she, Sue, had expected.

Sue laid her fingers briefly on her breast, where the precious letter lay, folded small inside her bra. She had rung Methuen's about an hour ago. At first she had talked too much from nervousness and wine, but then, fearing they might think her wildly unstable and change their minds about the book, she had clammed up entirely. She had hardly been able to choke out an acceptance of the first date suggested. When she tried to make a note of this, the pen had twice slipped from her fingers and she'd had to put the phone down while she crawled around looking for it. The editor, who sounded very kind, and neither impatient nor amused at Sue's ineptitude, then gave her the name of the nearest tube and directions on how to find the building, It was only after Sue's palsied hand had clattered the receiver back onto its rest that she realised the thirteenth was only four days away.

'I got buttered crumpets as well last night.' Amanda affected to gag on the cookie. 'My nan says I need—'

'I don't give a stuff what your nan says. She wants to try managing on my housekeeping. You'd be lucky to get a glass of water and a cream cracker never mind a buttered bloody crumpet.'

There was a long silence. Neither of them could quite believe their ears. Mandy gawped, mouth hanging open, sticky brown tongue clearly visible. Sue retired once more behind her screen, proud that, though her heart was riven with tremors, the sheets of newspaper remained completely still. She thought, I must be drunk. Was it possible that *in vino veritas* was not just some bibulous old soak's tarradiddle but a matter of simple fact? And that, beneath the self-preserving layers of submissive docility, slept a person capable of extreme nastiness? Oh God, prayed Sue, I do hope so.

She lowered the *Guardian*. Amanda had gone. Scooby Doo had come. As now had Brian, kicking his boots against the front step in an attention-seeking, exaggerated way for all the world as if he had just bid hail and farewell to Sir Ranulph Fiennes.

He came into the sitting room, grumbled at Mandy for throwing her things on to the floor, laughed over-heartily at Scoob then strode straight through the kitchen into the toilet. Here he withdrew his penis, which looked and felt as if it had spent the previous twenty-four hours marinading in a jar of chili paste, with extreme care. He urinated, tucked himself tenderly away and zipped up very, very slowly. Emerging from the bathroom he stared, much as Amanda had done, at the sight of his spouse sitting (lolling might be more accurate) with her feet up.

Brian gave the room a sharp once-over but everything looked clean and tidy and tea was, as usual, on the table. Propped against his mug was a letter. Brian picked it up. As soon as he saw the writing he knew it was from Edie. His stomach heaved. Feeling both excited and alarmed he wriggled into the piney niche and forced himself to sit calmly and make some show of eating.

The food nearly choked him. The food and apprehension. Coming to the house! He'd have to put a stop to that. That sort of thing could lead to trouble. She was obviously desperate to see him again. Understandable. He was pretty keen to see her too. In fact, during a day spent teaching on automatic pilot (not that his class had noticed the difference) Brian had done nothing but dream of the future. He had already decided that, once he had obtained his freedom, they would be married. His parents would kick up of course, because of the social gap, but they'd come round. And eventually he would want children, though obviously he and Edie would be all in all to each other for a long time first.

'There's a letter for you.'

'I do have eyes, thank you.' Brian picked it up and pursed his lips, casually judicious. 'Any idea who brought it?'

'No. It was here when I came back from play group.'

Brian was quite proud of the cool way he dropped the bulky envelope into his cardigan pocket and carried on munching his banana and walnut bap while it lay there, sizzling.

'Probably someone can't make rehearsal.'

'How's it doing? Your play?'

'Fine.'

Sue watched him poking food into the pink hole in the

middle of his beard, then priss up his lips and use his little finger to dab at the tight corners, checking for crumbs.

'I shall be going to London on Tuesday.'

'London?' He stared across the room without seeing her. 'What for?'

'My lunch. With the editor.'

'Oh. Right.' It was no good. He couldn't wait. Not another second. Not another heartbeat. Certainly not as long as it took to get out from the table and hide himself away. 'Could you do me a favour, Sue? Please.'

His wife could not conceal her consternation. She said, 'Are you all right?'

'Would you mind getting me some dry socks? These are soaking.'

She took forever. Twenty-four hours to drag herself to the edge of her chair. A week to attain the vertical. A month to make it to the door. Six more to cross the sitting room. A year to climb – God's truth! – she was coming back.

'Any special sort?'

'No, no, no. No. You choose.'

Somehow he waited, fists clenched and his body in a tight little ball. Holding his breath like a drowning man conserving energy. Then, when he heard her clogs clatter on the floorboards overhead he tore at the envelope, his fingers all thumbs. And drew out the contents.

When Barnaby got back to Arbury Crescent there was a postcard from Cully – in black and white, of the Radziwill Palace in Warsaw. The greeting was, as usual, dryly non-committal. Playing to great houses, invited everywhere. The weather was fine, Nicholas was fine, she was fine. Don't forget to video *The Crucible*. Love Cully. Cross, cross, cross.

Barnaby wondered, as he so frequently did, just how much she did love them. Or even if she loved them at all. Surely, she must. You couldn't devote years of protective tenderness and concern, gut-wrenching anxiety and supportive admiration to someone and not have that person reciprocate, if only to a modest degree, in kind.

But of course you could. Beloved children took their place in your heart carelessly for granted and your devotion as no more than they deserved. They did not see it for what it was, the best you could do, but merely as the least you could do. It was only the desolate and deprived, the youthful walking wounded amongst whom Barnaby spent so much of his time, who saw the truly colossal magnificence of such a gift.

Joyce watched her husband, frowning down at the postcard in his hand. He was wearing his 'better than nothing' look. Half resentment, half relief. The light caught his grizzled sideboards and his still thick, black and silver hair. Thirteen hours since he had left for work and she could tell from his absent and distracted movements that he was still there in spirit.

Some cases were like this. She simply lost him. Watched as he became subsumed into an alternative universe in which there was no honestly relevant part for her to play. It was not that he didn't, quite frequently, describe to her what was engaging his attention. But there was no way that these occasions could be mistaken for discussions.

Lying back on the sofa, Tom would ramble on in a shapeless, repetitive manner, with his eyes closed, rather on the 'how do I know what I think till I say' principle. And Joyce would listen with attentive and sympathetic interest even as she remained aware that, for quite long periods, he would have forgotten her presence entirely.

She had, very early in their marriage, seen exactly what a policeman's wife was in for. Loneliness, disorienting time patterns, stressful periods of isolation and the constant apprehension that today might be the day he would be brought home, like a Roman soldier, lying on his shield.

Wives had various ways of coping – or not – with all these aspects of police life. Joyce chose what seemed to her the safest, most pleasant and most sensible. Whilst Tom and, later, Cully remained the emotional lynchpins in her life, from the earliest days of her marriage she had looked constantly outwards, developing and sustaining friend-ships (virtually none within the Force) and working on the second most important thing in her life, her music. She had a lovely, rich mezzo-soprano voice and still sang frequently in public. Lately she had started to teach.

Her husband, having laid the brief communication from their daughter on the television set, was staring gloomily into a mirror over the fireplace.

'What's it a sign of when policemen start looking older?'

'That their wives are extremely hungry.'

'Is that a fact?' He smiled at her in the glass, turned, made his way to the kitchen. 'Did you get everything?'

'Nearly. I bought fromage frais though, instead of double cream.'

Expecting a rebuke, she was surprised when he said, 'Good. I won't use butter either.'

'Tom?' He was wrapping a blue-and-white striped tablier around his middle and didn't look at her. It barely met round the back. 'What's the matter?'

'Nothing.'

'Come on.'

'What?'

'Something's happened.'

'No.'

Barnaby set out his materials and *batterie de cuisine*. Copper bowl and pan. Whisk, kitchen scissors. Brown free-range eggs, smoked salmon, a day-old cob of French bread, pot of chives.

Best not to tell her. She would worry and fret and it wasn't as if he was not already mending his ways. When the case was over he would go back to the doc. Get his progress monitored. Start taking proper care of himself. Maybe even do a spot of exercise.

'Shall I wash the watercress?'

'Pour me a drink first, Joycey.'

'If you have it now you can't have wine with your meal.'

'I know, I know.'

'She opened the fridge, which was half full of glasses. Tom preferred a cold container to cold wine, saying he never had the patience to wait for the latter to warm up sufficiently to release its scents and savours whereas, the other way, within seconds the wine was just right.

Joyce opened a bottle of '91 Gran Vina Sol. Barnaby, scissoring open the salmon packet said, 'If I can only have one glass you might at least fill it up.'

'Any fuller and it'll spill when you lift it.'

'So I'll lap. Which reminds me – where is our guzzly little scumbag?'

'Tom!' She put some bread in the toaster before turning on the cold tap and holding watercress in the clear stream. 'You know you like him really.'

'I do not "like him really".' He covered strips of fish with fromage frais. 'I want him to pack his clobber in a red-spotted handkerchief, tie it on the end of a stick and sling his hook.' Barnaby drank deeply. Only once but with great

327

relish. 'Ohh . . . wonderful. This is wonderful. Try some.'

'Hang on.' She patted the watercress dry before sipping at her drink. 'Mmm . . . nice. But I preferred the other stuff. The one that smells of elderflowers.'

Barnaby whisked the eggs and tipped them into the pan saying, as he did so, 'Watch the toast.'

When it was crisp and pale gold Joyce painted all the slices thinly with low-fat spread.

'Aren't you having butter?' He tipped the salmon and chive snippings into the pan and agitated the wooden spoon, easing moist curls of scrambled egg from the sides and bottom of the pan.

Joyce said, 'Seems a bit flaunty when you can't.'

'Don't be silly. No point in both of us fading away.'

I can hack this calorie caper, decided Barnaby, sitting now at the table, his mouth full of peppery cress, creamy eggs and golden wine. It's all a question of attitude. I've been looking at it from quite the wrong angle. Like a prisoner facing a life sentence. In fact the only meal you need to diet at is the one you're eating. All the rest can be as fattening as you like. By the time he started on his huge, fat Comice pear and tiny shred of Dolcelatte he was feeling not merely resigned but almost content.

Joyce made some excellent Blue Mountain coffee and, after she had poured it out, stood behind her husband's chair, slid her smooth, soft arms around his neck and laid her cheek against his.

Barnaby turned his head, showing pleasure, wamth, a faint surprise. They kissed at some length like dear, close friends who were in love. Which is what they were.

'What's brought this on?'

'Good grief, Tom. Don't make it sound as if there has to be an R in the month.'

What had brought it on? That rapid disclaimer against her concerned question? That lying disclaimer. For that something had occurred to make him aware of his own mortality she had no doubt. He would tell her eventually, when he thought the danger was past. He always did.

Joyce experienced a vivid recollection. Herself at nineteen. A first-year concert at the Guildhall. Afterwards, on the fringe of a milling crowd of students, teachers, proud parents and friends, a slim young copper, ill at ease and hopelessly out of place, clutching a bunch of flowers. Waiting with dogged patience for his turn to be noticed.

He was getting up now. Turning to take her in his arms. His eyes moved intently over her face, as if stamping every individual feature to memory. And asking a silent question. Joyce laughed and said, 'If we were really imbued with the spirit of adventure we would fall to here and now on the kitchen table.'

'Eh?'

'I was reading this article on how to be sexually spontaneous. In the hairdresser's.'

'Who the hell wants to be sexually spontaneous in the hairdresser's?'

'Called "How To Keep Your Marriage Alive".'

'How to put your back out more like. No' – they linked arms and made their way into the hall – 'it's the boring marital bed again I'm afraid, sweetheart.'

'Dreary old missionary.'

'You knew my faith when I proposed.'

After they had made love Joyce fell quickly asleep, her head on her husband's breast, still cradled in his arms. Not wishing to disturb her he eased an extra pillow beneath his shoulders and half sat, half reclined, running over the events of the day, the previous day, the one before that.

Searching his mind for connections and resonances, hidden meanings, false interpretations.

He did not dwell at any length on that evening's debriefing, for it had been unprofitable to say the least. It produced only one new scrap of information and that from the outdoor team. In 1983 Beecham's Removals had collected Gerald Hadleigh's furniture and personal effects, neither from Kent nor London SW1, but from a storage depot in Staines.

This being the sum total on offer, Barnaby had then offered his notes on the interview with Mrs Lyddiard, plus his ideas on Hadleigh's feminine *alter ego*, which had been received with a mixture of wary caution and polite incredulity. Indeed, as he described the psychological persona that he had so confidently constructed earlier in the day, he started to wonder himself if it was not so much imaginative as imaginary.

Eventually he slept, dozing and waking intermittently, disturbed by the wind howling through the trees and a branch tapping on the window. At one point, in that dark hinterland between sleeping and waking, he found himself walking down a narrow street of bulbous cobblestones illuminated sporadically by pools of ochre-coloured light. He was carrying something very heavy. His arms were stretched out parallel and this heavy object lay, a dead weight, across them. Not that it was dead in fact for there were shallow, panting sounds emanating from it.

He halted beneath an overhead iron bracket holding a funnel, from which the strangely coloured light was flowing, to take a closer look at his burden. It was a seal. Lumpen and graceless on land, its prickly grey-brown fur was dull and dry. The head hung loosely down. There was a strange mark – a ring of darker fur, like a collar or noose

– about its neck. As he stood holding it, concerned and perplexed, it turned a pointed, doggy face and stared at him. The round eyes were also dull and covered with a gluey film. He realised, with a shock of horror, that it was dying.

He must find water. He started to walk as quickly as he was able. In his mind there was a picture, just around the bend of the street, of a river. He remembered the bridge, people fishing. He staggered along, knees buckling, sweat streaming from his face and hair. But, when he finally turned the corner, the river and bridge had disappeared. In its place was an open sandy plain on which strange animals roamed.

Barnaby looked into the seal's clouded eyes. They seemed to bestow no blame for his stupidity, only to be consumed by a quiet and terrible sadness. He could not bear it and began once more to struggle on. The world was full of water. Surely soon he must find some.

The surface of the pavement had become transformed. It was now spongy and yielding and his feet sank further in with every step. It was cold too. He felt the chill dampness of it seeping over the edge of his shoes. There was moisture on his hands and he saw that silvery froth had formed around the animal's mouth. The yellow lights were getting dim.

Then, just as he felt his back was breaking, he saw, shining at his feet, a puddle. He lowered the seal into it, feeling the muscles of his arms jump and quiver at the moment of release. The seal turned over and over in the water. Its fur sparkled, the eyes and whiskers shone. Then, as Barnaby watched, the beads of light on its coat and the reflected light in the puddle conjoined until the seal and the water were one oddly shaped mass of gleaming silver.

Trees, tall as telegraph poles, sprang up all around. Faxes chattered in their branches and reams of paper tumbled down. A woman, veiled all in black, appeared and disappeared, rushing through the air, draperies flying, on a high swing. The mysterious silver shape was becoming transformed into something longer and more streamlined.

Watching this process, so entirely out of his control, Barnaby was overcome by a strong sense of hazard. And yet, when the metamorphosis was complete, the result could not have been more ordinary. A motor car. Pearly pale with an interior full of shadows. As Barnaby bent to peer inside, one of the shadows turned a smiling face in his direction. He knew at once that he had found Max Jennings. And awoke hours later, with a totally numb left arm, a ball of fur dossing on his chest and a clamorously ringing telephone to hear that it was true.

Liam's Story

In the end it had simply been a stroke of luck. A motor-cycle policeman, himself a passionate admirer of the Mercedes Benz and the proud owner of a G-registered 230TE, had taken special note when the search had been first registered. Idling by the lights in the town of St Just he had seen the car, facing in the opposite direction, doing likewise. There was a couple inside and the man was driving.

As soon as he was able the patrolman wheeled round and pursued it, keeping a discreet distance, waiting to see if the driver had business in town or was merely passing through. The car took the road to Botallack. The policeman was about to radio in its exact position when the Mercedes suddenly turned left and disappeared down a narrow side lane. He followed, cutting his motor-cycle engine to coast silently.

They had parked outside a small cottage quite close to the furiously pounding sea and were unloading cardboard boxes from the boot. The wind blew the woman's scarf about and she had to keep pulling it away from her face.

Max Jennings expressed puzzled surprise (so Barnaby was later told) at an unexpected visit from the police, consternation at the reason for it and definite displeasure at the news that he would need to travel back to the Home Counties to answer questions rather than be interrogated in Cornwall.

'Surely,' he was now saying in the interview room of Causton CID, 'I might have gone to the station in St Just. Or, failing that, couldn't we have talked on the telephone?'

'I'm afraid that is not possible, Mr Jennings,' said Chief Inspector Barnaby. 'The case is being handled here.'

'I still can't believe it. How appalling.' Jennings reached out for his polystyrene beaker of station coffee and sipped with plain lack of appreciation. He took a deep breath as if to speak, moving his hand in emphasis, hesitated, then simply repeated himself.

'Appalling. Christ – what a terrible way to go.'

'Are you quite sure you knew nothing of this matter until today?'

'I've already told you. The cottage has no telephone, radio or television. It's very basic.'

'But surely your car has a radio.'

'Today was the first time we used the car. We took food and everything else we needed down with us. It lasted till this morning, when we ran out of milk and bread.'

He'd got everything off pat. And so he should have with six hours on the motorway to work it all out. Not that it couldn't have happened precisely as he described. If he had reached Cornwall before the evening after the murder, and not bought a paper since, his surprise could be genuine. Unless of course he was guilty, in which case he'd had even longer to get everything off pat.

Jennings opened a dark green leather case lined with pale brown gold-banded cigarillos. On being informed of the No Smoking rule he put the case away without comment, but did not look best pleased. Troy was impressed by the elegance of both case and contents. Far more than by Jennings' female companion, now shredding her hankie to bits in the outer office. Straight brown hair, frumpy camel coat, hardly any make-up. You'd have thought a famous writer could have done better for himself. In fact the only good thing you could say for her was that her name was Lindsay and not Barbara.

'So – what is it you want from me?' Max Jennings glanced at his watch, which was as stylish as the rest of him, with an air of slight impatience.

'I'd like you to tell us all you know about this matter.'

'Well, that won't take long,' replied Jennings. 'Absolutely nothing.'

'It does appear that you were the last person to see Mr Hadleigh alive—'

'The last bar one, chief inspector. Let's stick to the facts, shall we?'

'I hope we shall both do that,' said Barnaby and received a sharp-eyed glance for his impudence. 'Could I ask first when precisely you left Plover's Rest?'

'Plover's what?'

'Mr Hadleigh's cottage.'

'I don't honestly know. Lateish.'

'Do you remember when you arrived home then? Perhaps we could work back from there.'

'Eleven, twelve. I'm hopeless with time. Ask anyone.'

'Were you the last to go?'

'As far as I recall.'

'And how did you leave Mr Hadleigh?'

'Alive and well.'

'And in good spirits?'

For the first time Jennings paused. He looked down at his olive-green walking boots then across the room at a crime-prevention poster showing a disembodied hand creeping into an open handbag. 'Hard to say, really. He didn't strike me as someone who gave a lot away.'

'What did you talk about? After the others had gone.'

'Writing. That is why I was asked.'

'Do you often accept this kind of invitation?'

'Not as a rule, but Midsomer Worthy was quite near. Also I thought it might be amusing.'

'And was it?'

'No. A positive Valhalla of tedium.'

'Perhaps you could tell us—'

'For heaven's sake! What on earth have my impressions got to do with this shocking business? We'll be here all night at this rate.'

'As an outsider, Mr Jennings, you have a viewpoint that could be uniquely helpful. I'm not only interested in your opinions of individual group members but also in any cross currents or tensions you may have picked up during the course of the evening.'

'Relating to Hadleigh, you mean?'

'Not necessarily.'

Max regarded a poster on the other wall, this time seriously and at some length, as if gradually coming to terms with the notion that Neighbourhood Watch could change his life. Sergeant Troy, who had been leaning against the door, picked up an orange vinyl chair and sat just behind his chief. The room was very quiet. Just the hiss of tape and the occasional scraping of a chair leg as Jennings fidgeted about . . .

'In your business,' Barnaby nudged the conversation back on the rails, 'you must need a keen eye and ear. Your raw material aren't they, people? Surely you must have noticed something.'

'There was a woman with red hair – I'm afraid I forget her name – who was in love with Hadleigh. And extremely unhappy about it. A ghastly little man called Clapton. Hopelessly ineffectual and, I suspect, completely un-talented, with his poor squash of a wife. A sweet old chap so distrait it hardly seemed safe to let him loose without a keeper and a fearsome, barking-mad woman with legs like Nelson's column and a quite Laurentian idolatry for what she kept calling "true English blood".' He looked back and forth between the two policemen. 'Is the theory then that one of them came back later and did him over?'

Barnaby admitted to some surprise at this suggestion. 'You're the only person I've yet spoken to who didn't assume the murder was the result of a break-in.'

'Oh, no writer worth his salt's going to settle for that. Far too tame. Where's the plot?'

'Why did you go and visit this group, Mr Jennings?'

'I've already been asked that.'

'Your agent was frankly disbelieving. She implied it was the sort of thing you'd never do.'

'Talent? What on earth have you been talking to her for?'

'We were trying to trace you. After your wife had told us—'

'*You've been to my house?*' The words emerged in a tangled skein as if the man's tongue was so stiff it could not shape or separate them properly.

'Obviously. Mrs Jennings seemed to think you had gone to Finland.'

'Jesus Christ. What did you tell her?'

'At that stage there was nothing we could tell her. And in any case she was hardly in a condition to take much in.'

'It was your Mr Stavro,' said Troy, 'who described your

movements. According to his statement you asked for an early call, saying you had to drive to Heathrow. He also mentioned that you got home on the night in question at one a.m. and not, as you have just suggested, between eleven and midnight.'

'I told you. I never know what time it is.'

'Rather a waste of that beautiful watch then, sir.'

Jennings seemed not to have heard. 'Have you . . . ? Did you go back to the house? Talk to my wife again?'

'No.'

'So, as far as she knows . . .'

'You're still pussyfooting around Helsinki.'

Even as he spoke Barnaby wondered how true that was. He recalled the woman's bitter, wasted smile and eyes that could take no more yet knew that more was surely on the way. Saw her coppery limbs, banded with cold fire, cleaving through the water; up and down, up and down, like some glittering, cruelly constrained tropical fish.

Jennings' infidelities were his own affair (unless they had some bearing on the present case) and should have been a matter of complete indifference to Barnaby. Yet, momentarily, he felt both pity and disgust which he made no attempt to conceal. To his surprise, for the writer had struck him as self-contained to a fault, Jennings immediately started to explain and justify himself.

'It's not what you think.'

'Really, Mr Jennings?'

'If you've been looking me up you'll perhaps know that my wife and I had a son who died when he was small. He would have been nine this year. His death affected Ava terribly. Everything about her seemed to change. She became morose and occasionally violent. Spent some time in a mental hospital. She wouldn't let me near her

338

physically or emotionally. I couldn't comfort her and I had no one to comfort me. It was my child too.

'I'm not the philandering type but eventually, more out of loneliness than anything else, I became involved with someone. Over a long period of time we've grown very close and, I must admit, I now can't bear the thought of life without her. I wanted to tell my wife, but Lindsay wouldn't hear of it. She said Ava had had enough misery already to last a lifetime. We've been together, if one can so call snatched hours here and there and a few weekends, for five years. This is the first time we've attempted anything like a real holiday. The cottage belongs to Lindsay's friends. I was very happy there, but she couldn't settle. Kept fretting, sure something would go wrong.' Jennings picked up his beaker of coffee, by now quite cold, peered into it and said, 'God – what a mess.'

It was only too plain what mess he meant. The murder of Gerald Hadleigh seemed hardly to engage his interest at all.

'I hope this can be kept out of the newspapers, chief inspector. It's not as if it's relevant to your investigation.'

'That's really not in our hands, sir.'

'I can't believe that.' Then, receiving no response, he rose wearily to his feet, saying, 'Well, if someone will show me where you've parked my car . . .'

'I hardly think you'll need to know that just yet, sir.'

'I'm sorry?' Jennings, already moving towards the door, turned back in some surprise. 'Isn't that it then?'

'Not by a long way, I'm afraid.'

The chief inspector, more entertained than annoyed at this impromptu example of faux naivety, gave the machine the precise time and situation and switched off.

'In that case I must talk to Lindsay. Persuade her to go home.'

'You can have five minutes,' said Barnaby thinking, as Troy had done, thank God, Lindsay not Barbara. 'But I'm afraid it won't be a private conversation.'

'Why the hell not?'

'Rules and regulations.'

'I've never heard such arrogance. I shall complain about this. And at the highest level.'

'By all means. But I think you will find that such a procedure is quite in order.'

When Jennings returned, in rather more than five minutes, he looked both unhappy and distracted. It was plainly an effort, when Barnaby once more switched on the tape, to drag his attention back to the matter in hand. When asked if he wished to have his solicitor present he hardly seemed to register. It was repeated.

'No thanks. At one fifty an hour I keep him for high days and holidays.'

Barnaby chose his first question purely for its shock value. 'Tell me, Mr Jennings, had you met Gerald Hadleigh before last Monday evening?'

'What? I didn't quite . . .'

He had heard. He had heard perfectly. Barnaby kept his eyes on his suspect's face watching the play for time, and simultaneously guessing at the selection/rejection thought processes now whirring away in Jennings' mind. Why had that old buffer refused to go home? Could Gerald have possibly asked him not to? If so what reason had he given? Was my name mentioned? The police would have talked to St John by now – what had he told them? Alternatively, was there perhaps some letter or paper – perhaps and old diary – in the dead man's effects that proves some connection between us. Better play it safe.

'Yes, I knew him. Very slightly. Some years ago.'

'Was this perhaps why you accepted the invitation?'

'Partly. I suppose I was a bit curious as to how things had gone with him. You know, the way one is.'

'So that's why you made a point of staying behind? To catch up on old times?'

'Yes.'

'Not then, as you stated earlier, simply to talk about writing?'

'That as well. It was something we had in common.'

'Hardly to a comparable degree.'

Max Jennings shrugged. 'Writing's writing.'

'You seem to have gone to a lot of trouble to bring about a meeting of so little moment.'

'What do you mean?'

'I understand you stayed behind long after most of the others had gone, made a show of leaving, then virtually tricked your way back inside the house.'

'What dramatic nonsense. I forgot my gloves.'

'So why was it necessary to bolt the door?'

'I didn't.'

'And, if you only went back for something you'd forgotten, why were you still there over an hour later?'

'We got talking. All right?'

'About the past?'

'Largely.'

'Did Mr Hadleigh get upset?'

'I don't understand.'

'Then I'll put it more plainly.' Barnaby leaned forwards, resting his elbows on the edge of the table. Bringing his face closer. 'Did you reduce him to tears?'

Max Jennings stared at Barnaby then skewed his head round to look at Troy. He regarded first one man and then the other, all the while struggling to project the image of

341

someone utterly bemused at this preposterous notion that had been so crudely thrust upon him. But he did not answer and his eyes were bright and extremely concerned.

The interrogation started in earnest. Both officers took part and the rhythm was hard and relentless.

'Why were you so determined to get Hadleigh on his own?'

'Why was the murdered man afraid of you?'

'He wasn't—'

'So afraid that he begged St John not to leave the house *under any circumstances* until you did.'

'Everyone had commented on how tense he was.'

'Hardly spoke.'

'Wound up.'

'Like a watch-spring.'

'Been drinking.'

'You can hardly blame me for—'

'Why did you lie about the time you arrived home?'

'I didn't. It was a mistake—'

'Why did you lie about going to Finland?'

'I've explained that—'

'When did you discover that this cottage, supposedly belonging to your mistress's friends, would be available?'

'The exact dates, Mr Jennings. When did you learn those?'

'A while ago.'

'How long a while?'

'A couple of months.'

'Before you accepted Hadleigh's invitation?'

'Well . . . yes.'

'Convenient.'

'What do you mean?'

'To just be able to vanish like that.'

'After a murder.'

'I'd call that handy.'

'Very nice.'

'Why did you take all the clothes you wore that night away with you?'

'It's an outfit I'm comfortable in. I wear it a lot.'

'What happened to the brown suitcase?'

'The brown . . . ?'

'Belonging to Hadleigh.'

'Missing from his place. Not found at yours.'

'Why on earth should it be—'

'Where is it, Mr Jennings?'

'Dump it on your way to "Heathrow"?'

'What did you take from the chest of drawers?'

'I don't recall a chest of—'

'In the bedroom.'

'I was never in the bedroom.'

'Is that a fact?'

'I didn't go upstairs at all.'

'Why didn't you get in touch with the police once you knew of Hadleigh's death?'

'I *didn't* know—'

'That's your story,' said Sergeant Troy. 'Your girlfriend might be singing a different tune.'

'My God!' Jennings sprang to his feet with quick aggression, as if he had been physically invaded. 'If anyone's treating her like you're treating me I'll wring their bloody neck.'

'Sit down.'

'I feel like standing up. I assume I'm allowed to stand if I want to?' He glared at the two policemen in turn, his eyes and hands in perpetual motion. Then he sat down again in a curious, stiff way, balancing on the very edge of his seat as if to underline the transitory nature of his presence.

'Look at it from our point of view, Mr Jennings,' said the chief inspector and although the words might have been construed as conciliatory there was no hint of appeasement in his voice, which was unemotional to the point of coldness. 'Hadleigh was known to be afraid of you to a degree which led him to ask for what might well be construed as protection, albeit from a rather fragile source. In spite of this, and due entirely to your own machinations, he found himself in the very position that he wished to avoid at all costs. The following morning he is discovered dead and you, the last person to see him alive, have disappeared. And this after giving your wife false information about your whereabouts. By some freakish coincidence you then find yourself shut away in a cottage, miles from anywhere, which just happens to be minus all the usual lines of communication to the outside world. Really, you must think we were all born yesterday.'

Jennings received this dispassionate summing-up in silence and did not respond for some time. When he did speak he sounded nervy and uncertain.

'I do realise how extraordinarily things seem to have fallen out against me. But that in itself, though unfortunate, is hardly a proof of guilt. Isn't all of it what's known as circumstantial evidence?'

He was right, but Barnaby who was not running a comfort station had no intention of saying so. Instead he offered a mildly encouraging smile and turned the conversation around once more to face the past.

'Given that all these events could, by wildly stretching the bounds of possibility, have happened coincidentally, there is still the matter of your earlier connection with

Hadleigh. I presume you're no longer going to keep up the fiction that you knew him only slightly.'

'Our past relationship has nothing to do with this case. I give you my word.'

'I'm afraid your word isn't good enough, Mr Jennings. And, even if what you say is true, the fact remains that you are the only person known to us with any knowledge of Hadleigh's background. I'm sure you wouldn't wish to deliberately obstruct a police investigation.'

'Naturally not.'

'Especially when it is so plainly in your own interests to help us in any way you can.'

'Yes, I can see that.' His face folded in on itself. Barnaby watched him weigh and balance, assess a chance here, a dead end there, all behind a frown of deepening uncertainty. It was like watching someone trying to read a map in the dark. Eventually Jennings said, 'All right. But I need a smoke, a wash, something to eat and, if that was the best coffee you can produce, a cup of decent tea.'

It was almost half an hour later. Jennings had been escorted to the men's lavatory, where he had washed and shaved and smoked a couple of his cigarillos. Troy had gladly accepted one when it was offered, but found it a sad disappointment. Bitter, with a fragrance rather like rotting leaves. He smoked half, then, minding his manners for once, flushed the rest discreetly down the loo.

Settled once more in the interview room a WPC entered with a tray holding two rounds of sandwiches, three cups of tea and a fresh jug of water. It was a large tray and obviously extremely heavy, but Troy made no move to take it from her. If equality was what they wanted – the tray descended with a crash to the table – equality was what they could have.

Jennings ate a little, drank his tea and settled back, arms folded, looking more relaxed. 'So,' he said, 'where do you want me to start?'

'From the beginning,' said Barnaby, apparently not at all discouraged by his interviewee's renewed insouciance. He moved his chair slightly so that the remaining sandwich was outside his line of vision, for he was extremely hungry and had no wish to be distracted. 'From when you first met Hadleigh.'

'Right.' Jennings paused, his expression reflective and quite grave. Yet there was something anticipatory about it, too. He looked pleased that it was within his gift to unlock and unravel the mystery of another man's life.

'I met Gerald at my thirtieth birthday bash. A girl from Barts, where I was working at the time, brought him along.'

'Barts?' repeated the chief inspector. 'You mean the hospital?'

'Bartle Bogle Hegerty.'

'Ah.' He was none the wiser.

'The advertising agency. I was one of their copywriters. Had a garden flat in Maida Vale.'

'And you became friends.'

'Not spontaneously. In fact I didn't see him again for some weeks. Then we ran into each other – accidentally on purpose as I discovered later – in the booking hall at Warwick Avenue underground. I can see him now, feeding money into the automatic ticket machine. Knife-creased flannels, navy blazer, open-necked shirt and cravat. Barely forty and he looked like some retired colonel from central casting.

'We discovered we were travelling in the same direction and started talking about writing. We'd touched on this at our first meeting but only briefly, parties being what they are. Gerald was attending Creative Writing classes at the City Lit. I, in common with just about everyone else in advertising, was wrestling with my first novel. Before he got off, at Kensal Green, he asked if we could meet and talk further.

'My first inclination was to refuse. I don't really think there's much point in discussing the actual process of writing. It's a peculiar and essentially solitary business and you have to do it yourself to get the feel of it. Like swimming or riding a bike. But there was that about him which intrigued me. I can best describe it as a hugely concentrated carefulness. He was the most watchful man I ever met. So I agreed, largely out of curiosity. I wanted to find out more about him.

'I suggested a drink to keep things casual and he seemed happy with that. In fact on the first occasion he only stayed twenty minutes. Said he had a date and rushed off. We met a few more times. Had a meal once at his place, a completely characterless flat in a mansion block near Westminster cathedral. Mainly we discussed the authors we admired. He always talked about books in a purely technical way. He thought you could take them apart, discover how they'd been put together and then assemble one yourself rather like the engine of a car. He didn't understand their mystery at all. The fact that the best ones had a secret life that forever slipped through your fingers.'

Barnaby shifted restlessly. 'We seem to be drifting away from the main issue, Mr Jennings.'

'Not at all. This is absolutely germane, as you will shortly see. He read me a couple of his stories. Rigor mortis, inspector. Neatly typed. A beginning, middle and end and dead as mutton from line one. I did not respond in kind. I've never read my work to anyone. To do so would make me feel uncomfortable. Precious. Like one of those dreadful Bloomsburies.

'These casual meetings went on for about three months. I asked questions, the way one does with a new acquaintance, but he'd answer only grudgingly, a crumb at a time. I discovered he'd been brought up in Kent, the only child of middle-class parents now both dead. That he'd gone to a minor public school and had a dullish job in the Civil Service. I couldn't decide whether I'd lost my knack of being able to prise people apart and winkle out their secrets or if he was simply a bore with hidden shallows. God knows there's enough of them about. In any event I came to the conclusion I'd wasted enough time on him and decided to call it a day.'

Callous bugger, thought Sergeant Troy. He could see how the bloke earned a good screw telling stories though. Even though nothing very dramatic had happened so far Jennings had the trick of implying that, any minute now, it just might. Troy said, 'How did Mr Hadleigh take that?'

'I didn't put it so bluntly of course. Implied it was only temporary. Told him I was on a roll with the writing and didn't want to risk losing it. As I still had my day job and very little spare time that wasn't an unreasonable excuse. After I told him he hung up. Didn't say anything at all. There was this rather heavy silence then – click.'

'I must say, Mr Jennings,' said Barnaby, 'you have excellent recall for something that happened so long ago.'

'I remember it clearly because of what came next. I suppose half an hour must have passed. I was getting ready to go out. I had met Ava by then and was taking her to dinner at the Caprice. The doorbell rang. It was Gerald. He pushed straight past me into the flat. He was as white as a sheet. His face, always so smooth and tight, was all broken up. He looked crazed. His hair was on end as if be'd been tugging at it and his eyes were unfocused. He didn't seem to see me, just started striding about in a jerky way as if someone was goading him. Then he began shouting, disjointed questions and declarations all garbled up together in a sick sort of muddle. I tried to calm him down. To find out what the matter was. But every time I attempted to speak he drowned me out. Why was I doing this? What had he done wrong? Was I trying to kill him?

'Then he slumped into my armchair and started gasping. Desolate wheezing sounds, fighting for breath. Up till then, though annoyed at being held up, I must admit I was also rather excited by the eruptive and dramatic nature of the event. But now I became really alarmed. I thought he might be having a fit. I got some whisky, made him drink it and poured another. I suppose I felt that if I got him drunk I could calm him down and find out just what the hell was going on. He gulped the stuff, splashing it all over his shirt and trousers. His clothes already looked as if they'd been thrown on. One of his cufflinks was missing. His shoe laces weren't properly tied. While I was in the bedroom, ringing Ava, he started to cry.

'I had left the door slightly open and could see him, reflected in a looking glass, though he couldn't see me. He picked up a scarf that was lying, together with my coat, over the back of the chair. I remember thinking, he's going to mop his face with it which just showed how far gone he was, for his manners were always so archaically elaborate as to be almost a joke. But instead he laid the scarf against his cheek and then to his lips.'

Here Max Jennings paused, helping himself to some water, half filling a tumbler. Troy watched, his foxy features screwed up with distaste.

'You may all,' continued Jennings, once more seated, 'have been way ahead of me on this one. I don't think I was at all unsophisticated, yet it simply never occurred to me that Gerald might be harbouring such feelings. Firstly, there was absolutely nothing in his manner or appearance to suggest homosexuality – at least to a heterosexual like myself. Then there was the fact that, the first time we met, he was with a female date. Anyway, as you can imagine, I was now doubly determined to be rid of him. And, if humanly possible, without provoking any sort of declaration on his part. So I strode back into the sitting room, all brisk and rugger bugger, and said that my girlfriend had given me a hell of a rocket for keeping her waiting and I had to shoot off instantly.

'He took not the slightest notice. I didn't know what to do. I couldn't bring myself to touch him. To try and coax him out of his chair and through the front door. And I certainly wasn't going to leave him there. I decided to call a cab, thinking if I said he'd been taken ill the driver might help me shift him. But when I picked up the phone Gerald leapt up, ran across the room and snatched at the receiver. He cried out, "Don't send me away", burst into a positive avalanche of tears and fell to the carpet grasping me round the knees and practically knocking me over. It was ludicrous and pathetic and also a bit unnerving. I mean, he was a big bloke.

'I said fatuous things like, "Come on now, Gerald" and, "Pull yourself together" – all the while trying to walk away with him bumping on his knees after me. Then he seized my hand and when he did that everything changed.

Because there was nothing even remotely sexual about it. It was simply desperate, like someone hanging from their fingertips to the edge of a cliff. I stopped feeling threatened and helped him to his feet. We went into the kitchen, where I sat him down and made some coffee. Before he had a chance to launch into any sort of declaration I made it plain that the idea of being loved by another man was wholly repugnant to me. And that if he spoke a single word along those lines I would have nothing more to do with him. Of course this was my intention anyway but I could see he'd never go if I said as much.

'Once I'd made the decision to give this bizarre and rather unpleasant incident as much time as it took to sort it out and clear it permanently away the whole atmosphere lightened. Gerald became more relaxed, if still very anxious. He was by then extremely drunk. If he hadn't been I doubt very much if what followed would have taken place.'

'And what was that, Mr Jennings?' asked Barnaby.

'He told me all about himself,' said Max Jennings. 'But this time it was the truth.'

At this point in Max Jennings' revelations the tape ran out, illustrating, as he himself was the first to remark, a grasp of narrative technique that many a human storyteller might envy.

Barnaby inserted the new one in a highly ambivalent state of mind. He found it difficult to take Jennings' measure. The man seemed to be talking freely enough, but was that only because he had been pushed, almost threatened, into doing so? And although what had been said so far sounded convincing it had to be remembered that Jennings told convincing lies for a living.

Even so the chief inspector could not deny a slightly queasy frisson of expectation at the thought that the true life story of Gerald Hadleigh was (perhaps) about to be unrolled before him. He girded his attention and marshalled his wits. Concentrated listening, especially to an extended monologue, is a tiring business. The chief inspector was surprised to find he still felt quite crisp and wondered briefly if this could in any way be connected to his spartan diet.

As he started the tape, giving the date and time of the interview and listing those present, Barnaby watched Jennings closely. He had once more shifted to the edge of his seat, where he perched trembling slightly. His shoulders were hunched and his hands, fingers loosely meshed, lay motionless in his lap. There was no attempt to re-establish the previous 'candid' eye contact. This time, as he began to speak, he stared fixedly at the floor.

'The Gerald Hadleigh who came to my party was an invention. Even the name was false. He was born Liam Hanlon in Southern Ireland. The only child of a poor family. Literally a potato patch, a pig and a shotgun for the rabbits. His father was a monstrous man, a drunkard who beat his wife half to death on more than one occasion and the child too if he got in the way. As you can imagine, during this wretchedly cruel existence the boy and his mother grew very close, though they were careful never to show affection for each other in front of her husband. Somehow they both survived. The neighbours, such as they were, for it was a scattered community, knew what was going on but didn't interfere. If a man's fist sometimes slipped – well, that was between him and his wife. The priest, the Garda, all knew and did nothing.

'There was a single bright spot in Liam's miserable life.

He had a friend. An older boy, Conor Neilson, who lived on a farm a few miles away. Hanlon would drag his son over there when animals were being slaughtered, not all that humanely by all accounts. This was supposedly in order to "make a man of him". Of course it was just sadism. Once Liam cried when a lamb was killed and his father emptied a bucket of blood and intestines over the boy's head.'

'Bastard!' Troy was compelled into expectorating speech. He did not apologise for the irrelevant interruption, but compounded his felony by adding, 'I'd string the bugger up.'

Barnaby understood, even appreciated, his sergeant's intemperance. He too would rather not be listening. There was something dark and inexorable in the setting and unravelling of this already tragic tale. When bad paths were badly trod what good could ever come of it?

'Conor, by all accounts, was a strange plant to be growing out there in the bogs. Quiet and withdrawn, a great reader. When Liam could escape they'd roam round the countryside watching birds and other creatures. Sometimes Conor would draw – plants, flowers, pebbles in a stream. Naturally Liam's father despised the boy and his own parents weren't that far behind. Obviously,' (here Max Jennings looked up) 'I'm telescoping here. The next event I'm about to describe, which was to have such a traumatic effect on Liam that it changed the whole course of his life, took place when he was nearly fourteen and Conor three years older.

'It was a spring evening. Hanlon's fist had slipped even more savagely than usual and his wife had to be taken to the hospital. She was kept in and Conor's parents were asked if they would look after the boy. Liam was surprised and immensely relieved, for he had dreaded being alone with his father. He slept on an old canvas truckle in Conor's room, crying himself to sleep every night. Lonely for his mother, terribly afraid he'd never see her again. Eventually Conor took the boy into his bed. Cuddled and comforted him, kissed his tears away. One thing led to another.

'Liam believed, and persisted in believing in spite of all future evidence to the contrary, that Conor was moved on that first occasion solely by affection and pity. One can see why the poor little devil needed to think so. His sense of self-worth must have been virtually non-existent. How could he be expected to take on board the notion that the only friend he had in the world had taken advantage, at a moment of great desolation, to use and betray him? So, passively, out of affection and gratitude, Liam let himself be used. This dangerous union – for that's what it was, bloody dangerous forty years ago and in that community – continued. Even after Liam was back at home. Of course it was only a matter of time before they were discovered.

'His mother returned, but Hanlon didn't kick out the village girl he had installed when his wife was away. And it was she who saw the two boys one evening at dusk, "at it like otters" behind some corn stooks. Liam's father went after them with his shotgun and was never seen again. "Sucked into the bog" was the general opinion and nobody would have minded much had not the two boys also vanished. The Garda did some sort of search – not trying too hard, I imagine.

'After years of physical and mental cruelty the loss of her son tipped the balance of Mary Hanlon's mind and she became deranged, stopping people at random, staring with wild accusation into their faces, pleading that they return

Liam. Sometimes she would hammer on doors or scream through letter boxes demanding that whoever was inside bring him out. Eventually she was committed to an asylum.

'The two boys, like thousands before them, ran away to the big city. In this case, Dublin. Here, at least for Liam, things went from bad to terrible. It wasn't long before he and Conor were working the streets. And not much longer than that before it became plain that Liam's youth and beauty – for he was, in those days, extremely beautiful – meant that every waking hour could have been spent turning his back on opportunity. Conor quickly took full advantage of this situation. Soon no one came to the young Ganymede but by him. The rates were as high as the market would bear, but Liam only received food, a small clothing allowance and pocket money. This state of affairs continued for nearly three years.

'It may seem odd to you,' Max Jennings unmeshed his fingers and turned his palms upwards, as if to illustrate his own past unbelief, 'that Liam put up with all this for so long, but Conor kept him on a very short leash. The business took place at their flat, which meant opportunities to make other friends were virtually non-existent. And Conor would get very angry if Liam suggested going out and meeting other people. This was all that was needed to keep the boy in line for, not surprisingly, he was terrified of violence.'

For the first time ever Sergeant Troy, listening intently, found himself forced to think of an arse bandit – i.e. the rising scum on society's cesspit – with some degree of perceptive sympathy. This unsettled him considerably. Put out to a degree that rapidly became both irritating and uncomfortable, he was finally rescued by having resource to his 'Cliché For All Occasions' file. As always, it did not let him down. Under E (for excuses) there it was: Exception proves rule, the. Phew! Metaphorically, Troy mopped his brow. Things had seemed a bit unclear there for a moment. A touch on the complicated side. Relieved, he returned his attention to the story.

'Then, just a few months before he was seventeen, Liam met Hilton Conninx. Perhaps you may have heard of him?'

Even as Barnaby shook his head he experienced a distant tremor of acknowledgement far too faint to be called recognition. In any case a wander from the point was the last thing he wished to encourage. Outside it was by now pitch black. The rate things were going it looked as if they were going to be there all night.

'Conninx was an artist specialising in portraits. Extremely successful commercially he was poorly regarded by the critics though two of his paintings are in Dublin's National Gallery. A sort of Irish Annigoni. Having had Liam's remarkable looks glowingly described by a friend, Conninx made an appointment to visit the boy. The painter was not interested in what that same friend was cute enough to call "spreading the cheeky bits". Though homosexual, Conninx was by then in his seventies and hoarded what energy he had with careful scrupulosity to spend at his work.

'He knew straight away that he wanted Liam to model for him – in his autobiography, *Painted Clay*, he describes his first sight of the boy better than I ever could – the problem was Conor. He asked a large fee for each sitting, which wasn't a problem, but also insisted on not only delivering Liam and taking him home but staying in the studio thoughout. Purely to protect his protégé, or so the explanation went, from "that evil old pederast".

'In truth Conor could not afford to let Liam wander far and certainly not in the company of anyone as wealthy, intelligent and successful as Hilton Conninx. For it was only by constantly invoking their common memories of a cruel and poverty-stricken past, which he implied had equally cursed them both, that Conor maintained his hold on the boy. Both of them were in the gutter and one of them had better not be looking at the stars.'

Here Jennings broke off for a minute or two, resting his forehead in his hands as if the telling of the story was too much for him. When he started to speak again it was more quickly, giving the impression he couldn't wait for the whole thing to be over and done with.

'But in the end greed overcame Conor's struggle to maintain the *status quo*. As Liam's manager, or pimp, he had demanded a hundred guineas for each sitting. Conninx had indicated that at least twelve would be necessary. But, in the middle of the second session, Conninx suddenly put down his brush and said he couldn't possibly continue with a third person present. He would pay for both sittings, of course, but that must be an end to it. Liam discovered much later that this was all bluff. And that if Conor had called it, or even doubled the rate, Conninx would have given in. But twelve hundred guineas was a hell of a lot of money in the late fifties, particularly when you didn't have to lift a finger to put it in your pocket.'

Barnaby quelled a strong feeling of distaste at this latest exchange of a boy, already sold God knew how many times, as if he were a piece of meat. The chief inspector could not shake off the feeling that somewhere in this last heartless transaction a child was still present making mock of the words 'age of consent'.

'It was the beginning of the end for Conor. Within a few

visits Hilton Conninx had discovered Liam's appalling history and started to persuade the boy to break free. It wasn't easy. Liam had been in Conor's thrall for so long he found it almost impossible to imagine surviving without him. He had no other home and next to no money. But Conninx persisted. The painter had plenty of clout and not only financial. Conor, who had been living on immoral earnings ever since he arrived in Dublin, was in no position to call any shots. One evening Liam did not return from his sitting. Conninx's chauffeur arrived to ask for his belongings. These, such as they were, were handed over and that was that.

'Liam remained with Conninx for fifteen years and was treated in a manner that he had never known in his life before. That is, with kindness and respect. I am,' Jennings began to speak more quickly sensing (mistakenly) exasperation gathering in the breast of the man facing him, 'compressing as much as possible. Hilton tried to teach Liam about art and music without, it must be admitted, much success and also encouraged him to read. Many portraits of the boy were produced during their first four or five years together, when Conninx still had his sight. It was his conceit never to paint a sitter in contemporary clothes and Liam was portrayed as a Victorian cleric, a French zouave, a pasha, a Persian lutenist – that's one of the two in the National.

'He became Conninx's companion, amanuensis and friend. Though their relationship was never a sexual one there seems to be little doubt that Conninx cared deeply for the boy. Liam's reaction was more constrained. He was thankful, as I suspect deprived children remain all their lives, for the smallest affection shown, but he was not able to respond in kind. Perhaps his loving apparatus, if one can so describe it, had been irreparably damaged. Perhaps Conninx's attempts at healing never really reached the spot. Certain sufferings are untouchable, don't you agree?'

Barnaby had never thought about it. Now, doing so, he decided that Jennings was probably right. This conclusion depressed him beyond measure. Troy spoke into the deepening gloom.

'Did you say this Mr Connings lost his sight, sir?'

'Yes, some years before he died. Liam did everything for him after that and when Conninx became ill – at over ninety – he cared for him at home until he died.'

This didn't sound to Barnaby like a man incapable of love, but he had no wish to dam up the nicely running stream by saying so.

'When the will was read Liam was the sole beneficiary. He inherited the house, plenty of money and quite a lot of paintings. As is the way of things after an artist's death, the critics discovered just how versatile and under-rated Conninx had been and within weeks the value of his canvases went shooting up. Then something rather awful happened. The word on Liam's good fortune was round, of course. Dublin's not that big a place and in any case the bequest was published in the *Irish Times*. The day after this was done Conor turned up. Half of everything, or he threatened to tell the police that Liam had not only connived in his father's murder and helped to bury the body but had actually fired the shot that had killed him.'

'And had he?' asked Sergeant Troy.

'He swore not. His story is that he hid in the barn next to Conor's house while Conor went inside, supposedly just for some money and a change of clothes. But he was gone nearly three hours. When he returned it was to say that Hanlon wouldn't be bothering them again. He'd be drawn no further. No doubt Liam was so relieved to have escaped he didn't much care how dearly this freedom had been bought.'

'But surely,' said Barnaby, 'having been under-age when all this happened he would have had nothing to fear from the police.'

'Nothing serious,' agreed Max. 'He knew that and Conor must have known it too. But actuality, rationality if you like, had little to do with how Liam reacted to this new situation. It was the reintroduction of the past, you see. The terror of it. What frightens us as children frightens us all our lives.'

'So how did he handle this new turn of events?'

'Well, things were different this time round. Liam was older, pretty rich and with a widish circle of acquaintances, one or two of them quite influential. But Conor had also prospered, though not in ways that would perhaps bear close scrutiny. And his acquaintances were very unpleasant indeed. As to how Liam handled it . . . he did what he had done all those years before. Stalling Conor for as long as it took to put his own affairs in order, he ran away, this time making a thoroughly professional job of it. He went to England, chose a new name and completely re-invented himself.'

'That's a bit drastic, isn't it?' asked Sergeant Troy.

'You wouldn't think so if you'd heard *him* tell the story.' Here Jennings broke off and drank a little water. Momentarily he looked preoccupied, as if distracted by a quite different train of thought. He put the glass down and brushed at his forehead as if brushing away some irritating insect.

'This transformation was not only for reasons of concealment. He seemed to hold a rather touching belief that by determinedly altering external details and behaviour he would somehow be psychologically transformed.'

'Every day in every way . . .' quoted Barnaby.

'Exactly. Up to a point, and on a fairly shallow level, this may be possible, but the wounds Gerald had received were far too deep, and deeply infected, to be even adequately cleaned by such simplistic methods. But, as everyone you must have spoken to must have confirmed, as far as the outward shell was concerned he did a brilliant job. By the time I met him he looked and sounded like your quintessential Englishman. Any gentleman's club would have been proud to sign him on.'

Don't know about that, muttered Troy silently. Catch him on an off night in his frilly nix and saucy veil and you'd have all the old gaffers in intensive care. Mine's a triple by-pass, doctor, and easy on the rhino horn.

'Obviously, the telling of this story was spread over some weeks. Gerald made it longer than was strictly necessary embroidering, offering up extraneous scenes like tempting titbits. Dropping Irish names that neither I nor, I imagine, anyone else much had ever heard of. It was plain he saw himself as a Scheherazade. As long as his unhappy tale held my attention we would continue to meet. When it ended . . .' Jennings made a sudden awkward gesture of brutal farewell.

'So he made no further physical approach?'

'Of course not.'

'But if he had fallen in love with you—'

'He *loved* me, which is rather different. Said he had never cared for anyone is such a way before and, at the risk of sounding vain, I believed him.'

'Did he discuss sex at all?'

'Once, in passing. He described it as a degrading itch to

be scratched in degraded places with degrading people.'

'Sounds as if he might have been in the habit of cottaging,' said Segeant Troy.

'Not with you.'

Too bloody right not with me mate. 'Picking up men in bars, parks, public lavatories.'

'Perhaps. I think when it was a matter of really letting his hair down he went abroad. Certainly this aspect of his life was something he attempted to conceal.'

'Can't see why,' argued Troy. 'Not as if it's still illegal.'

'Because it was a matter of shame and misery to him,' cried Jennings angrily. 'I've just told you his life story. Christ – can't you work that out for yourself!'

Troy flushed angrily at this not entirely unfamiliar representation of himself as token insensitive clod. When he spoke again sheer perversity coarsened his voice.

'So what happened to break up love's young dream then, Mr Jennings? Turn you into the sort of person he was frightened to be left alone with?'

Jennings did not immediately answer. He seemed to flinch from a reply and Barnaby saw his mouth twitch and then tighten as if to trap any rogue words that might slip out. His eyes were watchful and his neck and shoulders unnaturally still.

Afterwards the chief inspector wondered at the provenance of the remark that he himself next made. He tried to trace its source. Had someone in the group talked to him about Jennings' books? Had Joyce? Perhaps they had been filmed and he, dozing before late-night television, had unconsciously absorbed some image or vision of a bleak landscape which was now prompting uneasy feelings of *déjà vu*. Whatever the reason, a conviction was growing in him that could not be put aside. He decided to test it out.

'Was Hadleigh aware, Mr Jennings, that you were writing everything he told you down?'

'No.' He looked up with tired resignation, as if they had reached this point, this mean, inglorious point in their discussion, only after long and weary argument. He said:

'Do me justice, Barnaby. I never pretended his story was my own.'

They took a second break there. More refreshments were ordered and this time the chief inspector succumbed. He was ravenous. He had been in the interview room for three hours, listening hard, and all on a pathetic helping of assorted greenery that wouldn't keep a rabbit up to snuff. In any case (some long-forgotten snippet vaguely connected with bedtime stories came to mind) wasn't lettuce supposed to be soporific? Couldn't have his concentration slipping.

And the sandwiches were so good. Thick shavings of rare roast beef, ham off the bone with orange-breadcrumbed rind and French mustard, Red Leicester and sweet pickle, all between satisfactorily thick slices of white or granary bread spread with pale butter.

'Are these from the canteen, sergeant?' said Barnaby, carefully pulling out a sprig of watercress and laying it to one side.

''Course they are,' said Troy, with some puzzlement.

'Incredible.'

'Really?' He watched the old man sinking his gnashers into sarnie number three. Troy himself had managed to snaffle only half a round before the remaining fatly bulging triangles had vanished. It had struck him as a perfectly ordinary sandwich. Jennings once more had eaten little.

'Must be somebody new on the job. Right.' Barnaby

pushed his plate aside and turned once more to matters of moment. 'Do you feel refreshed, Mr Jennings?'

'No.'

'Excellent.'

As Troy stacked the tray and put it on top of the filing cabinet he remembered that the point at which the conversation had broken off had left him floundering. He didn't like that at all. Being lost. Ahead of the game was where he liked to be. Or alternatively (rock-bottom basic minimum) running level with the other players. It seemed to him the goal posts had suddenly been moved, which was just not on. He sat down, tightening the level of his attention, hoping at least to spot the ball. Or rather, if he remembered correctly, the book.

'If you remember,' Jennings was saying, 'I mentioned at the beginning that I was working on a novel when I first met Gerald. Wanting to make lots of money, I was tackling formula fiction; stock situations, cardboard characters. No matter how hard I tried I just couldn't inject a flicker of life into it. Gerald's history, on the other hand, fired me. He didn't tell it well, yet I was completely involved from day one. I filled in all the emotional gaps, created the sour, black bogs and Dublin promenades. Wrote dialogue for Liam, and Conor too, knowing it was absolutely right, even through I'd never met the man. As soon as Gerald left I'd get it all down, cramming one notebook after another, whereas before I'd hardly been able to fill a page. By the time it came to an end I'd got two hundred thousand words.'

'At what point did you tell him what you were doing?'

'At no point. Don't you see . . . ?' Jennings, noticing Barnaby's expression of ironic distaste, became extremely defensive. 'He would have simply clammed up. This was the first time Gerald had told the truth about himself. I don't need to tell you how important, how therapeutic, that step can be.'

'I'd have thought,' rejoined the chief inspector dryly, 'that rather depended on the integrity of whoever they were talking to. And what that person did with the information received. A betrayal of the magnitude you were contemplating—'

'You have no right to say that! I had no such plan. Not then. In fact I tried to persuade him into proper analysis. I knew a couple of excellent people and he could have certainly afforded it.'

'How did he react to this suggestion?'

'He got terribly upset. Said it was absolutely impossible for him to ever tell anyone else. He only told me because he sensed I was on the point of abandoning him.

'I transcribed the notebooks into the form of a novel. It didn't take long. They were so fresh and full of life. I couldn't wait to get home after work and sit down at my typewriter. I became convinced, even before I was halfway through, that someone would buy the results. I tested Gerald out. Told him I'd taken a few notes – purely as an *aide mémoire* – after our meetings and did he mind? He immediately demanded to see them. I handed one of the notebooks over and when we met again he told me he had burned it.'

'So you were not unaware of how strongly he felt in this matter?'

'No.'

'Surely, then, that should have been an end to it?'

'Easy to say. Look,' his whole manner became more urgent. Imbued with the need to convince. 'There was no way he could have been connected with this book. All the names had been changed. And the—'

'Aren't you being a trifle ingenuous, Mr Jennings? That all sounds very logical, but theft is theft.'

'Writers spend their lives stealing. Conversations, mannerisms, incidents, jokes. We're completely amoral. We even steal from each other. Do it in the movies and it's called an *hommage*.'

'A very sophisticated argument I'm sure, but the fact remains that it was his story.'

'A story belongs to whoever can tell it.' He was becoming restless with irritation. While making an obvious effort to remain courteous, he was starting to sound like an instructor faced with a particularly obtuse pupil. 'Gerald had neither talent nor imagination. That wonderful tale would have been lost. Wasted. *Far Away Hills* made him famous. If there is such a thing as anonymous fame.'

Barnaby did not respond. Jennings' theory seemed to him both horribly feasible and subtly corrupt. Troy however, who had by now not only caught up with the game but spotted a chance to score, said, 'Seems to me, sir, all due respects, you made yourself famous.'

'So when did you finally tell him?' asked the chief inspector.

'I didn't. I tried. Many times. But my nerve always gave out.'

'I can't say I'm surprised.'

'In the end I sent one of my advance copies round by courier.'

'Good God, man!'

'With a letter, of course. Explaining, as I have to you, why I'd done it. Asking him to try and understand. I was expecting him on my doorstep within the hour, either livid with rage or suicidal. But he didn't show. I rang and got no reply. I thought perhaps he was away for the weekend. I wasn't sorry to put off the evil moment, to tell you the truth. But after about ten days I started to get worried and drove round there. The porter said Gerald had left in a great hurry. "Vamoosed" was his word. The furniture had been put in store and there was no forwarding address. I never saw him again. Until last week.'

'But surely you tried to trace him?'

'Of course I did. I put advertisements in *The Times* – even the *Gay Times* – the *Telegraph*, the *Independent*. I thought about employing a private detective, but it seemed a bit like hunting him down. I discovered later he'd been in a hotel round the corner.'

Barnaby pictured Hadleigh receiving his parcel, perhaps the very first gift from 'the only person he had ever really cared for'. Tearing the wrapper off, gradually comprehending the brutal ferocity of his friend's betrayal. Then hiding away from further hurt in some soulless hotel room. The chief inspector said, almost to himself, 'Poor bastard.'

'When the book came out I tried again. There was so much feedback, you see. Hundreds of letters. Supportive, concerned, totally understanding. Broken children grown into maimed adults trying somehow to make sense of the experience. They wrote so lovingly, wanting him to know he was not alone. I know this would have helped. But there was no way I could reach him if he didn't want to be reached. And that's how matters stayed until, as you are aware, I recently heard from him again.'

'Do you still have the letter?'

'I'm afraid not. I run a lean filing system. Everything but essential business correspondence and contracts gets answered and junked straight away.'

'You must remember the details, surely, Mr Jennings,'

said Troy. 'After what you've just told us it must have been a bit of a bombshell.'

'Hardly that. Ten years had gone by. I'd published several more books and garnered my own share of personal misery. It occurred to me once that perhaps my child's death was some sort of repayment for what I'd done to Gerald. Though that seems a bit hard on Ava.'

Not to mention the nipper, thought Troy in his corner.

'Anyway, as far as I recall, the note simply said that in his capacity as secretary he had been asked to invite me to give a talk. The rest of it was devoted to persuading me against the idea. "Painful memories, impossible situation, sleeping dogs". His prose style hadn't improved. At first my inclination was to take the hint and not go. But the more I thought about it the more certain I became that, in spite of his protestations to the contrary, this was not what Gerald wanted. So, as you know, I accepted.'

He was looking extremely tired now. Strained and somewhat lost and perturbed, as if he had followed a certain path and it had led him to a surprising and un-wanted destination. His smooth, tanned skin was mottled and chalky and stretched too tightly over his skull. The line of his nose jutted, sharp as a knife. Violet lines crisscrossed the fine skin beneath his eyes as if it had been savagely pinched. When, in answer to Barnaby's next question, he started to speak, his voice was quite without colour. He sounded almost bored.

The chief inspector wondered whether Jennings was genuinely exhausted or deliberately conserving his energy so that he would be alert throughout this, the most crucial stage in the whole interview. Barnaby had paused before speaking, withdrawing his attention momentarily from the immediate present to dwell briefly on the extraordinary tapestry that had so recently been unrolled before him. Namely, the tragic life and times of Liam Hanlon aka Gerald Hadleigh.

This burdensome knowledge, coupled with a recollection of the all-too-detailed blow-ups on the incident-room wall, stimulated in Barnaby's mind feelings of the keenest pity. In what a poignant light did the small child – escaping from one terror only to find, crouching at the end of his life another, unspeakably worse – now appear. And if you were responsible, Jennings, vowed the chief inspector, for twice stealing that life I will have you. By Christ I will! None of this showed on his face, which was entirely noncommittal.

'I assume, Mr Jennings, you will now be offering us an entirely new, or perhaps I should say "re-written", version of what happened on Monday evening.'

'I've nothing to change regarding the first half. Everything was exactly as I've previously stated, except for my feelings of course. I was surprised at how moved I was at my first sight of him. Driving over I'd felt nothing more than mild curiosity as to how he was keeping, coupled with a vague hope that I could somehow make him understand why I had done what I'd done all those years ago. Yet, though I was never conscious during our relationship of feeling affection, this latest meeting did evoke precisely that response. Gerald, on the other hand, hardly looked at me. But I was determined to speak to him. I'd arrived early hoping to do just that but St John was already there. As you know, I accomplished it eventually by getting him out of the house and bolting the door.

'I went back into the sitting room and what happened next was very distressing. He just went to pieces. Backed off from me, flailing his arms and shouting, "Go away, go away". I didn't know what to do.'

'Why not just do as he asked,' said Troy and was swiftly frowned on for interrupting.

'I started talking quietly. Saying how happy I'd been to hear from him, to see him again. That I meant him no harm and just wanted to explain things. Eventually he calmed down a little and slumped into one of the armchairs. I drew up a stool and sat with him. And then I told him what I've told you. I described my disappointments, my sad marriage, my lost child. I said if he had spent years thinking my life was nothing but success and happiness and all at his expense he could not have been more wrong.

'And then I talked about the letters that came after *Far Away Hills*. Sent to me but written to him. I had kept a few and offered to bring them over for him to read. Above all I tried to explain that I'd stolen his story to give it to the world, not for my own advancement.' Absorbed as he was in his narration, Jennings did not miss the sudden gleam of mockery in the chief inspector's eyes. 'OK,' he said, 'self-justification if you like, but not only that. I was trying to do something about his hurt, perhaps repair some of the damage. Give me some credit.'

Barnaby saw no reason to respond. Certainly he had no intention of demonstrating a shred of understanding, let alone approval. Jennings continued:

'Eventually I realised I was just saying the same things over and over again. He was still in the chair. His position hadn't changed, but he'd put his head in his hands, covered his face as though he couldn't stand the sight of me. Then I saw moisture rolling over the inside of his wrists and down into the cuffs of his shirt in a steady stream. I was so . . . I took one of his hands in mine. It was like a stone, cold and heavy. Tears splashed everywhere. The hollow of his palm was brimming with them, like a little pool.' He repeated himself, shaking his head as if this was still not quite within the bounds of belief.

He slipped then into a silence which seemed to have something of genuine shame about it and not a little mystification. His face was crowded with emotion. The silence continued for some time.

'It was this single moment that turned my thinking completely round. I understood then, for the first time, what a terrible thing I had done. For I had other stories to tell – even now my head's full of them – but *Far Away Hills* was all he had and the theft of it broke his heart.

'We sat there ohh . . . God knows how long. I asked him if there was anything, anything at all I could do to put things right, even as I knew there couldn't possibly be. Eventually he told me it was of no importance. His actual words were, "Who steals my life steals trash". Then he asked me, begged me, to go away. But I couldn't bring myself to. So, after a little while, he did. Quietly disengaged his hand and went upstairs. He looked so bloody lonely. And battered, as if he'd just climbed out of a boxing ring. Yet of the two of us he was the one with dignity. He'd had the courage to see my offer for the shoddy hypocrisy that it was and spit in its eye. I waited half an hour – by this time it had gone midnight – till it became plain that he was not going to come down, then put on my coat and left.'

'Pulling the front door to?'

'Yes.'

'You're positive it was properly fastened?'

'Positive. I made a point of slamming it loudly so Gerald would know I'd gone.'

'Did you see anyone at all when you left the house?'

'At that hour? In that weather?'

'Just answer the question, Mr Jennings,' said Troy.

'No.'

'Perhaps in a parked car?'

'Absolutely not.'

'Did you go upstairs during the course of the evening?'

'No.'

'What about any of the other rooms?'

'No.'

'The kitchen?'

'*Hell.*' He got up and poured some water, the glass clinking, trembling against the rim of the jug, then returned to his seat. 'What is all this? What do you want me to say? I've told you the truth.'

'You have told us two totally conflicting stories, Mr Jennings.' Barnaby leaned forwards and once more rested his elbows on the edge of the table. His thick neck and wide shoulders blotted out all else from Jennings' field of vision. 'Why should we believe the second any more than the first?'

'Oh God . . .' Fatigue had made him apathetic. He opened his arms and turned his hands upwards in resigned disbelief. He reminded Barnaby of the cauliflower man in Causton market chanting, 'You want my blood, lady? It's yours.'

'Think what you like. I'm finished.'

'There are one or two more questions—'

'Totally wacked. You're flogging a dead horse here, Barnaby.'

'Did you know that Hadleigh was married?'

'Married?' Bafflement and incredulity combined to revive Jennings' energies somewhat. 'I don't believe it.'

'There's a wedding photograph in his sitting room.'

'I didn't see that.'

'Put away before you came.'

'Must be a fake. A prop to flesh out the background. Where's the lady supposed to be now?'

'Dead of leukaemia.'

'Very convenient.'

'According to Mr Hadleigh, just before he moved to the village, which would be in 1982.'

'That's when I knew him.'

The chief inspector congratulated himself on his decision not to waste yet more man hours chasing up Hadleigh's marriage certificate or details of Grace's death. Jennings' suggestion would also explain why the dead man found it easy to tell anyone and everyone about this supposedly deeply painful episode in his life.

Jennings continued, 'I suppose that's why the picture was concealed. Because I was in a position to give the lie to such a story.'

'Presumably. The second point I'd like to clarify is rather more complicated. We've reason to believe that Hadleigh occasionally dressed as a woman. Appeared in public like this. Is that something you knew about?'

'How extraordinary.' But even as he spoke and gave a negative shake of the head Barnaby could see Jennings was preparing to qualify this response. 'Although . . . I did talk to a friend once, an analyst, about Gerald – anonymously of course – and he asked me a similar question. Did I know if the respectable middle-class civil servant was the only fake persona this man had adopted? He said living a lie, to this extent and degree, imposed tremendous strain and often the people who were doing so needed desperately to escape. As returning to their true selves was psychologically dangerous they would create a third personality, usually quite different from the first two. Obviously this chap used fancier terminology, but that was about the gist of it.'

Barnaby nodded. This sounded, given that they were discussing behaviour most people would regard as completely abnormal, not an unreasonable proposition. Someone came in to remove the tea tray and ask if they needed any refills. Replying in the negative the chief inspector got up and crossed to the window, opening it a little, breathing in the cold night air. As if in response to this move Jennings rose as well, commenting on how late it was and asking for his overcoat.

'I'm afraid there is no question of you returning home tonight, Mr Jennings.'

Jennings stared in amazement. 'You're keeping me here?'

'That is the case, sir, yes.'

'But you can't do that. You have to charge me or let me go.'

'Easy to see you don't write crime stories, Mr Jennings,' said Sergeant Troy. He grinned as he took down his black leathers. Middle-class outrage when the forces of law and order had occasion to tweak aside the velvet glove never failed to entertain. 'We can hold you for up to thirty-six hours. And apply for an extension if necessary. This is a serious, arrestable offence we're talking about.'

Jennings sank back on to his hard shell of a chair. He appeared numb with shock and was mumbling something that Troy did not quite get. He asked for clarification and was far from surprised when it came.

'I've changed my mind,' said Jennings. 'I want to see my solicitor.'

Hunting in Full Steel

It was the start of a new week and the weather had changed completely. Warmer, with a mizzle of rain. A sly day, as they say in Suffolk. When Troy entered the office Barnaby was on the phone. The sergeant saw immediately what was going on. The chief's expression was one he recognised, blank, self-controlled, constraining with some force the response he thought appropriate to the occasion.

'I am aware of that, sir . . .

'Yes, I shall be talking to him again this morning . . .

'It's hard to say at this stage . . .

'I'm afraid not . . .

'Naturally I will . . .

'I have already done so . . .

'I'm sure we all hope . . .

'No. At least nothing I'd care to put on the table . . .

'I am pursuing—'

Troy heard the crash as the interrogator slammed the phone down right across the room. Barnaby replaced his own receiver without any visible signs of irritation.

'Being leaned on from the top, chief?'

'The head lama himself.'

'Spit in your eye don't they? Llamas?'

Barnaby did not reply. He had picked up a pencil and was doodling on a large note pad.

'Jennings' solicitor, is it?'

'Just earning his hundred fifty an hour.'

'They got it sussed – lawyers,' said Troy, unbuttoning a cream trench coat of martial cut embellished with epaulettes, buckles, a belt of highly polished leather and pockets so wide and deep they could well have contained reinforcements from the US cavalry.

'Whoever loses they win. Crafty buggers.' He shook out the coat and placed it on a hanger, smoothing the fabric out and fastening the buttons.

'You're wasted here, sergeant. You should have been a valet.'

'Load of rear gunners. I suppose it's pressing trousers all day.'

'Well, when you've finished faffing about, I'm in dire need of a caffeine shot.'

'I'm as good as gone,' said Troy, who was indeed already opening the door. 'Do you want anything to eat?'

'Not right now.'

Barnaby was pleased with himself for not feeling peckish. Perhaps his stomach was adapting. Shrinking to accommodate the modest input that was now its daily portion. Of course, it could be that it was still only half an hour from breakfast time.

The kitten had, as usual, been present and making a nuisance of itself. After a polished performance of naked greed and winsome precocity it had climbed on to Barnaby's knee, displayed its bottom, sat down and massaged his trousers with its claws. All this to the sound of excessive purring.

'Why is it always me?' A cross demand to the room at large.

'He knows you don't like him,' replied Joyce.

'Dim then, as well as hoggish.'

'Oh, I wouldn't be too sure about that.'

This morning, perhaps recalling his previous manhandling over the marmalade, Kilmowski contented himself with simply looking at Barnaby's breakfast plate, looking at Barnaby, sighing a lot, yawning and turning round and round. Eventually, waiting till his wife's back was turned, Barnaby gave the kitten a small piece of bacon. Followed by a bit of rind for its cheek.

Joyce said: 'Why don't you just put him on the floor?'

The coffee arrived. Troy backed into the room with a tray holding a large Kit Kat and two cups and saucers. He put one of these on the desk before metaphorically licking a finger and holding it to the wind.

The atmosphere didn't seem to be all that bad. Not when you took into account the recent bollocking from the chief super. These were notorious. Poisonous bloody things, likened, by one recipient, to having your head forced down a blocked-up toilet.

Yet here was the DCI, barely minutes after the affray, swigging his drink and doodling with his pencil as if it had never happened. You had to admire him.

Troy, silently doing just that, wondered what was on the note pad. Barnaby was working with close, tiny strokes as if filling something in. Probably plants. Or leaves. The chief was good at that. Nature drawing. He said it helped him concentrate.

Troy unwrapped his chocolate, ran his thumbnail down the silver paper, snapped the biscuit in half. Then, munching, he eased his way around Barnaby's desk for a quick shufty.

He hadn't been far out. Primroses. Beautifully done, just like in a book. Tiny flowers softly shaded with grey, leaves with all the bumps on. Even dangly roots, thready and slightly tangled.

Troy felt envious. I wish I could do something like that, he thought. Paint or play music or write a story. Admitted, he could paralyse club cronies with a well-told joke. And his karaoke 'Delilah' at the Christmas party had been described as shit-hot. But it wasn't quite the same.

Seeing the chief's cup empty he tidied it away, saying, 'You come to any decision about Jennings yet, sir? Whether he's still in the frame?'

'I doubt it. We're checking out the story he told about Hadleigh's antecedents. If Conor Neilson had been leading the sort of life described he'd almost certainly be known to the Garda.'

'Plus it's an uncommon name.'

'Not over there it isn't. And this stuff from forensic is not encouraging.' He indicated several glossy photographs and closely typed back-up sheets. 'Jennings' prints are in the sitting room, on various pieces of crockery, the ashtray and the front door. Nothing upstairs—'

'There wouldn't be. The murderer wore gloves.'

'Don't interrupt!'

'Sorry.'

'Then there's the problem of his shoes. No fibres from the stair or bedroom carpet. No blood or other substances. No skin particles. They're absolutely clean. And you know as well as I do you can't do a job like the one we're looking at and take nothing from the scene. They're working on his suit at the moment but I can't say I have high hopes.'

'Bit of a blind alley, then?'

Barnaby shrugged and put down his pencil. Troy had

been quite wrong in thinking that the chief superintendent's sarcastic volley had been easily put aside. Though years of practice and a reasonably equable temperament enabled Barnaby to maintain an imperturbable facade he was, in fact, not unperturbed at all but experiencing the beginnings of a dark depression. A grey dried-upness of the mind.

The reason for this was not unknown to him. He had been indulging in the very thing against which his warnings to others had always been so stringent. Ever since the interview with St John – which meant virtually from the outset – his perception of the case had been subtly narrowing. Whilst giving lip service to this or that possibility he had, gradually, become convinced that it was with Jennings alone that the solution lay.

Either Max had killed Hadleigh and run away or he possessed some knowledge that would provide the key that could unlock the mystery. In any event Jennings' capture and the conclusion of the case had, in Barnaby's imagination, become so powerfully intertwined that he was now finding it extremely difficult to accept the fact that the first was quickly seeming to have little or no bearing whatsoever on the second. Which left him precisely where?

Well, once he had accepted that Jennings was telling the truth, there were three options. The first, that Hadleigh had been murdered by a passing opportunist who had then left with a suitcase full of women's clothing but without a Rolex watch worth thousands seemed barely credible.

The second was that he had been killed by someone known to him either in his feminine persona or casually as a homosexual partner. Remembering Jennings' description of the dead man's view of sex as an itch to be scratched in degrading places with degrading people this idea was depressing in the extreme. It meant they could be looking at someone who'd known Hadleigh for five minutes, maybe followed him home from some impersonal encounter, sussed the set-up and returned at a later date to see what was in it for him.

The length and breadth – not to mention the expense – of setting up the sort of open-ended investigation required should this be so meant it had virtually no chance of being undertaken. The case would remain a matter of record and permanently unsolved unless, and it could be years later, some sharp-eyed operative had their memory jogged and spotted a significant-looking connection or heard an echo. Sometimes it happened.

Option three, you worked further on what you'd already got, which was massively less complicated. If the door-to-door results were anything to go by, Hadleigh had remained aloof from village matters, received no visitors and mixed socially only with members of the Writers Circle, one of whom was in fruitless love with him. Barnaby scribbled their names beneath his primroses.

Brian Clapton. He could be further leaned on, which procedure would no doubt bring about some pathetic smutty little confession involving after-dark peepshows and furtive onanism.

Of Rex St John's innocence Barnaby was convinced. His story of Hadleigh's visit was confirmed by Jennings' revelations regarding their past connection. And St John's distress and remorse – intensifying daily, if Mrs Lyddiard was to be believed – was surely further verification. And he was an old man. Pretty fragile to have delivered that series of immensely forceful blows.

Although fully aware of the dangers of allowing sympathy for any particular personality to cloud his judgement, Barnaby was still inclined to view both Sue

Clapton and her friend Amy as completely uninvolved.

Honoria Lyddiard was something else. Physically more than competent to carry out the attack she was also psychologically capable, having the conviction, common to all fanatics, that their every thought, speech and action stemmed directly from some fundamental holy writ. Once a necessity for punishment had been established her sense of duty would allow her to inflict it without a qualm. But this crime – Hadleigh's mashed-up skull was suddenly, vividly present – was not some cool affair of obligation. This was red-hot rage, way out of control.

Which left him with Laura Hutton who believed herself to have been betrayed. A motive there all right. One as old as time. Barnaby recalled his two interviews with her; the anguished wails of pain and tears of sorrow. Could this flood of misery have been partially instigated by remorse? He decided to talk to her again . As far as he knew she was still unaware of Hadleigh's homosexuality and that her supposed rival did not really exist. These two revelations, if delivered in the right way at the right time in unfriendly, unfamiliar environs, could well bring about a genuine result. For it would surely take a much harder nut than Mrs Hutton to remain impervious in the face of the knowledge that she had committed a spectacularly gruesome murder for nothing.

Barnaby's attention was caught by a strange scraping sound as Troy cleared his throat preparatory to speech.

'Either cough, speak or sing, sergeant. I really don't mind which. That sounds like someone swinging on a rusty bog chain.'

'Just that it's twenty-five to, sir.'

'I've got eyes.'

Troy opened the door and a murmurous buzz from the

381

incident room filled the corridor. Barnaby heard it without enthusiasm. Thirty men and women awaiting instruction. Inspector Meredith would be present: sharp-eyed, snake-hipped, snake-headed, with his painted-on black hair and golden origins. Listening. Falsely respectful, offering ideas with mock tentativeness. Biding his time. Youth and high-riding ambition on his side.

'Right,' said the chief inspector. He picked up the SOCO file, dropped the pencil in his frog mug and got heavily to his feet. 'Let's go and pool our ignorance.'

Brian was still in a state of shock. His hands and feet, even his skin, felt numb. He had a throbbing pain behind his eyes that came and went with the force of a blow, as if his skull was being rhythmically struck. Getting out of the car, propelling himself, zombie-like, to the staff cloakroom where he now stood, he realised he had no recollection of driving to school at all.

He had been like this, more or less, since the photographs arrived. Since Sue had gone upstairs to find unwanted socks and he had torn the envelope half across in his eagerness to get at the contents.

At first, impossible as it might seem given the appallingly explicit clarity of the pictures, Brian had not understood quite what was going on. For just a microsecond he had stared at Edie's face, which peered fearfully back at him over someone's bare shoulder, without recognition. Her eyes were wide and staring and her teeth sank into her bottom lip as if to trap a cry. Brian, even while feeling touched that she should have sent him a likeness of herself, could not help feeling slightly disturbed at the dramatic intensity of the pose.

Explanation quickly followed. The next picture showed

white buttocks mooning high, if a trifle flatly, in the air. A third displayed Brian's profile grinning in an exultant, wolfish way as he apparently forced the thin, childish figure trapped beneath him. There were half a dozen more. The last was the worst. It showed Edie sitting on the very edge of the settee in an attitude of absolute despair, her face buried in her hands. Brian, naked in the attitude of a conqueror, stood over her.

He cried out then, awful, unclarified terrors confusing his mind, and dropped them all. Swept the photographs from the table on to the floor. He remembered that moment. He had been about to reach out and comfort her. How could such a gesture of compulsive consolation be made to look so threatening?

At that point Sue came clogging down the stairs. Galvanised by the fear of discovery, Brian scrabbled up the photographs, lifted the lid of the Aga and stuffed them inside. Knowing they must burn, he still stood there until they caught fire, blazed up, then folded softly into pale grey flaky layers. By the time Sue came in he was back in his chair and feeling as if a ten-ton truck had driven straight through him, leaving a jagged great hole behind.

Later, alone upstairs, Brian made some attempt to struggle out of the swamp of alarm and revulsion that was paralysing all coherent thought. It proved amazingly difficult, perhaps because he already had an inkling of the conclusion to which a rational assessment of the situation must inevitably lead.

All this while he was reliving the evening at Quarry Cottages. Kept seeing himself as through the camera's eye, drinking, prancing about, disporting his body with amorous abandon. For all he knew they had photographed him writhing in agony during his riveting struggle with the jeans.

Which brought him to the all important question, who did he mean by 'they'? Someone had been hiding with or without – oh God, please surely without – Edie's knowledge. The pictures jumped gleefully to mind again. Untruthfully violent, unspeakably obscene. They had not been ordinary snapshots. There was something blurry and one-dimensional about them, rather as if someone had been photographing a television screen. The paper on which they were printed was different too.

Brian didn't know whether to be more or less devastated by the fact that the envelope had contained no letter, directive or mention of further contact. In all the films he had seen featuring any sort of blackmail those on the receiving end had been given strict instructions to remain close to the phone and on no account to contact the police.

Brian's tormentors need have no fear of that. At the very thought of an official interrogation his viscera, already jelly-soft, started sliding and slopping uncontrollably about. He felt sick and cold and also very angry. Schooled though he was in the repression of all emotion, but especially any of an anti-social nature, Brian wept with frustration.

Eventually he dried his face and beard. It was then nearly six o'clock. There was no way he could sit there and sit there then go down and have his supper and watch the television and go to bed and lie there and lie there. He would go mad. He had to *do* something. To take, however briefly and spuriously, the reins of his wretched existence back into his own hands. He dragged on an old jacket, the one he used to clean the car, and his hat with the let-down fleecy ear flaps, then ran downstairs, shouted something incomprehensible to Mandy through the sitting-room door and left the house.

Outside it was dark and foggy. Footsteps rang out on the hard ground some time before the walkers themselves loomed and melted away almost in the same instant. Commuters edged their cars homeward, searching in the foglamps' glare for a familiar landmark or driveway. The lights around the Green were visible only as pale little smudges hovering in midair. The moon was a disc of dirty ice.

Brian was surprised afterwards with what a quick certainty his feet made their way to Quarry Cottages. Only once had he stumbled, falling into the gutter. A move which struck him as so symbolic of the whole sorry situation that he almost started to cry again.

When he could dimly see the outlines of the cottages Brian slowed up and approached the area where he guessed the paling fence to be. He walked on tiptoe. Every room in the Carters' house had the lights on. The windows, honeycombed by many little panes, glowed. Four square yellow eyes watched him out of the fog. Next door was dark.

Brian recalled standing there twenty-four hours ago – no, tell a lie, twenty-one. The emotions he had felt then faded to nothing beside the despairing lack of fortitude and terrible giddiness that engulfed him now. His mouth filled up with a sour liquid and he spat into his handkerchief. Quietly, so as not to disturb the dog.

Having arrived he had no idea what to do. Edie would be in there if, as was usual, she had travelled home on the school bus. And perhaps Tom. But what of the muscularly advantaged Mrs Carter? Conine the Barbarian.

How little, Brian now realised, he knew of the family's domestic arrangements. Did Edie's mother go out to work? Maybe she was a victim of the recession and had lost her job. Could such a misfortune conceivably be behind what Brian was now forced to view as a mere twisted parody of romantic dalliance? If so, what could the reason be but to make money?

Momentarily this understanding made Brian feel better. Self-preservation he could understand. It was certainly a kinder motive than wanton sport. And he could see how the idea that his interest in Mrs Carter's daughter was perhaps a little more personal than was strictly proper could have arisen.

For instance, it was possible that, in spite of constant vigilance, he had let the mask of professional director slip at some time. Anyone as perceptive and intelligent as Edie would certainly have noticed and Brian could just hear her, quite understandably, boasting a little about it afterwards.

Mrs C might well have put two and two together, creatively accounted the result as five and spotted an opportunity of sticking a nought, or even two, on the end. It certainly wouldn't be much more. They were small-time, sad people – low achievers, without vision.

Even so, assuming the worse (i.e. five hundred), it would not be easy to raise. Brian ran over his options. He could abandon his car and claim the insurance. But that meant notifying the police and they would probably find it and let him know, then he'd be committing fraud if he persisted. Perhaps he could damage it. Or leave it on a railway line.

Startled at the speed at which he seemed to be desecrating the Claptons' twin icons of law and order, Brian turned to the less dodgy notion of borrowing against the house. He had a thirty-year mortgage with twenty still to go, had never been behind with his payments and, as far as the Abbey National were concerned, must surely seem like a good bet for a top-up.

Option three: his parents. Brian, instantly a small boy again, rehearsed his mother's opening lines.

'You're not in any trouble are you, dear?'

And Brian, standing roughly in relation to trouble as might a pebble to the Boulder Dam, would reply, 'Of course not, Mummy.'

He knew nothing about his parents' financial affairs. His father had never discussed such matters. But surely Mr Clapton senior must have some sort of nest-egg? A small emolument to show for the years of drudgery at his boring little clerical job in the city. Or maybe there was an insurance policy that could be realised. Of course Brian would pay them back.

But there would be endless questions. And what reason could he give? Not improvements on the house, for that could be checked-up on, and would be too. Brian's parents, though timidly hesitant where the wide world was concerned, could be doggedly persistent when it came to the business of their close relations. Still, he could sound them out, perhaps under the guise of concern for their future financial wellbeing.

If all three sources failed he would be left with the bank, who would quite possibly cough up but would demand outrageous interest. But – wait a minute . . .

How about Sue? She was a proper author now. Going to be in print. Didn't they get given money even before publication? The writers' group were always going on about it. Jeffrey Archer's advance. Julie Burchill's advance. Telephone numbers. Noughts so numerous they ran off the front of the cheque and had to go swanking round the back.

Brian's breathing quickened. Nerve ends danced and jangled beneath his skin. He told himself not to get carried away. This was, after all, his wife's first book. She couldn't expect VIP treatment before they'd seen how successful Hector would turn out to be. Even so, there would be something. And, Christ knew, she owed it to him. Not only had he been keeping her for years but it was entirely her fault he had ended up in Quarry Cottage in the first place.

Brian screwed up his eyes and peered intensely into the fog, trying to discern signs of movement behind the windows. He removed his misted-up glasses and rubbed them on his jacket cuff. His teeth started to chatter and his beard to drip moisture. Then he sneezed.

Immediately the night was rent with the sound of ferocious barking. In an uncannily precise replay of the previous Thursday evening the cottage door swung open and a figure stood in the opening. On this occasion the spillage of light was almost non-existent, for the looming shape filled every inch of vacant space as if it had been inflated. History was repeating itself and, sure enough, the second time as farce. It was the giantess herself. She let out a coarse animal cry:

'*Whaahferkoodoonaer?*'

Brian immediately retreated quite a long way, covering the distance in a single backward leap of admirably fluid grace. Then he turned and ran blindly up the muddy track, stumbling over stones, slithering over iced-up puddles and occasionally being slashed across the face by whippy twigs.

Now a loudly clamouring bell returned him to a wretched present. It was time to abandon the safety of the staff cloakroom for the terrors of the gymnasium. About to leave, Brian caught sight of himself in the mirror and stared, aghast. Hair sticking out everywhere, eyes bolting, teeth chomping and nibbling at his lower lip. He looked like some weird variety of marsupial in the final stages of delirium tremens.

He bathed his face, patted it dry with a paper towel, smoothed his damp hands over his head and toyed briefly with the idea of not turning up. He could send a message that he was ill, which was no more than the truth. But he simply had to know what was going on, to find out what their plans were.

He forced himself out into the corridor down which he had once skipped so lightly and swallowed hard to keep his gorge from rising. The phrase 'choked on his own vomit' came to mind. It had always struck him as singularly silly. Who else's vomit could one possibly choke on?

Here were the doors already. The top halves were inset with thick, bubbled glass. Opaque but the shape and outline of those within could be seen, especially if they were in motion. Brian brought his face to the glass and squinted. Nothing. It was unnaturally quiet, too. Usually he would hear laughter and coarse shouts of aggro long before he'd reached the place itself. A great wash of relief left him trembling all over. He was reminded that the idea of blackmail was entirely his own. As for sending the photographs, that was probably no more than a malicious joke intended to frighten him. To get their own back for some imagined slight. Whatever the reason, they seemed to have chickened out. Best to make sure though. He pushed open the door.

Everyone was there. Down at the far end by the parallel bars. They were sitting cross-legged with stern, carved faces like warrior braves at a council of war.

Brian remembered explaining once that an empty space could be anything the actor cared to make it. Today there was no doubt about its function. It had become an arena.

As he began to make his effortful way over the vast expanse of gleaming parquet Brian's legs seemed to be attached to lead weights. He marched on and the gap between himself and the others seemed hardly to shrink at all. But finally this mysteriously slow and humiliating journey came to an end. Resisting the craven urge to tuck himself on to the more harmless tip of the semi-circle, in other words next to little Bor, Brian sat down alone and *en face*.

He immediately regretted this realising, just too late, that he had surrendered a great advantage. Namely the opportunity to look down at everyone from a five-foot-six vantage point. Still, he could hardly scramble up again.

Brian took a deep breath and tried to select from the frantic and tumultuous chatter in his head a few pertinent and cutting opening remarks. He still hadn't looked at anyone, which he recognised as another mistake, for the longer he refused to do so the more silly and cowardly must he appear.

Denzil said, 'You got here, then?'

'Yes, oh yes.' Brian laughed. At least that was his intention. But it was a poor patched shred of a thing. A mere tatter of the old hyuf, hyuf.

He braced himself to meet their collective regard, but at the last moment his nerve failed and his eyes slid across to where Edie sat, close to her brother, her face hidden against his shoulder. They were completely still, but Brian felt their concentrated self-perpetuating energy. They were all the same, waxing fat on group bravado. His mother would have called it 'egging each other on'.

'Well you lot,' began Brian and was shattered at the lack of authority in his voice. He sounded like a querulous child. He gave a little neigh, hoping thereby to release a deeper and more commanding timbre. 'What's all this about?'

Then, when no one replied: 'If it's some sort of joke I must confess I don't think it's very funny.'

'Joke, Brian?' Denzil frowned deeply. The movement tugged at the skin on his shaven skull and the spider wriggled. '*Joke?*'

'Seems to me,' said Collar, 'there ain't nothing even remotely funny about raping a fifteen-year-old girl.'

'Rape!' Brian nearly fainted. He remained upright only by placing his hands flat on the floor behind him and transferring his weight. There was a roaring in his ears and, though the beginnings of anger kept him conscious, his heart felt as if it was being sucked out of his chest by a vacuum pump.

'That's . . . Not . . . True . . .'

'You seen the evidence ain'cha?'

'The pitchers.'

He would never stop seeing the pictures. Her anguished triangular face staring directly at the camera. The slender figure crouching submissively on the edge of the settee as if awaiting further punishment. Brian recalled with much bitterness his earlier conclusion that Edie couldn't act for toffee.

'Edie? Look at me. Please.'

As if even the sound of his voice was a threat she burrowed even more deeply into the protective crook of her brother's arm. They sheltered together like orphans.

Brian, consumed with exasperation, cried, 'There was no rape. It wasn't like that.'

'You calling her a liar?' asked Collar. 'On top of everything else what you done.'

'No. Well. Yes, actually.'

'Oh sweet Jesus.' Edie began to cry. Soft moany little warbles, like a wounded pigeon. Her brother stroked the fiery floss of her hair, glaring at Brian in disgusted disbelief.

'*Edie* . . .'

'Leave her alone,' said Tom, his glance as cold as charity. 'We're looking after her now. I'm only sorry I never saw the need of it before.'

'We had no warning, Brian, you see,' said Denzil. 'No hint that you were like that.'

'I am not like that!' The calm contempt in their eyes, their brazen hypocrisy, was driving him mad. When he tried to speak he almost gagged. 'I would never have . . . She asked me round . . .'

'You do that, Edie?'

'Ask him round?'

Her response, though muffled in the folds of Tom's coat, was perfectly audible. 'He just turned up.'

'See? You're out your cranium, Bri.'

'You'll be saying next,' Denzil spoke through bared teeth, 'that you're going to refuse to compensate her for that terrible ordeal.'

Brian saw Edie whipping off her top, rolling down her tights, guiding his tentatively erect member with expert fingers, striking a match against her thumbnail.

'Too bloody right I am,' he cried.

'That's not very nice,' said Collar. 'Swearing.'

'Funny sort of example for a teacher to set.'

'Yeah, but he's a funny sort of teacher.'

'All them extra-curricular activities.'

'That he don't wanna pay for.'

''Course it's entirely up to him.'

'Absolutely.'

'If he can handle the consequences.'

'Now let's talk about this calmly and with—'

'He can handle anything.'

'A natural leader.'

'A born leader.'

'Plenty of bottle.'

'Where it matters.'

'That's not the way I heard it.'

'So. How does five thou strike you, Bri?'

'Five smackaroonies.'

'Five grand or all those juicy Awayday piccies turn up on Hargreave's desk.'

'He's fallen over.'

'I have *not*.' Brian picked himself up. Lifted his skin-and-bone haunches and adopted a trembly negotiating posture identical, had he but known, to that of the chacma baboon on finding itself up a similar gum tree. 'Look – can't we talk this through? Go over the pros and cons, as it were.'

'Them two words could be seen as highly insulting,' said Tom. 'Given the present circs.'

Brian mentally re-ran his last speech. He could see nothing in it to cause offence. Perhaps they were playing with him. Setting out to deliberately mishear or misinterpret everything he said as the secret police in totalitarian states were said to do. He really didn't think he could bear that.

'Don't try trashing us about.'

'Or pretending you got no money.'

''Cause this is serious shit we're talking here.'

'I certainly haven't got that sort of money.'

'You can raise it.'

'Your sort always can.'

'What do you mean – "my sort"?'

'Middle-class wankers.'

Brian closed his eyes to shut out, if only momentarily, the sight of them. He found it almost impossible to believe that something so unspeakably dreadful was taking place. Brian was not a brave man. He could not even read the word 'ordeal' without a symbiotic flutter in his chest. Now as his bowels gave a slow cold churn he squeezed them tight, praying they would not leak. So much for grace under pressure.

'Now listen, Cuntface,' Denzil was saying in an easy, conversational manner. Brian assumed an expression of unearthly alertness. 'See this?'

Denzil clenched his fist and the blue dots in the loose crinkly skin of his knuckles stretched themselves to read 'GT BTN'.

'Now you know,' quavered Brian, 'violence doesn't solve anything.'

'Don't see how you make that out,' argued Denzil. 'You mess with his sister. We screw you to the wall. You leave her alone. Problem solved.'

'But you can't live like that,' cried Brian, who would have been charmed by such disreputable logic had it surfaced in an improvisation.

'You know a better way?' asked Collar, with apparently genuine curiosity.

Brian stared around the ring of severe young faces and recognised his cause was hopeless. No point in searching for a flicker of sympathy or a weak link. As a last resort he started to whine.

'What have I ever done to you?' Silence. 'Except to try and open up your pathetic lives a bit.' The silence became slightly unpleasant. 'Show you a more glamorous world. Introduce you to—'

Tom cut Brian short by raising his own right hand in a formal and very serious manner. He looked implacable and right and deeply authoritative.

'There's nothing else to say. We want half now, by which I mean tomorrow afternoon. And half Friday.'

'And suppose I get it,' said Brian, knowing he supposed the impossible.

'We give you the tape.'

A tape! Of course. That explained the blurred prints and funny paper. Then, understanding this, various other incidents suddenly became significant. Her refusal to put the lights off. The music, which he had thought so romantic, was probably necessary to cover any sound from the camcorder. Oh! Edie of the sweet ginger ruff. Snake of my bosom. Viperette.

Hang about. Brian recalled the day, two terms ago now, when he had brought his brand-new Sanyo along to video rehearsals and it had disappeared. Could this possibly . . . ?

'What machine did you—'

'We got a contact in Slough.' Denzil had a nasty habit of running the tip of his tongue over the palm of his hand then stroking his scalp, repeating the movement over and over again. Brian had often wondered what his hand must taste like at the end of it.

'He runs a little business.' Collar took up the story. 'Educational films.'

They all looked at each other and then at Brian in a way that made it clear the meeting was at an end. Brian got up and prepared once more to travel that vast Sahara of sand-coloured interlocking blocks of wood. He had finally reached the door when Edie called his name.

'Yes.' Brian wheeled around and began to hurry back, suddenly light of foot. 'Yes, Edie – what is it?'

Edie, who had been fishing inside her Green Bay Packers jacket, now produced what looked like a piece of rag but was Brian's underpants. She threw them on to the floor. They were inside out and a thin, brown smear was clearly visible. The idea came to Brian that he would turn and walk away. Show his contempt by leaving them. Then he wondered if the group might tell everyone. Perhaps even pass them round. He bent and picked them up.

This time he had barely reached the halfway mark when the call came. He didn't turn round. Just stayed quite still, heart pounding with premonitory fright, stuffing his Y-fronts into his trouser pocket.

The voices started again. All of them at once. Not harsh and sneering as they had been before, but wheedling, seeming to beckon in a friendly way. Joshing him.

Brian, finding himself as he thought on the cutting edge of mass ridicule, almost ran the last few steps. Grabbing the handle, he swung the door open.

'Don't,' Edie cried. 'Brian? Don't go.'

Now she was hurrying towards him, seizing his arm, persuading him towards her. Brian sensed rather than saw the rest of them, approaching in a clump behind her. Within seconds they were all about him too, urging him back into the centre of the room in a vigorous but jovial manner, little Bor actually tugging at his hand.

'Whatcha think, Bri?'

'Was it good?'

'He really fell for it – didn't you?'

'He was in a recruitment mode in every sphere.'

'In every cocking sphere.'

'Can't see it in the play, though. Can you, Bri?'

'Nah. Can't see this . . .' Suddenly Denzil had in his hand a flat black shining case. He started throwing it up into the air, spinning it, catching it again. Winking at Brian. 'Actually in what you might call "the play".'

'You're not mad are you, love?' Edie linked up just as she had when they were drinking the Thunderbirds Mixed and smiled into Brian's face. An open, guileless smile, full of confidence, expecting praise. 'It was only an impro.'

Only an impro. *Only an impro.* Brian trembled and shook in an agony of hope and bewilderment and rage. Surely it could not be so. They would never have the wit or imagination or discipline to dream up and carry through such a scenario. They were too stupid. Thick. Cretinous. Moronic. Hateful in their vacuous self-esteem. Loathsome in their self-congratulation.

'You said we could do our own. Don't you remember?'

'Last week.'

'No harm done, ay Bri?'

Christ, they'd be asking him next if he couldn't take a joke.

'And we put a twist in the tail – like you said.'

'A coody theatre.'

'To "astound and amaze".'

'I know what he's worried about.' Denzil threw the tape. Brian snatched at the air and seized the box.

'Is this the . . . ?'

'That's it.'

'The one and only.'

'Refuse all substitutes.'

Brian unzipped his windcheater and put the tape inside. There was a long pause then, when Brian did not speak the circle around him started to break up. Denzil moved away to the parallel bars, released one of the ropes and started to swarm up it. The others, at a loose end, stared at Brian as if awaiting direction. They appeared, now that the fun was over, about to slip into their usual state of misanthropic lethargy.

'We got half an hour yet, Bri.'

'Don't call me "Bri".'

'What shall we do, though?'

'Do what you like.' Brian felt the tape, the one and only, hard and safe against his concave chest. 'Drop dead for all I care.'

He never intended to enter the gym again. All the stimulating and creative work that had taken place there was as ashes, dirty ashes, in his mouth.

'Aren't we rehearsing, then?' asked little Bor.

'I must have been mad to have ever wasted five minutes let alone five months of my life on any of you. Or to have thought that the stinking squalid sewers that pass for minds in your tiny pointed heads could ever begin to understand the first thing about literature or music or drama. I suggest you all crawl back to the gutter where you so obviously belong. And as far as I'm concerned you can stay there and rot.'

The briefing had been an arid business. Barnaby, having no definite lead, genuine insight or any sort of meaningful inspiration, was not a man to bluff and bluster his way towards giving the impression that he did. Nor did he blame the fact that he found himself thus high and dry on his team. That there were many officers, some far senior to himself, who would not have hesitated to do so was hardly a consolation.

Everyone had by then read the transcript of Jennings' interview. The immediate response divided the incident room fairly cleanly down the middle. Half thought the story too far-fetched even for Brookside or EastEnders and the rest were moved and intrigued by the darkly predictive nature of the tale and the way it shed light on their previous understanding of the murder victim.

But if Barnaby had hoped for the sort of positive feedback that would shunt his inquiry on to a more fruitful and revealing track he was unlucky. True the room was full of silent support. The wish to contribute, perhaps even to brightly shine, was plain enough and the frustration at being unable to do so equally palpable. It was clearly killing Meredith.

Eventually Detective Constable Willoughby wondered aloud if Jennings might not himself be Neilson and had told the story to direct the investigation away from the successful figure he had now become. Admittedly there appeared to be an age discrepancy but he himself had established that and could well be lying.

Barnaby pointed out that the author's CV was well documented and easily checkable and that he thought this probably made Constable Willoughby's suggestion something of a no no. He did not put this at all forcefully – the lad was brand new and only eighteen – but Willoughby, though managing to nod calmly in response, thereafter was seen to fall quietly apart.

'We shall have to start winding down here pretty soon if no new information emerges. We can't have thirty people twiddling their thumbs. Some of you will have to go back to your divisions at the end of the week. Watch the board for names. We can always jack things up should the tide turn.

'As for today, I'd like everyone who was present on the evening Hadleigh died re-interviewed. And before you do so go over their previous statements, including Hutton and Clapton's follow-ups, until you know them inside out.

Look for the smallest discrepancy or contradiction, especially self-contradiction. It's six days since they talked to us. They'll not only have forgotten most of what they said but they'll have remembered things that they may well regard as irrelevant but which might be very relevant indeed to us. Don't forget that though opinions won't stand up in court they can sometimes point the way to stuff that will. Try and establish an atmosphere where errors can easily be admitted or minds changed. It's often the fear of looking foolish that stops people backtracking and keeping what could be valuable information to themselves.

'I want you to try and get behind what has been said already. Apparently straightforward remarks can often conceal something more complicated. Compare different people's version of the same event. And easy does it. Five of the six people you'll be talking to will have committed no offence whatsoever.'

Unnecessary to add it could well prove to be six out of six. Everyone knew how much real meat was on the plate.

'I'd also like information about the day leading up to the meeting which, until now, has not been fully explored. Something untoward may have occurred but not been thought worth mentioning.'

At this point a uniformed sergeant asked if any decision had been reached regarding Max Jennings.

'He'll be released later this morning. I've nothing to hold him on.'

'I was wondering, sir.' Inspector Meredith spoke with a politeness so mannered and artificial he could have strayed in from a Restoration comedy.

'Yes?'

'I was going over both of Clapton's statements last night.' Well, bully for you, Ian. 'Could I ask if you yourself have any ideas as to what he might have been doing between eleven and midnight on the night of the murder?'

'Sergeant Troy seems to think he was hanging around a house in the village where a young girl, one of his pupils, lives.'

'I see. Thank you, sir.'

Meredith had the extraordinary ability to write his thoughts across his face with absolute precision and without moving a muscle. What he was presently thinking was, 'You should have mentioned that without being asked. Who now is hugging information to themselves?'

Troy said, almost matching the frozen politesse: 'There is a note to that effect on the back-up file, sir.'

After the outdoor team had gone about their business Barnaby withdrew to his desk at the back of the room. No need to seek the sanctuary of his office now for peace and quiet. The telephones, so clamorous a mere seven days ago, rang only intermittently. Occasionally someone used a computer, but to check facts rather than add new information. A good two thirds of the machines were idle. A winding down of energy was visibly taking place, a procedure satisfyingly normal at the successful conclusion of a case and depressingly frustrating otherwise.

Barnaby switched on his own monitor and brought up the detailed notes from Amy Lyddiard's interview. But he had hardly started to read when a call came in from the Garda in Dublin. This was far from being a rare occurrence. Contact was maintained almost daily, often in connection with the movements of known or suspected terrorists. But now the call was in response to Barnaby's request for information on Liam Hanlon's former companion and procurer.

The bottom line on Conor Neilson was about as final as

you could hope to get. A man going under that name for the past twenty years, which was as long as the police had known him, had been fished out of the Liffey eighteen months previously. His feet had been jammed into paint kettles filled with cement, his throat had been cut and his ears sliced off. He was known to have links with protection rackets, drug-running and prostitution.

Barnaby, asked then if this was the man he was looking for, said he wouldn't be at all surprised. Further details were promised by fax and the chief inspector thanked his informant, gave assurances that the matter was not urgent and rang off. It seemed to him that what he had just heard brought a dreadful symmetry to the matter under investigation. That two men, yoked together against a background of violence from their earliest years should, quite unconnectedly, end so.

Barnaby, disturbed and restless, got up and started to move about. Images proliferated in his mind. A little boy weeping through a mess of freshly bleeding offal. A man, blown apart by a shotgun, lying in an unknown grave, his mouth stopped by earth. Another standing upright, drowned, a great gash across his neck. Around him a floating stain suffused brown water and the gills of his wound, fish belly pale, gradually widened. Last and perhaps most terrible (Barnaby had fetched up opposite the Ryvita panels), were the battered remains of Gerald Hadleigh.

Old tags, quotations, half-remembered lines haunted Barnaby – thicker than water . . . who would have thought the old man . . . of coral are his bones . . . blood-boltered Banquo smiles . . . as old as Cain . . . every tear from every eye . . .

He couldn't stop staring at the photographs.

* * *

Directly after leaving the gym Brian also left the school premises. Pleading stomach cramps, he arranged for someone to double up on the only teaching period he had that afternoon and decamped. He couldn't put enough distance between himself and that terrible place where he had been so thoroughly eunuchised.

He was wondering if he could possibly work it so that he would never have to go back. There were barely three weeks to half term. He could fake an injury. Or develop his present supposed malady to a degree which would leave him virtually bedridden. If he could stretch this out to mid-June the little bastards would all have left. And it wasn't as if he'd lose any pay.

On the other hand (Brian braked carefully, drawing up at a red light) was there not perhaps a more positive way of looking at this diabolical misadventure, so spitefully thrust upon him? He had more than once read interviews with well-known actors and writers who had been forced, frequently quite late in life, out of some mundane occupation by an accident of fate, then found their true vocation. Why shouldn't this happen to him?

Of course the theatre wasn't an easy way to make a living. There would be difficult times, no doubt. Periods when he'd be resting. But how much better to be out of work doing something you really enjoyed. All he had to do was break in. Brian saw himself directing not hulking, talentless adolescents but a group of dynamically motivated young actors in a rehearsal room at the Barbican or Stratford. A parp parp reminded him the lights had changed.

He drove on, dreaming. The VW, like a tired beast of burden at the end of the day, wended its way home. They were on the outskirts of Midsomer Worthy when Brian, in the midst of assuring Kenneth Branagh that no, he had not made a mistake in tackling his first Lear so young and that together they would not only crack it but triumph, was recalled to the present by the sight of a small crowd gathered round the notice board in the middle of the Green.

Debarred by a couple of inconsiderate motorists from parking outside Trevelyan Villas, Brian fetched up almost parallel to the little gathering, got out of his car and noticed that quite a large proportion of it was staring in his direction. Intrigued, he looked carefully both ways and started to cross the shiny wet tarmac to see what the matter was.

As he did so Gerald's murder came into his mind. It had been days since he had given it so much as a thought and he only did so now because it occurred to him that something relative to the case might have been pinned up on the notice board. A 'Have You Seen This Man' notice for instance. Or an identikit poster of someone the police would like to interview.

The crowd parted biblically as Brian drew near. Some people turned away, others distanced themselves. One man leered and winked and Brian, puzzled, stared back. The board was covered with photographs of himself and Edie. They were all in transparent plastic covers to protect them from the elements and firmly secured by drawing pins. Though Edie's face was not visible the rest of her more than made up for it. Brian had been granted no such anonymity.

He stared at this lubricious display, resting a hand on the edge of the board to support himself. There was a roaring in his ears and he felt weirdly disoriented, as if on the verge of going under an anaesthetic.

The leering man said, 'Are you OK, mate?'

Brian did not hear. Slowly he tried to remove the pictures, but his fingers, large and thick with cold, could get no purchase on the drawing pins. He attempted to prise one out with his thumb but only succeeded in bending the nail savagely backwards, causing great pain. Eventually he just tore the things off, leaving shreds of plastic and triangular paper corners behind. He scrunched the photographs up, stuffed them into his pocket, turned and walked straight out into the road, which was fortunately empty. Then he made his way blindly towards the house, unaware that the bundle of villagers was following.

The gate seemed stuck. Brian pushed hard and noticed something behind it, blocking the way. It was his typewriter. He squeezed through the gap and bent down to pick it up. The latest episode from *Slangwhang* was still in there, sticking damply to the roller.

Now Brian could see all sorts of other things strewn over the straight and narrow path leading to the front door. Tapes, books, clothes. Records in bright sleeves. His silver cup for elocution. Ties, shoes. Oliver, his Gonk.

He moved slowly up the path, still carrying his Smith Corona. He picked his way carefully, but still managed at one point to tread hard on the bright, sweetly smiling faces of the Nolan Sisters. Rain began to fall.

He put the machine down on the step and searched for his key. It would not fit the Yale lock, which he now noticed was unusually bright and shiny. He moved sideways across the garden, muddying his trainers and trouser turn-ups, to tap on the sitting-room window.

Sue, her hair tied back with a velvet ribbon, was sitting at a table, painting. The oil lamp had been lit and her profile, serenely engrossed, was clearly outlined against a soft, golden haze.

Brian rapped again. The rain was coming down in earnest. His audience, standing around on the pavement, turned its collective coat collar up. One woman shook open a transparent plastic hood and covered her hair.

Sue dabbled her brush in a jar of clear water and wiped it on a cloth. Then she got up in a calm, unhurried way and left the room. Brian ran back to the front door. There was a soft little click as the letter box was lifted and an envelope fell on to the mat outside the door.

He snatched it up and, sheltering as best he could under the narrow lintel, tore it open. The message inside was brief. In future his wife would be communicating with him only through her solicitor, whose address and telephone number were enclosed. For the next few days at least Amanda would be staying with her grandparents.

Brian splashed his way back to the window and rapped for a third time. But Sue, staring fixedly well above his head, was already drawing the curtains.

'How do you feel?'

'OK.'

'Are you sure?'

'Yes.'

'You're shaking.'

'Only outside.'

'Can I get you something?'

'I'm all right, Amy, honestly.'

Sue turned away from the shrouded window. Amy got up from the old rexine pouffe which had been pushed into one of the alcoves. She had been tucked away there since the first enquiring scrape of Brian's key at the brand-new keyhole.

Realising her hands were still clenched, Amy slowly opened them and stretched her fingers. Then she looked concernedly across the room to where Sue was standing very upright, holding her shoulders rigidly, like a soldier on parade.

'Do you think he'll try the back door?'

'Perhaps. It's bolted.' Sue's voice was husky, as if she had a cold.

'Windows?'

'Locked.' She made a strange sound which could have been a cough or the beginnings of an exclamation. 'Don't worry. He can't get in.'

'I'm not worried.' That wasn't quite the case, though it would be true to say Amy was certainly a lot less worried than she had been when Sue had rung up nearly an hour ago and demanded that she come straight round. Honoria had answered the telephone and had been so taken aback by the urgent and uncompromising manner in which Sue had spoken that she had done little more than pass the message on. Amy had left immediately.

Arriving at her friend's she had found Sue in the front garden throwing shirts and pyjamas all over the place. Then she had gone back inside and Amy had followed, skipping and jumping over an assortment of garments.

'What on earth's the matter?' she had cried as soon as the door was closed. 'What's happened?'

Sue was panting slightly. She held out her arms, as if to prove to her own satisfaction they were really empty, then said, 'All gone.'

'What are all those things doing outside?' Amy tried to take Sue's hand but it was snatched away. 'Please, Sue – tell me.'

'Had the locks changed. A man came from Lacey

Green.' Sue stared around with stern purposefulness as if she were taking an inventory. Amy did so too. It seemed to her that several things were missing, although she could not have quite said what they were.

'Of course it will be temporary. My solicitor told me. Things will have to be sorted. But I'm entitled, he said. And why not? Earned it, I've earned it. They'll be at his mother's. Staying. See how she likes it. Jumping. Feet on cushions. Cartoons. Thump thump thump thump thump thump. Thinks they're angels. Do no wrong. See how she likes it. See how she—'

'Sue!' Amy gripped Sue's shoulders. 'You sent for me. And I'm here.'

'*Amy . . .*'

'It's all right.' She kissed Sue's icy cheek and felt a muscle twitch and jump. Sue eased herself out of Amy's arms in an indifferent way, as if resigned to the impossibility of comfort. Amy said again, very gently, 'Tell me.'

Sue told her. Amy listened, her bottom jaw hanging in disbelief, eyes round as saucers.

'On the village notice board?'

'Yes.'

'But . . . who put them there?'

'God knows. I saw them on my way to play group.'

'Where are they now?'

'I told you.' Sue sounded slightly impatient. 'On the notice board.'

'What . . . still?'

'Yes.'

'You left them there?'

'Yes.'

'*All day?*'

'Yes.'

'Ahhh . . .' Amy covered her mouth to check she was not sure what. A squeal of excited disbelief. A cry of horror. A whoop of satisfaction. Imminent laughter.

As they stared at each other, the frozen surface of Sue's face started to loosen, crumple, then fall into soft weary folds. She surrendered to a storm of tears. Amy guided her to the sofa, where they both sat down.

'Angry . . .' wept Sue. 'So angry.'

'I should just think you are.'

'Years of all that . . .'

'There, there.'

'Non-stop sneering.'

'I know.'

'How stupid I am. Not pretty, not sexy. Can't cook, can't drive. My painting's rubbish. I'm a rotten mother—'

'You're a wonderful mother.'

'And all the time . . . all the time . . .'

Amy waited until Sue became less distraught, then passed over a large silk handkerchief which had belonged to Ralph.

'Have a good blow.'

Sue trumpeted softly and dried the veil of moisture that had completely covered her face.

'Sorry.'

'Don't say that.' Amy reached out and retrieved the ball of wrinkled sog. 'It's good to cry.'

As Amy put the handkerchief away and watched Sue become more composed she wondered what would happen next. Had Sue asked her round merely for sympathy and moral support? Or to assist in some specific plan? Whatever it was was fine by Amy. Now that the first ripple of amazement on hearing of the notice board's farcical and outrageous montage was fading she became aware of her own anger, burning fiercely on Sue's behalf.

'Is there anything you want me to do?'

'Just wait with me until he comes.'

'Of course I will.' Amy imagined Brian's fury should he happen upon this latest news bulletin before arriving home. Always sanctimonious, his ability to instantly rewrite anything that showed him to a disadvantage would surely be strained here to the absolute utmost. And when habitual self-deceivers were forced to face the truth about themselves the consequences could be extremely dangerous. And not just for wild ducks in the attic.

'Do you think you might weaken and let him in? Is that why you want me to stay?'

'No.' Sue spoke from the kitchen, where she was filling her painting jam jar with water. She came back and put it on the table before lighting the lamp. 'I just want someone here.'

'Is he violent?'

'Only inside.'

It was Amy who saw Brian, earlier than expected, getting out of his car and trudging across the Green. By then Sue had finished setting the scene of quiet, creative solitude that her husband observed through the sitting-room window.

Amy held her breath when Sue responded to his urgent rapping by slowly rising, picking up an envelope, leaving the room and, on her return, slowly drawing the curtains.

Amy could not help noticing that, though Sue did this in a calm, controlled way, her head was tilted back at quite a sharp angle. Amy guessed that this was because Sue was afraid to look at Brian, but she was wrong. The truth was that Sue made this avoidance not out of fear but from the certain knowledge that if, even once, she had stared directly into her husband's eyes she would not be able to stop her fist crashing straight through the glass and into his stupid face.

After a dietetically correct lunch Barnaby returned to the incident room. Although it was barely three o'clock several members of the outdoor team were clocking back in, though Sergeant Troy was not among them. He had been detailed to harass Brian Clapton further, on the principle that the devil a suspect knew was more likely to slip past his defences than a devil he didn't. Especially if that first devil was already able to scare the shit out of him.

Barnaby was on the point of going over the statement Amy Lyddiard had made in his office for the third time. His previous reading had reactivated that earlier irritating niggle that there was something buried in there that did not quite add up but had not revealed precisely what it was.

He wondered if she had contradicted a remark made earlier, on the morning the murder investigation had begun. That interview would be under 'Lyddiard, H', for it was Honoria who had spoken at such domineering and bombastic length. Amy's contribution, as Barnaby remembered it, had been fragmentary to say the least.

Leaving his own screen, he applied himself to the nearest vacant keyboard and began his search. As he tapped away he was momentarily distracted by thoughts of his *bête noir*, who had elected at the morning's post-briefing sort-out to revisit Gresham House. To Barnaby's deep chagrin the malicious impulse which had prompted him to encourage Meredith to pursue the matter of Honoria's fingerprints the other day had sharply backfired. The man had returned with the news that, although Miss

Lyddiard would, under no circumstances, visit the station, she would be prepared, provided he himself was present at the procedure, to co-operate in this matter at her home.

Barnaby screwed his eyes up against the green dazzle. He recalled Honoria's responses as completely negative and, as he ran through them, it seemed that he was right. Amy had asked a single tremulous question and offered one contribution and that domestic.

'I made us a drink, cocoa actually—'

At which point she had been rudely cut short by her sister-in-law. Barnaby saw no significance in this. The interruptive mode of speech was natural to Honoria and he felt it hardly likely that a description of cocoa-making would reveal anything of moment.

The chief inspector slid his mouse about, scrolled back, then highlighted the context of Amy's remark, starting with his own question to Honoria.

B: Did you retire straight away?

H: Yes. I had a headache. The visitor was allowed to smoke. A disgusting habit. He wouldn't have done it here.

B: And you, Mrs Lyddiard?

A: Not quite straight away. First I—

Barnaby pushed his chair back in such a hurry it crashed into the desk behind and the policewoman sitting there jumped, staring at him in surprise. Mumbling an apology, he got back to his own machine and quickly found what he was looking for. It was right at the beginning. He had asked Amy if they had gone directly home from Plover's Rest after the meeting and she had replied:

'Yes. I made us some hot drinks then went upstairs to work on my book. Honoria took hers into the study.'

Well, it was a discrepancy all right, but a very small one.

Very small indeed. In fact, if it were any smaller ...
Barnaby felt his growing excitement dim before it had a
chance to really get going. For what was in a word?
Especially one as flexible as 'retire'. To some people it
could mean disappearing into the bathroom for a good
long soak, to others slipping away to the den, pouring a
stiff one and putting on the headphones. Why shouldn't
Honoria have used it to mean going into her study to read?

But it said here she had a headache. Barnaby cursed
himself for not being more specific. If only he had phrased
his question more precisely. Did you go to bed straight
away? Or even, did you go upstairs? Then, providing of
course Amy was telling the truth, he would have caught
Honoria out in a deliberate lie. Barnaby was mildly disconcerted to realise how pleased he was at the thought and
how much he would have enjoyed confronting her with it.

He ran through both statements again, but there was
nothing else that could explain his previous sense of
unease. That tiny contradiction was the grit in the oyster.

He sighed, closed both files and opened Laura Hutton's.
Quickly scanning through the first, unrewarding meeting
he turned to the follow-up, where she had drunk too much
and wept and railed against the man who had, as she saw
it, wilfully refused to care for her.

Barnaby read very closely, his concentration narrowed
till it all but blotted out the room. As before he looked for
incompatible, conflicting or just plain careless remarks.
Unfortunately, by the very nature of her admissions,
everything she described – the visit to Hadleigh's house in
the summer, the theft of the photograph, her love-lorn
nocturnal ramblings – were all unverifiable.

There was a rattle of china, a pleasant smell of coffee
and a cup and saucer were placed upon his desk.

'Ah.' Barnaby identified the bearer of his refreshment. 'You're back. What news from the Rialto?'

'Gone over to Bingo, last I heard.'

'Don't try my patience, sergeant. I'm not in the mood.'

Troy, wearing his what-have-I-said-now? expression, sat down and unwrapped a Walnut Whip. 'A right time I've had.'

'With Clapton?'

'Without Clapton, more like.'

'How's that?'

'Went to the school and found he'd left early. Went to his house and the wife says he's at his mother's. Go to his mother's and what do we find?'

Mr Clapton had opened the door and had been so devastated by the sight of a police car parked directly in front of his gate that, even though Troy was not wearing uniform, he had found himself seized fiercely by the arm and forcibly dragged into the house in a nice reversal of the usual procedure.

As the door was slammed behind him, Mrs Clapton appeared. Gift-wrapped in shiny nylon, she was wringing her plump hands and crying, 'He won't come out of the toilet.'

And he wouldn't either, in spite of Sergeant Troy's repeated knocks and crisply worded entreaties, spoken in a very loud voice over pop music pounding away downstairs.

When the sergeant had eventually given up, Mr and Mrs Clapton saw him off the premises as far as the gate. As he was getting into the car some people walked by and Mrs Clapton called out in a loud voice, 'We'll certainly keep our eyes open for him, sergeant. It's very sad when anyone loses a little dog.'

Troy told the story well and Barnaby laughed.

'Do you want me to get a warrant, chief? Bring him in.'

'Perhaps tomorrow.'

'I've found out what "Slangwhang" means.'

'Slang what?'

'You know – his daft play.'

'Oh yes. How did you do that?'

'Looked it up in the dictionary.'

'*You've*—?' Barnaby stopped himself – immediately but, he saw, not quite in time. Christ, what an incredibly patronising thing to think, let alone say. 'Sorry, Gavin. Really.'

'S' all right.' But Troy had gone very pink. 'Understandable. I'm no scholar, as you know. We got it for Talisa Leanne. For when she has homework, like.'

'So what does it mean, "slangwhang"?'

'Noisy or abusive talk. He's a pretentious git. That the right word?'

'Dead right.' Barnaby finished his drink, pushed his cup aside and was about to go into his mini-discovery on the Lyddiard front when several more men returned.

He saw at once that the crew brought no further revelations. They looked dull, bored and mildly resentful, as people do who have spent several hours getting nowhere and could have told you this would be the case before they started.

Detective Constable Willoughby approached Barnaby's desk and was relieved when Troy got up and walked away, for he had suffered more than once from the sergeant's abrasive manner. Barnaby indicated the vacant chair and Willoughby sat, placing his hat carefully on his knees and his notebook carefully inside his hat.

Barnaby prepared to listen with a mixture of sympathy and irritation. There weren't many pro cons as tender

415

round the edges as this one. The lad would either have to buck his ideas up or get out of the Force. Barnaby suspected it would come to the latter and only hoped this wouldn't be by way of a nervous breakdown.

'I've been talking to Mr St John, sir, as instructed,' began Willoughby. 'He hasn't anything to add to his account of Hadleigh's visit, or the evening and its aftermath. But there was something he noticed during the day, though I'm afraid it's very trivial—'

'I'll decide what's trivial, constable.'

'Yes, sir. As he was seeing Mr Hadleigh off the premises Miss Lyddiard came out of the gate at Plover's Rest and cycled away.'

'Do you have a time for this?' Barnaby picked up his pen.

'Eleven thirty. Mr St John remembers because he lost exactly half an hour from his writing period. She came back on two occasions that afternoon. If you recall, Borodino is almost precisely opposite—'

'Yes, yes. Get on with it.'

'Hadleigh didn't open the door, but that apparently was not uncommon if people knew who it was on the step.'

There was a pause. Willoughby, having reached his conclusion, started running his fingers round the rim of his cap, then gripped the peak tightly. In no time at all the silence became unbearable to him.

'He's a character isn't he – St John. As for that dog . . .'

'Thanks, Willoughby.' Barnaby smiled in a distracted way across the desk. 'Well done.'

'Oh.' Willoughby stumbled to his feet and tucked his hat beneath his arm. The notebook fell out. He bent down and retrieved it, his face glowing with pleasure. 'Yes sir. Thank you.'

Barnaby was not listening. Sitting back, eyes closed, he was already transported to the Green, Midsomer Worthy as it might have looked that cold, deep frosted morning on the last day of Gerald Hadleigh's life. He imagined a certain amount of excitement would have been present at the prospect of meeting a famous author. Food no doubt had to be prepared and packed up ready to go over to Plover's Rest. By mid morning the owner of this delightful residence would be disturbing an old man who only wanted to be left in peace to get on with his spy story. At eleven o'clock a woman, weeping her heart out and filling a basket with soggy tissues was due to be interrupted by an equally unwelcome visitor. After their meeting this person had gone straight to the home of Gerald Hadleigh. Finding him absent she had returned later. And then a third time.

Barnaby opened his eyes. His heart gathered speed as a possible reason for this oddly persistent behaviour occurred. He made himself wait a moment, breathing slowly and deeply until he felt more composed.

Laura might still be in the shop. He looked up the number and punched it out. She answered straight away.

'Mrs Hutton? Detective Chief Inspector Barnaby. I was wondering if you would do something for me.'

'I was just going next door for a drink. Is it urgent?'

'Yes,' said Barnaby. 'I rather think it is.'

Amy was in her room working on *Rompers*. She had been up there since five o'clock and so far had not been troubled either by a tinkling bell or any vocal demands.

At the moment she was worrying about her prose style, which was beginning to sound rather too cosily familiar. But was it, wondered Amy, chewing the tip of her Biro, worth constantly searching out fresh adjectives? Wouldn't

417

readers feel more at home with tried and true combinations? And this was not, she argued, simply an excuse for authorial laziness, for surely there were certain pairings so felicitous that even the most gifted scribe could hardly be expected to improve upon them.

A quick glance at the dawn sky from any bedroom window showed rosy fingers at their very best. Black hair, in certain lights, definitely took on the glossy hue of a raven's wing. And where was the besotted eye that did not shine exactly like a star when alighting on the object of its affection?

Amy was slightly comforted in the knowledge that this waning of writerly confidence was not entirely unknown even among the most successful. Max Jennings had described how he always started a new book convinced that this time the relationship was going to be one of unalloyed bliss and that they would be walking off into the sunset hand in hand with never a harsh work spoken. But it never happened. Long before the end of Chapter One they'd be back in the thick of it, screaming, swearing and throwing plates.

Amy sighed, gathered her thoughts and applied herself once more. The scene on which she was working was a dramatic one. Araminta had escaped from Black Rufus by leaping from his droshky (suitably clad in a Donna Karan jump suit) into a drift of newly fallen snow. Emerging, she had been reluctantly compelled to abandon her mock-ermine Versace throw with genuine amber toggles and rhinestone hood and was now fleeing across a frozen lake pursued by bloodhounds. Amy chewed her pen some more. Decided bloodhounds were a bit tame and substituted wolves.

She had no problem empathising with her perilously

placed heroine, for she herself was shivering in a sub-zero temperature. She got up and placed her mittened hand on the rusting radiator. Rather pointlessly, for it had been stone cold all day and, sure enough, remained so.

Amy jumped up and down a bit, the thick ridged soles of her fur boots bouncing on the threadbare rug. She blew on her fingertips and rubbed her cheeks hard, but the friction only made them sore. She decided, bearing in mind Honoria's promise that the heating would definitely be looked into, to go down to the library and have a word with her sister-in-law.

Amy made her way along the landing, her passage marked by dark, heavily varnished portraits of grandly robed Lyddiards going back to the sixteenth century. Her own particular aversion was a hawk-faced judge who looked as if he not only derived great pleasure from passing the death sentence but for two pins would roll up his sleeves and carry it out.

Honoria was at her desk severely engrossed in matters dexter and sinister. She looked aloof and far removed from worldly things. Though the one-bar electric fire was on, the big, high-ceilinged room felt almost as cold as the one upstairs. Amy hovered in the doorway but without attracting any response.

'I say . . .'

'Blood and bone.' Honoria was mumbling to herself. 'That's what counts. Blood counts. Bone counts.'

'Honoria?'

Honoria looked up. Her eyes burned into Amy's yet appeared not to see her.

'It's terribly cold. Could I—'

'Go away. Can't you see I'm busy?'

Amy went away. This was plainly not the time to ask if

Honoria had ordered the coke. Or if she would be prepared to down tools and bend the Neanderthal boiler to her will. As she crossed the ancient flagstones in the hall Amy stopped to pull out a couple of weeds that had seeded themselves between the cracks. The garden it seemed was trying to enter the house and, in this weather, who could blame it? She tried the cellar door, but it wouldn't open.

Amy frowned and tried again, sure that the door was simply stuck, for she had never known it to be locked. However after two more good pushes there seemed little doubt about it. Amy hesitated and wondered if she might not just make herself a nice hot-water bottle and sit with it on her lap. But then soon she would have to come down and start preparing dinner and she could hardly carry it round the chilly kitchen.

Honoria having made it plain she did not wish to be disturbed, Amy set off to find the bunch of internal house keys herself. Sometimes they hung on an iron nail in the lumber room, sometimes they were in the drawer of the kitchen table, occasionally Honoria put them down and completely forgot where. Once Amy had found them in a flower pot in the greenhouse.

Today they were not on the nail. Amy felt her way along the bench of drying dahlias and bulbs and old seed packets without success. She was moving Honoria's upright bicycle out of her way when she saw the keys lying in the bicycle basket.

The one for the cellar was an old-fashioned iron thing almost as long as her hand. She fitted it into the lock, where it turned smoothly. She switched on the light, which was so dim it made little difference and, holding the rail tightly, made her way down the steps.

The boiler took up so much space there was not much

room for anything other than its food. A heap of coal, a smaller heap of sticks, piles of old newspapers and parish magazines tied with string. Boxes of cardboard or wood, some rags and a can of paraffin.

Amy approached the monstrous apparatus – vast, round-bellied, black with age, neglect and bad temper – with some trepidation. Pipes sprouted from the back and writhed away through the cellar ceiling. There were three dials with red pointers like those on a speedometer. They all registered 150. She gave the glass an authoritative tap. The readings fell to 98.

Amy laid her hands gingerly on the metal. It was barely warm. She opened the door and peered inside. As far as she could make out there was a pile of ashes and little else. She took the raker, a piece of metal the size and weight of a crowbar but shaped like a long T, and poked about, activating one or two pallid sparks. Then she tore up several pages of the parish magazine and laid a few thin strips across the sparks before they expired. The paper browned, crisped, flamed.

Amy flung on some more paper and took a few sticks from the pile. She laid them carefully on top and picked up several more in readiness should the first ones ignite.

It was then she noticed there was something underneath. More paper? A label certainly – bright yellow with blue lettering: Hotel Masima, Tangiers. Amy swept the sticks aside. More labels, almost covering the top of a brown suitcase.

She dragged it out, laid it flat and pressed the catches. The lid sprang open. Amy knelt down, ignoring the grit and dirt beneath her knees and examined the contents. A black suit and veiled hat, lingerie, including a suspender belt and filmy stockings, high-heeled shoes. Two plastic tubs holding costume jewellery and cosmetics. And a shoe box crammed with photographs. How absolutely extra-ordinary.

She took a handful of the photographs out and started to look through them. Some were in colour, others black and white. Many featured a blonde-haired woman both on her own, with a couple of friends and playing with a dog. There was a relaxed holiday air about the snaps and several had actually been taken on a beach or around what appeared to be a hotel swimming pool. Two men wearing the briefest swimwear imaginable stood in front of a splendid boat.

And there was Ralph. Even in the poor light there was no mistaking his vivid smile, dark curls and direct gaze. He was with a crowd of people apparently at some sort of party. Certainly an air of jollity prevailed. They were all sitting round a table covered with glasses and bottles and paper streamers. Perhaps it was someone's birthday. The picture was a large one taken by flash. Ralph was wearing a square-necked, short-sleeved white cotton top, part of the Royal Navy's summer rig.

Amy peered more closely. There was something about the person next to her husband. A handsome man with blurry features, hair all over the place and a flower stuck behind his ear. Amy climbed the cellar steps and held the picture up to the light and gasped in disbelief. It was Gerald!

Full of excitement she ran into the hall. Words and phrases chattered in her head, primed her lips. 'You'll never guess . . . the suitcase . . . you remember . . . Mrs Bundy said . . . someone has put it . . .'

Honoria was standing, motionless, in the doorway of the library. The words curdled in Amy's mouth. She knew and understood the situation immediately. A pulse of apprehension fluttered, gained strength, then started to beat forcefully at the base of her throat.

For no reason the phrase 'save your breath' came into her mind. Might as well save your breath. She started to inhale slowly and deeply and exhale shallowly as if the air about her was already in short supply.

Her mind was cleanly split. Half ran underground, chattering with fear, making no sense. The other summed up the extreme danger of her position and hunted for a way out. Front door locked, bolted, not opened for years. Back door locked, bolted, would never have time to undo. Must not, *must not* be forced back down cellar steps to die like a dog. Ground-floor windows locked but she could break one and climb through, bleeding but alive. Alive.

The dark mass across the hall shifted slightly. Hardly a step, more a bulky cleaving of the air. The movement brought Amy's heart into her mouth.

Stairs. Same distance for us both. I'm smaller, younger, lighter, faster. Get to my room. Bolt the door. Open the window. Scream.

She tried to remember what you did before a sprint. Bend the knees? Up on the toes? It was vital that she got it right. It could mean the difference between . . . it could make all the difference.

But then all thoughts of preparation fled, for Honoria did something far worse than just redistribute her weight. She started to laugh. A soft, growly, vibrating thrum like the warm-up of a powerful engine, followed by a series of harsh barks. These were punctuated by honking noises when Honoria ran out of oxygen and snorted more in through her nose.

Amy ran. Hitting the stairs. Up the stairs. On to the

landing. Down the landing. Honoria close, so close behind. Panting, lumbering, grabbing handfuls of emptiness but once, when Amy stumbled, brushing the hem of her skirt.

Beneath their feet the ground flew. For Amy, reft of breath, all thought was stripped away. She was no longer even conscious of running, for other darker rhythms had taken her over. Into her room. Fall on the door. Close the door.

Too late.

Amy heaved and pushed but Honoria's iron foot was already implacably there. *She* did not push, for there was no need. Or apparently any hurry. Several seconds passed before she started to speak. Before she pushed her snout into the gap and contorted her mouth to spew out her dreadful revelations.

And Amy was forced to listen, for she dared not lift her hands from the door to cover her ears. Nor could she move away. Soon she was crying out at the horror of it but Honoria merely raised her voice, drowning the sounds of Amy's anguish.

And then, quite suddenly, the streaming poisonous flux dried up. And, shortly after, Amy's lamentations ceased. She listened intently in the silence, leaning hard against the door, praying that the terrible force on the other side would not decide to do the same. Her face was screwed up grotesquely with physical effort and her cheeks shone with tears.

Honoria punched the door with all her might. Amy hurtled away, falling on her back, and Honoria walked into the room. She stood, looking down at Amy. Honoria's rough, high-coloured slabby countenance was ghastly pale. Her eyes slithered and slipped about in their sockets or rolled so far back that only the whites showed. Glistening strands of spittle swung from her lower lip.

Amy scrambled up and moved away in a crablike manner, knowing that she must keep looking directly at Honoria, for that was what you had to do with wild things. Lions, tigers, mad dogs. Then they didn't spring. The pupils of Honoria's eyes were dark red. Her gross shadow stretched across the wall, the head lolling and wagging.

Amy fetched up against the sash window. She put her hands behind her and felt the cold glass and crumbly paint on the surround. If she could only open it. That would mean turning her back, but only for a second. And where was the alternative?

Amy swung round, reached up and started tugging at the catch. It was rusty and very stiff. She had to push and pull it hard to work it loose. Once she glanced over her shoulder. Honoria stood there, watching, wrapped in a terrible silence.

The window flew up with a crash. Clean cold air swept Amy's face. She put her hands on the sill and leaned out, looking down the long drive and through the open gates. Far below stretched an expanse of stone slabs.

As Amy stared down at their hard unyielding surface she remembered Mrs Bundy, doing the rough. Describing, as she scrubbed, what Gerald had looked like. What it had looked like.

Amy, feeling dizzy, closed her eyes. The stones rushed upwards. Slammed into her soft body, broke her bones. Sickened, she pulled herself upright and turned round.

Honoria said, 'Jump.'

Amy gasped aloud in horror and disbelief.

'Go on.'

Of course she would want that. The case and all that it

contained burned and Amy dead. What could suit her better? And a suicide would be perfect. Grief over her husband's death, I'm afraid. She never got over it. Talked about ending her life quite often, but I never really thought . . .

A bitter wind stirred Amy's hair. Ralph was in her mind and in her heart. Neither of them were believers. But what, Amy now wondered, if the believers had got it right and that, after the dreadful tumbling through that dark, yawning space, the slamming impact and spreading of tender flesh and breaking of bones, she and Ralph would be miraculously once more conjoined. How wonderful, how truly wonderful that would be. But Amy could not believe it. For her it wasn't true and there was no way she could make it so. The real truth was that she and Ralph would never meet again. Amy felt such extreme pain at this realisation that it was as if she had already fallen.

'*Jump.*'

'No!' Amy's profile was transformed into a hard, angry silhouette. 'I'm not doing it for you.'

Honoria glowered and her feet kicked and pawed savagely at the floor. She looked brutally sure of herself, less mad, much more frightening.

'I shall fight,' said Amy. 'And it will show. They will find you out.'

'Do you think I care.' Honoria's voice was thick with contempt.

'You will care,' shouted Amy, 'when you are in prison for years and years shut up in a cage with the sort of people you despise.'

'You're an even bigger fool than I took you for. Once your death is accomplished I shall seek my own. What else have I to live for?'

The appalling desolation behind this remark, springing from a hatred of life that Amy could not even begin to comprehend, evoked unwilling pity. For the first time she was moved to use her sister-in-law's name.

Honoria crossed swiftly over to Amy and spat in her face. Then she spun Amy round, seized her wrists and wrenched her arms together behind her. Amy kicked out backwards. A high strong kick like a spirited horse. It connected with Honoria's shins and hurt Amy's heel even through her boots.

Honoria began to drag her captive towards the open window. Amy's arms felt as if they were being torn from their sockets. She dug her heels in, rucking up the carpet but, like a chicken on the way to market dangling from tied legs could do little to help herself.

When they reached the window Honoria pushed Amy violently against the frame. The sash bar struck her hard on the nose and blood flowed into her mouth. Now she was being forced to the floor. Amy planted her legs astride, made them rigid and strong, braced the front of her thighs against the sill. Honoria let go of Amy's wrists, put both of her hands on Amy's shoulders and bore down with all her might. Amy's knees gave way with a crack.

Honoria grabbed the neck of Amy's sweater, bunching it up, pushed Amy through the window opening and half across the sill. Amy threw up her arms and gripped the sash, digging her nails into the wood. Honoria stopped pushing and began to prise loose Amy's fingers.

It was then that a vehicle appeared on the drive. Amy saw the headlights and yelled out. Screamed over and over again. Great shrieks so loud that her head filled up with the sound and rang like a bell.

Honoria hauled her back inside. Amy fought maniacally – kicking, punching, scratching. Fought with all her substance and all her strength. Far away she heard the sound of breaking glass. Honoria heard it too. Amy could see by the change in her expression. An acknowledgement that time was running out. Her hands closed around Amy's throat, the thumbs pressing into the windpipe. A spasm of mad joy made her body tremble and marked her face with a profane radiance.

Amy choked. She could hear humming, like the wind through telegraph wires, and saw redness everywhere. The pressure on her ears was terrible. The inside of her head expanded, pushing harder and harder against her skull until at last it gave way and she fell into the dark.

It was past midnight. Barnaby was in a private room at Hillingdon hospital staring out over the parking lot which, even at that hour of the night, was half full. He had been there for five hours. Unnecessarily, if he was honest with himself, for she wasn't going to run away. And she wasn't going to die. Thank God. Two bodies in one evening were more than enough.

They had been putting the first into the mortuary van as he pulled up outside Gresham House. The second, so much lighter, lay in its zippered polythene sheath in the hall.

Barnaby could see it as he got out of the Orion, for the huge doors, against which so many twigs and leaves had been piling themselves on his first visit, now stood wide open.

Laura Hutton's Porsche was parked at an oblique angle halfway round the back, as if she had drawn up carelessly in a tearing hurry, skidded in a half circle then rammed on the brakes. The keys were still in the ignition. Later Troy had driven it back to the little jewel box of a house and put it in the garage.

There was a sound from the bed, where Amy lay looking very small beneath tightly stretched, fiercely tucked bedclothes. Audrey Brierley sat close by, her white-gold cap of hair shimmering beneath the bedside lamp like a pearl helmet.

A staff nurse came in to take Amy's pulse and blood pressure. Amy had been sedated, but lightly, and the nurse's ministrations woke her up. Much as Barnaby wanted to talk he couldn't help feeling a pang of sympathy. After shining a light into both her patient's eyes the nurse said everything was fine and went briskly off, her shoes squeaking on the linoleum.

Amy stared at Audrey Brierley, who gently took hold of her bandaged hand. 'It's all right, Mrs Lyddiard. You're all right now.'

Barnaby picked up a chair and carried it over to the bed. He positioned it carefully. Not too near but not too far away, for he feared her voice might not carry.

'Hullo.'

'Hullo. It's you.'

'Again.'

He was right. It was little more than a whisper. He sat down and they smiled at each other. That is, he smiled. The corner of Amy's lips twitched very slightly, then gave up. And was it, he thought, any wonder? He began to speak, keenly aware that his opening words were hardly likely to improve matters.

'I'm afraid your sister-in-law is dead, Mrs Lyddiard. She took her own life. There was nothing anyone could do.'

'She said . . . she would . . . after . . .'

These few words seemed to exhaust her and she closed

her eyes again. Barnaby sat in silence for a short while but then continued, for he was anxious she did not drift back into sleep.

'I'll be as brief as I possibly can. We can talk at greater length when you're feeling better.'

'Hurts . . . to talk . . .'

'Of course. I thought I would give my ideas on what I think has been going on and you can just stop me, shake your head or whatever, if I've got it wrong. How does that suit?'

When she did not reply he began to speak, keeping his tone carefully prosaic, as if anything could reduce the impact of what he had to say.

'Honoria Lyddiard, until last Monday, had no idea that Gerald Hadleigh and her brother had ever met. But in Laura Hutton's kitchen she discovered a photograph of them both, together with some other people at a restaurant. Very excited by this, and eager to discover the whys and wherefores, she went straight round to Plover's Rest, but Hadleigh was out, calling on Rex St John. She tried twice more during the course of the day, but without success. Eventually, no doubt unable to wait until the morning, she returned late that same night.

'But the visitor was still there, so she stayed concealed in the trees behind the house, until she saw him drive away. Then, I suppose after knocking and getting no response, she went in. Knowing Miss Lyddiard's passion for correct behaviour we can only guess at the driving curiosity which got her, when she couldn't find Hadleigh downstairs, upstairs and into his bedroom. Then, and I don't quite understand how, I feel there must have been some sort of hiatus before they actually spoke. Enough time anyway for her to take in the photographs, some of which we now know were pretty explicit, and the clothes—Yes?'

'He . . . Gerald . . . was in . . .'

'The bathroom?' Amy nodded. 'She told you?'

'Yes.'

She told me everything. And spared me nothing. The vile words gathered again, infesting Amy's mind and fouling the calm, quiet room.

If you'd loved him enough he wouldn't have died. She knew now what Honoria meant. It seemed that years ago, when Ralph was in the navy, he had been unfaithful. Because she hadn't loved him enough he had loved someone else, who had given him the terrible disease that was to kill him. And Honoria knew this because the Spanish doctors had told her. But she had naturally thought it was a woman.

Gerald had been terribly drunk. When he came out of the bathroom and found her holding up the photograph of the group at the club at Marrakesh he had jeered and laughed. Then he had given her all the sordid details. How he and Ralph, who had never met before that night, had gone outside into the back yard and had sex, turn and turn about, up against the wall. How Ralph had loved it. Gone out again later with someone else. No wonder he'd ended up with Aids.

That was the moment when Honoria had struck. Seized the nearest heavy object and smashed it into Gerald's head, not just once but again and again until there was nothing of him left. Then she had stuffed the clothes and photographs into a suitcase and taken it away so that no connection between the obscene mess on the floor and her beloved brother could ever be made and because she was a law unto herself.

'It certainly wasn't Hadleigh who infected your

husband, Mrs Lyddiard,' said Barnaby. He had asked for a blood test directly after speaking to Laura Hutton and received a negative result. 'You had no idea what was wrong with him?'

'No . . .'

Honoria didn't tell me because she hoped I'd got it. Hoped and prayed that Ralph, before he died, had passed the sickness on. Watched and waited for the signs. Didn't tell me in case I sought help or, worse, was tested and found fit and well. In which case she would have killed me herself. Because that was the faithful promise she had made before God.

Weak tears started from Amy's eyes and WPC Brierley pulled some tissues out of a box on the locker. Barnaby decided to leave it there. By the time he had got his overcoat buttoned up and put his scarf and gloves on Amy seemed once more to be on the verge of sleep. He switched off the bedside lamp, leaving only the glow of a blue night light.

As they walked off down the corridor Audrey said, 'When will you tell her the rest, sir?'

'When she's up to it. I'd say she'd had enough for one night.' As they passed through reception he looked at the hospital clock. It was almost one thirty. 'And I think that goes for all of us.'

Coda

Nearly always, even when a case has, on paper, been solved there will be ramifications that remain forever unexplained. Characters on the fringe of the investigation for instance whose precise involvement remains mysteriously undefined. A tangle of snippets and loose ends that are fated never to be unravelled or neatly tied.

Accepting this, Barnaby had assumed the actual identity of the woman in Gerald Hadleigh's 'wedding' photograph would remain undiscovered and had dismissed the matter from his mind. Then one evening Troy, ringing up in great excitement, said that he had found her.

The sergeant had been re-running, not for the first time and to his wife's increasing annoyance, his video of *The Crucible*, in which the chief's daughter had so radiantly performed. In the court scene, when various women were racing all over the place and screaming their heads off, Troy had spotted a face in the background that looked vaguely familiar. He had pressed the freeze-frame and there she was. Mrs H. to the life.

They had traced her easily, first through BBC casting then via Equity. She was a registered film extra and, at the time of the photograph, had also been on the books of an escort agency. She certainly remembered the business with

Mr Hadleigh, for it had been the easiest hundred pounds she had earned in her life and all strictly Kosher. She had even been allowed to keep the hat and veil, but he had been quite short with her when she had tried to find out what lay behind it all. The church had been in the country not far from Burnham Beeches. It had all been pretty much as Max Jennings surmised.

All that was nearly a month ago. Barnaby, due for some leave, was now taking it, for Cully and Nicholas were about to fly home and he did not want to miss even a moment of their company. They would be staying a couple of days before returning to London.

As he sat now, engrossed in a relatively unclawed section of the *Independent*, he thought how very nice it would be to see them again and hear all about the on- and off-stage dramas that seemed to be permanently simmering in their closed and over-heated world. So different, thank God, from his own.

His left leg was going to sleep. He stretched it out, flexed his toes, then crossed the other leg over it with some vigour. The kitten, who had been playing with his shoe lace, went flying through the air to land on a cushion in the opposite armchair.

'Tom!'

'What?' He lowered the paper. 'What's the matter?'

'Try and be more careful.' She was running across the room and picking up Kilmowski, who immediately struggled to be put down.

'What have I done?'

'You could have really hurt him.' The kitten was already plodding back to the settee, where it started to make its way determinedly up Barnaby's trousers.

'Do you want your drink now or with your meal?'

'Now, please, love.'

A glass of Santa Carolina Grand Reserve was poured and very toothsome it turned out to be. Barnaby forced himself to sip rather than glug. Tomorrow, when the children were here, they would have champagne. A lovely smell was wafting from the direction of the oven. Rabbit casserole baked with lemon grass, capers and celeriac. Comice pears were in there too. He had made a sauce of half-fat cream cheese pushed twice through a sieve then flavoured with a dash of Madeira and some toasted amaretti crumbs.

Barnaby drank a little more and lay back, content. This, even with pins and needles being systematically pushed and pulled about one's upper arm, was definitely the life.

The phone rang. Joyce took it in the kitchen. She cried out with pleasure. 'Oh, hello darling – how lovely to talk to you.'

Barnaby's happiness went on hold. Something had gone wrong. They weren't coming. Or, if they were, they couldn't stay. If they could stay it was only overnight. Perhaps they were bringing people and he and Joyce would never have a chance to talk to their daughter or Nicholas properly.

'Tom?' There was the sound of the receiver being laid down and Joyce's face appeared in the serving hatch. 'Do you want a quick word? She's just ringing to check we've got the time right for Heathrow.'

'Might as well.'

'Don't come round. I'll pass it through.'

Cully sounded as if she was in the next room. It was going to be great to see him and Ma again. She had bought a super carved wooden rack in Poland for all his spices. What was he cooking tomorrow night? Had he remembered to video *The Crucible*? Tour had been terrific. Director an absolute toad. Nicholas utterly brilliant as Don John. She had never really got Beatrice right.

Barnaby listened to all this with a glad heart but, as she was about to ring off, thought it wise to inject a cautionary note.

'We may have a bit of a problem this end, Cully.' As he spoke his hand rested gently on Kilmowski, asleep on his shoulder and gradually slipping off. 'Regarding the kitten. I'm afraid your mother's getting terribly fond of it.'

'You don't have to go in, Amy.'

'I do, I do have to go in.' But she could not turn the handle.

They were on the landing outside Ralph's room. It was the first time Amy had entered Gresham House since the terrible night when she had so nearly died.

Walking through the kitchen, crossing the clammy, weed-infested flagstones of the hall, climbing the stairs, had been bad. But nothing like as bad as this.

'Shall I open it?'

'If you like.' But when Sue stretched out her hand Amy cried, 'Wait a minute!'

She was having second thoughts. Or rather twentieth, thirtieth and even fiftieth thoughts, for she had imagined this moment at least as many times. Now she asked herself why she was so determined. What sensible reason could there possibly be?

After all, he wouldn't be there. She would see the dappled horse with the worn leather saddle and scarlet reins that he had picked her up and put her on the first time he had brought her home. And the fire guard with narrow brass trim. Books and models and the beautiful scientific drawings at which he had excelled. But Ralph, or 'the remains' as the police had insisted on referring to him, was resting with his sister beneath the yew trees in St Chad's churchyard.

Sue had tried to understand what she viewed as Amy's amazing benevolence in permitting this, but without success. In her friend's place she would have arranged for Honoria to be cremated then flushed the ashes down the loo. Eventually Sue came to the conclusion that Amy, after the discovery that her husband was not only bisexual but occasionally unfaithful, had had a change of heart about him, but she was mistaken. Amy merely felt that if someone was prepared to kill, however madly or wrongly, to avenge the only person they had ever loved, the least you could do was let them rest in the same grave.

Sue now shuffled her feet, coughed to draw attention to the fact that time was passing and glanced sideways. Amy's face had become tight and expressionless and she was screwing up her eyes as if braced for some scene of visual devastation. A second later she flung open the door.

The candelabra were still there. The room was full of them. The whole place had been blazing with light apparently, like an altar in some great Romanesque cathedral. Hundreds of candles. Their congealed drippings sticking to the floor and all over the furniture.

Ralph's likeness gazed and smiled and laughed from every aspect of the room. As a baby, toddler and young boy. Many of the photographs were propped up, un-framed, against the candle holders. It was a miracle the place hadn't burned down.

Amy had been afraid the room would smell, but there was only the ever-present fragrance of mildew. Someone, perhaps the police, must have opened the windows. They had been very kind, as had everyone, especially Dennis Rainbird, the funeral director. He it was, after the first coffin had been raised, who had tactfully disposed of the load of heavy books it contained. He had also made a point, when Amy had refused to visit his premises to view the dear departed, of assuring her that Mr Lyddiard had been most beautifully embalmed. He appeared to be under the impression that this would be a comfort.

'This is where he was lying.' Amy went across to a large refectory table in the centre of the room. 'Under a white silk bedspread.'

Sue didn't know how to respond. The whole story had struck her as so completely revolting that she had nearly passed out when Amy first told her. To think of Honoria up here talking to a corpse, perhaps even holding it – God. It didn't bear thinking of.

'Did I tell you he asked for me, in Spain, just before he died? She said I'd gone away.'

'Amy – that's terrible. But surely he'd know it wasn't true.'

'Oh yes. He knew her very well. It's just . . . it would have been nice to say goodbye.'

Amy picked up a school report. One of many draped over the fire guard like little printed paper towels.

'Bright but mischievous.' 'Distracts other pupils.' 'A definite gift for languages.' 'Needs to concentrate more.' 'A popular boy.'

'Everyone liked him,' said Amy. 'It's all down here.'

Sue's feelings of intrusion and inadequacy deepened. Standing helplessly by she made a clumsy indefinite movement demonstrating a wish to comfort, then let her arms fall once more to her sides.

'I thought he didn't want children, but he knew, you see, what was wrong with him.'

That was why he had always taken the responsibility for contraception. Not, as he had told his wife, because he was worried about the side effects of the pill, but for her own safety.

He should have told her though. That was the hardest thing to bear. Not unfaithfulness or the fact that he had sexual inclinations of which she had known nothing, but this decision to carry alone the dark knowledge that their days of happiness were numbered. Perhaps he was afraid she would reject him.

'I'm sure that wasn't it,' interrupted Sue as Amy showed signs of increasing distress. 'He wanted to save you pain. We do when we love someone.'

Amy didn't seem to hear. She was moving around the room touching things – rocking the dappled horse, running a little green metal car backwards and forwards along the edge of a shelf, glancing through school exercise books. She was trying hard to invest these actions with emotion or meaning, but felt merely awkward and artificial. It seemed a ghostly place to her without even the memory of a life in it. Both sacred and pointless, like a mausoleum.

She pushed open the curtain and sunlight flooded the room, throwing into harsh relief the nursery artefacts so incongruously combined with ceremonial appointments of death. Suddenly the stifling atmosphere became unbearable.

'Let's go.'

'Don't you want to take something?' The house was due to be cleared the next morning by a firm from Princes Risborough.

'I have this.' Amy's fingers rested briefly on the locket. She was almost running down the landing. 'Come *on*, Sue.'

Sue was glad to comply. When they were once more outside she looked up at the great brooding mass of grey

439

stone, which now belonged to Amy, and was glad that she would never have to enter it again. They set off down the drive together.

It was a beautiful March day. The sky was a great stretched arc of cloudless blue. There were daffodils all along the drive and crocuses and aconites beneath the trees. As Amy closed the main gates Sue said, 'I've brought some bread. Shall we feed the ducks?'

'All right.' They crossed over on to the Green and the ducks immediately started quacking and waddling towards them. 'How is it they always know?'

'They spot the bags. You can give them the cake if you like.'

Sue couldn't get out of the habit of baking, even though there was only her and Amy and, more and more frequently, Amanda. The local wildlife, in all its varieties, had never been so well fed. She passed a huge lump of dried seed cake over to Amy, who crumbled it, saying, 'We mustn't forget that little one who always gets pushed out.'

'I'll see if I can coax him away while you distract the rest.'

Sue concealed her bread and moved off, leaving Amy surrounded by a bustling crew of eager birds. Then she crouched down by the side of the pond and tried to attract the attention of the very small mallard trying to push its way in, through or round the others but never quite making it. While tearing up a crust she thought about Hector, as she did most of the time now that she was a proper author, with a contract and commission for a second story. The working title for this was *Hector Learns to Rumba* and to say he looked remarkable in his Latin American costume would be putting it mildly.

Sue made little chucking noises, trying to attract the

mallard's attention, but without success. Perhaps it would be better to throw something so close to its beak that the others would not have a chance to snatch it. But they were packed very tightly together . . .

Amy was coming to the end of her cake. Sue watched as she distributed the final crumbs and reflected on how, in the space of a mere few weeks, their fortunes had both changed.

Amy was rich now. She had been offered what had seemed to them both an astonishing amount of money for Gresham House. And she was also, slowly, getting better. When she had first arrived at Trevelyan Villas from the hospital she had wept all through the daylight hours and had nightmares in the dark. Sue had felt quite desperate sometimes as to what best to do. But now, although Amy's sleep was never unbroken, she had at least stopped crying and yesterday had even started talking about the future, wondering where she should decide to live for instance. And how she must soon start thinking of getting on with *Rompers*.

Sue herself was fine. She had heard once, via her solicitor, from Brian. He had written suggesting that he move back in, just until Sue got over the shock of him moving out. She had thrown the letter on the fire.

'You're miles away.'

'Oh, yes.' Sue straightened up. 'Sorry.'

'What were you thinking?'

Sue, who had been thinking that she would never again have to watch Brian wrinkling the skin of his cocoa to the side of his cup with his tongue and then eating it, said, 'I was wondering if I should take my lenses out. My eyes are watering a bit.'

'It's the wind. Put some drops in when you get back.'

Sue distributed the rest of her bread. The mallard remained unlucky.

'I'm sure he's all right, actually,' said Amy. 'He may be small but he doesn't look thin. And his feathers are lovely and shiny.'

In the distance, as they walked home, they saw Rex exercising his soppy dog. He called out to them and waved and they waited for him to approach. Even from several feet away it was plain the man was consumed by happiness. His smile covered half his face and his eyes shone.

'What is it, Rex?' asked Sue. 'Down, Montcalm! You seem very pleased with life.'

'Well . . .' About to speak with great eagerness, Rex checked himself. The truth was that his current research into warrior traditions had just turned up the most amazing fact. It seemed that the Huns had used to cut the cheeks of new-born male babies with swords so the infants would taste blood before their mother's milk. Rex's pleasure in this arcane titbit had been only slightly diminished when he had been unable to find a place for it in *The Night of the Hyena*.

The women were looking expectant but, remembering what Amy had so recently gone through, Rex thought it wiser to keep his newly found discovery to himself.

'I'm afraid I didn't quite get the question.'

'We wondered,' said Amy, 'why you were looking so happy.'

'Oh, just life you know.' Rex beamed at them both. 'Just life.'

Then he touched his battered cord cap and walked away, Montcalm prancing and dancing at his heels.

* * *

Laura, studying her reflection in the Venetian glass in her yellow silk sitting room was well pleased. She looked beautiful, confident and, most surprising of all, happy. She, who had thought never to be happy again.

Turning slowly round, looking backwards over her shoulder, she admired her profile, noting with special pleasure the delicate, trembling sprays of diamonds in her ears. Her heavy mass of bronze hair falling around her shoulders, was held back by two pearl and marcasite combs. Laura thought she looked rather like a Burne Jones voluptuary, and smiled. She adjusted the accordian-pleated collar on her cape of heavy taffeta so that it framed her face. She was going to see *Der Rosenkavalier* and already her head was filled with music.

There was a spritzer of white wine and Pellegrino to hand. She had kept two goblets behind in case Adrian, one time owner of the Irish linen cupboard, decided to join her. He always got out of the car and came to the door. Never just sat there and tooted. She liked that. Laura drank a little and put the glass back carelessly, making yet another ring. The mantelpiece already looked like an Olympic logo.

Around her, as in every room in the house, were tea chests, cardboard boxes and shrouded pieces of furniture. Tomorrow she would be shaking the village dust from her feet. And not a moment too soon. Not that she had been there much recently. She had been staying with friends in Stoke Poges supervising work on her new house, which was close by, and paying only fleeting visits to Midsomer Worthy to pick up her mail and check for messages on the answerphone.

There had been several from Amy. They indicated a wish for a meeting so that she could express her gratitude to Laura for having saved her life. After the third of these embarrassingly tense communications, Laura had sent a postcard to say that it was really quite unnecessary and that, largely due to the move, she had very little time to spare. The hint seemed to have been taken for, even when her Porsche had been parked in the driveway, Amy had not stopped by.

The last thing Laura wanted was to be reminded of the gruesome tragicomedy she had witnessed at Gresham House. Afterwards, when the police had taken her to the station, they had insisted on giving her strong sweet tea which she hadn't wanted but which they kept saying was good for shock. Laura had tried to explain that everything had happened so quickly she had not had time to be shocked.

After smashing some glass and climbing through the gap she had run upstairs to the room from where she judged the screams to be coming. The second she dashed in Honoria had released Amy, crossed quickly to the open window, sat down on the sill and fallen backwards. One moment her legs were sticking stiffly upside down in the air and the next she had gone. She did not cry out, either when she fell or when she hit the ground. It was all over in an instant.

Laura still hadn't grasped all the ins and outs of what had been going on and wasn't sure she wanted to. All she really understood was that her decision to call on Amy instead of ringing up to propose that they meet elsewhere, as Chief Inspector Barnaby had suggested, was, in retrospect, a very good thing. She never had got a look at the picture in Amy's locket, supposedly the point of the whole exercise, but had been assured that this no longer signified. Now all she wanted was to put the whole messy business out of her mind, which she had succeeded in doing pretty well.

She was especially surprised at the rapid transformation of her feelings for Gerald Hadleigh. (She always used his surname now when referring to him in her thoughts.) Quite soon after being told about his strange double life and homosexuality the obsessional passion that had once so dominated her life had completely and mysteriously vanished. She seemed, like Titania, to have been released from some mysterious spell.

Laura wondered if this quick and easy recovery meant she was rather a shallow person and the thought was not entirely unpleasing. Certainly in many respects, the shallow seemed to have a far easier time of it.

The distinctive roar of a Jensen cut through these pleasant musings. Laura picked up her bag. On the way out she paused before her quattrocento princeling and frowned at his melancholy countenance. Always close to her heart today, for the first time, she felt irritation and wondered if she had not perhaps been too indulgent in inventing so many assorted tragedies to explain his mood. He was probably just having an adolescent sulk. Laura patted his hand and said, 'Cheer up. It might never happen.'

The doorbell rang. He was here. She reached for the little gilt chain which hung down by the side of the painting. Pulled it. And put out the light.

The Killings at Badger's Drift

Caroline Graham

The village of Badger's Drift is the essence of tranquillity.
But when resident and well-loved spinster Miss Simpson
takes a stroll in the nearby woods, she stumbles across
something she was never meant to see, and there's only
one way to keep her quiet.

Miss Simpson's death is not suspicious, say the villagers.
But Miss Lucy Bellringer refuses to rest: her friend has
been murdered. She is sure of it.

She calls on Detective Chief Inspector Barnaby to
investigate, and it isn't long until the previously unseen
seamy side of Badger's Drift is brought to light.

But as old rivalries, past loves and new scandals surface,
the next murder is not far away.

978 1 4722 4365 2

HEADLINE

Death of a Hollow Man

Caroline Graham

Backstage nerves are fraying, and revenge is on its way.

As Causton Amateur Dramatic Society prepares for the opening night of *Amadeus*, in the wings Esslyn Carmichael suspects his wife is having an affair with the leading man. And where better to settle scores than the stage?

Detective Chief Inspector Tom Barnaby expects an evening of entertainment, attending only to show support for his wife. But when someone turns Esslyn's final grand gesture into a gruesome *coup de theatre*, Barnaby's investigation suddenly begins.

978 1 4722 4366 9

HEADLINE

Death in Disguise

Caroline Graham

To the distaste of the Compton Dando villagers, the big house has been taken over by a group of New Age eccentrics. And when the first death is reported, no one is surprised . . . or disappointed. The Coroner rules it an accident.

But only weeks later, there's another death. And this time, it is murder.

Detective Chief Inspector Barnaby is called to the scene immediately, and there'll be no escape until he has sifted through the world of psychics, cult leaders and horrifying deaths to get to the cause of it all.

978 1 4722 4367 6

HEADLINE

THRILLINGLY GOOD BOOKS
FROM CRIMINALLY
GOOD WRITERS

CRIME FILES BRINGS YOU THE LATEST RELEASES FROM TOP CRIME AND THRILLER AUTHORS.

SIGN UP ONLINE FOR OUR MONTHLY NEWSLETTER AND BE THE FIRST TO KNOW ABOUT OUR COMPETITIONS, NEW BOOKS AND MORE.

VISIT OUR WEBSITE: WWW.CRIMEFILES.CO.UK
LIKE US ON FACEBOOK: FACEBOOK.COM/CRIMEFILES
FOLLOW US ON TWITTER: @CRIMEFILESBOOKS